Changeling's
JOURNEY

THE
Changeling's
JOURNEY

Christine Spoors

The Changeling's Journey

ISBN: 978-1-9997535-0-4

Cover art by Leesha Hannigan
Cover design by Eight Little Pages
Interior design by Eight Little Pages
Title design by Lauren Cassidy
Map design by Liza Vasse
Printed by IngramSpark

FOR KAREN,

I'D TRAVEL THE FAIRY KINGDOMS WITH YOU.

I AM SO GLAD YOU WERE BORN.

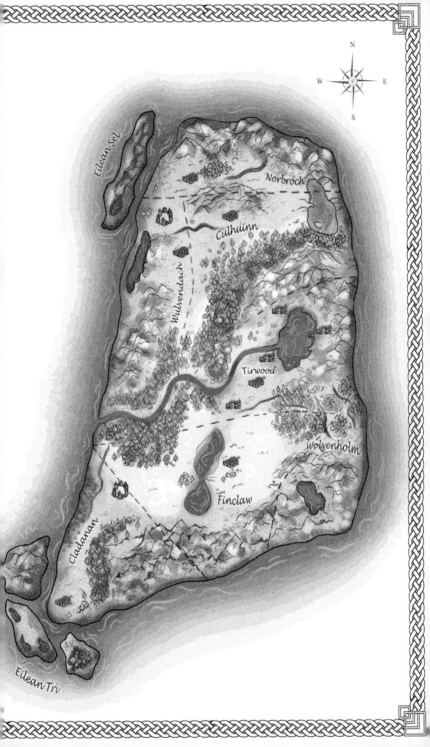

CHAPTER

I

Morven

I watched, vision blurring with tears, as Ailsa's da and two brothers piled stones on top of her grave. There were less than a dozen graves here in this part of the burial site, the family having only moved to our village a few decades back.

I had never spoken to young Ailsa much, but I could fondly remember the way she would weave flowers into her hair and paint the stump of her left arm with war paint. There hasn't been a call to war for years but paint could always be found at the market. Perhaps now that Ailsa was dead it would disappear.

Not that it really mattered. Ailsa was gone and that left me, the last changeling alive in the village.

My stomach churned with sadness at the death of a young girl of only ten years, but also with guilt.

It was horrifically unfair that every other changeling child died before reaching their teenage years, yet here I stood at the age of eighteen. Still alive, albeit usually gasping for breath as I clambered over the hills our village inhabits. Time and time again I found myself cursing the founders of this village for not settling on flat easy ground.

There was another boy who lived to be fifteen. He died before I was born but years ago I heard my ma and da talking about it when they thought I was asleep.

It was madness that I was still alive, and I could not help but wonder how much longer I would last. Over the years, we changelings weaken and die, no one knows why and no healer can stop it.

Glen once told me it was because changelings are made from magic and magic can't exist for a long time south of the Fairy Hills. I wasn't sure what I thought about that theory, there is magic all around us in Tirwood, despite it being a human kingdom.

I was jolted out of my thoughts by a gust of wind sending a spray of freezing water into my face. Shuddering, I pulled my cloak tighter around my body. Miserable weather for a miserable day.

A few weeks ago, Granny Athol had dramatically announced that spring was on its way. In my opinion, it couldn't come fast enough. I couldn't feel my toes and I wouldn't have been surprised if my nose had frozen solid.

The fairies stole children from their beds and replaced them with changelings without rhyme or rhythm, but some believed that they also helped the Others to change the seasons and ensure the growth of crops. As I stared at the growing pile of stones in front of me my thoughts soured.

If the crops failed and we all died they would have no babies to steal, and nowhere to leave the changelings they create. Maybe that would be for the best. Maybe they should just leave us all to starve.

A warm hand on my back made me jump, at once feeling guilty about my thoughts. A few sickly changelings were not a good enough reason to wish death upon the whole village.

If I hadn't been so cold I was sure my face would have been burning with embarrassment.

"Let's get you home Morven," da said, wrapping a strong arm around my shoulders, leading me away from the stones.

I was surprised to see that I was the last one, other than Ailsa's family, left. I had been so caught up in my thoughts that I hadn't noticed anyone leaving, I hoped I hadn't accidentally ignored anyone who tried to talk to me.

The death of anyone in the village is heart-breaking. Our farming village is small, compared to the town, and so everyone mourns each loss. The death of a changeling is always worse, anger and resentment adding to our sadness making it all the more sickening.

Nothing can be done to stop our babies being stolen, they are put to bed healthy the night before and in the morning, they are gone. If you were lucky, in their place a near identical child would lay with sickly pale, cold skin.

If not, the changeling would be missing a finger or maybe even an arm or a leg. Like they were created in a rush and vital parts were simply missed out.

No one knew what happened to the children the fairies stole, some of the more cynical villagers thought perhaps they were taken and used as sacrifices, or eaten. Most of the villagers held onto the hope that our babies were cherished. Welcomed into fairy families as if they were their own children.

Why they needed human children, our children, we had no idea.

Da helped me scramble back down the hill that separated the village from the graves. Everyone marching up and down the hill had transformed the green grass into a brown muddy death trap. If da hadn't been there to guide me down, I would have had to roll down instead, probably falling and breaking my neck.

Even with his help, I couldn't stop my feet from slipping in the mud as I shrieked and clung to him for support. He couldn't help but laugh at my struggle, but thankfully helped me reach the bottom without breaking any bones.

We hurried towards our family cottage, cloaks pulled tight around us against the freezing wind and rain. The smoke wafting out of the top of our cottage filled my heart with warmth. It may not be the fanciest or largest around, but our cottage had been in the family for generations. It was home and we all loved it.

The smell of ma's stew hit me as soon as we entered, making my mouth water. She had left the burial not long after the family had said their speeches about Ailsa and wished her safe travel to the Otherworld. It always upset her the most when a changeling passed away, probably because it made her think too much about when my time would end.

I hung my cloak by the fire, thankful to finally be out of the dreary weather and into the warmth. I waved at ma as I passed and made my way to the largest room, from which I could hear screaming and laughter.

Malcolm, my older brother, was pinned to the floor wailing whilst his twin daughters tickled him, giggling hysterically.

I had always been content with the size of our little family; ma, da, my older brother Malcolm, my younger brother Munro and me. We were a perfect mix of personalities who rarely argued and loved each other more than anything. Then four years ago, Malcolm brought home his wife-to-be Bonnie and a year later the twins, Morag and Mildred, were born and my heart grew

4

even bigger. Now I couldn't imagine our family without them.

Munro and I had laughed and laughed, until we were sure we would pass out, when Malcolm told us that he was continuing the ridiculous tradition that da started, calling all his children names beginning with the same sound.

"Tradition is important," he had shouted over Munro's snorting and my wheezing gasps for breath.

Important maybe, though pointless is the word that springs to mind when I think of that tradition. Unlike storytelling, now that is a tradition I cherish.

Bonnie had lived in Cladanan when she was wee. Her family had immigrated from the isles across the southern sea, generations before she was born.

Malcolm met, and fell in love with her, when he went to work on the ships in the south for a few years. Bonnie quickly became one of my favourite storytellers and I loved to hear her wild tales of pirates and selkies. I couldn't imagine the sea.

A river and a few streams passed by our village but it was impossible to imagine enough water to carry a whole ship full of people. It didn't take more than a few weeks to travel south, but da and ma always had work to do on the farm, so I'd never had the chance.

The second most important tradition for our family is going on adventures. When da was younger, he climbed every mountain around Loch Fai and a few of the mountains in south with his brother. He claimed that he once saw a wulver in the south, a man with hair all over his body and a wolf's head. That story is one of his personal favourites, but I am not sure I believe that he truly saw one and lived to tell the tale.

He decided that he wanted his children to go on adventures, and was eager to send Malcolm south when he asked. Ailsa's funeral made me even more eager to go on an adventure. I didn't want to die before I had a chance to see more of this land. I couldn't let that happen.

"Finally, you were out so long we thought you'd decided to dig your own grave already," Munro laughed until da smacked him, making me laugh.

"Don't let your ma hear you talking like that today," he said, frowning, although the amusement was clear in his eyes.

My mortality and likely imminent death had, over the years, become a source of jokes in our family. The only way to deal with the harsh reality that I could be gone any day was to laugh about it.

From 'Morven you slept so long we thought you were dead' from Malcolm or 'I can't sweep the floor... I've moved on to the Otherworld' from me whenever I was feeling lazy.

We always joked and laughed about it, and somehow that made it less real and less frightening. Ma always joined in, threatening to steal my clothes when I was gone, but not today.

Not whilst our neighbours were still piling stones on their daughter's grave. A grave, like the one I could be laid to rest inside any day now.

Ma's call to dinner roused me from my depressing thoughts as I joined the scramble for the first bowl of stew. After a steaming bowl, I made my excuses and hurried to bed, eager to hide amongst my blankets away from the miserable weather and my miserable thoughts.

I threw myself down onto the damp grass, taking deep breaths of the crisp morning air. I could feel the cold dew seeping in through my skirts but I didn't bother moving. Not after hiking up the steepest hill overlooking our village.

"Don't go dying on me Morven," Glen settled down beside me with a chuckle.

"You wish," I groaned, pulling myself upright. "I swear that hill gets steeper every time we climb it."

We sat in a comfortable silence for a while as I caught my breath. I loved it up here. From this high up we could look down on the village and watch people out in the farms, tending to their cows and sheep. We could see the small market in the centre, pillars of smoke billowing from the stalls roasting meat over their fires.

It was humbling to see our wee village spread out before us, a couple of dozen cottages and the market place, all circled by countless fields. Just beyond our village we could see the road.

It led off into the distance towards the town. Beyond that I could just make out the start of the Fairy Hills and the Fairy Forest to the west. Not the most exciting names but they were simply named because they were not ours.

No humans owned the land beyond the loch and the forest, there the fairies ruled.

I had never seen a fairy, although I had heard countless stories about them. As much as we hate them for stealing our children they are still our storytellers' favourite topic.

Glen loved stories even more than my da. That was one of the reasons he first became my friend when we were children. He wanted to know a changeling and one day decided that we were best friends. I didn't resist much.

According to Glen, the fairies are strong, beautiful and live much longer than humans. They live in grand castles and are gifted with more magic than any human could imagine. Then there are the fairies of the sky. No one has seen them down on the land, but sometimes at night we see bright lights in the sky seeping down from the north and know that they are fighting. Selkies, kelpies, wulver and the wee folk are all lesser types of fairy, according to self-proclaimed fairy expert Glen.

A few of them live down south here with us in the different kingdoms and look almost human, though they possess magic we could never dream of and unusual features. Like the wulver covered in hair, or the wee folk who are as small as an apple.

It's exciting listening to his stories and imaging these grand magical beings, but I could never quite stop my thoughts being pulled down a darker path.

"I wish I knew why the fairies steal our children," I sighed.

"Doesn't everyone?" Glen replied, scratching at his beard absentmindedly.

When he'd first started to grow that ridiculous bushy ginger beard he'd been so proud of himself.

"It would be great to just go and demand the answers. There must be a fairy somewhere that would tell us. Aren't they supposed to love humans?"

"Some say so, but then again, we all know the stories about human soup being their favourite dinner," Glen laughed. "I wish we knew for your own peace of mind, but also because that story would be brilliant to tell."

"It would make an amazing story. Morven and Glen crossing up over the Fairy Hills to demand answers from the fairies," I exclaimed, gesturing wildly as if to an audience.

8

"Yes... yes it would."

We turned to each other, our devious grins matching. What if we did just that? Went on an adventure north into the fairy kingdoms and found out what really happened to the children that were stolen. Maybe, just maybe, we could stop it from happening again.

"Your da would let you. He's been waiting for you to announce an adventure for months," Glen exclaimed as he jumped to his feet.

"And, your ma and da wouldn't miss you too much, not with Dougal and Donal working on the farm. I'm sure they could spare you for one short adventure," I allowed Glen to pull me to my feet.

"I'll fight my way through any beastie or evil fairy we encounter and you can smile and charm your way into inns and make sure we find food to fill our bellies," Glen grinned.

Almost at once I could imagine it, imagine the two of us travelling together trying to find answers. Perhaps even finding a way to stop any more babies being stolen and discovering a way to prevent changelings from dying so young. We could do it.

I grabbed his forearms growing serious. "Promise me we will do this," I said needing to hear him promise, needing to go on this journey and find the answers I had been longing for my whole life.

Glen took my face between his rough calloused hands.

"I promise."

CHAPTER

2

Morven

It turned out that Granny Athol was right, winter was finally ending. Today was my eighteenth Winter's End festival and the weather couldn't have been more perfect.

We had woken to the wind howling down through the chimney and the rain battering off the roof and doors.

Glen loves to tell stories about the Queen, who's name no one knows. It is said that she lives up beyond the fairy kingdoms in a land made of mountains, snow and ice. From there she controls the changing of our seasons.

It is said that awful weather at the Winter's End festival means she has fallen asleep, and that winter and the dark nights are over. The festival has no specific day, it's generally agreed that it's best to wait until the worst weather for it. Just to be sure that the Queen is asleep.

"So, my love, what are you hiding from me?" Ma asked casually, whilst hacking her way through one of the last turnips left in our store.

I cursed under my breath, ma always seemed to know everything before I told her. She always knew when I was keeping secrets. I'd more than once thought there must be some magic in her blood.

"I wasn't hiding anything," I said stubbornly, "though Glen and I are planning an adventure."

My ma's head shot up at that and as she stared at me with an unreadable, and slightly terrifying expression, I felt myself blush furiously. Maybe we were hiding it from our parents, but we had planned to tell everyone at the festival.

We decided it would be good to mention it whilst everyone was excited about the season ahead, and whilst they were all drunk.

Just as I was seriously considering running out of our cottage and finding somewhere to hide she threw down her knife and gathered me up into her arms.

"My wee girl, off on an adventure!" She exclaimed happily, doing her best to crush my internal organs.

I sighed with relief and wrapped my arms around her to return the hug. Ma had been the one I was most worried about telling, though she was always happy to let me live my life and do what I wanted.

It always helped to have your ma on your side, especially when announcing something as big as wanting to go off adventuring for an unknown amount of time. I was sure da would be happy for me, but just in case he wasn't ma could convince him.

We hugged each other a while longer until ma regained her composure and went back to destroying the rock-solid turnip. As exciting as it is finding out that your only daughter has decided to go on an adventure, standing around hugging won't get enough of your famous stew made to feed a village.

Feasts always took place in what we affectionately called the castle, I'd never seen a castle before but was sure that they were nothing like ours. Our castle was a huge stone hall that was built by the first settlers to arrive in our village, the largest building for miles around. It was used for everything, from feasts to meetings. Any event that needed a large building was held in the castle.

Without decorations, the castle was nothing more than a huge hall with sturdy walls made of stacked stones, a wooden roof and empty fire pits.

For the Winters End festival, it looked glorious. The fires were lit, filling the room with dramatic amber light. A welcome change from the cold blustery weather outside. Plates piled high with bread, scones, bannocks, butter, carrots, turnips and potatoes were starting to be brought in by our fellow villagers.

I could smell mouth-watering meat cooking, but there was no sign of it in the castle yet.

"Are we standing here all night?" Munro shouted disturbing my thoughts, to which I rolled my eyes fondly.

Munro, Malcolm and da were carrying huge pots of ma's famous stew behind me. I wasn't carrying one. I highly doubted I could have lifted one of the huge metal pots, and even if I had, the added weight would have made breathing and walking completely impossible.

Being a changeling did occasionally have some benefits.

I smirked watching them hurriedly stumble through the hall and slam a pot down on each of the largest tables. The tables and chairs in the castle were a sight to behold.

There were short stools, tall high-backed chairs, stools that looked ready to collapse at any moment, and chairs covered with the fur of an animal I couldn't even begin to imagine. There are no kings or queens in our village, we all sat together on our mismatched seats around scraped and worn tables that seem to have been in the castle forever.

After we finished preparing the stew for the feast we joined the other villagers, following the river that ran down from the hills and meandered through the fields.

Each family carried a small jug of milk and a bag of oats which were to be given up as an offering to the Others in the Otherworld. In return they would provide water, fish and a good harvest for the next year. The oats were scattered into the river at the point where it leaves the last field owned by one of our villagers. Then, the milk is poured around the fairy stone.

We all stopped and gathered near the fairy stone, which sat on the grass beside the river. I've never understood how this rock ended up amongst our fields and not up in the mountains. Da said it's the same colour as the rocks in the Fairy Hills and that magic carried it down to us so that we would know where to give our offerings. That is how it came to be known simply as the fairy stone.

Perhaps, the fairies had a different name for it. We'd never know.

An intricate pattern of lines, runes and knots had been carved into the rock, either by the first villagers or the fairies themselves, and it always filled me with awe to be standing beside such a huge piece of magic. Munro is the tallest in our family and still, the rock is as big as three of him standing on top of each other.

One by one the torches, carried by young children, were lit as the light began to fade from the grey cloudy sky. I always wondered if the sky fairies could see us from their home, with our burning torches circling and illuminating the fairy stone. I wondered what the fairies and the Others thought of our offerings of milk to the land and oats to the river, if they appreciated them or if they ever wanted something different.

One by one each family had their chance to offer up milk and oats to thank the fairies for our last harvest and hope that they would see fit to grant us another.

Da started off our family's offering. He took the milk jug and poured in a line around the now sodden and muddy ground at the base of the fairy stone, then he passed it to ma, to Malcolm, to his wife Bonnie, to Munro and then finally to me. Granny Athol and the twins had been left back at the cottage to boil the haggis. By the time I got the jug, there was only just enough left to complete our circle of milk around the stone.

Perhaps I just imagined it, but as the circle closed I felt a tingling in the air. Like the Other's magic came flowing out of the stone and onto my small family, thanking us for what we had given.

Next, we each grabbed two handfuls of oats from the sack Bonnie had carried with her from the cottage. There was never an order for the giving of oats and so families were simply throwing them randomly into the river. After da threw his, he picked ma up by the waist and spun them both around in a circle. She shrieked and threw the oats at random, thankfully managing to get them into the river whilst she twirled.

I glanced at my brothers and Bonnie and a moment later we each threw our oats high into the air above the river and watched as they fell like snow, illuminated red and orange by the torches, down into the rushing water.

Ever since we were children we always loved to do it at the same time, we felt it would be better for the Others to receive their gift from us as one. When Bonnie came along we quickly added her to the tradition.

After we'd given our gifts, and our family and farm was hopefully blessed for another year, we all piled in for a hug. Ma and da had been hugging so we crushed in with them, squeezing each other tight. I felt tears prickling at my eyes as we laughed together and enjoyed each other's company.

I felt so lucky to have a family made of such wonderful people, so full of support and love for each other. I could have happily stayed there all night, in the light of the torches. It was still wet and cold but I was comfortable in my thick cloak.

Soon, minds began drifting to the food waiting for us back at the castle and I decided that I didn't mind us leaving so much after all.

After the walk back to the cottage, which seemed to take forever, we met with Granny Athol and the twins before making our way to the castle for food. Each family sat in the seats beside the food they'd brought, but as the night progressed everyone ended up moving around.

There was no music yet, just the scrape of wooden spoons on wooden plates and the loud chatter of over a hundred-people happy and getting drunker by the minute.

There were no rules for the feast, simply grab a plate and fill it with as much as you can. Then eat until you are sure that your stomach will burst.

Watching my family eating, drinking and laughing together filled me with happiness and gave me the courage to announce my upcoming adventure with Glen.

"So, I have some exciting news," I said cautiously, out of the corner of my eye I saw ma nod, boosting my confidence. "Glen and I are planning on going on an adventure."

There was a moment of silence as everyone paused to take in what I had just said, then there were cheers all around and I found myself swept up in da's arms.

"Off on an adventure! My wee Morven off on an adventure!" He announced loudly, attracting the attention of the tables nearby.

"Alright Maddock, don't crush the girl before she has a chance to go," ma scolded with a laugh.

"An adventure you say! Where is my little lamb planning to go?" Granny Athol asked curiously.

"Glen and I thought we would go north to the town and then see the Fairy Hills and Loch Fai, maybe even the Fairy Forest," I explained, suddenly unsure I wanted them to know how far north we really planned to go.

"Oh lovely, what made you want to go north, rather than down to the sea or the mountains?" asked Malcolm, not realising he was putting me on the spot.

"Oh well... you know how much Glen loves to tell fairy stories. What better place to go so he can find out more? I just want to see the world, before it's too late," I said with a smile.

I hadn't lied to them, Glen was always on the lookout for more stories and I longed to see the world outside the village.

"Well, I think this announcement calls for more drink!" Munro declared before he pressed a wet kiss to my forehead and ambled off in search of drink.

"Drink!" shouted Morag waving her little spoon and splattering stew across the table.

"Drink! Drink!" echoed Mildred as if she was agreeing with her sister.

Thankfully the twins and their never-ending cuteness saved me from further scrutiny as Bonnie blushed furiously and frantically promised Granny that she didn't let her three-year olds drink.

The rest of the feast passed without a problem and Glen's family ended up joining us. Other than congratulating us on our decision to go exploring, nothing more was said about our destination choice. At times, I was sure I could see da glancing at me curiously but the drink made it hard to be sure.

After the food was consumed and we all agreed that we probably wouldn't need to eat for another year, it was time to light the fires. Every year we gathered spare wood to use in the Winter's End bonfires.

The fires signified the warmth returning to the land and the long bright days we would soon have. It was a beacon so the fairies and the Others knew where we were, to help ensure they granted us a good harvest and a good year.

Pipers and drummers dragged seats outside as the wood was piled up in a clear space downhill from the castle. We made sure that the fires were nowhere near the houses. We all remembered the story about the early villagers, they'd built their fire near their wooden houses and spiteful wee folk set their thatched roofs ablaze.

Wee folk are little fairies that live all over the land. They are apparently the size of an apple and look just like a strange little human. When I was a child I used to imagine that I had lots of wee folk as friends and I would name them and talk to them all.

Of course, that wasn't true. They dislike being seen by humans and only ever come out to steal food or accept offerings in the middle of the night whilst we are asleep. Some say that they are helpful and will clean and tidy your home, others say they are spiteful and mean like the wee folk that set the roofs on fire.

For this reason, bonfires are built far away from anything that could burn. Two large fires burn, and between them a much smaller fire that some can jump over with a good run up. Most chicken out before they reach the flames or end up landing in it and need to be hastily pulled out by their friends.

Maybe it's because the Others watch the flames, but thankfully no one has ever been burnt by the Winter's End bonfires.

This year both Glen and Munro were taking part in the jumping. I have never wanted to join in as I doubted I would make it over. Being a changeling made everything more strenuous than walking a struggle.

Glen was the first to jump, easily clearing the low fire after taking the most ridiculously long run up I've ever seen. Then it was Munro's turn.

He needed less of a run and when he reached the edge of the flames he jumped, springing up with his arms outstretched. I felt my mouth drop open in shock as he landed on the other side doing a forward roll onto his feet.

There was a moment of silence, as if no one could quite believe what he had done before the crowd erupted. Cheering his name and using what they had just seen as another excuse to drink more.

"Ma would have smacked you if she had seen you," I said with a grin.

"Aye but she didn't, and I'm sure I saw Rhona from the butcher's watching me," Munro winked before dashing off, presumably in search of the girl he risked setting himself on fire to impress.

The rest of the night was spent dancing around the fires to the music from the pipers and drummers. We took part in the group dances, which seemed never-ending and included far too many spins after a large feast. Then we broke apart and, although we danced alone, it was like one huge dance. All of us twirling and kicking and jumping together in a crazy rhythm, all moving to the beat of the same music.

As the night wore on the crowds slowly dwindled. Parents began rushing their children home before they got overtired and started wailing, couples thinking they were being sneaky hurried away together, elderly villagers complained about not being young anymore and demanded to be taken home and finally, those who had drank the most were wrestled from the castle and sent to sober up.

I walked home with da, we weren't sure where the rest of the family had wandered off to but they would turn up.

We walked together along the wide paths between fields and houses, both too happy to care about the light rain which was still falling.

As I turned to head up to the house he reached out for my hand and gently pulled me off into one of our newest fields. We sat across from each other on the stumps of cleared trees that had not yet been removed.

"So, my wee Morven is off on an adventure," he said with a smile.

"Not so wee anymore," I said with a slight laugh, a horrible sinking feeling in my gut telling me that he somehow knew our real plans.

"Where is it you're off to again?" He asked, his face not betraying any of his emotions.

"Just up near Loch Fai," I mumbled.

"Ah yes, a good place for Glen to hear stories, I remember now," he said leaning his elbows on his knees, looking into my eyes.

It felt like he could see every lie I had ever told and quickly looked away.

"Will his stories include lying to his family as well?" he asked and there it was.

He knew and now I was in trouble. I suddenly felt like my heart was ready to jump out of my chest.

"We didn't mean to lie," I said, then immediately regretted it.

"You didn't mean to lie to me and everyone else about where you were planning to go on your first ever journey, which you and Glen have clearly been planning for weeks?"

"We did mean to lie," I blurted out, "But... but that's only so you wouldn't worry!"

"Don't you think the obvious lies worry me more? A girl and a boy, not mature enough to tell the truth, journeying north by themselves gives me a lot more to worry about."

"I'm sorry. We wanted to tell the truth. You can trust me!"

"Tell me the truth then, and if you lie to me again, you will be going absolutely nowhere," he said leaning back and crossing his arms.

"We do want to go north and see the Fairy Forest and see Loch Fai, but then we want to keep going. Make our way up into the fairy kingdoms and see the fairies. Maybe... maybe talk to one..." I paused, breathing heavily but da's face told me nothing. "I just want to ask. Ask a

21

fairy about changelings. Ask them why they make them. Ask them why they steal babies. Why I am probably going to die soon even though I've never done anything wrong and if maybe they can stop it and..."

"Oh Morven, come here lass," da sighed dropping to his knees in front of me and pulling me down into his arms. "It's okay, I understand. I won't punish you, don't cry."

I couldn't help but cry into his shoulder while he held me.

Finally, the burden of lying to the people I loved most was gone and da didn't seem too angry, not angry enough to stop us going.

Talking about it made me remember just how much I needed answers, just how badly I wanted to find out why this happened and if I could save my life.

CHAPTER

Freya 3

Between the castle and the forest there were many meadows which filled with different flowers each season. Now that spring was approaching, the field we sat in was abloom with bright yellow daffodils, mixing with the few remaining snowdrops from winter.

Nieve and I loved to come to the meadows whenever I could escape from lessons and she could found time in between her chores.

Every time we visited, Nieve threaded the flowers she plucked into her long brown hair. She looked beautiful, especially when her hair shone almost auburn in the sunlight. I sometimes tried, but for some reason it just didn't look as good.

As Nieve was a human, she was never able to dress the way she would like. My father, King Ferchar, was insistent that the humans in our kingdom dressed in plain clothes and wore their hair in a simple style.

Unlike the fairies in Culhuinn, we fairies could dress however we liked and wear as much jewellery as we wanted. I longed for the day that Nieve could pick her own clothes and wear her hair as wild as she would like.

As Nieve roamed around in the flowers, I sat back on one of the tartan blankets we had brought with us and simply enjoyed being outside. At times the castle was stifling and I always found myself longing to be outside.

Not long after I sat down, I felt a little nudge at my leg. When I looked down I noticed one of the wee folk smiling shyly at me.

The wee folk didn't much enjoy the company of humans or fairies, but this little one seemed to enjoy mine well enough. She approached me whenever I came to the meadow, but she never stayed long. Today she held up a little white snowdrop that she had plucked. I gave her a grateful smile as I took it and her tiny little cheeks blushed a berry red.

Rustling from a nearby patch of flowers told me that her friend was impatiently waiting for her. Much like Nieve and I, they were always together. Unfortunately, her friend never came close.

"Thank you," I whispered as she waved her little hand at me and ran off into the flowers to join her companion.

I always wondered if she knew that I was the Princess or if she was simply curious about fairies and wanted to observe me closer. Whatever the reason, I couldn't help but feel special. I loved that our meetings were a secret no one else knew about. Nieve didn't sit still long enough to notice.

After she had her fill of the flowers, Nieve and I rode back through the gates of the castle, our hair windswept and her cheeks red from the wind.

After dismounting and leaving the horses in the care of the human stable hand, Berwin, we made our way indoors for a much-needed lunch.

As spring was only just beginning the weather was still mild enough that we got chilly sitting outside, especially Nieve. Despite the cold she never complained and loved nothing more than galloping across the open moors between the castle and the forest, her ears becoming so cold and red that I sometimes worried they would fall right off.

We raced through the halls laughing, occasionally having to pause to apologise to the servants whom we sent flying as we passed. As we went, we met mother who gave us a small smile but said nothing. I am quite sure that if we had stumbled across father we would have been in for a lecture about proper behaviour.

My heart pounded in my chest and my cheeks began to ache from smiling, as they so often did whenever I was with Nieve. If I had my own way, I would spend every waking moment with her and forget all about being a princess and lessons.

We swapped our thick heavy cloaks and dresses for lighter dresses, perfect for twirling and dancing, whilst remaining warm enough to keep us cosy inside the castle's thick stone halls. My dress was a light blue, whereas Nieve's was a dull shade of brown, which she still managed to look breath-taking in.

I knew it was foolish of me to spend so much time thinking about Nieve's lack of clothing options, but nevertheless I was always bothered by it. Any previous attempts to change father's mind had ended disastrously and so I gave up before I had even entered my twelfth year of life.

If I had a horse for every time I had wished that Nieve was a fairy like me, we would need a stable bigger than the castle.

"Come on Freya. I am about to die of hunger," Nieve complained making me jump in fright, not realising I had become so caught up in my thoughts.

"You scared me!" I accused as I followed her to the door.

She gave me an apologetic smile before leaning in and placing a soft warm kiss on my lips.

Over the last few years we'd begun sharing kisses more and more frequently. Although we never spoke about what there was between us, I knew that we both loved one another.

As children, we loved each other as best friends do, but as we matured so did our love. I often considered asking Nieve about us, but I was afraid to hear her response.

She was the more practical of the two of us, and I didn't want to draw attention to the fact that my father would likely behead us both the moment he found out I had fallen in love with the thing he hated most, a human.

"What were you thinking?" she asked softly.

"It's stupid," I mumbled, feeling foolish.

Nieve didn't waste her time on thoughts as silly mine.

"Nothing you think could ever be stupid," She insisted her eyes fierce and her grip on my arm reassuring.

I sighed. "I still hate that you can't wear bright dresses and plait flowers into your hair whenever you want. It's not fair."

Nieve gave my hand a squeeze. "It won't always be like this," she promised and the determined look on her face made me believe her.

I had to spend most of my afternoons in lessons, learning all I could about the different kingdoms and islands in this land. Father didn't think it was important that I know about the human kingdoms, but I could never stop myself from asking about them.

Thankfully my teacher Adair cared more about spreading knowledge than belittling humans and so he was always happy to oblige.

Nieve had lessons with me when we were children until a few years ago father decided that she didn't need to be learning. That was when she had to begin working in the kitchens. I always tried to tell myself that she still learned, but I hated that she wasn't with me.

I threw a fit when father told me of the changes but that brought me nothing but trouble and so I'd never mentioned it again. Perhaps it makes sense for a human to need less education than a fairy princess, but it still hurt.

A few weeks later, father invited me to lunch which made me nervous. I doubted he had anything good to say if he didn't want it said in front of mother or Nieve.

Unfortunately, you cannot ignore an invitation to lunch with the King, not even if he is your father. I had to drag myself away from Nieve and the patchwork blanket we had been working on together. Nieve was amused by how miserable the thought of lunch with him made me.

With a kiss for luck she sent me out the door, promising to catch up on her side of the blanket whilst I was away.

Far too soon I arrived at the table, feeling like I hadn't had nearly enough time to prepare myself for whatever he was planning to announce. It wouldn't be anything good.

"Take a seat my love," father said with a smile, gesturing at the seat across from him at the table.

We weren't eating in the main hall as there were only two of us, so we were much closer than I would have liked. I had nothing to distract me and all I could do was sit and stare at his harsh, lined face and worry about what would come next.

As the years passed, the worry my father caused me grew. Sometimes I wanted to hide from him. Wanted to go back to being a child without responsibilities and expectations to meet.

"Hello father," I said politely.

"Your teacher tells me that your studies are coming along well," he looked smug, despite having never taken any time to teach me himself.

"Yes, I am really enjoying it. Also, Nieve and I..."

He raised his hand to cut me off.

"I am glad to see that you are progressing better now that the human isn't distracting you during lessons."

"Nieve never distracted me. I've always been doing well," I protested with a frown, my nerves spiking at the mention of Nieve.

He glared at me and started picking at the chicken on his plate.

"You have always been far too distracted by that girl and so I've come to a decision," he paused dramatically, making my stomach twinge with dread.

"Yes, father?" I asked politely, his mental games never failed to infuriate me.

"I think it's time you prepare for your life as ruler of Culhuinn. That means learning more about ruling over a kingdom and spending less time distracted by humans. You're not a child anymore."

"There are humans all over this land, I doubt it would do me any good to avoid them," I tried to argue, wishing I could flee rather than stay and hear what he had to say.

"You doubt me because you are young and naive. Humans are lesser than us fairies, of course you know that. I think it's high time your little human friend moved out of your chambers and started staying with the other servants, where she should have been all along."

My mouth dropped open in dismay and I felt my earlier resolve to never again have a tantrum weakening. How dare he? Nieve meant everything to me and he wanted to discard her like she was nothing.

"I don't think that is a good idea father," I protested, frantically trying to search for a good excuse.

"I do not care. I am your father and I am the King, I know what is best for you," he didn't even bother to stop eating while he ruined the best part of my life.

"I can do extra lessons without Nieve having to leave," I insisted, dismayed that I had already sunk to pleading with him.

Father always emphasised the importance of not revealing your weaknesses to the enemy, something I was currently doing a terrible job of. If our situations had been reversed Nieve would know exactly what to say. If our roles were reversed she would save me.

"No," he said simply. "The human will be moved, along with some essential belongings, down to the servant's quarters where she will stay. Working like all humans in this castle should."

"This isn't fair!" I exclaimed, feeling my eyes prickling with tears of anger.

"Don't get emotional over a human. I never should have listened to your mother and let you befriend it anyway."

"Nieve isn't an it, she is my only friend," I cried, pushing my plate away and standing up. "I won't let you do this."

"It is done, and you better watch your tongue before I get angry," he looked almost amused.

I threw the chair out from behind me and ran out of the room. I heard father shouting at me to return but I ignored him.

He didn't care about me at all and, at that moment, I thought that I couldn't possibly hate him more. I hurried up to my rooms as quickly as I could, having to lift my skirts so I didn't fall flat on my face.

I must have looked ridiculous running through the halls, unable to stop the angry tears from slipping down my face, but no one made a move to stop me and I didn't hear father coming after me.

I threw open the door to the chambers Nieve and I shared but she was no longer inside, the blanket left discarded on the table. I rushed to the wardrobes and found that her clothes and shoes were all still inside. The discovery sparked a glimmer of hope, perhaps if her possessions remained then so did she.

I hurried to the door to check and see if Nieve had gone outside. I found the door locked which made me pause. The door was never locked.

I stood for a moment, completely unsure what to do before knocking timidly on the door. Perhaps Nieve was simply playing a trick on me.

There was no reply so I knocked as hard as I could, hurting my knuckles in the process. I was about to start shouting when I heard footsteps behind the door.

"Princess Freya, King Ferchar has ordered that the doors to your chambers remain locked until he sees fit to unlock them. He reminds you that you were warned about your behaviour and that he will see you when you have regained some sense. Meals and lessons will be continuing as normal within your chamber," said an unknown guard from outside.

"Can you get my mother?" I asked, feeling my lip quivering as I fought the urge to cry.

"The King said no visitors, I apologise Princess," the voice said before walking away.

I was trapped in my chambers. My only friend, my love, had been taken away from me and I had no one to help me, not even my mother.

With a hopeless sob, I ripped off my shoes and jewellery, throwing them across the room with as much force as I could muster before hiding myself under the bed covers to cry, holding our blanket close.

I hated my father and I vowed to never ever forgive him. Underneath my anger, I couldn't help but feel a twinge of hatred for myself.

This wouldn't have happened if only I had hidden my feelings and kept my temper in check. If only my mind was quick and sharp like Nieve's.

CHAPTER

4
Morven

Much to my relief, da explained to the family where Glen and I were planning to go whilst I was asleep. I think my emotional outburst the night before made him feel a little guilty for being firm with me, so he saved me the trouble of having to explain myself again.

Thankfully no one seemed to be angry with us for not being truthful and throughout the day, everyone took the time to approach me discretely and tell me how much they supported what we planned to do.

When I met Glen that afternoon, after another breathless climb up the hills, I had to tell him the bad news. I felt guilty for revealing our secret without asking him, for breaking his trust, but the feeling of relief was stronger. I was glad to no longer be burdened with our secret.

"Maybe I should cry when I tell them so my da doesn't decide to smack me for lying," Glen shouted from where he was sitting, perched upon a grassy ledge above me.

"Just bring up my impending death and hopefully they won't be too angry," I shouted back.

"I am glad you told the truth Morven. I don't know what we would have done if your da had stopped you going."

"Hopefully he would have eventually forgiven me and let me go," I said, aimlessly ripping up handfuls of grass.

Glen jumped from the ledge and landed on the soft grass beside me. From his bag, he brought out a loaf of bread and a blanket, which we settled down on to eat. I'd spent the morning helping ma and Munro clean up our part of the mess in the castle.

Once we'd finished the bread, and Glen told me more about the fairies we might encounter on our journey, we had to make our way back home. Glen had to go and tell his family about our lies and I had to help ma with dinner.

Glen never did say if his da punished him for lying, but they were still allowing our adventure to go ahead. Over the next few days we collected what food we could for our journey; mainly cheese, bread and dried meat as they would last longer than any vegetables. We were confident that we could forage or hunt small animals whilst we travelled and we planned to buy food whenever we reached towns or villages.

"Eat whenever you have the chance," had been Malcolm's main piece of advice for me. "You never know how long you'll go without food so it's best to eat often."

The days went by much quicker than I would have liked. Before I knew it ma, Bonnie and I were once again preparing her stew. We were having dinner with Glen's family to celebrate our last night in the village.

"It's alright to feel nervous or even scared," Bonnie confided in me, "I was terrified about leaving my family

34

and Cladanan to travel all the way up north to Tirwood with Malcolm, but it was the best decision I ever made. You just have to trust yourself and trust in each other."

As much as I tried to tell others that I wasn't feeling nervous and scared, I couldn't convince myself.

I kept imagining all the horrible things that could happen to us out on the road, the awful people we might meet and the wild beasts that could attack us. I tried to remind myself that I wanted to go on this adventure, that I wanted to learn more about the fairies and changelings.

Malcolm told me that he had been nervous before he set off but that once we were on the road, we would be far too busy having fun to bother thinking about everyone back home.

We gathered in Glen's family's cottage, which was bigger than ours, so both of our families could be together to have one last feast. Ma had made her stew as per usual and Martha, Glen's ma, had baked bread and bannocks for us all. Glen had two older brothers Donal and Dougal. Dougal was married, but luckily his wife was visiting her sister in a nearby village so that made the room slightly less crowded.

I had always felt like Glen's family was my second family. I'd known them my whole life. Da and Glen's da, Graham, had known each other since they were born and went adventuring together when they were younger. They were both overjoyed to see their children following in their footsteps.

As we ate they told us stories about the mountains in the south, we'd all heard about their encounter with a wulver before but the story never lost its excitement, no matter how many times they told it.

"We've been working on a gift for you both," Martha announced once the food was finished.

A moment later ma skipped through from the next room with two wrapped bundles, one for Glen and one for me.

I felt myself blush as we took our gifts as all eyes in the room were suddenly on us, watching expectantly. Inside the bundle was the most gorgeous dress I had ever seen. The tartan at the bottom was green and brown, the top half brown with long sleeves.

Granny Athol had knitted a thick woollen scarf which was dyed a rich deep brown. The final item was a thick travelling cloak of a darker shade of green. They were the nicest clothes I had ever owned and could tell they must have cost a lot of coin.

"I love them!" I exclaimed jumping up to throw my arms around ma who looked equally as ecstatic.

"Only the best for my wee lass on her first adventure," da said patting me on the back.

"Aye and only the best for my wee lad," Graham agreed, Glen had also received new clothes for travelling.

"We should make bets on how long it takes before they fall in some mud and ruin them," Munro laughed.

"I can't see them making it out of the village," Donal said.

"Not even out this cottage," Dougal added.

That night, after the meal, ma and da let me sleep in their bed with them. I think ma was more upset about me leaving than she was letting show and if I was honest, so was I. Da seemed excited for me but I knew he must have been slightly worried, especially with me being a changeling.

We were just about to get into bed and sleep when wee Morag wandered in, her big round eyes filled with tears as she told ma about her nightmare. As ma left to go fetch Bonnie I snuggled under the piles of blankets.

"I don't think anything bad will happen to you Morven, you're a brave girl and together you and Glen make a perfect team," da paused sighing and running a hand over his face, clearly unhappy about what he was going to say. "If something does happen and either of you die somewhere up in the north, I will find you. I'll bring Malcolm and Munro and we will come get you. We'll bring you home. I've told Glen this as well. I won't let a child of mine die and be buried away from the family."

I pushed my face into the blankets in an attempt to stem the tears now falling. It was comforting to know that they wouldn't simply leave me, but the thought of never seeing any of them again broke my heart. Da placed a kiss on my head and began rubbing soothing circles on my back, like he did when I was a child. Sometime later I felt ma join us again and she cuddled up beside me.

"Sleep well lass," I heard her whisper just as I started to calm down and fall asleep.

The next morning was awful. As I got dressed, ate my breakfast and packed my bag, my throat was tight and sore as I tried not to cry. My eyes burned and I had to keep reminding myself that I did actually want to go on this journey. I wanted answers and I wanted to try and save my life. I eventually lost the battle against the crying when it was time to say goodbye.

"You have a good time and look after each other," ma said in between hitching breaths and sniffles.

"Yes, keep yourselves safe. Make sure you have fun whilst you travel, no one will blame you for not being able to find the answers you seek," da added, the two of them hugging me tight.

Thankfully ma and da were the last people for me to say goodbye to. By now my nose was sore from wiping it and my eyes must have been red from all the crying.

Glen and his family weren't handling our departure much better and so there were red faces, blotchy from crying, all around.

After our emotional goodbyes, we travelled with a farmer da knew. He was taking wool to the main town where there was the largest market in the kingdom and the royal castle.

It was strange to leave our little village behind. I watched and waved until our village became nothing more than a little cluster of stone cottages in the distance. After crying out all my tears, I began to feel less upset about leaving them. Instead I was anxious to get our journey started, although I still dreaded not being able to talk to them every day.

Everyone goes on journeys, I told myself whenever I felt sadness creeping in. Everyone goes away and everyone eventually comes back, it would be fine. Glen must have been feeling the same as he wrapped an arm around my shoulders as we sat amongst sacks full of wool.

"What do you think it will be like?" I asked as we travelled along the worn road, through gently sloping hills without a cottage or person in sight.

"Busy I reckon, and loud," Glen admitted.

"I can't imagine seeing so many people in one place. Da said it's much bigger than our village and that the market is even busier than our castle during festivals."

"Aye that's true, but I am sure we will love it," Glen laughed. "We'll probably be amazed and wander around with our mouths open staring at everything."

"As long as we don't catch too many flies we should be okay."

Talking about all the sights we might see helped pass the time and made me forget about what we had left behind, at least for the moment.

We were lucky that the weather stayed dry as we travelled, there was a slight chill in the air that made me glad for the new thick travelling clothes ma and da had given us.

I was used to living amongst fields, with only a few hills to break the monotony. I found myself awestruck by the lands we were travelling through. We passed increasingly huge hills with outcrops of grey rock bursting from the grass. We passed more rocks like the fairy stone, each with carvings similar to the ones back in our village.

"Morven, look over there," Glen suddenly pointed over to one of the rolling green hills.

There, beside a winding river, was the most magnificent animal I had ever seen. Back home we had cows, sheep and chickens but never had I seen an animal like this.

It had thick brown fur covering its body and pointy ears. Though the feature that struck me most were the two huge antlers protruding from its head, twisting and curling towards the sky. I had heard about the stags that roamed the hills and forests but had never been lucky enough to see one with my own eyes, until now.

"We've hardly even left the village and already we've seen things from the stories," Glen said his eyes bright with excitement, "Just think about everything we might see as we go north."

After one overnight stop, which Glen and I spent curled up together in a pile of blankets beside the fire, we arrived at the town.

As we approached the town, the road became busier with farmers and families from other surrounding villages, all heading in to visit the markets. We passed many people on foot, heading in from the cottages on the very outskirts of the town, which we had seen scattered amongst the hills.

The cart pulled to a stop just before entering the town to let us go exploring on our own. We took our leather bags and bundled up our blankets.

Then, we were off on our own, for the very first time in our lives. I took Glen's hand as we approached a larger crowd of people and he gave it a reassuring squeeze.

The main town in Tirwood sat near the foot of the southern part of the Fairy Hills. I couldn't stop staring at the giant mountain peaks visible behind the market and the castle.

The castle sat atop a hill behind the market, at the edge of the town, and was the closest thing to the mountains. It was the most glorious building I had ever seen. It must have had at least three floors with stone turrets, like we'd heard about in the tales.

Unfortunately, before we could see the castle up close, we had to brave the bustling market.

There were stalls we could recognise in the market selling meat and bread and seasonal vegetables. Then there were stalls dedicated to specific items like knitted hats, gloves and little pieces of metal jewellery. One even sold expensive looking gems that Glen was sure weren't really the blood of the sky fairies, but he had a long look anyway.

The market traders called out to passers-by and we found ourselves trying soups, a strange herbal tea and even ended up being pressured into buying a little piece of carved wood which showed an engraving of the castle. Not essential, but I knew ma would appreciate it as a gift.

After spending the afternoon wandering around the market we went looking for somewhere to eat. Malcolm had told me about pubs and inns where you could trade coin for food, drink and a bed for the night. Glen and I had never had a reason to spend much of the coins we had earned doing work on the family farms, so we were sure we had enough to last us the whole journey.

We found one inn that we both agreed looked quite respectable. It was a stone building with two floors and a thick thatched roof which, for some reason, made it seem a lot safer than the others we had passed.

We quickly made our way inside as the night was starting to draw in and my hands were numb from the cold, despite spring beginning.

The inn's owner was a cheerful man with a shaved head and a beard even larger than Glen's. He laughed heartily as we asked about a room and food. Apparently, it was obvious that neither of us had ever done this before but he was eager enough to help us. Probably thanks to our coin.

With our room purchased for two nights, and a hot dinner waiting for us, we stored our bags and blankets under the rickety bed before locking the door and heading down for dinner.

Dinner consisted of slightly stale bread, some pork and boiled nettles to wash it down. The nettle tea made Glen cough and splutter but we decided that it was better if he drank what he hated, rather than wasting our coins on more expensive drink and ending up drunk.

The wooden tables in the inn were long with many seats and we soon found ourselves drawn into conversations with the locals. They were eager to share gossip about market sellers we had never heard of and news about King Torin.

Unfortunately, they soon ran out of things to tell us and became curious about what villagers were doing up here in the town.

"So, ran away to get married did ye?" A man with hardly any teeth asked, giving us a sly grin.

"Oh no, just thought we would see the town. Not much where we live but grass and animals," Glen said while I just rolled my eyes.

We didn't act like lovers and anyone paying attention would see that it was not women that held Glen's attention.

"Aye well there's lots to see here," said the toothless man's friend, his defining feature being a pair of the largest ears I had ever seen.

"Lots to see and hopefully lots of stories, I love to collect tales," Glen explained.

"If it's tales yer after then ye want to be seeing the wee old lady," Toothless said gesturing left and spilling his drink all over Ears.

"Aye, she'll tell you a tale or two," Ears agreed, absentmindedly shaking the drink off his arm like he was used to it.

"Where does the lady live?" I asked, suddenly a lot more interested in the conversation.

"Across the river," said Ears.

"Aye, across river and down the road," agreed Toothless.

"Across the river, down the road and up to the hill to the last wooden cottage," Ears finished nodding seriously.

That was the most ridiculous way I had ever received directions but I was excited to see what she would have to say. I hadn't been sure how Glen was going to find stories, unless we had encounters with all sorts of magical beings, likely risking our lives.

An old lady in a cottage seemed like a much safer way for Glen to find what he was after and I could tell from the smile he gave me that he was excited as well.

CHAPTER

Euna[5]

"I do wish you would stop that," my twin, Aelwen, called from across the hall where she stood in her travelling clothes, ready to leave. She was helping her youngest child Prince Elath, a small boy of only 10 years, to fasten his cloak despite his protests that he was old enough to do it himself.

"Maybe if you wish harder, it will come true," I replied with a smirk, continuing to absentmindedly gouge grooves into the table with a small dagger.

"I suppose, if it makes you feel better, then you can just stay here and continue carving up the table," she smiled calmly as she slowly approached me, as if approaching a small animal and trying not to frighten it.

"Yes. I am sure taking up carving will solve all of my problems," I threw the dagger down onto the table and stood to embrace her.

Despite how much I attempted to distance myself from everything, it was impossible not to love my family.

"I will miss you." she whispered, wrapping her arms tight around me.

I let myself smile as her snow-white hair tickled my face. We were born to the same mother and father, but where she had white hair to match our pale skin, I had hair blacker than night, matching our dark eyes.

"If you don't travel down to Wulvendach then they might come north to Norbroch. Considering the mess our last royal guests left behind, that is something I definitely want to avoid," I forced a laugh.

"You know as well as I that the wulver never leave their kingdom. Are you sure you won't come with us? The children would be so pleased."

"We should leave one queen in the castle, just in case we receive unexpected visitors."

Our father was killed during a battle when we were young, leaving our mother with two twin girls to raise and a kingdom to rule. She did a marvellous job and Norbroch prospered and found peace during her reign. Her one fault however, was that she neglected to ever tell us which twin was the heir to the throne.

There was much debate between the Lairds and Ladies, about who they thought most deserved the throne. Instead of waiting for them, we came to our own decision.

What better way to rule a kingdom than to have two queens, two people to share the burden, two people to council and guide each other. Much to the dismay of many, there was nothing that could be done to stop us and fifteen years ago we were both crowned Queen of Norbroch.

"Take care of yourself Euna. Tormod will be making sure you do," Aelwen placed a gentle kiss on my forehead before joining her family in the courtyard where they were mounting their horses, ready to journey south.

I watched as they prepared to leave, along with their guards and servants. My nieces and nephew looked excited about journeying south but I did not envy them. Not when it was safe here in the castle.

"Stay safe on the road," I called as they began to leave.

I watched from the large wooden doors as Aelwen, her husband Laird Ronan and their three children rode out of our castle which sat at the foot of the frozen mountains.

They would travel south, crossing the border into Wulvendach. From there they would follow the border between Wulvendach and Culhuinn before heading inland to the castle. There they would meet with the wulver King and Queen.

The wulver were fairies that had a covering of hair all over their bodies and possessed the strength to crush a human, and possibly even a fairy, with their bare hands. Despite their unusual strength and power, they are quiet people who keep mainly to themselves.

Unfortunately, this means discussing anything of importance with them requires a long tiring journey as they avoid leaving their homes and families.

In the past, I too travelled south to visit. Now those days were long gone and the thought of travelling out of Norbroch filled me with an uncomfortable mix of dread and fear.

I preferred to remain here in my kingdom, safe in the knowledge that no one would ever be allowed to hurt me in this castle, never again.

Once I had watched Aelwen and her family ride south and out of sight I returned to the main hall and took my seat. This time, with nothing to distract me the dagger was left discarded on the table.

I could not help but cast my mind back ten years.

10 YEARS AGO

"The journey here was awful," King Ferchar declared loudly as he took his place across from Aelwen and I at the table.

His wife, the Queen, had the decency to look somewhat embarrassed by her husband's outburst and offered us an apologetic smile.

"I like the snow," chirped the young Princess Freya from her seat beside her mother.

Unlike my nieces and nephew who were too young to sit at a table, and so spared from an evening of dull conversation, the Princess was ten years old.

Despite my annoyance at her family's visit I had to admit that she looked precious. She wore a thick woollen dress with a fur collar. Such thick clothes were useful outside in the snow, but they made the poor girl look awfully uncomfortable inside our warm hall. Her blonde hair was gathered behind her head and she had snowdrops threaded amongst her intricate plaits.

"You are in luck Princess, it is to snow for the whole duration of your stay here. You will have plenty of time to go out and play," Aelwen replied with a kind smile at the young girl.

"You should move further south, it's much less harsh. The moment we passed through the mountains into Norbroch I thought I was going to freeze stiff," complained the King, much to the amusement of the Princess.

"It makes a lovely change," the Queen swiftly changed the topic of conversation before her husband could insult us and our home any further. "Is that venison I see?"

The feast carried on that way, the King making snide remarks about us and our home, his oblivious little Princess finding it amusing and his wife frantically offering compliments.

Aelwen did not seem to mind and laughed along with the King's jokes, easing some of the tension. I, on the other hand, stabbed viciously at my meal and glared icily at him.

"I think perhaps our discussions can wait until the morning," Aelwen said with a smile as we finished the last of the feast. "I am sure a night's rest will do you all the world of good."

The King agreed and we were finally able to retire for the evening. After hastily saying my goodbyes, I made my exit from the hall and began heading up to my chambers. Tomorrow our discussions regarding trade and farming would commence.

The battle that killed our father was fought between Norbroch and Culhuinn, the climax of years of war. Our agreements would be the beginning of a new friendship between our kingdoms. Though the King's attitude was making me wonder if we would live to regret this decision.

As I was rounding a corner on the upper floor I found myself colliding with a human. The human was knocked to the ground whilst I merely had to take a step back to regain my balance. I glared as he took his time getting up off the floor, grinning as he went.

"I apologise my Lady," the man said after he found his feet again

"Your majesty," I corrected.

His cheeks turned a rosy red, which reminded me of the berries that grew close to the forest floor as he gave a low bow. I had seen only a few humans in my life, mainly in passing as we travelled.

There were no humans here in Norbroch. To me humans were strange, so like us fairies, but so fragile.

49

To the human eye, or to a fairy with poor vision, we appeared the same. However, I could see that there were numerous differences between us.

Where my skin was like a blank sheet of undisturbed snow, free from imperfection, this human had little brown freckles covering his nose and red cheeks. Blue veins were visible beneath his skin in areas, and he had wrinkles around his eyes as he smiled. I wondered why he was smiling, until I had the sudden horrible realisation that I was staring at him and found myself scrambling for something to say.

"I apologise your majesty, although it seems I was the one in danger during our encounter," the grin never left his face.

"Yes well, you are a human," I pointed out, "What did you expect?"

He laughed then as if he had never heard a more humorous comment in his life.

"I do hope I survive our encounter, me being a mere human," he teased and I had to fight the urge to smile myself.

"What is your name?" I enquired, unsure why I even cared.

"Lachlann, I came here to Norbroch with my King and Queen, whom I hope won't need to hear about this. King Ferchar would be displeased to hear that one of his servants had been foolish enough to run into you, your majesty."

"I do hope you will be more careful walking through my halls in future, Lachlann," I said before continuing down the hall towards the stairs which took me up to my bedchamber. "King Ferchar will not hear about this encounter from me."

I did not look to see if he would reply, or if he watched me go. It was oddly difficult not to turn back, but I managed to control myself.

Why did it matter if a human servant was watching me leave? I decided that I must be tired from the long day getting ready for the King and Queen's arrival. That explained my foolish thoughts.

PRESENT DAY

A decade later, I could still remember the way I felt that evening as if it had been mere moments ago. As hard as I tried I could not get the human, Lachlann, out of my thoughts. I convinced myself that it was simply because he was different and new. I thought I would soon tire of him.

How wrong I was.

I should have known, as I lay in bed that night thinking about those freckles, that I was already lost.

The arrival of the cook demanding to know what I wanted for my evening meal roused me from my thoughts. I quickly dismissed her, the thought of eating anything with my churning stomach made me feel nauseous.

My guard Tormod, who had joined me whilst I was lost in thought, frowned until I promised to eat something later.

Thinking about Aelwen and her family riding south along the coast made me sigh. As much as I did not want to leave the castle, I felt quite sure that if I never left, then I would never escape my grief.

CHAPTER

6

Morven

After a night spent crushed together in the small straw bed at the inn we had a quick breakfast of porridge, which was so lumpy ma would have died had she saw it.

We then headed out to find the home of the old lady we'd heard so much about the night before. I couldn't help but feel nervous as we made our way over the small river that ran through the village and out amongst the cottages on the other side.

I was quite certain that witches didn't exist, but, from all the tales I had been told I was sure that if we did encounter a witch on our journey, this would be when it happened. An old lady living alone on the edge of a town who knew more about fairies than anyone else, I couldn't help but be worried.

"What if she is a witch?" I asked deciding to voice my thoughts before we walked straight into a witch's lair.

"I've never heard of a witch living in the town, but I suppose this does seem like the place," Glen said gesturing towards the little wooden cottage we were approaching.

"I'd rather not be murdered by a witch before we even make it north of the town," I said, my stomach churning more and more the closer we got.

"I'm just messing with you. I am sure she isn't a witch, just an old lady with some stories. That will be me one day, alone in my little cottage telling stories about my adventures in the north."

"You better mention your wonderful, beautiful accomplice Morven in these stories," I elbowed him lightly in the ribs.

"My most popular story will be about the time I let a witch eat you whilst I ran away home," Glen said, making us both laugh.

He was always good at making me feel better when I was afraid.

All the talking and laughing made the walk to the old woman's house pass much faster than I would have liked. The next thing I knew we were passing through a small garden filled with white snowdrops. The flowers making it look as if her grass was covered in snow.

Surely a witch wouldn't plant a garden? Or at least that's what I tried to tell myself. Though the tales never mentioned what witches thought of flowers, maybe they all had gardens?

I bumped into Glen's back when he stopped. He had to grab my arm to stop me toppling down into the flowers I was so caught up thinking about.

Glen gestured that he would knock, and the silence as I waited made my nerves grow again. What would da say when he found out that we'd travelled all the way to the town, only to be killed and eaten by a witch that we'd approached ourselves?

Glen knocked on the wooden door and we waited nervously for it to be answered. The door flew open without warning, revealing a tiny woman with curly grey hair and a chest so large that I was completely powerless to stop eyes being drawn to them.

"I thought you two were going to stand out here in the garden all day, and I'm bloody glad you didn't crush my snowdrops!" she said, breaking our stunned the silence.

"Oh... well... we are sorry," Glen mumbled.

"Don't you worry, well come on into the warmth. No point standing out here in the garden all day like a pair of scarecrows," she wandered inside, gesturing for us to follow.

I felt my tension ease and almost wanted to laugh. We were expecting a malevolent witch and instead it was the sassiest old lady I had ever met. Granny Athol would have been horrified by her.

We quickly followed her in, Glen shutting the door gently behind us. Her cottage wasn't filled with cauldrons and potions like I had anticipated. Instead there was an old wooden table with matching chairs, each had a little straw cushion and a fabric covering. There were mismatched old woollen rugs strewn across the floor and tapestries pinned to the walls.

The burning fire made the whole cottage feel cosy and the pot, of what I guessed was soup, on the table made my mouth water immediately.

"I assume you are here because you want some stories from me?" The old woman said with a smile, picking up the ladle and beginning to fill the two bowls in front of her with the chunky soup.

"Yes, we heard you are something of an expert on fairies," I said as we sat ourselves down on the seats across from her, glad to finally put my heavy bag down.

"If you want an expert then you are definitely in the right place. A story and some piping hot soup is just what the two of you need. A wee bit of looking after on your first big journey," she passed us each a bowl and a spoon before sitting down to start her own.

"How did you know that?" Glen asked looking just as shocked as I felt.

"When you've been around as long as me you just know these things," she replied with a wink. "Now, what would you like to ask me about the fairies?"

"We wanted to know more about why they create changelings and what they do with the babies. If you know anything about that," I asked before shoving more of the soup into my mouth.

The soup was perfect, the vegetables were just the right softness and the meat was so tender.

"Ah yes, I thought you might have been a changeling lass."

"I'm the last one alive in my village so I just want some answers." I replied, pretending I wasn't freaked out that she knew so much about us.

Would a witch know this much? I really should have listened to the stories better.

"Well, going up north will definitely do you some good. I've heard some say that it's good for you to be up nearer the fairies and their magic. You might even meet your twin."

"My twin..." I mumbled shocked enough that I managed to stop eating.

"Morven doesn't have a twin," Glen explained.

"Oh, yes she does. Up in the north there will be a girl with wavy brown hair and big blue eyes who looks just like your friend Morven. A changeling is simply a copy of the human baby that the fairies took, so there is an identical girl to you somewhere up there," the woman said, looking pleased to have shocked us both again.

"What will she be doing? What do they want her for?" Suddenly I was worried for this girl who looked just like me, a girl I had never even met.

"She will be old enough to be working for a family of fairies by now I suppose. Fairies don't much like working and humans make good workers, especially if they can be raised from birth to do a certain job."

"That's awful!" Glen said.

"Oh, it won't be too bad. She will have food and clothes and a nice warm bed to sleep in. Much better than being eaten by a fairy don't you think?" the woman said kindly, obviously trying to soothe the disgust we were both feeling.

"Who do they think they are?!" I exclaimed, horrified.

Realistically I knew that there were fates much worse than a life of arduous work, but it made my chest ache to think of her alone, working for fairies with no family around her.

No choice about what she wanted to do with her life. No adventures. I was also sad for ma and da, they would be heartbroken when they knew what really happened to their baby.

"Oh hush, eat your soup. The girl might even like it," She said with a smile that definitely wasn't as reassuring as she intended it to be.

I couldn't help but feel shaken by our visit to the wise old lady, we realised after leaving that we had never even asked her name. Everyone has always known that the fairies take our children, but never the reason why. It was horrible to finally know.

Before it was easy enough to speculate and dismiss all the upsetting suggestions, now we couldn't be ignorant and it was awful. I almost wished we had never asked.

Glen pointed out that the old lady could have been lying as we had never asked how she got her information, but she'd known so much about us without being told which me believe her.

Before we left, she used a piece of charcoal from her fire to sketch us a map on a piece of spare fabric. It showed the journey we would be taking and she explained that, although it wasn't very common for people to travel north, there were still paths we could follow.

After another night in the inn, we decided to go and see the castle. The streets leading towards the castle had banners draped from building to building, proudly showing the tartan favoured by King Torin. We followed the banners down through the streets until we came out at the bottom of a steep grassy hill. There were a few worn paths leading up to the castle gates.

As we slowly walked up the path we spotted many guards wandering around in pairs, watching the people closely, looking for any trouble. We could also make out guards on the castle walls.

I wished there was some way for us to get up there with them as the view must have been spectacular, overlooking the town and all of its surroundings. I wondered if they could even see our village from up there.

We strayed off the path and made our way around the front of the castle walls. Glen pointed out a large patch of grass which was sparse and trampled compared to the rest. He explained that was where the annual games were held.

During the games hundreds of people, from villages all around, travelled to the town. We had all heard stories about the caber tossing and the hammer throw where the strongest men and women from all over Tirwood gathered to compete. Then there were the dancers with their flowing skirts and of course, the unimaginable feast. Glen and I would be long gone by the time this year's games occurred, but I could almost imagine what it would have been like as we stood there on the field.

We overheard a group of women complaining about rain being on the way and decided to stay one final night before setting off. It would take a few days for us to travel from the town all the way up to the small village beside Loch Fai, where we would be taken across the loch in a boat, for a few coins.

From there, we would have to travel through the Fairy Hills, but I decided not to think about that until nearer the time. The thought of spending days in amongst the mountains was strangely nerve wracking.

Glen suggested we have another look through the market at the stalls, rousing me from my thoughts. The sellers changed every day and so did the items on sale.

As we were looking at one stall which sold wooden runes and an especially peculiar set of stones, that the owner claimed they were from the queen of the sky fairies, we heard raised voices coming from the street we had followed towards the castle.

Glen grabbed my hand and we hurried off towards the source of the noise to see what was happening.

People were lining the streets and so Glen had to pull us both up onto a stack of barrels so we could see over their heads. I leaned my head against his arm and closed my eyes for a moment, taking deep breaths and cursing my changeling body for becoming breathless so quickly.

"Morven look!" Glen exclaimed pointing down the street where riders on horseback were making their way through the streets. "It's the King."

At the front of the procession sat King Torin, he had grey hair and a beard that Glen was likely jealous of. It reached halfway down his chest. I decided at that moment that if Glen ever tried to grow one as long I would cut it off whilst he slept.

Beside the King sat two younger men that I assumed were his sons, the Princes. Both looked to be around the same age as Malcolm. The eldest had his dark hair tied back like the King, whereas the younger of the two had curls which seemed to stick up in every direction.

They all wore their favoured tartan of purple and blue. Some of the men carried bows and knives, making me wonder where they had been and why they needed to be so heavily armed.

"Probably returning from a hunt," Glen explained as if reading my mind.

As they got closer the noise grew to an almost deafening level as people cheered and shouted all around us, as if they would somehow attract the attention of the King or one of the Princes. People were holding their children up towards them and it made me smile to see that the younger prince was waving and smiling at the children he passed. I could imagine that for years they would be retelling the story of the time they met the Prince of Tirwood.

I couldn't wait to tell da about the King, he often spoke of him and from what I could gather he was a good ruler.

We hadn't been called to war against another kingdom in a lifetime and he was fair with the coin he gave in return for food and wool from the farmers.

As I watched him ride past, I wondered if the King knew about the changelings and if he had ever tried to stop our babies from being stolen. It didn't look like his own sons were changelings and for a moment, I had the horrible thought that perhaps he worked with the fairies and allowed them to steal our babies. I hoped not.

"Wave Morven!" Glen shouted over the noise as he grabbed my hand again and waved it wildly in the air, making me laugh.

The youngest Prince waved in our direction as he passed, although almost definitely not at us. Glen cheered ecstatically and was likely already creating the story he would tell. We had only travelled to the town and already we had gathered so many stories to tell.

After the excitement of seeing the royal family, we decided to head back to the inn for food. It was still strange not to return home every evening to see what ma had cooked.

We decided to drink, as it was our last night in the town, and with it we got a soup so thick I didn't even want to know what it was made of. Taking a seat at the long table, in the same place we had the previous nights, I was excited about the intriguing people we might meet.

We didn't have to wait long before a man with long black hair sat beside us with a bowl of equally thick looking soup. His skin was brown, darker than Bonnie's, so I knew he was from the far south. His worn clothes made it clear that he was on a journey like us, or had at least been travelling for a long time. He seemed to sense me watching him for he looked up with a smile.

"First journey away from home eh?" He asked with a grin.

"How is that so obvious?" Glen asked frowning.

"When you've been around this land as many times as I, you just get to know people, and you two are far too excited to be here in this shit little inn," he said before laughing at himself.

"Where have you journeyed?" I asked, eager to hear all about his adventures.

"Where haven't I been? I've been wandering since I was younger than the two of you."

"Well, we are heading north into the fairy kingdoms," I said, wanting to impress him.

"Good thing you decided to go in the spring. It's a dangerous place to be in the winter, almost froze solid so I did."

"Did you ever meet a fairy?" Glen asked, hoping he could have useful information for us.

"Aye met a few. Not the nicest of folk, they look down on humans, even the more gifted of us," he frowned.

"Are you? Gifted I mean," I asked, feeling my eyes grow wide.

Granny Athol had told me stories about a woman who visited the village once, she could make the ground crack and crumble simply by touching it.

The man smiled, looking pleased to have been asked and looked around for something he could perform his gifts on. He plucked a wilted flower from the pot halfway down the table and held it out in front of him, making sure we both had a good view of it.

Then, before our eyes the flower straightened, the petals uncurling and losing their brown hue. It was as if he had just plucked the flower from the ground.

He had brought it back to life.

Beside me Glen choked on his drink and spat it across the table before having a coughing fit. I simply gasped and then froze. What else could I do, seeing magic for the first time. The man looked even more pleased with himself and placed the flower back into the pot amongst the brown and wilted ones.

"Don't see much magic, do you?" he chuckled.

"No, not at all," Glen explained between coughs.

"Where do you come from?" I asked curiously, his question making it seem as if you often saw magic wherever he was from.

"I grew up in a village, west of the twin lochs in Finclaw. They say the link to the Otherworld is just through the standing stones in our land. You see a lot of gifted folk down there, a gift from the Others I reckon."

I glanced at Glen, who looked absolutely thrilled to learn more about magic. I thought to myself that if our first adventure went well, perhaps we would make our way down south to Finclaw. To see more magic and maybe even try to learn some ourselves.

"You would make a great farmer," I blurted out without thinking.

The man howled with laughter.

"Aye, maybe I would. One day I might settle down and start my own farm when I get bored of travelling."

To my relief, the subject changed from his magic to Eilean Trì as Glen was eager to hear more about the islands.

Bonnie had told us stories about them in the past, but this man seemed to know all about the trouble brewing down there. Three kings were after one crown, he told us. It all sounded very exciting but I soon found myself wishing for bed.

Depending on the weather, it would take a few days for us to reach the village beside Loch Fai and so we wanted to make the most of comfortable beds while we could.

CHAPTER

7

Morven

The weather was thankfully dry when we woke the next morning, meaning we were free to leave and start the next part of our journey. I couldn't help but be nervous about leaving the town. The loch-side village would be very different to what we were used to and too far for us to quickly return home. As we travelled north we would soon be entering the fairy kingdoms, which was more than a little terrifying.

Before leaving, we had one last browse of the market and bought food we hoped would last, plenty of bread and dried meat. We wanted to have a good supply in case our journey to the loch-side village took longer than expected.

As we bid a farewell to the inn keeper we mentioned that we were heading north. He helpfully suggested we go to the northern exit of the town and look to see if there were any traders or farmers travelling north who would agree to take us with them.

We decided to listen to his advice and found a man returning to a small farming village like ours, halfway between the town and our destination. We gave him a few coins to take us and he seemed very happy to have company for the journey.

Our day was spent listening to stories about his wives, whom he still couldn't believe let him into their lives, and their numerous children.

Unlike during our journey to the town, he let us sit at the front of the cart with him, instead of sitting in the back amongst the supplies. That meant we had an even better view of the landscape and made me glad to have new travelling clothes as the wind was freezing.

The further north of the town we travelled, the more we could see the peaks of the Fairy Hills. Although the day was dry there was a thick fog in the air surrounding them and so the uppermost peaks were hidden from view. Our travelling companion, Wallace, said that the fog would soon clear. I hoped that by the time we reached the loch we would be able to see them in their full glory.

Wallace seemed very curious about our journey and had many questions. Glen wisely decided to say that the loch was our final destination. We both silently agreed that Wallace didn't seem like the type who thought highly of adventures or the fairies.

"Does your village ever have any trouble with changelings?" I decided to ask.

"Aye," Wallace said simply with a look of sorrow that made me immediately regret asking. "My wee lad Clyde was a changeling. Had only one leg on him but he was a jolly wee thing, died in his fourth year though."

"I'm sorry. We've known quite a few changelings to die in our village as well," Glen said sympathetically, reaching out to give my hand a squeeze.

"I reckon it's worse in our village lad, rare to find a family without a changeling these days," he sighed, his hands clenching on the horse's reins.

"Is that because you are closer to the fairy kingdoms?" I asked, hesitant but hoping he was still okay to talk about the subject.

"Aye probably, not sure how many changelings they have up beside the loch but I'll bet it's a lot more than in the villages down south."

The conversation ended after that, each of us lost in thought about changelings that had died and cursing the unfairness of it all. With so many children being stolen in the north, it was reasonable to assume that Glen and I wouldn't be the first people attempting a journey like this.

I hoped that those who'd journeyed north before us simply hadn't found an answer. The thought that they might have died at the hands of the fairies made me want to turn and run back home. I decided not to ask Wallace about that. I knew I wouldn't like the answer.

We rode on for about half the day before Wallace suggested we stop for a break. Apparently, his horses had been carrying him up and down this road for the past seven years, but needed to stop every now and then.

He insisted on sharing his food with us and so we ate bread with cheese and washed it down with strange, cold herbal tea. I could hear Malcolm in my mind, reminding me to eat whenever the opportunity arose.

Wallace wouldn't take any coin for the food so I pretended not to notice when Glen snuck a few coins into his bags when he went to relieve himself. That was one thing that annoyed me about travelling as a girl, men and boys could just piss wherever and whenever they liked.

Unlike many girls, I didn't bleed with every moon and so we wouldn't have to worry about me slowing down our journey with cramps and sickness. Ma said she thought it was because I was a changeling, but we weren't sure.

We were all rejuvenated after the food and so Wallace decided to sing for most the afternoon. He claimed that his horses liked it, but I highly doubted it.

He sang songs Glen and I had never heard before about kelpies in Loch Fai and the Fairy Hills. His happiness was infectious and soon Glen and I found ourselves awkwardly clapping along and attempting to shout out the parts of the songs that we could pick up.

Just as the light was beginning to fade, we spotted a little village, much like ours, in the distance. We were closer to the mountains and I couldn't wait to see them in the morning light.

"There isn't any room for you two in my cottage, not with my two wives and the children," Wallace explained, "but my brother has a small shed he uses for storage that you two could sleep in for a few coins tonight, if you'd like?"

"Of course, thank you Wallace," Glen answered for us with a smile. "We'll be sure to tell stories about you and your family when we return home. You've been so helpful."

Wallace made a face that told me he didn't care whether anyone told stories about him and I had to avert my eyes to stop myself from laughing. Glen often forgot that not everyone cared as much about telling tales as he did, some people didn't care at all.

That night we ate a strange combination of meat and thick sticky porridge before we slept. Beitris, one of the women Wallace had told us so much about, was going to give us fish but Peigi, the other, said that we would be sick of fish after staying up beside the loch and so we'd best eat some meat whilst we could.

His brother's shed was surprisingly comfortable and warm so we made our bed on a pile of sacks, filled with the remains of their winter grain stores, and used our blankets to keep warm.

"I'm not sure I would trust two strangers with my winter grain overnight," Glen commented once we had settled down beside each other.

"Neither would I," I laughed, "I think this is how they make their money. He brings travellers from the town and then his brother gives them a place to sleep."

After gratefully wolfing down more of Beitris's porridge, we left. The sun was still rising and the sky beside the mountains in the distance was streaked with pink, orange and blue. The sky was often like this at home, but the way it looked above the mountains was one of the most beautiful things I had ever seen in my life.

We had shown Wallace our wee map from the old lady and he pointed out that we simply had to go north. There was a path we could follow and so long as we kept walking straight, with the Fairy Forest on our left, we were going in the right direction.

His instructions seemed simple enough and he guessed that, if we left soon, we would make it to the loch-side village by nightfall. I had my doubts that we would make it that quickly, but Wallace didn't know that I was a changeling and just assumed we were two healthy young humans. If we'd had horses we could have made the journey a lot quicker, but neither of us liked the thought of being on horseback all day.

We packed up our bags with the trinkets from the market and our blankets. Glen took the bag filled with food and leather pouches of water as it was the heaviest, sparing me the extra weight for the first part of our journey on foot.

Glen now had a short dagger attached to his side which we'd picked up in the town. When we were planning the journey, we decided that it would be good to carry a small weapon for protection as we didn't know what beasts we might encounter on the way.

We didn't risk buying one in our village, word would surely have travelled back to ma and da and they wouldn't have been pleased.

The first part of our walk was pleasant enough. The road was quite flat and so we managed to maintain a good quick pace as we marched along it. Every so often we had to move to the sides to let horses and carts roll past but I didn't mind, it gave me a chance to stop and catch my breath.

Soon the Fairy Forest came into view on our left and it was a sight to behold. Our village had trees, which gave us apples in the summer, but the scattering of trees we had encountered before was nothing compared to this huge dense forest.

As we walked alongside it, I got a sense that the forest was somehow alive. I couldn't decide if I wanted to run away from the forest or if I wanted to run into it and completely lose myself. I resisted both urges and our conversation soon turned back to home.

"Did you see Munro trying to impress the butcher's daughter at the Winters End Festival?" Glen asked with a chuckle.

"I did, bloody idiot. Ma would have been furious if she had seen him," I said shaking my head. "Do you know if it worked? Was Rhona impressed?"

Munro was two years younger than me and so was Rhona, I had spoken to her as our da's argued over the price of meat. Rhona seemed like a nice girl but I didn't really know much about her. Her hair was a curious mix of blonde and ginger and so I could see why Munro would fancy her.

"I wouldn't be surprised if it did. It impressed me," he grinned.

"Perhaps you should ask him out? That would surprise your ma," I teased, "Maybe by the time we get home Rhona will be joining us for dinner."

"That would give my ma a shock. She just can't seem to understand that we don't want to kiss, have babies and be together forever," Glen said whilst I loudly pretended to vomit.

"Who do you want to kiss and have babies with?" I asked curiously.

He shrugged. "Not sure I want to kiss and have babies with anyone. Anyone I want to kiss I certainly can't have babies with anyway. I'm hoping Dougal and Ceitidh have a baby soon so she'll be distracted by that for a while."

"It's so strange to be away from home and not know what's happening. They could all be pregnant, or in love with new people, and we wouldn't even know," I said, suddenly feeling homesick.

"Aye but it's worth not knowing for views like this," Glen gestured towards the mountains growing larger and more impressive with every step we took.

By now we could make out the snow on the top of the mountains as, like Wallace had predicted, the fog had cleared.

As the day wore on, the journey became progressively more difficult and less enjoyable. The flat ground first became slight hills and then small mountains. The climb making my legs ache and my chest feel tight.

Thankfully, Glen was patient. Happily waiting whilst I panted for breath and regretted every choice I had ever made which lead me to this road.

To make matters even worse, the previously cloudless sky was starting to turn cloudy and we could see some very ominous looking dark clouds heading in our direction.

After stopping for a short lunch break, and a chance to run into the edge of the creepy forest to relieve ourselves, we felt the first few drops of rain.

"It's going to start pissing it down soon," Glen said with a sigh, frowning up at the sky.

"Well we could do with a wash, you especially," I laughed.

I wasn't laughing for long, much too soon the rain arrived... and it poured. The road quickly turned from crunchy dirt to a muddy puddle under our feet as we hurried along. The road was deserted and I cursed every human who was at home, I hoped they all knew how lucky they were.

The sky darkened as the clouds continued to roll in and our clothes became heavy with the weight of the water. I hoped our leather bags were sturdy enough that our food and the fabric map would be protected, losing them was not what we needed.

"I've never hated the rain more!" Glen shouted over the roaring of the rain pouring down onto the leaves in the forest and the deepening puddles at our feet.

"What did we ever do to make the Others send this rain down on us?!" I shouted, shaking my wet hair as if I was a dog to get it out of my face.

It felt as if we were hurrying along that road for weeks. The ache in my legs and my lack of breath became less important in wake of my new longing to be dry and warm.

As the rain continued to pour down, the sky continued to darken and night began to draw in, although spring was here the nights were still long.

"Morven, hurry!" Glen called from the top of the next hill that he had ran up.

He had slipped quite a few times and in my misery, I had desperately hoped he would fall. I could imagine him sliding all the way back down to the hill and it made me cackle.

"I can't!" I screamed back as I furiously stomped through the mud.

I did in fact make it up that hill and it felt like the happiest moment of my life when I did. From up there we could see that the path continued down the hill and then onto flat ground which would take us to the loch-side village.

There the buildings looked warm and we could see smoke and light coming from within cottages. Loch Fai stretched out behind the village, the Fairy Hills beyond it were difficult to see through the blinding rain and darkness, but the view was still spectacular.

Glen lifted me onto his back and then took off running down the hill, both of us laughing and shouting as he did. Miraculously he didn't fall, and soon we were at the bottom feeling elated. He put me down and we hurried to the village, as fast as our weary legs could carry us through the puddles.

I was exhausted when we arrived and barely took notice as we entered the first inn we found, quickly purchasing a room for the night. We threw our sodden mud-covered clothes on the floor and then fell into the bed, wrapping ourselves in the warm blankets.

I barely had a chance to appreciate the soft bed before I was fast asleep.

CHAPTER

8

Freya

I spent the next week, in between lessons and meals, moping around my chambers feeling lonely and sorry for myself. I was furious at my father for leaving me here in my rooms like a prisoner, simply for attempting to reason with him.

Mother came to visit me every night to talk through the door. Telling me about the day and her numerous meetings. Thankfully, the guard at my door was nice enough to let her speak to me although he wouldn't allow her to enter, probably out of fear of my father's reaction.

Mother told me that she had seen Nieve around the kitchens carrying plates, and that she looked happy and well. I doubted that. Nieve had spent her whole life with me and neither of us had ever completed what could be considered a full day's work before, she was probably miserable.

A selfish part of me hoped that she was missing me just as much as I missed her.

At the end of the week, after I had completed my final lessons and was considering retiring to my bed, there was a knock at my door which made me jump. It was much too early for mother to be visiting.

I called for them to enter and the door opened to reveal the guard who had been outside my door all week. At least I assumed it was him as the voice sounded the same, albeit less muffled without a door in between us.

He told me that the King had requested my presence at dinner that evening and I was to make myself presentable. Then, much to my surprise, my maid was ushered in to help me get ready. Before I could think about what I was doing, I had thrown my arms around her and buried my face in her neck.

"Oh Mae, it's so good to see you." I beamed, choking back a sudden rush of tears as she patted my back sympathetically.

I was used to secret kisses with Nieve and rare hugs from mother, so the feeling of another person in my arms made me realised just how alone I had been all week.

"I've missed you as well, Princess." she said with a smile, pulling me over to the mirror and shoving me down into the chair to begin working on my hair.

Mae was wonderful. She could create intricate plaits and hairstyles and, as a child, I had truly believed she was gifted. A simple three strand plait required a lot of concentration from me. Of course, my father had been quick to correct me when I had told him of my suspicions, unable to let his dislike of humans go long enough to allow his daughter to believe they could be gifted.

Mae's magic fingers quickly worked my hair into a presentable half up and half down style. I then hurried to dress in a simple skirt and bodice decorated with flowers in muted colours. I didn't care much about my appearance now that Nieve wasn't there to see me.

Those first few steps out of my chambers into the hallway made me realise just how much I had missed wandering around. I found myself smiling at everyone we passed in the halls, eager to take in the castle and see everyone I had been kept from. Some of the human servants I frequently met smiled back but others simply ignored me and continued with their work, as per usual.

The closer we got to the hall, the more nervous I became as I remembered who I was meeting. It was sad that a simple meeting with the man who raised me made my stomach churn and my legs fidget with the desire to run away. Upon arrival, a wash of relief flooded through me as I saw that mother would also be present at dinner.

She hurried out of her seat to place a kiss on my forehead when I entered. A small voice in my head noted that this was the first kiss she had given me in a while. Perhaps me being locked away made her realise how little attention she gave me the rest of the time.

"Freya! Good to see you," father spoke as if I had simply been away visiting friends, not locked in my chambers by his command.

He was sat at the head of the table whilst mother and I sat facing each other on either side. My confidence was boosted by the mere sight of her and father didn't seem prepared to lecture me any further. I slowly felt it was safe to assume that the matter was dropped. I truly was free from my temporary confinement.

He clapped his hands dramatically and then human servants carrying food began to swarm in from their hiding places. We enjoyed a course of soup and then another of meat and I thought that even food tasted better now that I was free again. It was ridiculous, but I allowed myself the delusion.

Father said we would be trying something new after our plates had been cleared away. Foolishly, I thought nothing of it. He was a curious man, always looking to broaden his horizons. That was until the servant carrying the plates walked in. It was Nieve.

Mother had been right, Nieve did look well. She was clean and clearly still being well fed, although I wasn't sure if a week was enough time for the effects of food deprivation to start showing. She didn't make eye contact as she wandered around the table diligently putting plates in the appropriate places. She always was a quick learner.

She reached my side of the table and I couldn't help but smile at her presence. When she didn't lift her head to look at me or even acknowledge me, I felt my smile fade. The same Nieve who had kissed me until my lips tingled and I felt lightheaded now wouldn't even look in my direction.

"Nieve," I said, trying to catch her attention, but she simply slipped past me and headed back towards the door. I jumped out of my seat and rushed after her.

"Freya, return to your seat." I heard father shout from the table but I ignored him.

I grabbed onto her wrist to stop her moving any further away from me. When I tried to pull her back towards me she resisted, which made my eyes sting and a feeling of rejection settle heavily in my stomach.

"Nieve I'm sorry." I mumbled, panicked by the way she ignored me. Desperate to make her forgive me and see that this wasn't my fault.

"Freya if you don't get back here right now you will be sorry," I heard father shouting furiously and the sound of mother talking frantically, trying to soothe him.

I tugged on her arm again. "It wasn't me. Nieve, please."

Nieve winced as my voice cracked and turned to me. What I saw when she lifted her head made me gasp.

Her beautiful face was injured. It was clear that someone had struck her hard as her cheekbone on one side displayed a dark, but fading, bruise.

"What happened?" I asked at once feeling panicked and frantic, my father's angry shouts only adding to my anxiety.

"I must return to my work Princess." Nieve said emotionlessly, her eyes darting to the scene behind me.

I slid my hand down until I was holding her hand, in the hope that she would trust me enough to let me help her. I wouldn't have let her go, needing to find out what happened and make sure she was safe, but father's hand latched onto my upper arm and harshly pulled me away. In my shock at his sudden violence, I lost my grip on her hand.

"How dare you disobey me," father spat, shaking me roughly.

"Get off me." I cried, uselessly trying to pry his tight bruising fingers from my arm.

When it was clear that wouldn't work, I used what little strength I had to push his chest, making him to let go. It worked for a moment and I turned in time to see that Nieve was almost at the door and about to leave me again. Before I could even take a step towards her, father turned my roughly by the shoulder and struck me hard across the face.

I froze, dazed by the force of his strike and stunned by the blossoming pain developing across my cheek and mouth. I couldn't remember ever being hit in my life. No one would dare harm the Princess, not even whilst playing. I had never felt anything like this before.

I lifted a shaking hand to my face and winced when I touched my now sore lip. I felt warm wetness on my fingertips and when I looked, I could see bright red blood which made my stomach churn and my legs feel week.

I was used to the sight of blood, having seen it every moon ever since I was a young teenager, but this was different. This made my head spin with disgust and fear.

Father seemed momentarily just as stunned by what happened but he quickly recovered, reigniting his anger. He grabbed my wrist and roughly pulled me back to my seat. He pushed my dazed form down into the chair before pushing it in tight, so I was trapped between it and the table.

"This is what happens when you disobey me," he hissed as he took his own seat. "You will not talk to that human again. Do you hear me?" he demanded.

I nodded absentmindedly, my mind whirling in horror at the revelation that someone was hurting Nieve and possibly had been all week whilst she had been away from my protection.

The thought of my own blood made everything worse. I could feel it trickling slowly down my chin but was unable to make a move to stop it or wipe it away. I flinched when a slice of the sweet bread was jammed roughly into my hand.

"Eat. This is a family meal," father said, sounding pleasant again as if his only daughter wasn't sitting bleeding on one side of him and his wife stifling sobs on the other.

As if I was a wooden puppet with someone controlling my strings, I chewed the bread. I silently went through the motions of eating. My only thought was that the sweetness of the bread mixed oddly with the tangy metallic taste of my blood.

Mother never did mention what happened that evening at dinner and I didn't blame her. Father became more and more temperamental as time wore on. I felt as if I was walking on eggshells whenever I had the misfortune of being near him.

Mae sighed unhappily at the sight of me when the guard brought me back to the room after the meal was over. I wandered over to my bed and lay down feeling exhausted from the evening's events. The throbbing on my face was more noticeable when I was lying down and I felt my eyes burn with tears again.

"You're alright lass," Mae said, sitting down beside me and rubbing my back gently.

I rubbed at my eyes feeling foolish, I had thought she was still at the door with the guard. Princesses should never cry. Father always said that, but recently crying seemed to be my main hobby.

Mae didn't laugh at me or tell me to get a grip, even though there were thousands of people out there with bigger problems than my own. She just sat with me, rubbing my back soothingly until I felt better. It occurred to me that this was something my mother should be doing and I desperately hoped that father would never take Mae away from me as well.

"Let's get you into bed," Mae said after a while, gently pulling me up and directing me over to the wardrobe so she could help me change into a nightgown.

She frowned at the dark, finger shaped bruises on my upper arm but made no comment. As she carefully took the plaits out of my hair, I felt hopeless, but she chattered away about her day anyway. Once I was ready, she directed me back over to my bed and tucked me in like she used to when I was a child.

I flinched as a cold wet cloth wiped my tears away and washed the dried blood from around my lip and chin. The water stung my cut lip but it soothed me to know the blood was gone.

Mae said that by the time I woke in the morning the cut would barely be visible as it was already starting to heal a little. That was one good thing about being a fairy, quick healing.

With a final goodnight and a soft kiss on my forehead Mae blew out the candles and left me. I thanked the Others that I was tired and quickly fell into a blissfully dreamless sleep.

CHAPTER

9

Morven

When we woke up the next morning my legs ached and there was no way I could have forgotten about yesterday. The journey from Wallace's village to this village beside the loch was the furthest I had ever walked in my life.

"I can't believe we made it." I said, voicing my thoughts to Glen who burst out laughing beside me.

"Bloody glad we did Morven. I considered leaving you behind and just running for the village when that rain started," he teased.

"I considered just lying down and waiting to drown," I said, throwing my arms out as if I had dropped dead in the middle of the road.

"Well, thank the Others we made it and didn't decide to abandon each other to the elements."

The inn was by far the nicest place we had stayed on our travels so far. The straw bed was bigger than the previous one and so Glen and I had more room to stretch out whilst we slept. The room was warm and cosy as there was a fireplace and, for a few coins, we were even able to have water heated so that we could wash. I was glad to finally wash away the dirt and dust from our travels. My hair had become a disgusting matted mess and I was overjoyed to have it untangled and clean.

Another coin saw our clothes bundled away by a girl who worked in the inn, she promised to have them returned to us by tonight. Thankfully we had some spare, albeit less warm, clothes with us in our bags so I didn't have to see Glen's naked body for too long. We were both comfortable around each other but it's difficult not to stare at the parts of your friend you don't normally see.

We didn't do very much with our first day in the village, wanting to rest and recover from our near-death experience in the rain.

The next day, Glen and I were both feeling refreshed and after a quick breakfast we decided to head out and explore. It wasn't raining anymore but the streets were still muddy and so we had to be careful not to fall and ruin our newly washed clothes. This village was a lot larger than our own and it felt like a whole new world.

They had markets like ours, but with vastly different items on sale. They sold multiple kinds of strange looking fish that I wouldn't even know how to eat, there were people selling jewellery made of little pearls from the loch and stalls filled with all sorts of equipment for boats and fishing.

Even the accents of the people here were different from ours, despite it only being a few days away from our village.

We saw sellers from the village which lay at the foot of the Fairy Hills, to the east of the loch. You could tell who had travelled from there as they were paler than us from further south and they all wore furs from huge monstrous looking beasts. I desperately hoped those beasts could only be found high in the mountains and that Glen and I would never be unfortunate enough to encounter them.

Our day was much the same as our time in the town, without the added excitement of the royal family and a wise old woman who was probably a witch.

We wandered down to the loch where we saw rows of wooden boats tied with thick rope to huge wooden pegs hammered down into the stony shore.

There were many people, who I assumed were sailors, wandering around shouting instructions at each other whilst they unloaded and loaded the boats. It was fascinating to watch and we spent most of our afternoon sitting looking out across the water. We could see boats in the distance heading north to the most northerly human town as well as east.

"Scary, isn't it? The way the boats just float on top of all that water." Glen frowned.

"A wee bit. Bonnie says boats hardly ever sink, unless there is a storm," I attempted to be reassuring.

"We better hope the Others don't send another storm after us then," Glen smirked, only half joking.

The village was a windy place, because it was so close to the water Glen explained, so before it became too dark we decided to find somewhere to have a hot meal before we slept. We also needed to find a boat to take us across the loch.

We wandered along the shore as the sun began to set until we came to a wooden path that stretched out over the water, leading into a round building supported by wooden poles. It was as if the building was floating, with only the little wooden poles to support it and stop it tumbling down into the water.

"Here?" I said eyeing it warily. Glen nodded but made no move to step onto the unstable looking path.

We could hear voices inside the strange building but that did nothing to inspire confidence in us. What if the added weight of Glen and I sent us all crashing down into the water? A group came up behind us and we awkwardly moved out of the way to let them past. They strode out into the building, seemingly unbothered by the danger

One of them, a tall man with dark hair tied low behind his head paused to look at us.

"You two alright?" he asked with a friendly smile.

"Yeah just... thinking..." I answered lamely.

"The crannog isn't about to collapse, if you're worried about that," he said with a knowing grin.

"Isn't right to float a building like that," Glen said gesturing towards the building like it was the most horrifying thing he had ever seen.

"I've lived here all my life and the crannog has been on those wooden poles since long before I was born. It will be fine. Come on," he said before confidently wandering in.

I grabbed Glen by the hand and pulled him onto the wooden path alongside me. It was disconcerting to see the waves crashing around the poles through the gaps between the wooden planks. Instead I tried to keep my eyes on the back of the helpful, and not unattractive, man.

We made it into the building, which had a good thick floor so it was easy to forget that we were out over the loch. We bought a strange, thick fishy soup for a coin and some ale as that was all they had to drink. Large tables were scattered around the central hearth and surprisingly, I could see there was a second floor to this strange building.

"This will definitely make an interesting story," I said to Glen with a laugh.

The soup was the most disgusting thing I had ever tasted and even Glen, who could eat just about anything, had to chug down multiple cups of ale to remove the taste.

Whilst Glen was purchasing more drink to chase away the horrid fish flavour, the man from earlier dropped down into the chair beside me.

"Glad to see you were brave enough to make it inside," he smiled.

"Glad to be warm, although I could have happily lived my whole life without tasting that," I said gesturing towards the bowl.

He burst out laughing. "I won't tell my Aunt what you think of her cooking."

"Oh no, I'm sorry!" I hurried to apologise, feeling my cheeks burning with embarrassment.

"Don't worry about it. Not a lot of fish where you're from I take it?" he asked, looking genuinely interested.

"We live in a farming village a few days south of the town." I explained and before I could catch myself, ended up explaining all about our livestock and farms.

"Sounds great, not a fish in sight," he grinned. "My name is Finnian by the way."

"Morven." I said simply which made him laugh again.

"Pleasure to meet you Morven, your ginger friend over there seems to have been distracted so how about I get you another drink?" he offered, gesturing over to where Glen was talking to a man with hair almost as ginger and vibrant as his own.

"Yes please," I said, glaring at Glen who didn't seem at all phased and waved heartily back at me from across the room looking very pleased with himself.

Whilst I sat there alone at the table I really started to feel the effects of the hurried drinking from earlier. It had been worth it though; the fishy taste was only just lingering. When Finnian returned, I was patting my tingling face with my equally tingling hands.

"My face feels tingly." I explained as I accepted the cup from him.

"Maybe not a good plan to drink too much more then, eh?" Finnian said, pulling his chair up closer to my own.

He was a very large man, I couldn't help but note, with well-defined muscles on his arms and chest, from working on the boats his whole life I assumed.

Markings on his arm caught my eye and before I could think about what ma or Granny Athol would say about me stroking the arm of a stranger, I had done it.

Finnian rolled up the sleeve on his shirt to reveal a tattoo which ran from his shoulder all the way down to his wrist. It showed symbols, like the ones on the fairy stone back home, and it was as if they flowed along his arm as he moved.

"It's beautiful." I gasped, mesmerised.

"Glad you like it, it was bloody painful," he said patiently, letting me stare at his arm.

"It's like the fairy stone in our village."

He nodded. "The fairy symbols are spread all over the land. We all see the same ones and it doesn't matter where you go, you'll find them everywhere. Or so I am told."

"We are planning to travel north into the fairy kingdoms." I admitted, for some reason eager to hear his opinion on our adventure.

"To explore?"

I hesitated, unsure if I wanted to tell him my secret. I really felt I could trust Finnian despite only just meeting him, although that could have been due to the drink.

"I am a changeling." I blurted out before I lost my nerve. "We want to go north to see if we can learn why they keep stealing our children."

Finnian was silent and I couldn't bring myself to look at him and see his reaction. He startled me when he lifted me, as if I weighed nothing, onto his lap and wrapped his arms around me.

"That's a bloody brave thing to do," he whispered as he hugged me close. "You go and you find those answers for us all." He said, nodding to himself. Clearly also feeling the effects of the drink.

I wondered if he had a changeling in his family and remembered Wallace saying that the further north you travelled, the more changelings you would meet. Instead I wondered how many people in his family were changelings, and how many of them survived.

I didn't voice these thoughts as even my drunk mind knew it would ruin this moment we were sharing. I was strangely comfortable in the arms of a man I had only just met, and I was quite content to stay there.

Glen screaming my name woke me from my sleep with a start and I leapt out of the bed to help him with whatever was wrong, only to find him sitting at the small table in our room laughing.

"What?" I whined, lifting my hands to shield my eyes. My head felt as if there were wee folk stamping around and crushing my insides.

"Little too much to drink last night Morven?" Glen teased.

"You drank as well," I accused, not liking my inability to remember much past Finnian holding me in his arms in the crannog.

"I am not a skinny wee changeling though. I'm a big strong man who can handle his drink."

It was my turn to laugh. "You wish."

I hurriedly dressed as the cold started to give me goose bumps, every movement made my head pound and my vision swim. Once I was dressed I threw myself back down on the bed with a groan.

"I'll never be well again," I complained, feeling sorry for myself. Suddenly very homesick for my ma who could cure anything, or at the very least give you sympathy until it went away.

Glen pushed a cup of water into one hand and some bread into the other as he always did when anyone had drunk too much. I would bet coin that bread did absolutely nothing to help, but I accepted them gratefully anyway.

He explained that the night before he had been speaking to that man, Raibert was his name, but made sure to keep an eye on me as we were both drunk. He had thought that perhaps I would spend the night with Finnian but even whilst drunk, I wasn't prepared to take that risk.

Finnian had ushered me back over to Glen when the crannog started to empty and Raibert, assuming that Glen and I were a couple, quickly left. Glen had been drunker than he thought and so Finnian had to help us find our way back to the inn whilst we loudly complained that everything looked the same.

"He probably hopes that he never sees us again then," I groaned, unable to hide my disappointment.

"He actually said he would meet us for food at midday, if you feel up to it," Glen said wiggling his eyebrows suggestively. "Seems like you made a good impression."

"Wheesht." I complained, unable to stop myself from blushing.

That afternoon, once I was sure that I wasn't about to die, we made it out of the inn and met with Finnian in the crannog again. This time we managed to make it across the wooden path, which looked just as unstable as it had the day before, without too much hesitation. The meal contained fish again, but luckily this one had a much milder taste and so we managed to eat it without the drink to wash it down.

Finnian looked just as handsome as he had the night before and I couldn't help but stare at him as we had our meal. He didn't laugh at me or tease me for getting drunk, and I was glad to notice that I felt comfortable being around him even whilst sober. He had a good sense of humour and thankfully didn't seem like a very serious man.

Thinking of him as a man and not a boy made me wonder what age he was, so when Glen nipped out to relieve himself I decided to find out more about him.

"How old are you? I didn't ask last night."

"I was twenty-two during the winter there, how old are you? I'm guessing not an old man like me," he answered with a warm smile.

"Only eighteen, quite an achievement I think, with me being a changeling," I said with a humourless laugh.

"You should be proud of yourself. Or proud of whatever it is your ma keeps feeding you that keeps your heart beating."

"That'll be the stew," Glen said as he returned and caught the tail end of our conversation "Famous for her soup Ailis is, it's worth travelling south for."

"Maybe I will visit your village once you return."

"I look forward to it," I said with a smile which turned into a glare when I noticed Glen raising his eyebrows suggestively, loving every moment.

Luckily Finnian didn't seem to notice as I attempted to kill Glen with my eyes.

"If you haven't yet found transport up to the northern village then I would be happy to take you both across in my boat, it'll cost you a few coins though," Finnian said with a wink.

"That would be great," I said, after a glance at Glen to wordlessly confirm our choice.

Finnian looked embarrassed for a moment, "It's just a small boat. Not as big as some of the others you've seen tied up on the shore. She's still fast though."

"Oh, that's alright, size doesn't matter does it Morven?" Glen said with a smirk which quickly faded when I kicked him hard under the table.

We decided that we would spend one last day in the village before heading out across the loch as we needed to ensure that we had enough supplies for our journey north.

We'd have a chance to buy things in village on the northern shore of Loch Fai, but Finnian often mentioned that the market here in the south was the best so we felt it was only polite to spend some more coins.

I was glad that Finnian was taking us across the loch as being with him helped to distract me from the homesickness I so often felt. Glen said that he thought Finnian was looking to make me his wife and the thought made me burst out laughing.

I couldn't imagine living up here beside the loch, eating fish that I hated all year round. The idea of staying in his company was a pleasant one, but I knew that as a changeling I wouldn't live long enough to be a good wife for anyone.

I wasn't even sure why I was thinking about marriage whilst in the middle of a life changing journey north. We were heading into the fairy kingdoms to demand answers, not looking for husbands. I decided not to think any more of marrying tall, muscular, tattooed men until the journey was over. Although I still allowed myself to appreciate his company and the rather impressive sight of him.

It would have been a waste not to.

CHAPTER

10

Euna

The weather took a turn for the worst causing Aelwen to invite King Ferchar, his family, and all of their travelling companions to stay in the castle until it cleared. As Norbroch was prone to long spells of heavy snow and raging storms, there was no way of knowing when they would leave us.

As hard as I tried, I could not find it in myself to be angry about that. To my dismay, I was finding it increasingly difficult to hide the smile on my face whenever I spotted the tall curly haired human heading in my direction.

Since our first meeting, that evening in the hallway, I saw Lachlann almost every day. Our daily routines meant that we were often in the same areas of the castle at the same time. I was not sure if I should curse or thank the Others for that.

The days passed and the weather continued to worsen, Lachlann and I spoke often and I found myself getting to know him. He had no immediate family, having been raised with a small group of human boys in Culhuinn. All of whom unfortunately now worked on various tasks for the King. Lachlann did not seem too fond of his king and I did not blame him, I could not imagine being raised to work for such a rude and arrogant man. Then again, I could hardly imagine myself working for anyone.

I had many acquaintances around the castle and across Norbroch, but never had I felt anything close to affection or love for any of them. Never the giddy feelings I experienced whenever I saw Lachlann.

When we were younger Aelwen was prone to falling for boys, and the occasional girl, after knowing them for only a few weeks and I refused to believe that I was doing the same. It was ridiculous.

A week after the King's arrival, Aelwen brought up the human whilst we were having a family lunch together. I should have expected that Aelwen would notice my fondness for him. She always seemed to be able to guess every emotion I felt. If I was not already all too aware of her gift, I would think she could somehow read my mind.

"I notice you've been talking to that man a lot," she commented, completely out of the blue whilst we ate a thick stew that the cook had brought for us.

"What man?" I asked, feigning ignorance whilst wrestling my spoon back from her youngest daughter Princess Aoife, who was now two years old.

Her eldest daughter, Princess Elspie, who was three years old, had given up on lunch and was instead drawing shapes on the table with the gravy.

"Oh, I don't know, just a certain tall, handsome, curly haired human from Culhuinn," Aelwen answered with a sly grin.

"Handsome, is he?" teased her husband Laird Ronan, whose family resided in a small castle east of the Verch forest.

"We have only spoken a few times," I focused on my reclaimed spoon and not Aelwen and Ronan's amused expressions.

"It is good to see you making friends Euna. You are always cooped up alone here in the castle," Aelwen continued, her expression turning sombre as she spoke.

"I enjoy life here in the castle," I hurried to assure her "and Lachlann is not my friend."

"I'm sure he could be. Wouldn't that be nice?" she encouraged.

"It would be inappropriate for me to become friends with one of King Ferchar's servants," I said feeling exasperated, that very thought had been reoccurring in my mind for days.

"There is nothing stopping you. Although, meeting without the King noticing would be the wisest choice," Aelwen hurried to reassure me.

"I doubt he would notice, not if your friend Lachlann continues to complete his work," Ronan added.

"I am... unsure how to make him my friend," I admitted, the admission sounding far too much like a complaint for my liking.

Aelwen laughed, "For a start you don't make anyone do anything. He has to want friendship."

"I cannot just walk up to him and ask him to be my friend, can I?"

"Ask him to join you for a drink perhaps, as if you are simply two strangers, rather than a Queen and a servant," Ronan suggested, the two of them looking far too excited about their plan.

"That may work..."

PRESENT DAY

The castle was eerily quiet without Aelwen and her family roaming its halls, despite most of the servants and guards still being present. Unlike my sister, I never found myself forming a close bond with them and so I could not start up conversations now.

To alleviate my boredom a few days after they left, I donned a heavy navy cloak and headed out of the castle. My wandering took me to the Verch forest, a small forest which lay near the foot of the mountains. I remembered learning as a child that this was one of the smallest forests in the whole land and that shocked me. The trees were so huge and so old that I struggled to imagine a larger forest.

A vast forest sprawls across the land from Culhuinn down into the human kingdoms. Aelwen once visited and said that the forest was alive with magic. Despite knowing this, I was perfectly content with our little forest, with its usually snow covered evergreen trees and the little red berries that grew throughout the year.

Occasionally I would spot a will o'the wisp floating amongst the branches and made a point of not following them. It was well known that those tiny little fairies followed the commands of the Otherworld. They could spy to their hearts content, but I would not be taking anything to do with them.

The thought of travelling anywhere filled me with dread but I loved to be outside amongst the animals and magic. The wind blowing my hair and cloak behind me brought with it all sorts of curious sounds and smells. None of which you could experience from within the stone walls of the castle.

As a child, I had often dreamt of leaving the castle and my lessons behind to become an explorer. I would imagine myself going off on an adventure across the land with nothing but a little bag of food and my horse. A ridiculous notion, but still, I often wondered if I would have been happier had my life had taken that course.

10 YEARS AGO

I asked Lachlann to join me for a drink the next time I met him, near the servant's chambers. I certainly had not been waiting there to see if I would meet him. His freckled, finely wrinkled face burst into a huge smile the moment I asked and he readily agreed to meet me. His smile was infectious and I could not help but share his happiness. That was until I realised I was horrifically unprepared.

What was I expected to wear? Were there any formalities I was unaware of? As soon as Lachlann went back to work I hurried as quickly as possible, without breaking my composure, to Aelwen's chambers in search of her advice. I ended up with my arms full of the wriggling squirming baby Prince Elath, but it was a small price to pay for her insight.

Her first piece of rather unhelpful advice was to wear something I was comfortable in, which helped me in no way. What if I had been comfortable being naked as a newly born baby? Comfortable could mean anything. Thankfully she picked out a simple, navy dress for me.

Her next piece of advice was to not wear anything too regal, which would make Lachlann uncomfortable, but also nothing too below my station so as not to rouse suspicion.

Her final piece of advice was to simply be myself. Another ridiculous suggestion, how could I be anything other than myself?

That evening, I met with Lachlann in a rarely used room on the opposite side of the castle to where King Ferchar and his company where staying. Ronan had suggested it as the room was unlikely to be disturbed and none of the King's staff would be at that side of the castle to see us. My personal guard Tormod grinned when I told him of my evening's plans and seemed more than pleased to be on guard outside the door to ensure no one entered.

Whilst I waited for Lachlann to arrive I lit the fireplace, not that the room was particularly cold, but I knew that humans felt the cold more keenly than us fairies.

I shuffled and reshuffled the two bottles of whisky on the table, I could hardly tell the difference between the varieties but Aelwen insisted that different Lairds produced slightly different variations. I then found myself anxiously organising bannocks into a pattern on the plate before quickly stopping myself.

Ridiculous that one meeting with a human man had me acting like an infatuated young girl.

I took my seat at the table and vowed not to move or do anything ridiculous until he arrived, which had better be soon. Unless he had simply lied about wanting to meet. That thought made my stomach churn uncomfortably and so I forced it from my mind.

My wait did not last much longer and Tormod was soon opening the door to let Lachlann in. His hair was ruffled from his day's work and his cheeks red from exertion, as if he had run all the way here.

"I apologise my Queen. My work took longer than anticipated although I hurried here as fast as I could," he said, taking the empty a seat across from me.

"Euna." I blurted out abruptly, which made him smile. "You may call me Euna when we are together, no need to be quite so formal." I explained.

If I had been a human my face would surely have been burning red with embarrassment.

"Well then Euna, how about I pour you a drink, any preference?" he gestured towards my well-arranged bottles.

"Oh no, I can hardly tell the difference between them," I admitted, which made him laugh heartily.

"We can start with this one then," he grinned, choosing the fullest bottle of the pair.

I found that, despite my awkwardness and new habit of blurting out single words in response to his questions, Lachlann was very easy to talk to. He seemed to be genuinely interested in what I had to say and happy to be in my company. I often noticed that whilst acquaintances within the castle listened to me speak, I could see in their eyes that their minds were wandering.

Lachlann was different. I was the recipient of his full attention.

"I love spending time outside, especially in the Verch Forest near the castle," I explained to him as we tried the second type of whisky, his cheeks were now flushed red from the drink and his curls wilder as he kept running his hands through them.

"I would love to visit Verch, maybe you could take me?" he looked so eager I could not say no.

"Well, it is nothing like the large forests you are used to in Culhuinn. You may not find it very interesting," I explained, suddenly worried that I had made it sound too impressive.

"We servants have little free time back in Culhuinn and so I've never really had much of a chance to explore. I would really like to see a place you love, if you would share it with me."

"Being Queen does not leave much time for enjoying things, but I would enjoy showing you the forest, so long as the King remains unaware."

"Luckily, I am not one of his personal servants. I'm sure I could easily spare time for you Euna," he said with a smile that I returned.

"Perhaps that should be our next meeting then?" I asked hesitantly.

"That sounds perfect." Lachlann replied as he stood, taking my hand as if I for some reason needed help getting out of my chair.

Human hands were much warmer than a fairy's hands I noticed.

We started towards the door, Lachlann never letting go of my hand. He paused and turned to smile almost shyly at me. His smile was radiant, like the sun breaking through the clouds after a storm, sparkling on the snow.

"I really enjoyed spending time with you this evening Euna."

"As did I. We really should do this again," I smiled, reaching out and attempting to flatten his dishevelled curls.

He stepped closer and I felt a little twinge of nerves when I realised how close we were. His expression was happy but questioning as he moved closer still. I found myself frozen, unable to respond or do anything a normal person would do when they found themselves pressed up against a handsome young man such as Lachlann. I cursed the Others for making me so awkward around him.

Gently, Lachlann leaned his forehead against mine and I was quite sure that my heart was about to burst right out of my chest and ruin this perfect moment.

He seemed to be waiting, silently asking for permission to move closer, and so I nodded against him. He smiled and gently pressed his lips against mine. He attempted to move back when I did not respond and so I quickly placed my hands on his shoulders to pull him back. This gave him courage and his hands slowly found their way down to my hips. Our kiss was brief, but we were both smiling when he pulled away.

"Goodnight Euna." he placed one last kiss on my cheek, slipping out of the door before I had a chance to regain my senses and reply.

Not long after, Tormod opened the door, presumably to check in case I had been murdered without him noticing. I had not moved from the spot I was standing in.

"Will you be returning to your chambers tonight my Queen?" he asked with a grin on his face.

"Yes, let us go back. Thank you Tormod."

"I am glad you had a good night," he said, surprising me as we reached my chambers.

I was going to correct him until I realised that this truly was one of the first evenings I remembered enjoying for a long time.

PRESENT DAY

Despite my thick cloak, I was chilled to the bone by the time I managed to pull myself out of my memories of our first kiss. I was exhausted and cold when I returned to the castle and was planning to head back to my rooms for a warm bath when Tormod spoke up, halting me.

"Perhaps my Queen it would be wise to have a meal before you retire?" he questioned, the sympathetic look on his face made me feel oddly guilty and so I agreed, requested that some hot soup be brought to my rooms.

I had a feeling that he and Aelwen were conspiring against me and that if I avoided too many meals they would be sure to discuss it when she returned.

Tormod was not allowed to shout at me, as he was my guard. Aelwen, on the other hand, would have no trouble scolding me until I saw the error of my ways. I knew that from experience.

It was not that I did not want to eat food or that I thought I could go without it. It simply held no real appeal and I found all food bland and uninteresting these days.

It simply did not matter anymore, nothing much did.

CHAPTER

II

Morven

"You can both swim, can't you?" Finnian asked as he lifted me by the waist and helped me into the wooden boat. Glen jumped in beside me and we shared a look before nodding.

It was a good morning for sailing across the loch, or so that's what we kept hearing from the sailors and fishermen we passed. There was a strong wind out there and no sign of the kelpies to create storms. I listened out for any suggestions that a storm could be brewing as we prepared to leave.

There was no way I was risking being out in a flimsy wooden boat whilst a storm raged. I didn't think Finnian would have appreciated me calling his first boat flimsy, so I kept that thought to myself. The look on Glen's face told me that he was thinking something similar.

We hadn't thought that crossing the loch would be something that made us feel frightened and uneasy, but then again, we had never travelled any distance on water before. Our feet had remained firmly on the ground since the day we were born. We were now realising just how much we'd like to keep it that way.

Far too soon for my liking, the boat was being pushed away from the stony shore and floating out into deeper waters.

Finnian had tried to explain how the boat worked but I couldn't really understand what was going on. Ramsey and Thorfinn, friends of Finnian's, would row the boat out into the loch as he steered. Then the two huge fabric sails would catch the wind and help send us across to the northern village. I couldn't really see how that would work or even properly comprehend the fact that we were floating.

His two friends seemed nice enough, I think they could tell that we were uneasy being on the boat and so tried to tell jokes to cheer us up. They hoped to one day have a large sailing ship, like their families, so decided to start their own little crew with just the three of them.

Ramsey tried to joke that they once had a fourth crew member who was dragged down into the depths by a kelpie, but that joke didn't make either of us laugh. I felt we should leave joking about drowning until we had both of our feet back on land.

After our initial fears about floating in a small wooden boat on a vast loch ebbed a little, the journey became quite peaceful and I found myself starting to enjoy it. The strong wind blew my hair around and made me regret not tying it back in a plait. We all had red cheeks, ears and noses from the frigid wind but it was refreshing. I could see why Finnian and his friends would pick this life over working in the mines down in the mountains.

Once the boat was caught by a good wind we were sailing across the loch without much work being needed and everyone on board relaxed. Glen made a point of speaking to Ramsey and Thorfinn, with an obvious wink, which left me free to go speak to Finnian who was at the back of the boat, controlling the direction we sailed in.

"It's beautiful out here." I said, watching the view of the north and the Fairy Hills grow clearer as we floated onwards.

The mountains were a mixture of green grass and grey rock, some of the larger ones even had snow at their peaks. I could just make out little stone houses from the other villages and was sure I could see little white dots when I squinted my eyes, probably sheep.

"Aye, nothing like being out on the open water for a good view," Finnian said looking pleased with himself. "You two picked a good day for sailing."

"I really like your boat," I praised awkwardly a few moments later, feeling guilty that I hadn't yet commented on the boat he and his friends so clearly loved.

"You wouldn't if you'd been on the huge boats before, but thank you anyway."

I sat down near where he was standing and was content to simply watch the landscape change as we neared the middle of the loch.

As we sailed, the weather began to change. It happened slowly at first. Glen and I didn't notice until Finnian and his friends started discussing wind patterns and looking curiously up at the gathering clouds.

They didn't look particularly worried about the weather worsening, but there was a sense of unease on the boat as the clouds continued to develop and rain started to fall.

"I never wanted to see rain again after that walk," I complained to Glen.

"Me neither, this is definitely far too soon for us to be soaked again. Perhaps spring wasn't the best time for travelling," Glen sighed, frowning at the sky as if he could stop the rain by scaring it away.

"It's always raining though. The weather is never good enough for travelling."

We were starting to be able to see the northern shore of the loch by now and so I tried not to feel too worried about the weather. I hoped that it wouldn't take too long to reach the village and that we would be in a nice warm inn before the weather got too bad.

Almost as soon as I had those thoughts, the exact opposite happened. Out in the loch there was a sound which we looked towards but couldn't see anything. Then again, the unmistakable sound of a man laughing heartily seemed to echo all around us.

"You've got to be joking," groaned Ramsey who had wandered over to us, shaking his head furiously as the laughter continued.

I was completely confused until I spotted movement in the loch and then, from underneath the surface, a man appeared. Or at least he looked almost like a man. When he appeared again I noticed that his skin was a peculiar mix of grey and blue. He had strange rounded facial features and not much of a nose.

He disappeared under the surface again and everything was silent until three men appeared, twisting and diving in and out of the water, laughing as they went. As they jumped it became clear that the bottoms of their bodies were scaled like a fish and that they had strange tails instead of legs.

"Kelpies." I whispered in shock and Ramsey beside me confirmed my thoughts.

"Happy kelpies are always a bad sign, there's a big storm coming and we've run out of time to get away from it," he complained, rushing off to prepare for the coming storm.

I looked to Finnian, feeling as if my breath had been replaced by panic. He didn't look particularly worried, just annoyed, as if he couldn't be bothered to deal with the storm. Not like there was a possibility of the boat sinking and drowning us all.

The rain was falling in big fat drops now, and the wind was churning up the loch, creating larger and larger waves.

"What do we do?" I asked frantically.

"You'll be alright lass, just find yourself something to hold on to and stay in the boat," he grinned gesturing over to the side of the boat where rope around the edge would make a good thing to hold onto.

Glen had already found himself a place to sit and was holding onto the edge as if his life depended on it. As I hurried to find a spot, a wave hit the boat causing it to rock violently from side to side. I fell painfully to my knees, cursing as I went. I scrambled over the deck and grabbed onto the rope, gripping it so hard that my cold fingers ached and protested.

A burst of laughter over the sounds of Finnian and his friends shouting to each other, the wind howling and the rain pouring down startled me. Slowly, taking care to grip the rope tight, I looked over the edge and gasped in shock as I stared directly into the black eyes of a kelpie. The kelpie stared back at me with an amused expression.

"Morven, move!" I heard Finnian shout and as I turned to ask why a colossal wave slammed into the boat, spraying water all over the deck and knocking Thorfinn onto the ground.

He quickly scrambled back to his feet before the next wave hit, this one impossibly larger than the last.

Needing to shake out my aching hand I loosened my painful grip on the rope, just as the next wave hit.

The boat swayed violently, sending me slamming into the edge and overboard. I felt as if I was falling slowly and could hear multiple people shouting my name before I slammed painfully into the water.

I gasped as the icy water soaked me, instantly chilling me to the bone. It was so cold it almost stopped my heart and I began to choke and panic as the water rushed into my mouth. I remembered Bonnie talking about swimming and tried uselessly to kick my legs and swing my arms, but to no avail.

I could see the light of the surface through my burning eyes, but every movement I made seemed to pull me deeper down into the depths of the loch. I felt, but did not hear, a hysterical panicked laugh burst its way out of my mouth and bubble towards the surface as I realised that I was going to die here.

My head was pounding and my throat and chest were burning as my body tried to cough and rid itself of the water. I thrashed around for what felt like hours until black spots began appearing in front of my already blurred vision and my desire to fight against the water began to fade.

Perhaps drowning here in the loch wouldn't be that bad. My body was being pushed and pulled by the waves and my hair floated around my face, tickling my cheeks. As I began to close my eyes, in the distance I thought I noticed the kelpies. I couldn't hear their laughter over the water in my ears, and the pounding in my head, but I thought they looked happy as they twirled and danced.

I woke slowly. I was in a warm and comfortable bed with, what felt like, a whole flock of sheep's worth of blankets on top of me. As I breathed I became aware that my throat was dry and sore. More worrying, though, was my chest, which felt like it had been crushed, like I had been sat on by a cow.

I wriggled underneath the blankets, wanting to feel what was wrong and find a drink. A gentle hand on my forehead stopped me and I opened my eyes to see Glen. He was smiling fondly but I could see that he was exhausted and I wondered why, until I remembered.

I remembered the storm, the shock of the freezing water, the realisation that I couldn't swim and sinking deeper down into the loch. The most unsettling memory was of a strangely scaled hand latching onto my arm. The blurred creatures I saw swirling towards me, with torsos like men and tails like fish, as I ran out of air and passed out

"I fell in." I said hoarsely, wishing for a drink.

"Yeah you did, almost gave me a bloody heart attack when you went under," Glen said with a humourless laugh. "Thought you were dead when you disappeared."

"I'm sorry." I whispered, feeling guilty for putting him through so much worry and stress.

"I know you didn't mean to fall in Morven, you don't have to say sorry. You're lucky Finnian jumped in after you. I wouldn't be surprised if that man was part fish or part kelpie himself. He swam down into the loch so fast and before we knew it, he was back at the surface holding you," Glen explained, shaking his head as if in disbelief.

"I'm alright, though?" I asked hesitantly, feeling much too sore and exhausted to think of much else.

"Yeah, you're alright. Get some sleep, Morven. You'll feel better when you wake up," Glen placed a gentle kiss on my forehead and left me alone in the warm bed.

It didn't take long for me to drift back off to sleep. Back into strange dreams of churning waves and laughing kelpies.

When I woke a second time, my throat was even drier and when I tried to speak I could barely make a sound. My lips were dry and cracked, and my chest ached with every breath I took. A hand gently lifted my head and helped me sip some warm milk which instantly helped soothe my throat.

I expected to see Glen, but instead Finnian was there helping me. The look on his face reminded me of da whenever he was trying to hide his anger.

"Hello," I croaked, unsure what else to say and fighting a growing urge to hide under the blankets until Finnian and his accusing eyes had left the room.

"Hello Morven," he answered, his expression lightening slightly.

He gave me one last drink of the soothing milk before getting rid of the cup and sitting down beside me, on top of the blankets. He propped himself up and sighed.

"You lied to me."

"When?!" My mind whirled, trying to think of any lies I had told.

"When you stepped onto my boat and told me you could swim." he said, looking angrier now that he had voiced the reason behind it.

"I thought I could swim," I explained feeling foolish, which made him pause for a moment.

"You thought you could swim... but you've never tried?" he asked slowly.

"No, never, but my brother's wife told me you have to kick your legs and swing your arms." I explained, wishing I'd asked more about swimming when I'd had the chance.

Finnian gave a small laugh at that and I was glad to see amusement erasing the last of the anger on his face.

"You should have told me that Morven. I wouldn't have let you both so close to the edge of the boat if I'd known you'd start drowning as soon as you hit the water."

"I'm sorry. I didn't think," I mumbled weakly.

"I bet you are. I had to jump in and rescue you. Your clothes were so heavy they'd started dragging you down. I had to pound your chest when I got you back on the deck to make you cough up the water you swallowed. I bet you're feeling pretty sore now."

I nodded and looked down at my chest. When I moved the shift slightly, I could see dark black and blue bruises forming on my chest where Finnian had hit me. No wonder I was hurting after going through all that.

Something about seeing my injuries and knowing that I had upset Finnian and scared Glen made my eyes burn with tears. I found myself sniffling to try and keep them at bay.

"Aw lass, you're alright now," Finnian said, pulling me close gently so he could hold me without hurting me. "I should punish both you and Glen for lying to me on my boat, but I think the shock of what happened taught you both a lesson."

I nodded in response and turned my face into his chest to hide that it was now red with embarrassment and streaked with tears.

He didn't say anything else, simply held me close and ran his hand comfortingly through my hair until I felt better. A sudden yawn surprised me, I had spent so much time sleeping recently but it made him chuckle.

"You can fall asleep. I'll stay here with you, and when you wake, we can see about getting some food in you," Finnian said, and with that, I slept.

CHAPTER

12

Freya

The following morning I was surprised when Mae woke me and helped me dress and get ready for the day. I had assumed that I would once again be confined to my chambers, but father was unpredictable, which made it impossible to know what he was planning. Although, I knew it would likely be awful.

The cut on my lip looked as if I had been struck days ago, not simply the night before due to how fast fairies healed, so I didn't bother trying to hide my face from anyone. I knew from seeing Nieve's cuts and bruises over the years that they took longer to heal on humans.

Throughout the day, I felt sick with dread that father would appear, but he never did. I went to meals, attended lessons with Adair and even had a stroll through the grounds with no sign of him. The only change to my life, apart from the disappearance of my love, was the guard who now trailed after me like a shadow.

I found myself wandering aimlessly through the castle. I hadn't realised just how much I relied on Nieve for company, and to think of things to do. Now I was alone and I longed to speak to her. I shook my head to banish the thought, unless I found a way to disguise myself and sneak into the kitchens I couldn't speak to her.

The guard, whom I had started referring to as my shadow, and I left the castle as I quickly became bored of its halls. It was the perfect day for riding but, unless my shadow suddenly became good company, I didn't feel like going alone.

My eyes drifted over to the stables and I decided perhaps the horses would be better company than a silent guard. Berwin was inside the stables when I arrived, and he simply bowed to me before continuing with his work. Usually we spoke, but his silence made me wonder if he had only ever spoken to me because of Nieve.

That caused a flicker of jealousy to run through me. No one knew of our love, and I selfishly hoped that she wouldn't find someone better than me now that she was in the company of other humans. The very thought made my eyes sting.

"How are the horses today?" I asked, startling Berwin.

"Good and healthy, Princess, just like they always are." he answered, clearly confused by my sudden urge to have a conversation with him about horses.

I noticed his eyes flick to my healing lip but then he quickly looked away. I couldn't tell if he was simply very perceptive, if the servants had been gossiping about what happened, or if I was just paranoid. I hadn't exactly hidden it as I walked through the halls with blood all over my mouth and chin the previous night.

Whilst I was lost in my thoughts, Berwin headed into one of the stalls and I made the sudden decision to follow him in. Kicking the door shut before my shadow could move from where he was leaning at the other end of the stable looking bored. He was probably storing information away to report back to my father.

"Is Nieve alright?" I whispered, hurrying over to Berwin. He didn't answer and looked completely confused so I continued. "Tell her I'm sorry. I didn't know what my father was going to do."

I then hurried over to pat the nearest horse's face and stare into its eyes. When my shadow pushed open the door, he found Berwin shovelling hay whilst I appreciated the beautiful animal before me. I deliberately didn't look at him, I just hoped my risk had paid off.

If Berwin gave my message to Nieve then maybe I could help her. Perhaps we could meet in private and continue to love each other before she forgot about me, or decided that I was to blame. I loved the thought of having a secret romance. The thought of the consequences, for both Nieve and I, should we be caught quickly soured those thoughts.

The days and weeks passed rather uneventfully. I gave my father no further reason to strike me and my days were spent repeating a boring routine of meals, lessons with Adair and walking around the castle in the hope that I would lose my shadow.

Unfortunately for me, he was a tall man and so I had to rush around to keep a good pace ahead of him and his long legs. He never enquired as to why we spent our time practically running through the halls to no particular destination, and I supposed that he probably didn't care.

I often considered starting a conversation with him to relieve my boredom, but then I remembered that he worked for my father and so would report back anything I said to the King without a moment hesitation. He couldn't be trusted.

I assumed that he reported back to the King during the night whilst I slept, as that was the only time in which he wasn't guarding my door.

One day after lessons, I was planning a new route for us to hurry along when my shadow spoke.

"Princess, King Ferchar has requested that the full court gathers in the main courtyard."

"Why?" I felt a twinge of nerves. I doubted this would be for fun and games.

"I am unsure Princess. I was simply told that we were to make haste once your lessons ended," he handed me my thick outdoor cloak.

We hurried off through the halls and made our way to the largest courtyard, near the entrance to castle. As we entered I could see that all the human servants, and even some of the fairies who worked in the castle, were gathered.

My mother and father stood on the raised stone platform at the door. Mother looked pale and nervous, as she always did these days, whereas father looked as if he was having the best day of his life. He heard the door open and gestured for me to stand at his side, my shadow moving to stand behind me.

"I am sure you are all curious to know why I gathered you here this afternoon," father said sounding very pleased with himself.

No one in the crowd responded but there was an unmistakable feeling of tension in the courtyard.

Realising nothing would be said, he gestured over to a set of small doors, one of many which led down into the prisons. A place I had never been and hoped I never would.

The doors opened and two large guards brought out a human I had never seen before. He had blonde plaited hair and I was sure he probably had a very pleasing face, beneath the cuts and bruises.

I took a deep breath to calm myself, but my heart was pounding in my chest. Something awful was going to happen and there was no way I could escape it.

The man was forced to kneel, facing the crowd in front of my father, and I hoped desperately that he had no family out there watching. No one should have to see their family member go through whatever was about to happen.

"This human was caught conspiring against my kingdom." father shouted suddenly, making me flinch.

The crowd stayed silent but I could see growing panic on some of their faces as we all began to realise what was coming.

"This pathetic human, who goes by the name Alasdair, wanted to see me dead in the ground and this good kingdom in ruins. So, he will be paying the price for that today. As you can see, he has already been punished," he laughed, kicking the human in the back, making him grunt in pain.

I took another shaky, not so calming, breath and tried to avoid looking at the man. I was sure that if I just found something else to focus on I could pretend this wasn't happening.

My shadow and I would soon be back to our normal routine as if nothing had ever happened.

One of father's guards handed him his sword and he kicked the man down onto his front, placing a foot on his back to prevent him moving. The human, Alasdair, was lying with his head near me and I fought the urge to close my eyes and run blindly away from this horror.

"Thankfully, my beautiful daughter managed to trick this human into revealing his plans and aid in his capture," father revealed with mock pride as he readied his sword.

I flinched as he mentioned me and stared at him with undisguised confusion, why was he lying? I had never seen this man before in my life, and now everyone in the castle was going to think that he was killed because of me. I clenched my fists, feeling my breathing become more erratic, would Nieve believe this?

The thought of her hating me for causing the death of one of her people made me want to burst into tears. Father knew I hated the execution of both humans and fairies and now he was putting the blame on me. I opened my mouth to deny his accusations but at that moment he swung his heavy sword down.

With one clean cut the prisoner was dead. Human flesh, bone and muscle no match for the strength of a fairy.

I felt the sickeningly warm blood spray onto my boots and ankles, where the wind had lifted my skirts slightly, and almost added my own vomit to the mess now covering the platform.

I glanced down to see a trickle of blood running steadily towards my feet and hastily took a few steps back. I bumped into my shadow who placed a hand on my back to steady me, and prevent my retreat.

Father picked up Alasdair's head by his bloody blonde plait and held it up high for the whole crowd to see. To my horror, he took my hand and pulled me forward, my feet sliding on the slick stones where blood was pooling around us.

I thought the sight of a trickle of my own blood had affected me, but that was nothing compared to the pool of warm sticky red which made my eyes blur and my chest feel as if the air was being choked from my body.

"This kingdom is united against human traitors. Remember that," father shouted, throwing the head down in front of the now weeping and furious crowd.

He then turned on his heel and stormed back into the castle, my mother and their guards following him.

I could hear mumbling in the crowd as I stood frozen and I wondered what they must think of me. I could hear their angry voices and knew that they thought this was my fault.

I tried to see Nieve, but the lights dancing in front of my eyes made it difficult and I felt as if I was swaying on the spot trying to find her.

I wished that she would appear before me and take me away from this, wash the blood from me and hide me from the crowd's anger. Hold me in her arms whilst I cried. Fix the hole in my life where she should be.

I needed her, but she did not come for me.

"Princess," my shadow murmured behind causing me to flinch.

When it was clear to him that I had forgotten how to make my legs work, he took my shaking arm and gently pulled me back inside the castle. He kept a hold of my arm as we walked through the castle to my chambers. There was no sign of the King in the halls and I was glad. I doubted I could have looked at him without bursting into tears, vomiting on him, or both.

"Get them off," I whispered hoarsely to Mae as I was delivered to my room, frantically pulling at my blood covered boots and socks.

The sight and feel of the blood on my hands made me feel worse and I wanted everything off. I pulled at my dress frantically, feeling tears on my face.

I could hear my breathing loud and panicked but I was trapped.

121

I couldn't get away.

"Calm down." Mae shouted sternly as she rushed to help me, ripping the dress in her hurry to free me and remove the bloodied clothes from my sight.

Once I was in nothing but my thankfully bloodless shift, not caring that the guard was still present, I ran to pour the water for washing all over my hands and legs to clean them. Rid them of human blood.

Alasdair's blood.

Blood that the humans of Culhuinn blamed me for, all because the King lied.

CHAPTER

13

Morven

I slept through the night without any more disruptions and felt much better when I finally woke up. Careful not to slip I slowly lowered myself into a bath of heated water, which we'd had to pay coin for, and instantly my aches and pains felt soothed.

The bruises on my chest now looked awful, but it was a small price to pay for my life. My knees were scraped and cut, and a dark bruise had blossomed beneath my ribs where I'd hit the edge of the boat, before tumbling overboard into the loch. Finnian had carefully poked at the bruises and luckily none of my ribs had been broken.

After soaking in the warm water, I slowly made my way down to the inn's main hall where food was being served. After a bowl of piping hot porridge and a mug of heather tea, I felt considerably better. I was still shaken after having had such a near death experience, but the nice long cry the previous night had helped me feel better.

I was glad to see that Glen looked less stressed and exhausted after getting a good night's sleep, and gladder still to notice that Finnian didn't seem to be angry anymore. I hoped he realised that we hadn't meant to lie to him, but I didn't bring it up again.

We had originally planned to only spend a few days in this village north of the loch, but after yesterday's events we decided it would be best to stay until I was fully recovered. The next leg of our journey would include mountains and forests, if our map was to be trusted, and so we didn't want to encounter anything dangerous whilst I was still injured. The fact that I was a changeling, so less fit than Glen, was problem enough.

The inn we were staying in was owned by a man called Hamish. His wife Eithrig felt sorry for me, after hearing about my fall into the loch, and stopped charging coin for the warm water to help my aches and pains. Hamish had laughed when he heard about my ordeal, but there was no malice in it.

I would have happily stayed in their inn, rather than continue our journey. It was clear just how in love they were and their happiness seemed to spread to everyone who stayed in the inn.

I had never really thought about growing older and marrying, I'd always assumed that I would be dead long before that could happen. Seeing Hamish and Eithrig together made me secretly wish for something similar. Not for the first time, I found myself hoping that the fairies would be able to stop my life from ending any time soon.

Finnian told us stories about Hamish and Eithrig. Apparently, they'd acted like enemies for years before realising that they loved each other and marrying a few days later, much to their families' confusion. He told us stories about his childhood, spent sailing across the loch, and visiting the three loch-side villages with his da. His stories helped the days pass, and I was glad that Glen had a chance to learn whilst we were stuck in the inn.

A few days later, just as I'd gently lowered myself into the bath, the door opened and to my horror Eithrig wandered in, humming cheerfully to herself. She froze when she saw me there in the water but instead of leaving, like I thought she would, she gently closed the door and came over to help me.

I blushed furiously at revealing my naked body to a woman I had only met a few days before but I relaxed as she tutted sympathetically at my bruises and sat down beside the bath. Clearly, she was used to seeing people naked.

She used a soft cloth to help wash my back and arms, telling me about her day and the inn. Her voice was soothing and the water was working wonders. I was so relaxed I could have fallen asleep, if it wasn't for her voice keeping me present. She paused for a moment clearly debating saying something, then bluntly asked her question.

"Are you a changeling?"

I flinched at her words, wondering how she could possibly know that about me. Changeling's tended to be paler than others, especially when they were younger, but I wasn't sure if Eithrig would notice. Her skin was darker than mine or Glen's, likely because she'd moved from Finclaw or Cladanan. I'd hoped that she would simply think I was pale because my family was from Tirwood. She seemed to notice my panic and hurried to reassure me.

"I had two sisters that were changelings. You learn how to notice a changeling after spending so much time with them. I can always tell," she explained with a sad smile.

"Do you think everyone can tell?" I asked, before realising that she had spoken about her sisters as if they had passed away. I cursed myself for being so insensitive and selfish.

"Not at all lass. I'm just good at noticing these things," she said with a wink.

"I'm sorry about your sisters," I mumbled.

"Thank you, but it was a long time ago now. They didn't live past five years, sadly. Unlike you, you lucky thing," she beamed.

I wasn't sure I felt particularly lucky, but I smiled anyway. Her happiness was infectious and I couldn't help but feel happier after spending time with her.

Having spent so much time with Glen and Finnian, recently, it was nice to spend some time with another woman, especially one who understood what life was like as changeling.

I found myself growing closer to Eithrig as the days passed. She revealed that she had always longed for a child, but sadly, they'd never managed to have a baby. Instead, they dedicated their time to their inn and making sure their guests had a good time.

It's funny the way you can meet someone and within a few days you are spilling your deepest darkest secrets to them, as if you have known them your whole life. I was glad that we would get another chance to stay at the inn as we made our way home.

Glen was making a name for himself as a storyteller and every evening after we ate, he ended up telling stories to the other guests, whilst learning all he could about their myths and tales.

He had asked me every question he could think of when I told him that I was sure I had spotted the kelpies. Unfortunately, he hadn't noticed them as he'd been too focused on not falling out of the boat and drowning, unlike me. He kept insisting that we went back down to the loch in case they came to the surface again, but we had no such luck.

He was great at telling tales though. The lack of detail, and the fact that he didn't even see the kelpies with his own eyes, did nothing to hinder his ability to weave them into a story.

The chance to spend more time getting to know Finnian was an unexpected bonus of almost drowning to death. He introduced me to his friends in the village and his sister, Fraoch, who moved there a few years ago, with her new husband. He also helped me try new foods whilst we stayed in the village. Thankfully, I found the brown trout that swam up here edible so could eat without needing lots of drink to wash it down.

Glen continued to be something of an attraction to the locals with his stories from the south, which he loved, so there were always people eager to hear him talk. One afternoon I decided to take the opportunity to escape and have some time alone.

It was nice to walk through the markets and have time to think about everything that had happened on our journey so far. We hadn't even left the human kingdoms yet and already, I felt changed by our experiences. I could understand now why da was so determined for us to go out and see more of the land. Homesickness crept in whenever I thought of home and my family, but tried not to dwell on it.

As I wandered through the stalls, I thought about what I would like to buy for everyone on our way home. My eyes were drawn to some smooth round stones, the seller told me they were from the very bottom of the loch, which were strung together to make jewellery. Ma would love it and I promised to return and purchase some soon.

The market was less exciting now, as we had been wandering around it all week, so I headed down to the water and found a seat on some barrels.

From there I sat and watched the different people as they worked. It was easy to see the difference between the travellers from each of the three villages. The villagers from the east all wore their thick fur cloaks and hats, whereas, the villagers from the south tended to wear layers of woollen clothes, like Glen and me. I also noticed that more of them had tattoos of the fairy symbols, like Finnian.

The villagers here in the north were a mix between the two and seemed to enjoy shaving parts of their hair into strange patterns, men and women alike.

I felt invisible sitting on the barrels, wrapped in my warm cloak and watching everyone else go about their day. I was all too aware that soon the most dangerous part of our journey would begin, so I was glad for some rest.

As I looked out across the loch, I tried to imagine that I could see all the way down south to our village. The loch looked peaceful today, unlike the day of our crossing. The mountains were free from clouds and so I could make out all their harsh jagged features. Some larger waves rippling far out in the loch drew my attention as the rest of the water remained peaceful.

With a splash, something flicked out of the water for a moment before disappearing back down to the depths. I couldn't hold back a gasp as I crept closer to the water's edge for a closer look. The waters splashed again and, for a moment, I could see a colossal creature with a huge flat body and a neck as long and thick as a tree.

It seemed to glide along the surface for a moment, its small beady eyes surveying the shore, before sinking back down below the waves.

"There she is," said a gruff voice beside me, making me shriek in fright.

I had been so captivated by the sight that I hadn't even heard one of the sailors walking over the stones towards me.

"What is she?" I asked, completely flabbergasted.

"That's our monster, beautiful she is," the man said with a proud smile, before wandering off along the shore whistling to himself.

I watched the waves for a while longer, hoping desperately for the surface to break and reveal the monster again, but I was out of luck.

Soon my growling stomach was too loud to ignore and I headed back to the inn for a much-needed meal. I smirked as I walked, thinking of how furious Glen was going to be when he heard all about yet another creature he missed.

"You are never going anywhere without me again," Glen complained. "I can't keep missing out on these stories!"

I laughed, "stop leaving me then."

"Leaving you? You're the one who threw yourself out a boat to get away from me!"

That night they were hosting a dance and a small feast in the inn. While Hamish hated to invite in large crowds, Eithrig grasped every opportunity to celebrate and invite in the village. She confided in me that she didn't host anywhere near as many dances as she would have liked. She unfortunately had to compromise with Hamish.

I was beside myself with excitement at the thought of a chance to celebrate. As we journeyed, Glen and I would likely miss the Queen's Light festival and so I threw myself into helping Eithrig prepare food and tables for the guests. This would be our only chance for a night resembling a festival and I wanted to make the most of it.

We spent the afternoon making an odd soup, which needed endless different ingredients and had to be left to boil for ages. Then we baked bannocks and bread, even some with berries Eithrig had collected.

To enter the inn that evening everyone, apart from small children, had to pay a coin and so the food was simply spread around the hall for everyone to take whatever they wished.

A band arrived, much to the locals' delight, and took their place in a corner of the hall to play. The songs were familiar but had a strange twist to them, unlike when they were played at home. Hearing songs that reminded me of the festivals in the castle back home made me feel desperately homesick again, so I went to find Finnian, who would be a welcome distraction from my thoughts.

He was sitting with Ramsey and Thorfinn enjoying a bowl of that soup we'd cooked earlier. He quickly made an excuse to leave them when he spotted me hovering nearby.

"Evening lass," He greeted me with a kiss to the cheek.

"Evening," I replied with a grin, "I can't believe you enjoy that soup."

He laughed, "there's so much of it up here, I would have a pretty hard life if I didn't."

"True, but I'm still doing my best to avoid it."

"Let's get some drinks instead, that sure took the taste out of your mouth last time."

I elbowed him playfully and agreed. Eithrig was only too happy to serve us both. She oversaw the drinks as she didn't quite trust Hamish not to get carried away. It wouldn't do for the whole town to be sick and hung-over tomorrow, not with sailing to be done and fish to be sold.

We found seats and watched as the locals started to clear a space in the middle of the room. I could see Glen on the other side of the hall, talking to an old man with a beard so long it reached his elbows and fairy symbols tattooed on his arms and neck.

"I wonder what my ma and da would do if I came home tattooed like all of you here."

"You'd suit a tattoo Morven, just something small to remember this journey," Finnian said nodding seriously at the idea and I loved how willing he was to agree to things. He made everything more exciting.

"Perhaps on the way home," I agreed.

"Perhaps." he teased, mimicking my voice.

The music picked up its pace and the drumming got louder as the locals came together to dance. They clapped and cheered as they spun each other around, stamping and switching partners quickly. I noticed Glen watching intently, probably trying to memorise the dance so that he could teach it to everyone back home.

Finnian stood abruptly beside me and grabbed my hands to pull me out onto the floor.

"I don't know this dance," I protested, shaking my head wildly.

"I'll teach you." and with that, I was part of the crowd.

I was quite sure that I looked ridiculous, flapping my arms about and hurriedly switching to new partners whenever directed. Luckily the locals seemed amused by it and not at all annoyed about me ruining the steps.

Despite feeling flustered and mortified, I found myself laughing and enjoying the dancing. I felt like we had been welcomed into their little community here. It was almost like stumbling across another home.

The dance changed to one where you stayed with the same partner and so I was glad to be back with Finnian. I think we were both glad for an excuse to spend some time close to each other. Despite my joy, I couldn't help but be angry that I was to be a changeling.

If I wasn't a changeling, then this would likely be the extent of Glen and I's travels. Finnian and I could consider a relationship, but no. Because of the fairies in the north we had to keep travelling north into wild kingdoms full of unknown danger, all to try and stop me from dying. It wasn't fair.

The dance slowed and I rested my face on Finnian's shoulder, focusing instead on his warmth and our gentle swaying.

The days passed, and with them my bruises faded. The pain in my chest eased and even my cut knees scabbed over and began healing, as if nothing had ever happened. I was happy to be back to my usual self with only breathlessness to worry about. Glad to have survived the experience. However, I was less pleased about having to leave the villages around the loch, which I had grown to love.

Eithrig and Hamish packed us many weeks' worth of bread, dried fish and cheeses. We filled leather pouches with water and had our travel clothes washed again before we were finally ready to leave.

"I'll miss it here," I said to Glen one night, as we lay beside each other.

"Miss the village or miss a certain tattooed young fisherman?" he teased.

"Both." I admitted with a sigh.

"Aye, I'll miss it as well. Especially when we're running from bears, fighting wulver and sleeping on the cold hard ground. Then I'll miss it all." Glen said making us both laugh, half amused and half nervous.

"At least we can return after we have our answers."

"Hopefully we can let the villagers here know how to stop their babies being stolen as well. Somehow spread the word and save them," Glen said making me proud.

I had almost forgotten that we could help more people than just me. I was glad that Glen was here with me, for the times when I was so busy feeling sorry for myself I forgot that I was not the last changeling in the land.

The next morning, we filled up on salty porridge and bread. Then we paid Eithrig and Hamish what we owed them and gave them a tearful goodbye.

We would be following the road north, which was rarely used. If the map was correct, we would travel up through the Fairy Hills and then through the Fairy Forest, before arriving at a castle at the base of a mountain range. We would hopefully come across a few villages on our travels, but the woman had not known their precise location.

Glen and I decided to pay coin for two horses to take us up the road to the Fairy Hills. The horses we purchased were used only on these roads, and the seller assured us that once we dismounted they would wander back down the road and return home. It seemed unlikely to me that a horse could do that but he was confident enough that we didn't question it.

The climb through the mountains would be exhausting, and we didn't want to be tired before our climb even started.

"I'll be seeing you on your way back then Morven, just ask around for me. I'll be somewhere around this loch," Finnian said, as we were saying farewell.

Glen had already gone out to the horses to give us some privacy, much to my embarrassment.

"We will. If I don't come back, then just know that I had the best time here at the loch with you," I said, blinking furiously to stop myself getting emotional again.

Goodbyes were always so difficult.

"None of that! You'll come back down that road having sorted out the fairies in the north, and you'll be full of tales about the adventure you had. Alright?" he said stubbornly.

"Alright," I agreed.

Before I could say anything else, his arms were around my waist, pulling me close. Then, to my surprise, he leaned down to gently kiss me.

Distracted by the feeling of his warm lips against mine, I realised that my arms were hanging limply by my sides. After a few moments of debating what to do, I settled for gripping his leather coat tight. It was only when I felt him smile against my lips that I realised I was stopping him from moving away.

Reluctantly, I released him.

"Now you go have that adventure Morven." he placed one last quick kiss on my lips before pushing me gently out of the door to face an amused looking Glen.

"Ready to go?" he asked with a smirk, to which I could only give a dazed nod.

CHAPTER

14

Euna

Meeting with the Lairds and Ladies was never my favourite thing to do, and I liked it even less when Aelwen was away. I resisted the urge to roll my eyes as Laird Lus, who was unfortunately in charge of overseeing crop growth, approached me.

I already knew what he was going to ask me, thanks to Aelwen's warning before she left for Wulvendach. She had said no to his suggestion the moment he voiced it, but still he thought trying me would be a promising idea. He was a surprisingly large fairy, and I often wondered how much of the crops he consumed himself.

"My Queen," he greeted dramatically, performing a ridiculously low bow in front of me.

Beside me I heard Tormod cough to hide his laugh. It always amused me to see just how low some of the Lairds would bow, especially when they wanted something. I was not sure who started the rumour that the closer to the ground you got when you bowed, the more likely the Queens were to agree to your proposal. I was grateful for them anyway, it was the only fun part of these meetings.

"Good to see you Laird Lus," I said, although I was sure my expression conveyed just how unhappy I was to be in his presence.

"I had been hoping to see you here."

He clearly thought that small talk would make me more likely to agree to his request. Oh, how wrong he was.

"This is the designated meeting time in which Laird's, like yourself, can raise issues with the Queens of this kingdom. Last time I checked I was one of those Queens." I said scathingly.

"Yes, your majesty," he forced a laugh, "I will get straight to my point. The kingdom of Culhuinn has a much larger crop yield than us here in Norbroch, and I think I know how we could improve our own."

"That is because Culhuinn is a much larger kingdom than Norbroch. But do tell me your wonderful plan," I mentally prepared myself for what the fool was about to suggest.

"I think, your majesty, that with the use of humans for labour, we could vastly improve our crop yield and farming practises. Perhaps even improve all aspects of our kingdom."

I felt Tormod stiffen beside me and I sighed heavily. Even with Aelwen's warning and time to prepare myself, I felt a surge of anger and had to fight the urge to slap the stupid fairy right across the face. How dare he.

"How exactly would the employment of beings weaker than ourselves improve this kingdom?"

"You misunderstand me, my queen. Not employment, we would simply take the humans from their land. Give them no choice but to work here for us, like they do in the south."

136

"Has it ever occurred to you that we do not produce as high a yield because here the weather is less suitable for crop growing? Not to mention the fact that we have much less space free for crop planting?"

"Each of those are problems we can't control, but we can control the labour. Free labour is exactly what we need. Trust me, my Queen."

"I do not trust you. In fact, I am beginning to doubt you are who this kingdom needs in control of crop growth. I seem to recall you inquiring about this with the good Queen Aelwen not more than a few weeks ago and being told the exact same thing," My last slither of patience was gone. "Our answer is no. The answer will always be no."

The Laird's face paled slightly and he looked increasingly flustered. He had clearly assumed that Aelwen and I did not converse about the proposals made, so had hoped to convince me, and that I would then convince her.

He should have realised that I was the Queen least likely to ever agree to use feeble humans as free labour, and that he would soon be looking for a new job.

"Come Tormod, this audience is over," I said, striding from the room without a backwards glance.

Aelwen and I ruled Norbroch together and we would until the day we died. No pathetic Lairds or Ladies would divide us, no matter how hard they tried.

10 YEARS AGO

"Are you not angry that you were stolen from your family?" I asked, as Lachlann and I wandered through the Verch forest, careful on the snow which had frozen and turned icy overnight.

The ever dutiful Tormod was trailing slowly behind us, attempting to pretend he was not there and give us privacy.

"I am angry, but what can I do about it? There's nothing to be done," Lachlann answered with a frown.

"Are you sure there is nothing you can do?"

He sighed, "I wouldn't want to abandon everyone I know, and there is nowhere we could all go to escape the King. He would find us before we could make it far enough to hide."

"I could hide you here." I said, surprising myself. Though I knew that I meant it.

I did not care if it risked the new and fragile relations between our two kingdoms. The more I learned about King Ferchar, and the way he treated the humans, the less I wanted anything to do with him.

Lachlann took my hand, "I know you would Euna, but I can't."

We wandered in comfortable silence for a while longer, the snow crunching beneath our feet echoing loudly through the trees. Lachlann's hand in mine felt like the only source of warmth in the whole, vast forest. I was anchored to him.

A short time later, we came across an area of the forest where huge stones, carved with the symbols and runes of the Others, were scattered. I always sensed a higher presence of magic here near the stones, and today was no exception.

I became aware that I could sense another being nearby and tensed, as did Tormod who hurried to my side. I knew that I could always count on him to be quick when he thought his Queen was in danger.

We stopped walking, which caused Lachlann to throw a confused glance at me. I simply shook my head and placed a finger to his lips so he maintained his silence.

I never felt worried about danger. I trusted Tormod with my life and I knew that I could likely defend myself against most threats. Lachlann, on the other hand, looked horrifically fragile and human all of a sudden. I worried that he would not be able to defend himself, should we be attacked.

Both fairies and humans were mortal, although we fairies age much slower than humans and can heal much faster. The realisation that I was worried for Lachlann, and that I might not be able to protect him, turned my insides to ice.

He flinched beside me as the source of all our worries suddenly revealed itself and the silence was broken as Tormod laughed.

From amongst the trees a will o'the wisp appeared, a tiny flying fairy carrying a bright lantern. As a child, my father told me that the light was so bright to human eyes they could see nothing but a floating burst of magic. Often, they were tricked into following it to their doom. Thankfully, Lachlann made no move to rush off towards the will o'the wisp and it looked to me with a questioning glance, waiting to see what I would do.

The will o'the wisp watched at us curiously. Floating in a circle around the three of us, waiting to see if it could persuade one of us to follow. I always feel wary of them as it is well known that they speak with the Others and the Otherworld. That they obey the commands of the Others when they are not spending their free time trying to trick humans. It is an odd mixture of habits.

"It wants to see if you will follow it. If you do, it will lead you off into the forest. You will become so lost that not even your King will be able to find you," I explained to Lachlann, who still looked bemused.

It saddened me to realise that he was never told these stories as a child, as he had no parents to raise him. I highly doubted King Ferchar took any time to teach his human servants about the Others and magic.

"You could find me." he smiled, still watching the little fairy and its lantern curiously.

"I would send Tormod to find you whilst I sat and enjoyed a nice drink back at the castle," I teased.

Lachlann made me feel younger than twenty-two. As father died whilst we were still young, I felt a duty to our kingdom to mature and become wise as quickly as possible.

Aelwen did also, but she still managed to find the time to fall in love with multiple men and women, and sneak out of the castle to go on romantic evenings with them. She would come back smiling and seemed to float around the halls happily for days after. Her strange, almost obsessive, behaviour had always confused and annoyed me until now.

Now, I noticed my thoughts turning to Lachlann when I should be focusing on more important things.

I felt happier. It was as if a weight I had never known I was carrying had been lifted. I realised that I was happier than I had been since before Aelwen and I became orphans, before the responsibility for this whole kingdom fell on our shoulders.

The will o'the wisp eventually lost interest in us and floated off amongst the snow frosted trees, whether to trick some unsuspecting wanderers or to obey the silent commands of the Others, we would never know.

Seeing it made me wonder just how much the Others cared about the lives of us here in Norbroch and across the land.

We returned to the castle a few hours later, by then Lachlann's nose was bright red from the cold and I was eager to get him a hot meal. A human I had never seen before was waiting for us. He had blonde hair, which was pulled back into multiple plaits, and he was smirking. I had a moment of panic as I wondered why he looked pleased to see us. Imagining him telling the King about us. Our whole relationship ending in disaster before it even began.

Fortunately, Lachlann embraced him when they met, so I assumed he was another stolen child that Lachlann had grown up with. Tormod and I were left as awkward bystanders for a few moments whilst they greeted each other.

"My Queen, this is Alasdair, another servant of the King," Lachlann eventually introduced him.

"Pleasure to meet you," I said stiffly, wanting to make a good impression but unsure how.

"The pleasure, is mine your majesty. Lachlann speaks very highly of you." he said as he gave a low bow.

"Lachlann should not be speaking about me at all," I gave Lachlann a glare which made him laugh. "I am sorry to say I have heard nothing about you."

"Ah well, not much exciting to say about me I am afraid. Just a humble servant," Alasdair said, making Lachlann laugh.

"He definitely isn't."

"It was lovely to meet you, though sadly I must leave you both now. There is much planning to be done for the upcoming Queen's Light festival, which your King has decided to attend at our castle."

Aelwen had threatened to seriously harm me should I miss the meeting to discuss festival plans.

Alasdair gave one last bow before heading off into the castle to complete his day's work. Lachlann returned to me, his cheeks still flushed from our walk, and placed a quick kiss on my lips. Then he was darting off after Alasdair and soon vanished into the castle.

"Perhaps it wouldn't do to keep Queen Aelwen waiting," Tormod reminded me in an amused tone which earned him an unamused glare.

CHAPTER

15

Morven

Apart from aching thighs and sore legs, our journey on horseback to the foot of the Fairy Hills was pleasant. We had now left Tirwood behind and entered the fairy kingdoms. Having never spoken to a fairy before, we didn't know what this land was called.

It was a relief that we'd managed to enter the kingdom without any trouble and hadn't encountered any horrific beasts or human eating fairies so far. With no reliable information to go on we couldn't afford to let down our guard, just in case something did happen.

We chatted about our different experiences in the loch-side villages as we rode and only stopped to relive ourselves and have small meals. We didn't want to risk running out of food in the mountains.

When eventually the mountains appeared in front of us, we were in awe. We knew they were huge, but nothing really prepares you for standing at the foot of mountains so large that their peaks are obscured by clouds.

The Fairy Hills were mainly brown, with patches of green grass growing around them as summer crept closer. We could see sheep on the hills we were closest to and kept a wary eye out for their owners who could be lurking nearby, ready to turn us into their next meal.

The path we were on continued up into a valley between two of the mountains. Thankfully it went nowhere near as high as the peaks and, although it was steep, it would be much easier than trying to walk over one of the mountains from top to bottom.

It was a worn path, despite how little it was used, and it made me wonder if in the past humans and fairies had travelled between kingdoms more often than they do now.

We dismounted from the horses distributed our bags evenly between us. Then we shouted "home" and gave the horses a pat on the shoulder, as instructed by their owner. To my surprise, they turned and headed off back to the village.

As we watched them go I wondered what Finnian was doing today, if he was back out on the loch in his boat fishing for brown trout or if maybe he waiting to see the horses return.

The sun was setting quickly and so we found a gap between some large boulders at the entrance of the valley to shelter from the wind. It wouldn't help us if the rain started, but lying in each other's arms we'd be warm enough throughout the night. The cold hard rock was uncomfortable but we managed to sleep eventually, the day's riding having tired us out.

The weather was mild and dry when we woke to start our first day of clambering through the Fairy Hills. Before setting off we made sure that we had our food provisions and that Glen's small dagger was easily accessible. There was no way of knowing what horrible beasts we could encounter up amongst the rocks and the clouds.

The path, which wound in between the Fairy Hills, was made up of jagged pieces of rock which moved whenever they were stood on. This made our progress slow as we didn't want to risk falling and breaking our ankles on the first day.

I was surprised by how enclosed I felt, surrounded by huge walls of rock. Although the valley was large enough to fit one or two carts at one time, I still felt trapped within the stones. The only way to escape would be to go forward or back.

My unease grew as the day progressed. Glen and I didn't speak much as our voices echoed all around us and we didn't want to risk attracting anything's attention. Better to silently move through this stone prison as quickly as possible.

The path became steeper as we walked and we both ended up falling on the uneven stones, scratching our hands and hurting our knees, before the day was over. For a while, the path was so uneven and dangerous that I started to think we were never going to make it, but then it reached a peak and suddenly, we were looking down over a valley.

It was breath-taking, a terrain unlike anything I had ever seen before. The valley grew wider after the small mountain of stones. The path led down into a wide, gently sloping valley which, to my surprise, even had a small river running through it. The river came from high up in the mountains and ran through the middle of the path, disappearing into the stones we had climbed at the end of the valley.

The small trickle of water helped to lift my mood. In the stories, the adventurers always found what they were seeking when they followed a river, or if they were lost, a river always brought them home. We had found our river and at once, the stone walls seemed less ominous and the suffocating silence was broken by the calming sound of water running past us towards its goal.

Our night was uncomfortable, although we were warm, our woollen blankets did little to cushion the solid rock we lay on. No grass grew down in the valley and so we had no choice but to rest uncomfortably. Glen drifted off to sleep not long after we had a quick meal of dried fish and some of the bread from the village, which was starting to harden.

I had to fight to keep my eyes open as I lay staring up at the sky. It was strange to see the sky bracketed between two huge mountain peaks. Instead of brown and grey the mountains looked black and mysterious in the moonlight.

I could see faint wisps of bright green and blue light and I wondered what the fairies in the sky could be fighting about. I wondered if we would wake up covered in their blood jewels if their argument turned into a battle. I soon lost my own battle with sleep, and spent the night dreaming of the castle I would build once I had an abundance of coin from selling the jewels.

Morning arrived, bringing with it a pain every time I moved my neck and stiff limbs from a night lying on a bed of stone. The fairies must have settled their dispute without bloodshed as there was not a single jewel in sight, much to Glen's disappointment.

More bread for breakfast, washed down with water from the stream, and we were ready for another day wandering through this seemingly never-ending valley.

The longer we spent here, the less I was amazed by the size of the mountains. Instead I became bored of their similarity. Glen thought he spotted some sheep at one point, but that was the most exciting thing to happen that day. Another night on the crippling rocks, watching the stars pass, and then finally it was our last day in the rocky prison.

We wandered alongside the river, grateful for the light rain which helped clean the dust and dirt from our skin and make the journey somewhat more exciting. A wind started to pick up, which was unusual, the valley had been calm and almost airless up until this point. Before long a wind, that simultaneously chilled us to the bone and refreshed us, was whistling through the valley.

As we walked the valley sides began to change, and soon grass and plants grew on either side of us, blowing around in the wind. After spending so long in near silence, I felt as if the wind was howling within my head and it was all I could focus on.

"Morven, look!" Glen called from ahead of me.

So distracted by the noise, I had failed to notice the valley ending in front of me. In between the rocky walls I could see the river running through gently undulating hills and into the forest.

I assumed this was another part of the Fairy Forest, which we had passed many times now on our journey. The old woman's map had shown that the Fairy Forest travelled across half of the land.

Exhilarated by the wind and freedom I rushed forward to take Glen's hand, and after a few minutes of running happily, we were out.

We ran for a while, laughing, until I was completely out of breath. With a happy sigh, I sank down onto the cool damp grass and lay down for a rest. I had never been so happy to see trees, grass and open space.

Glen and I spent the remainder of that day wandering through the hills, which seemed like an easy stroll compared to the uneven stone hill we had encountered on our first day in the mountains. We chatted happily about the sights we hoped to see and laughed about our time in the valley as if it was a distance memory, not less than a day ago.

The green grass and hills made me feel as if we were back in our village, wandering around to avoid doing work. We had travelled so far, but still the land and the nature around us felt the same as it did back home.

Home... I felt a twinge of homesickness at the thought of home, but we had been away so long now that my longing for our wee village had lessened to a dull ache. Perhaps it was the thought of another walk in that valley, or the risk of falling back into the loch, which made me less eager to begin the journey home.

After hearing so many stories about how dangerous the fairies were, it was almost disappointing that we hadn't been chased or attacked yet. In fact, we were yet to see anyone or any signs of life, other than the path which led off into the forest. Unless of course, the path simply formed itself by magic.

"Are you nervous about entering the forest?" I asked Glen as we lay beside each other on the grass.

It felt luxuriously soft in comparison to the rocky ground in the valley. I wanted to stay there forever.

"Well there aren't many stories about the forest so I'm not sure what to expect," he admitted, "Why? Are you nervous?"

I shrugged. "It just seems so huge, especially on that map. I don't want us getting lost in there."

"If we follow the path we will be fine," Glen said confidently, and stupidly, I believed him.

"You got us lost!" I accused, throwing my hands up in despair.

"Me?" Glen shouted incredulously. "It was the will o'the wisp that led us here."

Which was true, we had entered the forest the previous day and had an easy day walking. The weather was pleasant as we followed the winding path through the trees without a problem. It was difficult to tell which direction we were going as everything looked the same. Still, we felt confident that eventually the path was going to bring us out of the forest on the other side.

By the end of the day we were sure that we had managed to travel a large distance, though we had no way of knowing. One benefit of being surrounded by trees and bushes was the ability to go relieve ourselves in private. The valley had been far too enclosed to get any sort of privacy.

That night we settled down to sleep near a fallen tree. The luxury of the soft ground was still amazing, but because of the strange animal sounds and creaking trees I slept fitfully.

Glen and I both woke multiple times throughout the night, fearful that some hideous creature was about to come crashing through the trees and attack us. No attack came, but by the time morning arrived we were tired, weary and becoming sick of the sight of trees.

That afternoon, as we were grumpily trudging through the forest, clambering over fallen logs and cursing the fairies for not taking the time to clear their paths, a bright light flew across the path in front of us. We both froze, waiting to see if it would return, but it was gone and we decided that we must have imagined it.

Our ignorance didn't last long and soon the light was reappearing continuously. I felt as if we were being circled and watched. We were.

I watched the light, expecting it to disappear out of sight, and was startled when it floated towards us. Before I even realised what I was doing, I reached out, as if to touch it. My fingertips warmed the closer I got, like it was a tiny little fire floating in front of me.

"A will o'the wisp." Glen gasped beside me, mesmerised.

I nodded, that made sense. I had heard the stories about them ever since I was a child but I hadn't recognised what was floating before us.

It suddenly darted away from us and we hurried to follow it. I wanted to look at it more. The light was so bright that I could barely make out what it was.

Soon Glen and I were following the will o'the wisp as it flew, seemingly randomly, through the trees. It ignored the path, and so we went from chasing it along the path to scrabbling through bushes after it.

The chase was the most fun we had had in weeks and I could finally understand why dogs loved to chase after sticks. The thought made me laugh, which in turn made Glen laugh.

I had to stop and clutch my chest after a while, my changeling body making the prolonged chase difficult. I watched in amusement as Glen scrambled after the will o'the wisp looking ridiculous and elated.

My smile faded as I realised just how strange his behaviour was. Why in the name of the Others were we wasting our time chasing after a light? We were supposed to be heading north in search of answers.

How many babies had been stolen and replaced with changelings whilst we remained here in this forest, aimlessly chasing a light?

As the light, and then Glen passed, I grabbed onto Glen's hand and pulled him away. If we continued following this will o'the wisp we would surely be lost until the day we died.

Like everyone else, I'd heard the stories about travellers who followed the will o'the wisps forever or of those who ended up travelling to the Otherworld as they chased them. I had always thought of those people as foolish and couldn't understand why they would follow something for so long. Now I understood. I had never felt so drawn to anything in my life.

We made a point of walking away from the will o'the wisp and ignoring it whenever it passed by us, trying to reclaim our attention. After a while it grew bored and eventually left us alone, presumably to find someone else to trick. I hoped whoever it found had more sense than the two of us.

Eventually we found the path again and continued on our way. We hoped that we were still heading north but only time would tell.

If we came out of the forest back at the mountains I was going to scream.

"I'm sorry I blamed you," I said after a while.

"Don't you worry, Morven. I'm just glad you had enough sense to stop the chase," Glen said, wrapping his arm around my shoulders.

CHAPTER

16

Euna

10 YEARS AGO

In Norbroch the Queen's Light festival, celebrating the longest day of the year, has always been important. In the years since Aelwen and I gained the throne, the celebrations have only grown. Aelwen loves festivals and takes every opportunity to throw a feast and bring in musicians.

I remembered my teachers telling me that the humans celebrated the same festivals as us. They have little magical ability to ensure crop growth, so they must focus on appeasing the Others by giving multiple offerings.

Here in Norbroch, we give offerings and take care not to anger the Others. It is rumoured that on the days of festivals the Otherworld is closest to our realm, so we always take care. I had even heard rumours of people stumbling across places in the hills where you can travel to the Otherworld, though I was not sure I believed that.

Culhuinn throws a small feast for the festival but King Ferchar cares little about offending the Others and so their offerings are always small. Queen's Light is the time to ask for protection for livestock, making it especially important for us here in Norbroch where we grow less crops.

It dawned on me that this festival would be the first proper Queen's Light experience that Lachlann would have. Unashamedly, I became almost as bad as Aelwen when it came to planning and organising, much to Ronan's dismay. I wanted it to be perfect for him.

To begin with, I had been angry that the King was staying in our castle for so long. We could not agree on new trading terms as he was even more stubborn and greedy than we could have imagined. Now though, I was beginning to dread us ever reaching an agreement as that would mean that Lachlann would be forced to leave me.

The morning of the Queen's Light festival always starts the same. Everyone leaves the castle and goes out to the largest meadows near the Verch forest, where the morning dew collects in the grass.

It is said that anyone who washes in the dew, on the morning of the festival, will become beautiful and so everyone does it. Not many people, apart from some of the younger fairies looking for love, care much about the dew improving their appearance but it is a tradition we all follow.

The Queen's traditionally go first and so Aelwen and I were the first to kneel in the damp grass and begin covering our skin with the dew we could collect. I noticed the Queen was helping the giggling Princess Freya to cover her skin whilst the King stared at them with a look verging on disgust.

Aelwen's children were still too young to properly take part and so that morning they were being cared for back at the castle.

"He should take care to be more respectful," Aelwen commented.

"Especially with one of the Others living so close," I added with a laugh.

Some, who believed the more obscure rumours and stories, say that deep within the frozen mountains north of our kingdom there is huge castle in which the Queen of the Others lives. I am not sure how they know this as anyone who tried to cross the ice would surely die. Why their Queen would choose to live in our realm was also baffling. Perhaps it was simply a representative sent to watch over us. The thought made me laugh again.

Festivals were a time for hope and optimism, and I was eager to put aside my worries and duties until tomorrow.

After everyone had a chance to roll in the grass, we spread out through the meadows and forest. We were collecting the yellow flowers which had started growing now that the weather was a little warmer and the days were longer.

For the next few days yellow flowers would decorate the castle and homes across the land. For the feast later many people, including Aelwen and I, would add them to our hair or wear them as jewellery.

I spotted Lachlann and Alasdair looking amused as they collected their own flowers. King Ferchar had tried to insist that his servants did not take part in the festival. However, Aelwen had been so furious he had had no choice but to allow them.

It was disrespectful enough to not honour the festival, but refusing to allow your subjects to celebrate was a sure way to anger the Others.

People began making their way back to the castle whilst Aelwen, our guards, Tormod and I had to ride out to where the cattle and sheep were being moved to new summer fields. Many torches were lit to draw the attention of the Others and ensure that they protected our livestock. Bonfires would be lit later in the evening.

We oversaw the movement of the animals and had to talk to the farmers. I always felt unsure about what to say but thankfully everyone was in good spirits and so the conversation flowed.

By the time we returned to the castle, preparations for the feast were in full swing. Huge tables had been brought out behind the castle to the large space used for events. There was a grassy moor which lay between the back of the castle and the mountains in the distance. It did not need to be protected, which meant that even the guards could enjoy the festivities.

Not that anyone would risk committing crimes today. Not with the Otherworld watching us so closely.

We wandered leisurely through the preparations, complementing servants on their work and wishing everyone well. Luckily, Aelwen no longer wanted to spend as long doing that as she had when we were first crowned. Now she was eager to help her children get ready for the festival.

I was glad to return to my chambers and have a few moments peace before my maids arrived, full of laughter and excitement to help me get ready.

I picked a dress of dark blue. My dark hair was then plaited at the top, so the yellow flowers could be added, and the rest left cascading down my back.

Aelwen looked beautiful. She wore a white dress that matched her hair, which was plaited up intricately and looked like she wore a crown of flowers. Her girls looked equally as beautiful in their matching dresses and I assumed that Elath was with Ronan, dressing in matching kilts.

Tormod was eager to get to the feast and I found myself feeling guilty that he had waited for me. We headed out early and I could not help but keep adjusting my dress and fretting over my hair.

I wanted to make a good impression to Lachlann tonight. I was not ugly by any stretch of the imagination, but the sight of my sister had made me feel somewhat underwhelming.

"He would be a fool not to think you beautiful, my Queen," Tormod commented after noticing my uncharacteristic fretting.

"Let's hope so. Go enjoy your evening Tormod," I dismissed him with a smile, whilst cursing how observant he was.

As I walked through the crowds of people I was reminded why I loved our kingdom so much.

Norbroch has always been a kingdom of hardworking and friendly fairies. It warmed my heart to see so many of them together. It made me happy to think of the fairies, all over this kingdom, celebrating together and offering thanks to the Others without fear, unlike in Culhuinn.

It would be clear that we deserved their protection and I hoped that the next year would see our livestock growing fat and our crops growing tall.

After meandering my way through the crowds, I took my seat at the table, which was on a slightly raised wooden platform. The platform had been hastily constructed so we royals could watch over the celebrations as we ate. I think the people liked to see us there enjoying ourselves and I hoped that they viewed us in a good light.

Much to my surprise, Aelwen had not asked for the platform to be extended to fit King Ferchar and his family. Instead they had a table amongst the Lairds,

Ladies and servants. The King could not refuse our hospitality, but I had a feeling that he would be leaving the festival once the feast was over.

The feast was exquisite and I found myself eating an obscenely large amount. I was so full that I doubted I would ever need to eat again.

When I was sure I could not manage another bite, I watched fondly as my nieces and nephew ate and vowed to spend more time with them. They were the future rulers of our kingdom and they deserved more of my attention. Aelwen caught me watching and beamed in response.

Festivals were always a time for making promises and vows. This was probably because of the large volume of drink consumed, but also because everyone was so happy.

I could imagine people up and down the land making wild promises and vows with their neighbours and family, only to wake hungover in the morning or forget every single one.

I wanted to promise the kingdom that they would have a good year, the best in generations, but this was not the time for grand speeches and so I kept my thoughts to myself.

Once the main meal of the feast was over, we headed to the two huge bonfires which had been constructed over the last few days.

Aelwen and I took heavy torches, and with a nod, ignited the bonfires. Everyone stood back and there was a sense of awe as we watched the flames destroy the pile.

It was humbling to witness such a powerful force, more powerful than any of us could ever hope to be. Tomorrow the ash from the bonfires would be scattered throughout the fields that grew crops, and around the fields in which the livestock were kept. This would protect them throughout the year, if the Others were pleased with us.

After the excitement over the lighting of the bonfires was over, I decided to have a wander around the festivities. I did not plan on staying out all night but it was good for the people to have a chance to speak with me and see me enjoying the festival.

I headed over to a table giving out cups of a thick drink made with uncooked oats, whisky, cream and what I assumed was honey. It was warm and sweet and so, despite being full after the feast, I forced myself to have one whilst I spoke with the stall owners and then paid coin for another to take away with me.

Aelwen's favourite drummers, pipers and fiddlers began playing out on the field and the dancing began. It was always interesting to watch the movements made by some of the drunkest, or simply most daring, dancers. I was not a dancer, not unless it was required. I loved the music but I simply did not feel the need to twirl and jump like some people.

Aelwen was twirling and laughing with her children. I took another sip of the warm drink as I watched, and felt content. That feeling doubled when I felt warmth at my back and noticed Lachlann standing there.

"Enjoying your first Queen's Light?" I asked.

"It has been the best night of my life," he admitted truthfully. "Even better now that I am in the company of such a beautiful fairy." he reached up to touch the flowers in my hair.

Deciding that I did not care about the consequences, I turned and kissed him before he could speak again. His surprise made me laugh.

It was strange to be able to kiss him in public and as I closed my eyes, I imagined that we were simply two lovers enjoying the festival, rather than a fairy Queen and the servant of another King.

We broke apart after what felt like too long, and not long enough. It would not do for too many people to notice us. Not everyone would be too drunk to remember and, though the King had retired early, not all of his servants had gone inside.

"Come back to my rooms?" I did not want to leave his company so soon.

Lachlann grinned mischievously, "I'll meet you there," and with that he slipped away, disappearing into the crowd.

I was sure that by this time no one would miss me when I left the festivities, but I made a show of saying goodbye to a few people and announcing how tired I was after such a long and joyful day.

Then, once I was sure no one would care, I hurried off into the castle and up to my chambers. The halls were deserted as everyone was out, either enjoying the dancing or hiding away somewhere with their own lovers.

Lachlann was already waiting outside my door when I arrived so I grabbed him and quickly pulled him inside, locking the door behind us.

Our kiss resumed once we were away from curious eyes, and I felt a twinge of nerves in my stomach at the thought of finally bedding a man. This could be our only ever opportunity, and I was suddenly worried that I would ruin it with my lack of experience.

"We don't have to do this Euna," Lachlann noticed my hesitation.

"I want to," I mumbled feeling foolish.

I was the Queen of Norbroch. I should not be falling prey to my nerves like this.

"We have all night, there's no rush," he said with a comforting smile as he started to pick the yellow flowers out of my hair.

PRESENT DAY

I cursed myself for allowing my mind to wander back to that perfect night as I wiped the tears from my face. My bed felt empty and cold in comparison to that night when it had been full of laughter and love. I stared at the space beside me and tried to remember everything about him, every last freckle.

We had woken the next morning to Tormod knocking the door, curious as to why I had slept in and checking to see if I had been murdered whilst he enjoyed his evening.

Lachlann had blushed furiously when I made him answer the door, refusing to move from under the warm blankets. Tormod had simply laughed at Lachlann's embarrassment and said that he was glad we had a good night.

Now though, Lachlann was gone and I was left alone here in the cold with nothing but my memories to torment me.

I wanted to hate him for leaving me.

Everything would be easier if I did not long for him to return to me.

CHAPTER

17

Morven

I felt as if the path was going to continue winding through the trees forever. Never again would either of us see the sky or the loch or our families. I cursed the old lady back in Tirwood for not giving us more information about navigating our way through this forest.

This path must end somewhere. I tried to reason with myself, but my aching feet and the weariness in my bones weren't making me feel very reasonable. Glen felt the same and our conversations had stopped what felt like a whole forest ago.

It was difficult to think of anything to say when all you could see were trees. All you could hear was the wind blowing through the leaves and the faint chirping of birds. All you could smell was that damp smell of leaves and rich soil, a smell you only find deep inside a forest.

I decided that if I never saw another tree in my life I would be very happy about it. I hated trees.

Rustling in front of us startled me out of my tree related thoughts. I thought perhaps it was another will o'the wisp, come to try and trick us off the path again. I would have some very harsh words to say if it was.

Instead a girl, who looked to be the same age as Glen and I, stepped out from between the trees.

She wore a dress made of a fabric I had never seen before, which seemed to float around her skin and move with the rhythm of the forest. Her long auburn hair had been allowed to grow down to her knees and she was the most beautiful thing I had ever seen in my life.

I realised that we'd stopped walking and simply stood, mesmerised, watching her approach us. The Others had truly blessed us with this sight. She made all the walking worthwhile.

"Are you lost?" the girl asked, her voice seeming to float on the wind.

It was like a song I had been waiting my whole life to hear, and hoped to listen to forever.

"We are." Glen and I replied at the exact same time which made her smile.

"I can show you the way. Follow me."

With that she turned on her heel and seemed to float off in amongst the trees, leaving the path behind.

Glen and I hurried after her with a lot less elegance. I didn't want her to leave me. I felt quite sure that my life would end if she left us here alone in the forest. I had to stay with her. Forever.

As we hurried along, stray branches scratched at my face and arms, but I didn't care. Nothing would stop me following her. Nothing. Every so often she would stop and smile over her shoulder at us, making the sting of my scratches and the aching in my legs fade.

Her happiness was more important.

At once we were back on the path and, a few steps later, we had broken out from underneath the cover of the trees. She had helped us escape the forest, just as she had promised. Now we were free.

A refreshing wind picked up and her hair drifted around her head, adding to her startling wild beauty. I was never sure if I would ever fall in love with a girl, although I always thought I might, and finally here I was. I doubted I would ever have room in my heart for anyone else ever again.

"Come along now," she called as she drifted towards a small stone cottage I had not noticed before.

It had a large strange smelling garden, in which herbs and plants I had never seen before grew. The thatched roof was covered in grass and had beautiful flowers growing in it as if it were alive.

Our rescuer kind enough to invite us into her home. It was warm and cosy, and there was a pleasant herbal smell drifting around the rooms from the plants she was burning in wooden bowls scattered around the house. I couldn't quite recall where we had been planning to go before we arrived here. I just knew that I would be happy to stay in her cottage.

After feeding us a hearty stew, she told us about the problems she had been having recently, trying to complete all of the household chores. I felt tears welling in my eyes at the very thought of such a beautiful, perfect being struggling so much. Glen and I jumped at the opportunity to prove our usefulness and be of assistance to her.

I was quickly given the task of sweeping the floors in the cottage, whilst Glen was sent off to wash various oddly shaped bowls and plates.

Once I had completed my work I was rewarded with a smile. The most beautiful smile I had ever seen. Her smile made me feel like my chest would burst from all the love I felt.

She hasn't smiled at Glen like that, I thought to myself smugly.

Time passed as Glen and I continued to help our breath-taking saviour. She often referred to us as her humans and so I concluded that she must be a fairy, which made sense considering we were in the fairy kingdoms. Not that it mattered.

She could turn into a fish at this very moment and I would still care for her until the day that I died. Thinking about my death sparked a flicker of anger in the back of my mind, yet I had no idea why I would be so angry at the thought of dying. I supposed that before the fairy came into my life, things like that must have been important to me.

Thankfully, I was now free from that burden.

Although Glen and I often worked together to complete chores and spent almost all our time with each other, there was a growing tension between us which was becoming impossible to ignore.

He seemed to follow me everywhere I went and his desperate attempts to gain the fairy's affection sickened me. It was clear that I was her favourite.

I could barely think of any reasons why he needed to be here, other than to reach the high shelves and lift heavy things.

As the days passed by the animosity between us built and soon we were pushing and shoving each other. Doing our best to make things difficult for our rival. The fairy, bless her, didn't seem to notice any problems and so we were free to let our hatred grow.

Soon I had lost track of the time and days. Not that it mattered, not whilst I was here with the fairy.

My fairy.

One morning, or afternoon, Glen and I had been tasked with cutting up a strange leafy vegetable which grew in the garden. It was a deep purple colour, like a new bruise, and seemed to fight against us as we tried to cut it.

My eyes burned with tears and my head began to pound as we chopped. I hoped I wouldn't have to eat it, something told me that I wouldn't survive the meal. The tension between the two of us was now at its worst and, with the addition of this ridiculous vegetable, we both snapped.

I snorted with malicious laughter as Glen hacked at the vegetable, cutting all kinds of mismatched shapes from it. The fairy wouldn't be pleased with his work, maybe now she would finally realise how useless he was and send him away.

I couldn't recall where he had come from, but I hoped to see him out of the door and on his way back there very soon. Angered by my laughter, and talent, Glen slammed the knife down on the table, narrowly missing my fingers.

"Get away from me," I hissed, wanting nothing more than for him to disappear.

"Feel free to leave," he replied.

"I can't," I said smugly, "the fairy loves me."

Glen let out a bark of laughter so loud it hurt my ears.

"She loves me the most and I can prove it," he stepped close enough that I could feel his breath on my face.

"Fight me for her then." I shouted, pushing him hard enough to make him step away.

"If you want a fight, I'll give you a fight."

"Good." I screeched.

I knew the fairy wouldn't be angry if I hurt or even killed him. She would understand that he deserved it. That he didn't love her. Not like me.

I stormed away from him and threw open the kitchen door. We wouldn't disrespect her by fighting and breaking anything in her cottage. Not after everything she had done for us.

I didn't bother to look back and see if Glen was following me because I could hear his loud angry footsteps behind me.

He was going to be so sorry he ever made me angry. I would show him and then she would love me the most. I doubted she would even notice that he was gone.

We exited the garden and stormed out into the moors, where our fight wouldn't risk breaking anything my fairy owned.

My anger began to dwindle as we walked and I struggled to get it back. I had to fight Glen. I had to, but... but why?

I wasn't sure I could remember why we were fighting anymore. I knew it was important. That's right, I had to fight for her.

The little voice in my mind telling me that I shouldn't fight grew louder and louder as we walked. When it became impossible to ignore I stopped suddenly to turn and look at Glen. His expression of confusion showed that he felt the exact same way as me.

Standing there in amongst the long grass, I felt as if I was looking at him for the first time in weeks. I noticed just how dirty and unkempt he looked and assumed I was the same. I couldn't remember feeling anything but adoration for the fairy.

When was the last time either of us had slept, or ate properly? My mouth was dry and my lips were cut and chapped, as if I hadn't had a drop to drink in years.

"What happened to us?" I whispered, almost scared to speak up and ruin our moment of clarity.

"Enchanted." Glen whispered back, looking pale.

"What do we do?" my heart was racing with panic in case the enchantment suddenly came back.

"We have to get away from her," Glen said. "Hit me."

I flinched, thinking the enchantment had returned but he shook his head.

"We'll pretend to fight and then go back. One day we can sneak away when we are ready, she won't be watching if she thinks we are still unaware. You can't enchant someone who knows about it," he explained, and I was glad that he had spent so much time learning all he could about fairies and the north.

I noticed the fairy's auburn hair in the distance. She was returning from a walk in the forest and would soon be close enough to see us.

Before she could notice us chatting, I let out a shriek of anger and charged at Glen. Who in turn wrestled me to the ground, growling and snarling as if he was some sort of wild animal. I would have laughed, had I not been so terrified that she would notice the broken enchantment and simply chain us up.

I punched Glen as hard as I could in the mouth, giving him a bloody lip. Having never punched someone in my life, I felt as if I had broken every bone in my hand on his hard face.

Before I could think of what to do next, he backhanded me, knocking me sideways onto the grass. Just as I was scrambling to my feet I felt it. It was akin to being submerged back into the loch.

Rather than being freezing, the enchantment was like a numb tingling all over my body. My eyes struggled to focus on anything but my fairy and the urge to give in, sink into the blissful feelings of adoration for her, was almost overpowering.

It's an enchantment. I reminded myself over and over as I rushed towards her when she beckoned us both. She looked amused at our fight but tried to hide it behind a mask of sympathy.

"Oh, my poor humans," she cried, cupping both of our faces.

I pushed my face into her hand as if I was her pet, desperate for affection. This must be what she wanted. Two human pets to do her chores after she'd enchanted them into loving her.

The thought made me feel sick.

"Come, let's get you both back inside." she said in a voice that sounded much less musical than I remembered.

I nodded eagerly and hurried after her, making a point of not even glancing in Glen's direction. I worried that he may have fallen back under her spell, but I could only hope that we were both still free

.

CHAPTER

18

Freya

Although Mae tried to tell me I was wrong, I could tell from the expressions on the servants' faces that they blamed me for what happened that day in the courtyard. I still could not understand why my father had named me responsible me for his death.

My theory was that he had finally grown tired of me being friendly towards the humans, even after Nieve was stolen away, and so decided to make them hate me instead.

If only I had followed his wishes. That poor man Alasdair, whose beheading haunted my dreams, would still be alive today.

I could never have imagined how difficult it was to live with the guilt of killing a man. I could hardly sleep and when I did, I was plagued with nightmares. Thankfully, my appetite wasn't affected, although the sight of blood in undercooked meat was enough to make me want to vomit.

Father didn't seem to notice the troubles I was having, but I often noticed mother giving me sympathetic glances. I no longer wondered why she didn't intervene with father's plans. Now I understood how dangerous he really was. I wondered how many people died before he had managed to scare my mother into submission.

Life without Nieve had been lonely and empty, but that was nothing compared to how I now felt. The servants didn't speak to me and so my only interaction was with Mae or my teacher, even then I found it difficult to concentrate long enough to learn much from him.

My shadow was always present but, now more than ever, I was wary of him. I still didn't know when he reported back to father about my activities, but I confidently assumed that he must.

Spending time rushing around the castle in the hopes of losing him, or at least annoying him, no longer held any appeal. Everywhere I went in the castle, I met humans who now despised me. Instead I began spending most of my time outside.

Today's location for avoiding everyone was the large open meadow which lay a short ride away from the castle, and the town, to the east. It felt wrong to be there without Nieve the first few times I'd visited, but now it was the only place I felt close to her, or rather my memories of her. There were farming villages nearby, but luckily this land was always left to the animals and wild flowers, so I was never disturbed.

I dismounted and allowed my horse to wander freely, knowing that she wouldn't leave and honestly not caring much if she did. I heard my shadow dismount behind me as I made my way to the middle of the field.

It was peaceful here, away from the servants and their accusing stares. The breeze in my hair was pleasant and comforting, compared to the stifling air inside the castle, which choked me from the moment I woke up to the moment I fell into a fitful sleep.

With a sigh, I sank down onto my knees, rolling onto my back and simply lying there. The warm sun on my face, and the soft grass beneath my body, was more comforting than my bed had been in weeks. I closed my eyes and let my mind drift off, feeling like nothing could trouble me here in this meadow.

Unfortunately, it was not to last. The sound of someone running through the grass towards me ended my moment of peace.

Frantic hands grabbed me by my upper arms and pulled me upright. I panicked, opening my eyes and coming face to face with my shadow.

"Are you alright Princess?" he asked, his eyes sweeping over me as if looking for an injury.

"What are you doing?" I was both bemused and irritated at the disturbance.

"I was tending to the horses when I saw you go down, I thought something had happened to you," he explained, looking calmer now that he knew I was not in mortal danger.

"I just wanted to lie down," I said, realising that sounded ridiculous.

He let me go and I sank back down onto the cool, comforting grass. My shadow stayed on his knees beside me and made no move to leave which made me glare at him.

"You don't have to stare at me. I'm not going to do anything you can report back to the King," I added bitterly.

"I don't report to the King. My job is to keep you safe and protected," he said with a sigh, sitting down on the grass beside me.

"I don't believe you."

"You may complain and have me fired if you want. He would find you a new guard straight away."

I noticed that he sounded somewhat unhappy at the thought.

"No." I hurried to assure him, the idea of a stranger following me around, and my ever-present shadow leaving, made my stomach churn. I was tired of people leaving me. "I'm sorry, you can stay."

"You don't have to apologise to me Princess."

"I doubt it is fun for you, having to follow me around. Even I wish I could get away from myself," I explained, closing my eyes.

"I understand, these past few weeks have not been kind to you, but it'll get better. You'll see."

He sounded so confident and determined that I felt the tightness in my chest loosen a little. Maybe he was right.

His determination reminded me of Nieve and as I closed my eyes once more, I let my mind wander back to happier times spent here amongst the flowers. Away from the watchful eyes in the castle. Free to be whoever we wanted to be.

We stayed there enjoying the peace for the remainder of the afternoon. The warm breeze blew strands of my hair gently, making them dance and tickle my face. The sun was warm, despite the breeze, like it was trying to burn away the darkness inside of me.

I was sure I heard the small feet of the wee folk in the grass, but they never came out. Probably because of the stranger beside me. I hoped that if we kept coming back, my little friend would feel brave enough to approach once more.

The sun moved across the sky as I lay there, and I felt my shadow beside me shiver a few times. It was starting to get chilly as it was only spring, not the middle of summer. I didn't want to be selfish, especially after his attempts to comfort me earlier, so I suggested that we go back to the castle we both unfortunately called home.

As we arrived back at the stables, I spotted Nieve talking to Berwin. Making a split decision, I jumped from my horse before they could see me. Silently gesturing for my shadow to take the horses into the stables himself.

Thankfully he understood my wild hand movements and I managed to sneak behind the stables. I crept as close as I could to the doorway where they were standing to listen. Realising that, had either of them noticed me, it would have been proof that I couldn't be trusted and was spying on humans for the King. I had to take the chance to see Nieve again.

A wave of relief washed through me when I noticed that she didn't look injured. She had no new visible bruises or cuts, and didn't stand as if she was in pain. I allowed myself to hope for the best. She hadn't lost a considerable amount of weight in our time apart, so I felt it was safe to assume that she was being fed well down in the kitchens.

I felt another wave of emotion, this time embarrassment, as I caught my eyes drifting over her figure appreciatively.

"Have you seen much of her? Does she look okay?" Nieve was asking, sounding concerned and I hoped desperately that she was asking about me.

"Almost every day, she is always out riding. You can probably see for yourself that she looks exhausted. It doesn't look like she is coping very well," Berwin answered with a sigh.

"Things will only get worse." Nieve replied which made me worry.

What would get worse? Was it really me she was asking about?

"She asked about you, not long after King Ferchar separated you," Berwin admitted hesitantly, and I wanted to cry with relief. My risk was paying off.

"Tell her nothing," Nieve ordered in a tone so harsh it made me wince.

Never had I heard her speak like that to anyone. I blinked furiously and tried not to think about what she said. I could cry over it later, for now I needed to listen.

"I haven't," Berwin continued unfazed by her tone, "I think you should consider it though, consider speaking to her."

"You know I can't. Contact would put everything at risk. We need to wait, to plan and then I will consider the Princess."

I flinched at being mentioned so directly. They were talking about me. I was helpless to stop my eyes from burning with tears as I realised that Nieve truly didn't want to speak to me.

Her talk of plans confused me, unsure what the humans could be planning in the kitchens, but I didn't dwell on it.

I had cried more times that I could count over her, and here she was refusing to even consider speaking to me. What had I done?

Of all the humans, I had expected that Nieve would hate me least for the execution. That she would be the most likely to believe that I had nothing to do with it. I was wrong.

"Is there anything I can do? I can't stand all this waiting, tending these horses and watching as the Princess looks worse and worse each day. I want to help."

Nieve shook her head looking somewhat pained at the thought. "We have to wait."

At that moment, my shadow appeared with our two horses, he gave a nod of greeting to Berwin before directing them into the stables, without so much as a glance at Nieve.

The walk to the stable entrance should have taken mere moments and I realised, gratefully, that my shadow must have walked as slowly as possible to allow me time to listen.

"It's the Princess's new guard, you better leave," Berwin whispered once my shadow was inside.

Nieve turned on her heel and hurried off without so much as a goodbye.

It took all the strength I had not to chase after her and beg for her forgiveness. Beg her to speak to me. Even if she simply wanted to tell me how much she hated me, if she wanted to shout at me, hit me. It would be less painful than this.

I rushed back around to meet my guard. Hoping it simply looked as if I was too lazy to return my own horse to the stable, not like I had been eavesdropping. I had been avoiding eye contact with the humans around the castle since the execution so it wasn't unusual behaviour for me to avoid Berwin, not wanting him to see my red eyes.

Luckily, he also seemed to be lost in thought about his conversation with Nieve, so my shadow and I slipped out without needing to make conversation.

I tried not to worry myself with trying to understand their conversation. Instead I focused on being content in the knowledge that Nieve was unharmed and eating well. That was the least I could wish for until I found a way to get her to communicate with me, or my father to let her come back.

Both of which now seemed unlikely.

I found myself growing to like my shadow. I finally learned that his name was William and that his father was a Laird living between the rivers in the east.

I trusted him, now that he had sworn he wasn't simply here to spy on me and report back to the King. He could have lied about that, but I decided to trust him anyway. I had so little company these days. I couldn't afford to be picky.

Father demanded that I attend another meal with him. This one, thankfully, passed without disaster. I was seated beside Laird Brochan who spent the duration of the meal telling me about his son Tomas.

Like almost every Laird I had the misfortune of being forced into conversation with, he wanted me to visit his son, probably hoping he could marry his way into the royal family.

I wanted to laugh, for the first time in weeks, at the thought of marrying. The woman I loved refused to even speak with me. I had no room left in my heart to care about anyone else.

There was an undeniable tension growing amongst the humans in the castle. I thought that perhaps I was imagining it, but it continued to grow. I just hoped it had nothing to do with me.

I admitted to my shadow that I was worried they would target me for revenge, but he dismissed the idea and promised to protect me. Father could fight his own battles with his people. I just wanted to be left alone.

The beheading continued to haunt my dreams. Sometimes the grieving crowd ripped me to pieces and sometimes, Alasdair's bloody head simply rolled after me wherever I ran.

As the weeks passed, my shadow and I rode out to the meadow as often as possible as I was able to peacefully sleep there. My shadow never complained about it. He simply sat by my side, watching out for danger whilst I slept amongst the flowers.

CHAPTER

19

Morven

After our fight, the fairy seemed to be watching us more intently. I was sure that before we had been left to our work without the fairy lingering, but it was difficult to remember what had happened during our time in her cottage.

Trying to think about our time under the enchantment was like trying to see the bottom of a muddy puddle. We continued to work as hard as we could, although now that the enchantment was broken the work was difficult.

Without a haze of love and devotion clouding my mind, I was all too aware of the burning thirst I hardly ever had a chance to quench and the ache in my empty stomach from the irregular meals.

I felt dizzy the whole time we worked and Glen's pale face and shaking hands told me he was the same. We couldn't break our routine and eat whilst we pretended to be under her enchantment. Soon we were stumbling around as if drunk from lack of food, drink and sleep.

The urge to throw the broom I was using away, curl up in a ball and accept my fate was growing stronger with every floor I swept. As we worked throughout the night I got closer and closer to giving up.

Thankfully, the fairy finally acknowledged our loudly growling stomachs and we were given porridge the next morning. We made sure to thank her profusely before shovelling the food into our mouths as fast as humanly possible.

Almost straight away, I felt the fog of dizziness leave me and I was faced with the new problem of trying not to vomit. It's never a clever idea to stuff yourself full of food after days without any.

I doubted the fairy would believe that I was still under her enchantment if I threw up all over her kitchen. The porridge never did make a reappearance, and we were able to garden and whisper our plans that afternoon.

"We can leave when she goes into the forest," Glen whispered as we worked. Pulling nettles from in amongst the fairy's strange herbs.

I'd never seen herbs and plants like the ones that grew here, not even whilst in the middle of the Fairy Forest. Many of them produced the bright purple vegetables that Glen and I fought over. However, most unnerving of all were the flowers, with drooping purple petals, which turned to follow whoever was closest to them.

Soon our hands were lumpy, red and stinging furiously with a rash from the nettles, but there were no dock leaves in sight. Which was strange. Whenever I had encountered nettles in the past dock had always been growing somewhere nearby. A part of me wondered if this was a test and so I made sure not to complain.

"We just take our bags and go?" I mumbled quietly, ripping up handfuls of nettles and pretending they weren't making me want to chop off my own hands.

"They are untouched, still sitting beside the door where we left them the day we arrived," Glen said with a nod, discretely looking around and planning our escape route.

Realising Glen needed a distraction so that he could get a better look, I took my basket, full of the strange and frankly disgusting looking plants I had picked, and wandered around the garden to a new area. The purple flower heads watching me as I went.

I swung my basket merrily and hoped that, if the fairy was watching us, her attention would be on me.

"The river bank," Glen whispered, before he hurried back to the cottage to continue his work.

Half a basket full of weeds, and several new nettle stings later, I positioned myself so that I was facing away from the cottage and could look out across the land we would have to cross.

If the fairy went into the forest behind the cottage then we could hurry out across the moor, hidden by the cottage if we walked in a straight line. From there, we could jump down onto the riverbank. The river was in a very shallow valley, and so you would not see someone crawling along the banks if you were standing watching from the cottage.

I thanked the Others that Glen was with me. Had I been alone, I would have just started running through the grass in hopes of escape. I would never have thought of hiding so close to the cottage.

The next morning the fairy provided us with another meal, which was lucky as today we planned to leave for the river bank. Our work for the day included more weeding in the garden, as well as washing and mending in the house. This would mean that the fairy wouldn't get suspicious when I was inside, checking on our supplies.

We worked anxiously all morning, Glen weeding and surveying our escape route, whilst I chopped up more of the purple vegetable.

Just as it was reaching midday, the fairy called us inside. I had to remind myself to fight her enchantment whilst making sure to stare at her in adoration. The enchantment was always strongest when we had her full attention.

"I must go into the forest today my humans," she said, and I gave a small whine of complaint, as if I was upset about being left behind.

"I must," she repeated, patting me on the head. "It's dangerous in there, far too dangerous for you two."

I wondered if she really didn't want us hurt, or if the enchantment was simply messing with my mind. We followed as she headed for the door until she stopped us with a firm no.

"You two stay here and do your work for me. I promise to return before darkness falls."

With a parting kiss on each of our foreheads, she was gone.

We watched from the doorway until she was a tiny dot of white in the distance, and then we watched until we were sure she wasn't about to change her mind and come running back to the cottage. When Glen sighed in relief sometime later, I finally let myself look away. She was gone, and it would be hours before it got dark.

"Now?" I asked Glen hesitantly, almost too anxious to break the silence in case it brought her back.

Glen jumped when I spoke and then nodded, looking resolved. He pulled me close and, for the first time in what was probably weeks, possibly even months, we hugged.

Glen and I have always been close, and we had grown even closer whilst we travelled. For weeks, we had cuddled together at night for warmth and safety, and it was as if my very bones had missed this human contact.

Soon I was clutching him so tight my fingers hurt and sniffling pathetically into his shirt. It felt so good to hold him in my arms and have him hold me back. Clinging to each other felt like holding on to home, and family. His warmth thawed a part of me that I hadn't even realised had frozen, whilst we worked away under the fairy's enchantment.

"We can do this," he promised, gathering our bags whilst I watched the tree line for any sign of our captor. Taking a moment to wipe away my tears.

The fairy did not return, and soon Glen and I were closing the cottage door and heading off through the long grass towards the river.

The purple flower heads turned to watch us go and I wondered if they could somehow tell her that we were leaving. They remained silent as they watched Glen and I hurry away as fast as we could.

If the fairy was to exit the forest right now, she would have a view of the cottage but not us walking away behind it. We hadn't stolen anything from her, though our bread and cheese supplies were now hard and almost inedible we decided to simply make do with it.

Perhaps it was the lingering effects of the enchantment, but the thought of stealing from her when she hadn't lifted a hand to hurt us made me uncomfortable. It also terrified me that perhaps she would hunt us down if we took something, rather than simply letting us go.

We kept up a quick pace as we made our way through the grass. I kept looking behind us at the trees, which grew smaller and smaller as we went. I expected to see a furious fairy chasing after us, and felt sick to my stomach with nerves which refused to be calmed even as the distance between us grew.

There was never any sign of her. She was probably deep in the trees, completely unaware that her humans were escaping. After, what was perhaps the hundredth-time, Glen grabbed my hand and stopped me from looking back.

"We can do this," he repeated, squeezing my hand. "Just a wee while longer and we'll be down on the riverbank where she can't see us. We are leaving her behind, for good."

Glen was right. Soon he was grasping my arms and helping me jump down onto the sandy bank of the river.

It was steeper than we had expected and, if Glen hunched over slightly, we could walk along the river without our heads being visible over the top. This made it easy to peer over the edge at the grassy moor behind us and the tiny cottage in the distance.

Not wanting to risk being caught so close to freedom, we walked until the sky was darkening and we were beginning to stumble and trip due to exhaustion.

When we did finally stop and peek over the top, the forest was now far away in the distance behind us and instead, we were facing the mountains of some fairy kingdom we did not know.

The map showed us that we should now be south of the town where we would find our first castle. The royal family lived there, and we hoped that we would finally find the answers we were looking for.

"Can we stop?" I begged Glen, who nodded eagerly and collapsed down onto the river bank with a sigh.

"She won't find us now. She has no way of knowing where we went and she might not be back from her day in the forest yet."

"She doesn't seem to like leaving her cottage anyway. I doubt she would chase us this far," I said and for some reason, I was sure I was right.

My worries had faded as we put distance between us and, unless I thought about it, I was finally free of the sick churning nerves I had battled all afternoon.

We had managed to escape. We were free.

CHAPTER

20

Euna

10 YEARS AGO

I always thought that, if I ever did fall in love, it would be romantic and perfect. That the people would tell tales and sing songs about forever.

I never imagined that it would happen whilst I spoke to the repulsive King of Culhuinn, watching out of the corner of my eye as Lachlann and Alasdair played with a few children. I had to fight down a smile as they laughed and enjoyed themselves, glad to see them all happy for once.

The sight made me wonder if Lachlann and I would ever have a child, something I had never longed for before. I hoped that they would have his freckles if we did. I blinked the thought away. Wasting my days daydreaming about babies was pointless.

I forced my attention back to the King. The last thing I wanted was for him to become aware of my affections for one of his human servants. If only Aelwen knew what I was thinking, she would be so proud. Daydreaming about romance had been her favourite pastime as a young fairy.

"I wish I could stay with you," Lachlann had said from where he lay beside me, earlier that morning.

"You can," I insisted, rolling over to face him with a smile. "You could stay here safe in my castle forever and never go back to Culhuinn."

He smiled and gently pulled me to rest against his chest, running a soothing hand through my hair.

We were silent for a while, content to listen to the early morning birds singing outside and the servants getting the castle ready for the day. I knew he was thinking over our problem and so I waited for him to speak.

After a while he sighed, "The King would never let me stay."

"You would not be asking him. You do not need his permission," I replied stubbornly.

"He would notice if one of his servants suddenly went missing. He may not like us, or care about us, but he does watch us."

"He knows nothing about our relationship, we could hide you here in Norbroch and deny even knowing that you existed. Aelwen would agree and the King could not risk accusing us of lying."

"I think he could and would accuse you," Lachlann sounded increasingly unhappy as the conversation progressed.

"He could not," I insisted, "Not if you left with them then found a way to return north whilst the other humans continued south."

A plan was beginning to form in my mind as we spoke. Lachlann was silent again, he too thinking over this new possibility. I trailed my hand in leisurely circles over his torso, which was freckled and muscular from a life of challenging work outside, much like the rest of his body.

Cosy in bed together was not a bad place to plan to deceive a king. I did not feel any guilt about it. King Ferchar had proven himself to be rude, arrogant and uncaring for those he ruled. I would not feel guilty about saving someone from him. Even the Others could not blame me for that.

"Perhaps that could work. I would need to explain it to Alasdair though. He knows of my affection for you, but I don't know what he would think about me deserting the kingdom."

"I think he would encourage you. I have seen him watching us," I said, and laughed when Lachlann attempted to jolt upright suddenly.

"He what?!" He demanded, sounding horrified.

"I simply mean that he has spotted us around the castle and the grounds. He seems like a clever man so I have no doubt that he will have realised the true nature of our relationship by now," I explained, patting his chest to make him relax back down onto the bed.

"He has never mentioned it to me." Lachlann still looked troubled.

"Just like you failed to mention it to him. He never looks angry or disgusted when he notices us. Just smiles in my direction and carries on with his work. He probably failed to speak up about it because he thinks you do not want him to know," I explained, amused.

"I will mention it today then. See what he thinks about it."

"Good idea, just not quite yet. I have no desire to move anytime soon."

And with that, I wrapped my arms around him and held him tight. It would take a great deal of effort for him to move me. A fairy's strength was much superior to that of a human, even one as muscled as Lachlann, so we lay together, content, until we could ignore our responsibilities no longer.

"So," Aelwen said, I could practically hear her smirking so I did not bother to look up from my lunch, "How is life treating you?"

"Life is treating me well," I said with a smile, which blossomed and grew on my face until I was grinning like a fool.

"I am so happy for you," Aelwen exclaimed clapping her hands. "I just knew this would work out well."

"Oh? I did not realise you were able to see into the future," I teased gently.

"Well it seems I can," she laughed, shuffling her seat closer to mine and lowering her voice seriously. "Have you any plans to get Lachlann to stay?"

"I have had some ideas."

"Tell me!" She cried, forgetting her momentary seriousness as her excitement got the better of her again.

Aelwen was in love with the idea of love. She always had been and always would be. She loves freely with all her heart, which is magical. A wonderful thing to experience when you are her family, but it was like a self-imposed curse when she was younger. Falling in love with every fairy that showed her a moment of kindness.

I explained what little plans I had managed to come up with on my own. Lachlann would leave with the royals, and the other servants, when they began their journey south to Culhuinn. Then, at a currently undecided point in the journey, he would sneak away from them, perhaps in the dead of night. From there he would return to Norbroch and back into my arms. There were still many aspects of the plan which we had not yet resolved, so I let my explanation trail off.

"This is wonderful," Aelwen said as she busied herself with pouring us each a small nettle tea to end our meal. "Clearly you need my assistance, so I will think about it today and let you know a finalised plan later."

"I do not need your help," I replied stubbornly before smiling, "but if you insist then I am sure I could make time to speak with you tonight."

"Oh, thank you Queen Euna," Aelwen cried sarcastically and with that, she downed the rest of her tea and was gone, probably away to feed our family's newest addition, Prince Elath.

"I like your dress," I heard the Princess Freya say from across the table.

Embarrassingly, it was not until a nudge from Aelwen roused me from my thoughts that I realised the complement was directed at me.

"Why thank you Princess, you look beautiful this evening," I answered with a smile.

Why she was even bothering to complement me I had no idea. Perhaps her mother had insisted that she attempt to befriend us as one day she would be the ruler of Culhuinn.

"Of course she does," interrupted the King with a barking laugh. "Just look at her father."

His deliberate exclusion of his wife from his statement created an uncomfortable silence, which thankfully the Princess did not notice. I had to fight, with every ounce of strength I possessed, not to roll my eyes at him. Beautiful is not a word that springs to mind when thinking about King Ferchar.

I did not trust myself to do more than give a smile, which I hoped looked more genuine than it felt.

It was easier to listen to the King's pretentious drivel, and the Queen's empty complements and praises, now that they were starting to discuss their journey home. Negotiations regarding trade between our two kingdoms were finally nearing an end.

The previous night, Aelwen had come to me with a plan so brilliant I could not banish it from my mind. She had allowed for multiple escape attempts for Lachlann and had even managed to rope Tormod into helping us.

Aelwen struck up a conversation regarding our wulver neighbours in the west, so I allowed my mind to drift back to the plan. Already planning everything that Lachlann and I would do, once he was safely back in the castle.

PRESENT DAY

Tormod and I stood at the main doors of the castle and watched as the ambassadors from Eilean Sel, which lay across the sea to the west, rode up. A messenger had arrived the previous night and alerted us that selkies had been spotted on the western coast of Norbroch a few days prior, and were travelling towards the castle.

The selkies never sent their own messengers. They would simply arrive unannounced, if not for the messengers in the coastal town of Selport who watched out for them.

"The Others must be angry with me, why else would the selkies arrive whilst Aelwen is still down south with the wulver?" I complained as we stood there.

Tormod did not seem pleased by their arrival either, but he ignored my complaint. Whilst I had never seen him be cruel to another before, I knew that he distrusted the selkies.

Perhaps it was due to their strange accents, or more likely, it was because of their ability to transform their lower bodies whenever they wished. When they tired of walking on two legs they formed a tail, which allowed them to swim like a seal in the sea, or even lochs and deep rivers.

I had no problem with them. Though their visits were infrequent and unannounced, they were surprisingly easy guests to please.

"Queen Euna," The female ambassador called happily, dismounting from the horse she had purchased with surprising grace for someone who spent much of their time with a tail.

The small village of Selport thrived during visits from the selkies. They swam across the sea to reach Norbroch and so never carried many belongings. This meant that once they reached land they had to pay coin for clothes, food and horses. This created a small amount of trade between our kingdoms and over the years many children with striking black eyes had been born in Selport.

It originally caused panic and fear. Villagers fearing the babies were born cursed because of their unusual grey seal-like skin. Soon, they realised who the fathers of such children were and the new skin tones and black eyes were explained.

That had been during my Grandmother, Queen Kathlina's, reign. Now there is a high population of half selkie-half fairy folk living in the north, which I will admit has been wonderful in helping our two kingdoms bond.

"We were not expecting you," I scolded lightly, as the two ambassadors climbed the few steps to where we were standing.

They seemed to be moving as slowly as possible, just to ensure that Tormod and I were thoroughly soaked through by the rain.

"Our King and Queen wished to send news regarding the events occurring in the southern human islands," the male selkie explained.

"Yes. Our King and Queen also wished to send gifts for the royal family of Norbroch," the female selkie added, nodding enthusiastically.

"Let us move this discussion somewhere more comfortable," I said, eager to get out of the rain.

My dress was now clinging, heavy and uncomfortable, to my body and chilling me to the bone as the rain pelting down outside was freezing.

Before discussions began I insisted on a small feast, the selkies never asked for much whilst they stayed here in Norbroch, but over the years I had found that food always helped.

One of the most frustrating things about selkies, was their distrust of warm cooked food. They would much rather eat a fish raw than have it cooked and served with vegetables and buttery potatoes. My appetite was fragile enough without the addition of two selkies, devouring raw fish directly across the table. From the looks they gave my soup and warm bread, I could tell they found my choices just as odd.

As Aelwen was still down south conversing with the wulver, eating cooked food and not wearing a soaking wet dress, I had to endure it in silence.

After the two of them finished I politely waited, feeling faintly nauseated, until they had picked the fish bones from between their teeth before beginning the conversation.

As polite as I tried to be, whilst the two ambassadors filled me in on the situation down south, it was hard not to stare. I was so used to seeing fairies in Norbroch, not selkies.

Rather than possessing two rows of similarly shaped teeth, like humans and fairies, the selkies had teeth which were sharpened points. Their front teeth were longer than those at the back and I was sure that, should they wish to do so, they could bite through my arm with no trouble at all.

Where a fairy or human eye contained a black circle, ringed with colour, a selkies eyes were completely black, like the glossy eyes of the seal, with which they had much in common. The reflection of the candles burning throughout the room flickered and danced in their eyes.

As I watched, I realised just how much freer they were than us fairies, with their ability to travel both land and sea without a problem. I wondered why the Others had saw fit to confine the rest of us to the land.

"Our source doubts that the conflict in Eilean Trì will be settled without much human blood being shed," the female said, concluding their tales of the human islands in the south.

"They very rarely are," I sighed, the loss of human life was not a route I wanted this conversation to go down.

I found it difficult to guess what the selkies thought of the situation unfolding. The fight for a human throne had no impact on us here in Norbroch, but Eilean Sel traded with the human isles and so the situation was of interest to them.

Why they sent two ambassadors across the sea to tell me I did not know, but I assumed it was simply an excuse to spy on us, on me.

The last selkie visit had occurred whilst I was still caught up in my storm of grief. Trade with a kingdom, ruled in part by a Queen who can barely muster the will to hold a conversation, is not ideal.

I did my best to appear alert and competent. I had had years of practice hiding how I felt. The selkies would see me as a calm and capable Queen, someone they could trust enough to continue trading with.

Not the person I was on the inside.

CHAPTER

21

Morven

Throughout the night we took turns sleeping on the cold, uncomfortable river bank. We were both exhausted after our day's work, and the constant fear that we would be caught. The stress we'd felt as we hurried away from the cottage, in which we had been held captive, lingered.

Nothing out there suggested that the fairy was chasing after us, but we took turns keeping watch anyway. She didn't seem to like travelling much further than her cottage and the forest, so I hoped that she wouldn't leave them behind to search for two runaway humans.

Still, it would have been awful for us both to fall sleep and wake to find ourselves recaptured. I was tense as I sat up on the riverbank, listening to the occasional screech of foxes and the water rushing past below me.

The night passed, turning the sky a startling mix of orange and blue as the moon disappeared and the sun rose. Although it was sometime between spring and summer now, the nights were still harsh and cold this far north. I couldn't wait to get moving and soak up what little warmth the sun had to offer us.

Before we left, we choked down some of our bread, which was now so dry and old that it scratched my throat as it went down. Luckily the river looked clean and clear, so we had an abundance of cool water to wash it away.

"I hope we find a market up near the castle," Glen complained as we walked. "Can't remember the last time we had a hot meal."

"Me neither," I agreed, "I'd kill for some of ma's stew right now." My mouth watered at the thought of warm gravy with vegetables, potatoes and soft tender meat.

I shook my head furiously to get rid of the thought, now wasn't the time to be thinking about stew.

"Don't talk about it," Glen gave a pained groan.

Neither Glen nor I could remember exactly how long we had been enchanted. Travelling made it difficult to keep track of the days, especially whilst in a mountain valley, or lost in a confusing magical forest. Despite that, it felt good to be on our way again.

We left the river, and its banks behind, and started to walk north. Behind us we could see the forest to the east and the river leading towards distant mountains in the west. Our map showed that if we continued heading north we would reach the castle eventually.

The journey didn't take as long as I expected and by around mid-afternoon, we were following a road into the town. The castle was built in front of huge mountains, which made the Fairy Hills look miniscule. Their peaks were snow-capped, and the contrast between the harsh black rock and bright green grass was striking.

Somehow it made sense that even the mountains in the fairy kingdoms would look more menacing.

Spread out on either side of the castle was the town. The town was comprised of stone cottages, not dissimilar to the one we had just escaped, and had a market near its centre. We watched fairies going about their daily lives, working in the market, riding in and out of the town on horses and most importantly, heading into the castle.

At the entrance of the castle there was an arched doorway, through which people could wander freely as the large wooden doors were throw open. Glen and I decided that the best place for us to try and find answers would be in the castle.

Even if we didn't get a chance to speak to anyone, we could hopefully observe them and try to learn about what they did with the babies they stole.

Too nervous to waste any time, we passed through the markets without so much as a glance at the goods and headed for entrance.

No one gave us any strange looks as we headed in, which meant that seeing humans must not have been unusual. It made me wonder if they all had humans enchanted in their homes.

The courtyard we ended up in was magnificent. It was larger than my cottage back home and, although it was simply paved with stones, it was grander than any human built building I had ever seen. The courtyard had many doors, leading off in all directions, which made our plan to charge in and find answers suddenly seem foolish.

We had no idea where to go.

Everyone around us was hurrying off without a moment's hesitation, allowing us no time to stop and think about where we wanted go. Not unless we wanted to attract attention. Glen pointed towards the first door to our left and so we headed through that.

It made sense not to go charging into the centre of the castle, just in case we needed to escape. Although, I highly doubted that two humans could outrun a whole town filled with fairies. We would be found in minutes, especially if the stories about fairies and their magical powers were to be believed.

The door we passed through led us to a set of stone steps. We crept down as quietly as we could, half expecting to hear the footsteps of malicious fairy guards chasing after us at any moment. We made it down the steps without hassle and found ourselves in a large storeroom filled with sacks, which I assumed must have been food stores

"Och, you scared the life out of me!" a girl shrieked behind us, causing us both to jump out of our skins.

We spun round and were faced with a short girl, the generous sprinkling of freckles across her face made her immediately stand out as a human. The girl was dressed in a simple brown woollen dress, unlike the fairies we had seen strolling through the town in patterned dresses of a much higher quality.

"You two here to help me load the carts?" she asked, dragging a sack out a door at the other side of the room which I hadn't noticed.

"No." Glen said simply and grabbed my arm to pull me away.

We hurried out of the room before she could ask why we were there. Back up the stairs we went and out into the courtyard, the sun making my vision blur as the storeroom had been almost pitch black in comparison.

As we headed through a doorway, directly opposite the one we had just left, a hand, which I noted was much colder than someone should be at this time of year, grabbed my upper arm. I turned to see one of the fairy guards we had been hoping to avoid, his companion grabbing hold of Glen. I made a move to try and free my arm but Glen shook his head.

We were led away from the doorway and across the courtyard. No one glanced in our direction. Humans being manhandled by guards must have been a common occurrence here in the castle.

We were taken through another one of the numerous doors, passing many guards, before we were forced into a small room containing nothing more than a wooden table and a chair. The sudden increase in guards suggested that we had been brought to the guard's quarter of the castle, or worse, the prison.

By this point my stomach was churning unpleasantly and, although I could feel myself sweating, I was chilled to the bone.

There was no way Glen or I would be able to leave, unless the guards decided to free us. I wasn't sure I wanted to know what we would have to do to earn that freedom.

The guards who caught us left and a different fairy stepped through the door. He had a presence about him that made me want to confess every little thing I had ever done wrong. Being under his scrutiny was even worse than da at his angriest.

We stood in silence, waiting anxiously until he finally spoke.

"You two are not humans employed by King Ferchar, correct?" his face gave us no indication of what his feelings were about this fact.

"Correct." Glen and I answered simultaneously.

The way he said employed made a weight lift from my shoulders, it had settled there when we saw the human down in the storeroom. Employment indicated that the humans were all here by choice, and being paid coin for their services. Not forced to work as I had feared.

"What exactly are your intentions here in the castle?" he asked.

"We want to meet the King and find out what happens to the babies you fairies steal," I blurted out before I had a chance to think about the possibility of my words offending him.

The guard's emotionless mask slipped for a minute and he raised an eyebrow in surprise. He didn't seem surprised that I had just told him our plans without hesitation, instead that our intentions here weren't what he was expecting.

My sudden willingness to tell all reminded me of the enchantment we had been under and the reason for my loose tongue suddenly became clear.

Magic.

CHAPTER

22

Morven

Instead of being sent down to a dark, disgusting dungeon to face all manner of torture, as I had been expecting, a well-dressed servant entered the room and beckoned for us to follow.

After sharing a glance, we did, although I made sure to hold Glen's hand to make sure he stayed close. Two of the fairy guards followed as we passed through a maze of corridors and rooms.

In each, the decoration grew grander and the furniture fancier. Lit fireplaces became common, as did comfortable looking chairs with tartan throws and servants ready to serve food and drink at any moment. Most impressive though, were the huge floor to roof tapestries depicting battles and landscapes. Clearly the dungeon was the last place Glen and I were going.

I was beginning to enjoy the tour of the castle when the servant stopped in a small room and looked us over, not bothering to hide his disgust. I felt myself blush with embarrassment.

We hadn't had a chance to wash, other than in the river we'd followed, and I could feel that my lips were still horribly dry and chapped.

"King Ferchar has requested your company at dinner. You would do well to remember whom it is you dine with and take care to give his majesty the respect he deserves." the servant advised, striding off the way we'd came.

Our guards motioned for the doors to be opened, and we were hurried into a grand hall before we had a chance to prepare ourselves.

King Ferchar standing, ready to receive us, was what caught my attention first. I had always imagined that the fairy King would look regal, grand and strong. This fairy was all of those things and more. He looked as if he could quite easily snap the both of us like twigs.

"Take a seat." he gestured to the wooden table and I silently cursed, neither of us had thought of something respectful to say.

We were both speechless.

We hurried to take our seats and at once a human servant appeared out of nowhere, pouring us various drinks and herbal teas. Once we were comfortable, and had enough drink for a whole family, they retreated to wherever they had come from and our questioning began.

"What brings two humans to Culhuinn?" the King asked, his expression unreadable.

I couldn't tell if he was angry, or merely curious.

"We travelled here from Tirwood in search of answers. We hoped to learn about why fairies create changelings and to find out what is done with the human children." Glen answered as my stomach churned with nerves.

"Ah, changelings are what you call the babies left behind, yes?"

We nodded, too nervous to say more.

"Well, I'll admit that I know a little about the whole business. The changelings are created by magic and left behind whilst the human baby is taken north to be raised, and then put to work." he answered, sounding almost apologetic.

"Thank you, anything you know is helpful as we know very little. All we know is that we are unable to stop our children being stolen, and our changelings die so young." Glen explained, and for a moment the King looked amused.

"Occasionally fairies are born gifted with magical abilities. Some can encourage crops to grow or affect the weather. Some can influence the minds of others or make themselves appear changed," the King explained, pausing dramatically to ensure we were listening, which of course we were.

"Very rarely, a fairy is born with the ability to create new life from their magic. These magical creations do not live as long as those created by the Others. That is why your changelings die so quickly."

The story was interrupted by the castle's servants hurrying in to fill the table with food. There was so much food that I felt as if I was attending a festival.

It was uncomfortable, having people arrange our food for us, but they did not pause to let us to help.

I noticed a few of the servants paused to stare, or do a double take. They must not have been used to seeing new humans around the castle. Which I supposed was a good sign.

"Do you know who makes the changelings?" I asked once we had started our meal.

"Unfortunately, I do." he replied with a sigh, "Up north in the kingdom of Norbroch they are obsessed with humans. Nothing I do stops them from stealing human babies for their own sick purposes."

Glen and I glanced at each other. If Norbroch was responsible for the creation of changelings, and the deaths of so many humans, then we had to travel even further north.

We couldn't simply end our journey here. Knowledge of how and why our babies were stolen would do nothing to prevent it from happening again.

"I think then, that we should travel north," I said carefully, unsure what the King's reaction would be.

Fortunately, he seemed to agree with our plan and at once looked pleased.

"Yes. I think that would be the best way for you to find the answers you seek and, dare I say it, put a stop to this horror. In the morning, I shall provide you both with food and a guide to help you travel through the mountains."

Glen and I hurried to thank him and assure him that his help would not be forgotten by either of us. How we humans could ever repay him for his help I had no idea. Telling us where we would find those responsible for so much death gave us a chance to save lives.

His help was the greatest gift either of us had ever received.

He raised a hand to silence us. "Tell me more about your journey, what have you encountered thus far."

Glen, the storyteller, was in his element as he retold our journey. The King seemed especially amused by our experiences in the Fairy Forest and intrigued by the enchantment we both fell under.

"Finally, my darling daughter arrives," the King interrupted as the door opened and a fairy stepped through, he hurried to collect her and sit her down across from me.

It made me smile to see that even a fairy king cared about his daughter, like my da cared about me. Our first experience with a fairy had been awful and proved every story about evil fairies right. However here in this castle, the fairies we had met were forgiving and helpful, despite our unannounced arrival.

His daughter was beautiful. She wore a fine dress made of a material I had never seen before. It looked so soft that I had a sudden desire to lunge over the table and touch it. There was no doubt that it was expensive, and I wished that I could bring some home to ma and Bonnie. She wore delicate jewellery around her wrists and neck, which caught the light as she moved.

The addition of polished metals and jewels really set the fairies apart from Glen and I. Made it clear to all that we were from a farming village, not royalty.

The princess had a kind face, but I noticed that she had dark circles under her eyes and looked as if she needed a week of sleep. Life as a princess must be tiring. Her blonde hair was long and loosely curled, making me all too aware of how dirty and tangled my own was.

As I studied her face, I noticed with a start that she was also watching me. My expression must have been one of awe and wonder as I stared. The princess, on the other hand, was looking at me as if I was a ghost. Something from one of her worst nightmares.

I felt my cheeks redden under her scrutiny and quickly diverted my attention back to the meal in front of me.

The King seemed to realise that his daughter wasn't planning on speaking and so resumed the conversation with a smile.

"Enchanted you say?" he looked amused.

Glen nodded. "Aye, we weren't aware of the enchantment until we were half a meadow away from her."

"How strange. I really must send someone to investigate further."

Something about the way the King spoke told me that it was unlikely anyone would ever be looking into it.

We spoke about our journey, and the sights we had seen, as we enjoyed a hearty meal. The two of us still starving after our escape from the enchantment.

There was a thick vegetable soup, warm bread and roast meat. Then we were served a pie filled with spring berries. I was nearly finished before I realised that I had forgotten all about making a good impression. I must have been eating like some sort of beast. Good thing ma wasn't here, she'd have had some stern words for me about that.

The Princess didn't touch the food in front of her. Simply continued to stare off into the distance, lost in her thoughts. The King didn't acknowledge it, and I wondered if perhaps this was simply her normal behaviour. I had met people before who's minds didn't work quite like mine.

"I am sure the both of you would benefit from a good night's sleep before beginning your journey north in the morning." the King said once the food was finished, dismissing us from his presence.

"Thank you," Glen said, as we left the table and were directed towards a newly opened door that I hadn't even noticed previously.

"Thank you." I mumbled awkwardly.

Glen and I were likely the first people from our village to ever meet royalty, definitely the first to meet fairy royalty.

I hoped we weren't being rude in our ignorance on the proper ways to communicate with kings. To my relief the King never seem offended by us, simply amused.

"I will not see you again before you leave Culhuinn so I wish you a safe journey. Do remember to inform the Queens that it was King Ferchar who sent you to their door."

CHAPTER

23

Freya

After the day's lessons I had hoped to hurry up to my chambers, where I could curl up with Nieve and I's patchwork blanket and pretend that nothing existed.

Instead, we were greeted by a flustered Mae, who hurried to get me ready for yet another meal with the King. My shadow tried to make small talk and give me supportive smiles as we walked to the hall where the person I hated most waited, but I didn't bother to respond.

He left me at the doors, with what I assumed was supposed to be a comforting pat on the back.

When I entered, I was mildly surprised to see two strangers sitting at the table alongside my father.

"Finally, my darling daughter arrives," he exclaimed, rushing to sit me down across from the guests.

I felt a flicker of panic at his happy demeanour and when I looked up at our guests I understood why.

The man across from me had a heavily freckled face and a scruffy ginger beard, matching the hair he had tied up. They were clearly travellers, human travellers.

I would have wondered why father had invited them to our table had I not looked at the girl. She was young and looked exhausted from travel, but what made my heart stop was her face.

I thought Nieve was sitting across from me, until I noticed that this girl had more freckles, like someone who had the freedom to spend time outside.

She wore, clearly handmade, woollen clothes and her long brown hair was wild and unkempt. I knew that, was the sunlight to hit it, strands would glow red in the light.

Those minute details aside, there was no way that anyone could deny that this girl was the exact double of Nieve. I felt sick to my stomach as I stared at her.

I couldn't help but imagine Nieve being free like this girl. Her hair wild and filled with flowers. Her face freckled and flushed by the wind, riding through the kingdoms without a care in the world.

It was strange that a girl who looked so much like Nieve could, at the same time, look so different. I felt no desire to kiss those near identical lips, or wrap myself in those arms.

I realised with a jolt that I had no idea how the human children, who arrived at our castle to work for us, came to be here. None of them had parents but I'd always just assumed that they were orphans.

Did the King steal babies that were twins?

Was it only twins he stole, or was it all babies?

My mind spun in confusion and I found it impossible to drag my eyes away from her face. I was barely aware of the conversation going on around me.

I couldn't imagine human families giving up their children for a lifetime of servitude, and I knew that the King would never pay to buy humans.

What kind of monster would steal children like this?

The conversation around me faded to an end and I awoke, as if from an enchantment, as the humans were

214

leaving. The man bowed to me and the girl gave an awkward curtsey before they were ushered out of the door by guards.

I stood, wanting to grab the girl and demand to know all about her life. To find out if she knew about Nieve. They were gone before I had taken more than a few steps.

Instead, I rounded on the King, suddenly furious about whatever was going on in this kingdom. I had to speak up. I couldn't allow him to continue with whatever evil was allowing him to steal these human babies.

"Don't be foolish," he smirked.

"What have you done?"

He laughed, "I have done many things."

"How dare you steal those babies."

"I dare because I am the King." he said, the humour in his eyes slowly being replaced by anger.

"Why is that human girl here?" I demanded to know.

"She is leaving to travel north tomorrow, and the deranged Queen in Norbroch will kill her the moment she crosses into her kingdom, so do not think of her."

"You are disgusting," I spat. "No wonder the humans all hate you."

He was on his feet and stalking towards me before I could think of anything else to say. He didn't stop like I expected. Continuing forwards, grabbing me as he went, and slamming me hard against the wall.

Holding me there with his hand around my throat.

"Is that what the humans have told you? Is it?" he hissed furiously, his face only inches from mine.

"I don't need anyone to tell me that." I refused to back down, "I can see it with my own eyes."

His hand tightened around my neck and, for a moment, I was sure he would strangle me.

"You better watch yourself, little girl."

"You better watch yourself." I threatened, "I hate you and so does this kingdom. I hope someone kills y..."

I didn't manage to finish my sentence as he punched me hard in the stomach, stealing the breath right back out of my lungs.

Unused to pain, my legs buckled. His hand around my neck became the only thing stopping me from falling.

"I have been far too lenient with you. That ends tonight. You will obey, or you will be disciplined. I've had enough of you, and your mother," he shouted, so close it hurt my ears.

He dragged me away from the wall and started towards the door, shouting for my shadow to retrieve me. I saw my shadow enter, and the flicker of concern on his face, before the King threw me forward.

I stumbled unsteadily before falling. My head collided excruciatingly with the wooden table, and my vision blurred as my head then hit the stone floor.

I was aware of a peculiar warm wetness on my face and head, but couldn't move to investigate it further.

My shadow was moving me, but the pain in my head was unbearable, and I slipped into unconsciousness.

CHAPTER

24
Freya

My footsteps echoed around the halls, my halls, as I walked towards the courtyard.

A door to my left opened and my shadow, William, joined me. His hair was tidier than usual and his clothes looked new, which was strange but I didn't dwell on it.

For some reason, I was eager to head outside. I was eager to join the festivities? I wasn't sure what we were supposed to be attending, but I hurried along anyway.

I pushed open the heavy doors and stepped out into the courtyard, greeted by cheers and applause. It should have been unusual to see both humans and fairies together in the courtyard, but instead it felt right.

Everyone was dressed in dark warm clothing, which told me that we were no longer heading into summer. The strange costumes, worn by both human and fairy children, caught my attention. Every child wore a costume, lovingly handmade by family members, and I realised with a smile that it was the Queen's Dark festival.

I was sure that it had only recently been spring, but now the year was ending. The harvest season was over and the nights were long and cold. The farmers would have spent their day slaughtering livestock to store, and moving the rest to new fields for the winter.

I could not remember what I had done earlier that day. My only memory was of the spring and King Ferchar's anger. I pushed the confusion from my mind as tonight was about the festivities.

We were celebrating. Thanking the Others for the crops, whilst hoping to encourage them to protect our animals through the frosty winter.

I paused on the stone platform to welcome everyone to this year's Queen's Dark festival. I spoke about new beginnings and alliances, thanking them for their patience and acceptance.

I must have put time and effort into planning what I would say as the words rolled off my tongue without a moment's hesitation.

As soon as I finished speaking I found it hard to recall what I had just said. I ended with a flourish, calling for the small bonfires in the corners of the courtyard to be lit. The flames would attract the attention of the Others to our castle and villages, ensuring their protection and cleansing our kingdom of all evil.

Once the bonfires were burning, the feast could begin. More food than I had ever seen was brought out of the castle kitchens. Never before had both fairies and humans been invited to the festival. Luckily this year the Others had looked kindly on us, ensuring that we could provide for everyone.

Festivals were a chance for the best cooks to bring out their finest food and receive praise, sometimes even employment. I spent a long time trying new foods, most containing turnip.

I ate without restraint, eager to try everything I was presented with. The smiles and blushes that my compliments caused made me laugh heartily.

Never in my life had I see the King interacting with his subjects as I did now. He had never given any indication that he enjoyed festivals, which was something I could never understand.

Turnips, carved in all manner of strange faces, were scattered throughout the courtyard. All throughout the kingdoms, hundreds of turnips were carved every year for the Queen's Dark festival. They looked haunting once illuminated by a small candle.

The castle was never usually decorated with many turnips, as the King didn't care for traditions. However, this year he was nowhere to be seen, which meant that we could celebrate properly. It was strange, but wonderful.

As we feasted, groups of children wearing painted masks and homemade costumes wandered amongst the tables, singing songs and telling stories in exchange for food or, if they were lucky, coin.

In the villages and town, the children would go guising and visit each cottage. Here they had no doors to go to, so they simply visited each group of revellers. Their stories amused me and I laughed as I wished them all a good winter.

As I laughed, I realised that this was the happiest I had been in months. I couldn't remember any reasons why I would have been unhappy before, simply that this was a joyous night.

I was aware of a presence in the air throughout the festival. It was not aggressive or threatening, simply lingering. Hanging over us as we feasted, drank and laughed. Adair told me once that on the night of the

Queen's Dark festival the dead watch us from the Otherworld.

Some say that the realm of the Others is closest to us on this night. That if you were to travel to the standing stones in Wulvendach, you might fall through and be dining in their halls forever.

Some families, who were especially eager to speak with their dead loved ones, left empty chairs and plates of food in the hopes of attracting them back from the Otherworld. How much of this was simply a story meant to scare children I didn't know, but there was no denying the presence of the deceased all around us.

The King never arrived, and I noticed more and more traditions occurring in the courtyard, traditions which had been frowned upon in the past.

I watched as human and fairy children dunked their faces into barrels of water, trying to catch apples in their mouths. The luckier of them finding a coin inside.

With the Others so close to us during the festival, it was believed that some of the gifted among us could see things which hadn't yet happened, or see into the past. I was asked to join in with the roasting of hazelnuts but declined politely. That was for those looking for romance.

They would roast a nut in one of the bonfires and, if it stayed whole, the man or woman they loved was sure to return their feelings. If the nut split and broke, then it was unlikely that they loved them back.

I will admit that I doubted burning nuts told anyone anything, but it was amusing to watch the drunken emotional reactions of those burning them. It made me smile to think of all the new relationships which would start tonight.

The thought of romance brought images of a beautiful woman to my mind, with flowers in her long hair and not nearly enough freckles. When I tried to focus and remember her name, it vanished.

A young human woman, with runes tattooed all over her body, stood near one of the bonfires. She was rearranging a pile of stones and claiming that she could tell people what the coming years would hold for them. I decided it would make a good impression if I took part in at least one of the traditions.

I also wanted to see if she could tell me why I felt so uneasy and confused. Why I had forgotten so much. She greeted me with a warm smile and it made me happy to see such acceptance from a human, although I couldn't remember why.

"I would love to know what the stones are telling you about me," I said with a smile.

She shook her head and gave me a sympathetic look.

"Not yet," she said simply, before shuffling the flat stones which I noticed were carved with runes I could not understand.

"Oh, should I come back later?" I asked, feeling somewhat embarrassed at her refusal.

"The future is uncertain, you might not be back," she gave me an apologetic look which made me want to laugh. Perhaps this woman had drunk far too much at the feast.

"Freya!" I heard a voice call, a voice which made my heart pound and my vision blur with tears.

I turned to see the girl from my thoughts coming towards me. She looked fiercer than I had pictured her, her body more muscular and her hair plaited intricately behind her head.

She looked like a warrior.

I felt a pang in my chest as if I had not seen her in a long time and stumbled forwards towards her.

"My love," she whispered with a smile, reaching out to take my hand.

As I reached for her, I was left breathless by a sudden agony in my head. I lifted my hand and was surprised to find my head bleeding. Warm blood running between my fingers and down my arm.

My head had not been injured tonight.

Had it?

All of a sudden, I was dizzy. Swaying as the ground rushed up to meet me.

I woke with a jolt and struggled to sit upright. Both the blinding pain in my head, and hands pushing me down, made it impossible. I opened my eyes slightly but the pain made it difficult to focus. The light from the candles was so bright, I could see little past their glow.

"You are alright Princess, let Mae clean your wound," I heard my shadow say, as memories of the night rushed back to me.

The fight with the King and my head smacking off the wooden table.

"What..." I mumbled confused, the festival had seemed so real.

It was as if I had been out in the courtyard just moments ago though it dawned on me that it couldn't have been anything more than a dream.

"I brought you straight to your rooms after you fell. I know it hurts but it should start healing soon," he reassured me, wiping at the blood on my face with a damp cloth.

I tried to explain to them about the festival, and how happy everyone had been, but I was so sluggish that I could barely get the words out.

They continued with what they were doing as if I hadn't even spoken, scolding me lightly whenever I tried to bat their hands away or get up.

"I'm sorry I couldn't protect you," my shadow whispered, stroking a hand through my hair.

"No one can be protected from him." Mae answered with a humourless laugh.

I didn't try to answer either of them. My mind and body were exhausted. I felt as if I had lived two different evenings at once, and the pounding in my head increased whenever I tried to make sense of what had happened.

All I knew was that I wanted desperately to fall back asleep and go back to that perfect night at the festival, back to Nieve.

Perhaps my dream meant that we would be lucky. That the King would be away visiting another kingdom by the time it was Queen's Dark, or even Summer's End.

I doubted it though.

The King despised the wulver, thinking them unnatural, so would never visit Wulvendach. The kingdom of Norbroch hadn't allowed us to return since our visit when I was a child, so I assumed that they hated him just as much as me.

Exhausted by the events of both evenings, I let my eyes drift shut, hoping to fall into a nightmare free sleep.

I heard Maw saying that she would wake me soon, to check my head, but couldn't muster a response.

CHAPTER

25

Euna

10 YEARS AGO

Lachlann and I were lucky enough to have one final chance to visit the Verch forest before he left for his journey south. Before his escape from the King.

King Ferchar was busy preparing to leave so we were able to slip out of the castle unnoticed. Aelwen would lie for me should the King call on us, and Alasdair would make sure no one missed Lachlann.

Thinking about what would happen, should our plan fail, made me so scared I could barely breathe. Instead I focused my attention on him. On my love.

We were sitting as close to each other as possible, his arm wrapped around my shoulders, our legs intertwined. Despite Tormod watching out for danger and passers-by, I still felt on edge.

The closer it got to Lachlann leaving, the sicker I felt and the harder it was for me to relax.

Despite my worries, we were content in each other's company, as we watched the sky begin to darken. Half of the sky was covered with dark grey clouds, but as the time passed they slowly changed.

Before long it looked as if half the sky was aflame with vibrant hues of orange and red, the likes of which I had never seen anywhere but the fires which burned during our festivals.

"I often wonder if a red sky means that the sky fairies are burning. The stories tell us that when they are fighting the sky is alive with blues and greens," I explained to Lachlann.

"The stories don't explain why the sky burns red?" he asked curiously, to which I shook my head.

As we spent more and more time together, I realised just how sheltered Lachlann's life had been. He never had anyone to tell him the fairy and human stories as a child.

It made me sad to think that no one had taken the time to tell him about the sky fairies, or the wulver or the selkies in the west. No one in Culhuinn knew anything, other than that they were alive to serve the King. It was heart-breaking, and I had no way of stopping it.

Culhuinn was a much larger kingdom than Norbroch meaning their army was also much larger than ours. Despite not having had a war since our fathers battled, the King still spoke of his army as often, and as loudly, as he could. There was no doubt that he was exaggerating his strength, but still our army was too small. We could protect the border and stop invasion, but we could not travel south and liberate hundreds of humans without being slaughtered.

"What are you thinking about?" Lachlann asked, pulling me from the log to sit on his lap.

"I wish I could free you all," I whispered, my voice choked with emotion.

"One day, I hope we can free ourselves," Lachlann replied in between placing soft kisses on my cheeks.

"Norbroch would help you," I promised taking his face in my hands. "We will help the humans should they ever gain their freedom."

As we sat there, the sky burning bright above us and the trees rustling in the wind, I knew that I meant it.

Before Lachlann could reply, Tormod came back through the trees. He looked sombre and I wondered if perhaps he was as nervous about tomorrow as we were. He inclined his head towards me, letting me know that the forest was empty, before mounting his horse and riding away.

"He's leaving you?" Lachlann asked, his confusion making me smile.

"Follow me," I slipped from his lap and held out my hand for him to take.

He smiled fondly and did as I bid. I tried not to squeeze his hand too tightly as we walked through the frost, but I wanted to savour every moment we had together. He radiated warmth. It was as if a bonfire burned bright within him.

We pushed our way past frost coated bushes, our feet crunching on fallen needles, deeper and deeper into the forest. Eventually we emerged into a small clearing, surrounded by tall trees which seemed to glisten against the burning sky. I froze, waiting to see how Lachlann would react to what I had planned.

His smile grew as he took in the secluded clearing, the furs and blankets strewn across the ground, the small bonfire burning and the basket of food Aelwen had insisted I bring.

The idea began as a dream. A dream I could not get out of my mind, no matter how long I was awake. Aelwen noticed of course, and I ended up admitting what I had dreamt, much to my embarrassment. Aelwen was in love with the idea, and took it upon herself to scout out a location where we could be alone together.

Tormod had lit the bonfire for us before he left, but I could not bring myself to be embarrassed that he knew what we would do here. Not as I watched Lachlann, the bonfire illuminating his face in its amber glow, smiling like I had never seen him smile before.

"You did this, for us?" he breathed, and I nodded.

Slowly, I undid the latch on my thick furred coat, letting it fall to the frosty ground. Then, without breaking eye contact, I began unlacing the front of my dress. I forced myself not to laugh as I watched him fidget.

Soon his impatience won and, before I knew it, we were together on the furs, my dress abandoned somewhere in the frost. I had to laugh as he almost knocked himself over in his haste to unlace his boots and throw them carelessly behind us.

"We have all night," I reminded him.

This night was all we had.

"Hey, don't worry," he whispered, gently cupping my chin. "Once I am free we can spend the rest of our lives tangled together here in this forest."

"Aelwen would probably allow it," I smirked.

With that, I relaxed and let myself enjoy our night together.

Despite the bonfire being small, it burned bright throughout the night. I was sure that at times I saw it flicker and dance as we did.

I just hoped that the Others could see us. That they witnessed our love and would protect us.

Morven

We spent the night in a room almost as large as our cottage back home. Servants brought us warm water to wash in and plates of food, in case we were hungry throughout the night. Not that I could manage another bite after the feast with the King and the strangely silent Princess. The more I thought about her, the more I wondered why she didn't speak.

The straw bed was the most comfortable thing I had ever slept on. It made our beds at home seem as if they were made of rock. The blankets were made of wool, so soft I considered stealing one, just so I could let everyone back home feel it.

Glen and I were used to falling asleep to the sound of other people moving in rooms nearby and the wind, whistling through gaps in walls and doors. There was none of that last night, not in a castle built by fairies and fit for royalty. The walls were solid and the only sound in the room came from our steady breathing and the crackling of the dwindling fire in the corner.

I was glad they let Glen and I sleep in the same room, had I been alone, the silence would have been suffocating.

After our lack of sleep under the fairy's enchantment, and then the stressful night spent on the sandy riverbank, we slept like the dead until servants woke us early the next morning.

I hadn't realised quite how exhausted I was until I woke feeling better than I had in days, maybe even weeks.

"I am never leaving this bed," Glen complained the next morning and I agreed, refusing to move until the servant ripped the blankets away from us with a laugh.

They quickly helped us dress and pack our bags ready for the next part of our journey. We were given so much food that our bags, which were already filled with trinkets from our journey, were close to bursting and I couldn't help but feel guilty.

Surely there were villagers somewhere in the kingdom that needed this food more than us.

Every servant we saw during our short stay was a fairy and it was surprisingly easy to tell. Their skin was oddly smooth and where our skin showed freckles, veins and flushed with colour, theirs remained one solid colour.

I hurried to dress as quickly as possible. Foolishly embarrassed in case the fairies, with their perfect skin, could see something wrong with mine. Glen noticed my haste, but also noticed my embarrassment, and didn't mention it.

We wandered through the courtyard at the front of the castle, the one we had entered in the previous day. Now that we weren't scared we would be arrested or killed at any moment, I could admire how beautiful the castle was.

It was built out of brown and grey bricks, their size so uniform that I couldn't help but be amazed by their building skills.

I felt a pang of homesickness at the thought of our little cottage back home, with its mismatched stone walls and thatched roof.

The courtyard wasn't as busy this early in the morning, but we got another glimpse of some humans. They were all dressed in simple outfits, much different from the fairies we had encountered during our brief stay.

Even if the King did disagree with the creation of changelings, it was obvious that he did not value his human subjects as highly as the fairies, or pay them as well.

One of the servants, who had helped us get ready, directed us towards the stables near the main gate before hurrying away. I was ashamed to realise that neither of us had learned their names, despite all the help they had given us.

When we reached the stables, we met with our guide, who was striking to say the least.

He wore his dark hair in three thick plaits which reached down to his waist. His face and neck were so scarred that, if he told us he'd once fallen onto a pile of knives, I would have had no trouble believing him.

Unlike the other fairies we encountered inside the castle, his clothes looked old and worn. He looked more like the humans back in our village, with mud covered boots and dirty clothes from a life of working outside.

"They call me Swift." he bluntly announced as we approached.

I couldn't have stopped my snort of amusement if I tried. Luckily it was muffled by Glen's burst of laughter.

I elbowed Glen hard when I noticed Swift's anger at our response... he was being serious.

"Why do they call you Swift?" Glen asked, fighting down more laughter.

"Because I am. I have travelled the length and breadth of Culhuinn, and of Norbroch in the north. I have journeyed to the ends of this land and back again."

"Well they call me Glen, and they call her Morven, because that's the names our ma and da gave us."

"This is our first journey, so you'll have to excuse us novices," I added with a smile.

"So long as you do not die, I do not care." Swift said and with that cheerful comment, he called for the stable hand to bring out the horses which would be taking us north.

The horses were beautiful. The smallest of the three seemed to be a sprinkling of different greys, its brown mane tied up away from its face. The two other horses were so dark they looked almost black and had light brown manes and tails.

I was relieved when Swift told me I would be riding the smallest of the three, although it still intimidated me a little. Apparently, the horses were powerful, strong, sure footed and perfect for navigating through the mountain pass into Norbroch.

The stable hand helped me attach my bags before allowing me to step on his hands and struggle my way into the saddle.

Embarrassingly, it took two attempts for me to even mount the horse. I only managed it the second time because the stable hand practically threw me up onto the horse.

Unlike the horses we borrowed to get to the Fairy Hills, these horses obeyed with the slightest pull of the reins or squeeze of the thighs.

"She'll see you safe through the mountains," the stable hand said, giving her an affectionate pat.

"Is it that obvious that she scares me?" I nervously laughed, to which he grinned.

"Just a bit. Might I ask your name?" For a moment, I thought I noticed a hint of disbelief on his face as he looked at me.

"It's Morven, what's yours?" I wanted to learn the name of someone who helped me whilst I was here.

"Berwin. What sends you up to Norbroch?"

"I'm just looking for some answers," I explained weakly, wondering why he was so interested.

I didn't have a chance to ask as a moment later Swift spoke, and once again we had to fight down laughter.

"The journey begins." he called dramatically, and somewhat ominously, before heading out the gates.

This journey wasn't going to go well if we burst out laughing every time our guide spoke. I wouldn't be surprised if he just left us behind somewhere.

Berwin laughed, "You better follow him. You have a good life Morven, find your answers."

He gave the horse a pat on the rump and then I was away, unable to question his somewhat dramatic statement.

Have a good life?

I had a horrible feeling that he could tell I was a changeling, and knew just how short my life was going to be.

"Hurry!" Swift shouted as we pushed our horses to maintain a fast pace.

I fought the urge to ride up beside him and kick him right off his horse. Despite the horse doing the galloping, I still felt exhausted.

My forehead and upper lip were disgustingly damp with sweat but I couldn't muster up the energy to wipe it away. I hoped I was simply imagining it, but I was so breathless I seemed to be panting louder than the horse.

There was no denying that Swift was an expert when it came to adventures. Glen and I had ambled at a slow pace towards our previous destinations, with no planned route or timescale in mind. Swift, on the other hand, charged towards Norbroch determinedly.

He paid no mind to the humans struggling to follow him. Humans who were moments away from falling off their horses and simply lying down in the long grass to die.

"I regret everything." I shouted to Glen in between loud wheezes.

"I can't feel my arse." Glen sounded almost as exhausted as I did.

"You should thank the Others for that. I'll never walk again."

Looking back, our journey from Wallace's village to the loch-side village, which had seemed tiring and painful at the time, was a dream compared to what we were currently experiencing.

My arse, lower back and thighs were burning as I failed miserably to find a comfortable rhythm to match the horse's. My thick woollen dress was pulled up almost indecently and my thighs were rubbing painfully against the saddle.

The further north we travelled, the more aware I was of the falling temperature. My poor legs were only covered by the long woollen socks ma had knitted me.

The valley between the mountains couldn't have been more different from the one we travelled through in the Fairy Hills. The valley floor was wide enough for our three horses to move side by side, although Swift hurried ahead of us for the whole journey.

The horses were not as eager to run straight to Norbroch as Swift was, so we spent a few hours on the frosty rocks, resting.

Glen and I bundled ourselves up together in our blankets whilst Swift sat across the fire from us, staring into the darkness. Occasionally he glared at us, but other than that he was silent.

When we finally left the mountain valley, the land before us was a welcome change. I felt I could breathe easier, just as I had after we left the Fairy Hills. The walls of rock were suffocating, and so the sight of Norbroch made me smile.

We could see green rolling hills, covered with a thick layer of early morning frost. Further north we could even see snow, despite it being summer. I could only just make out a dark forest lying across a river to the east, and it surprised me to see that the trees still had thick green leaves.

Despite the snow and frost, Norbroch reminded me of our village down in Tirwood, with its rolling hills spotted with sheep. The main difference here was that the green was broken by jagged stumps of black rock. It looked as if the rock was bursting out through the grass, attempting to take over.

Leaving the shelter of the mountains was like being plunged into the icy waters of Loch Fai all over again. The temperature difference between Culhuinn and Norbroch was so unbelievable that Glen and I agreed it must somehow be the work of the Others.

Swift had barely spoken during our journey through the valley, though he was kind enough to warn us that we would soon be freezing. We'd layered on our extra set of clothes and it was only just enough to keep out the biting cold.

"Welcome to Norbroch." Swift said, in the least welcoming tone I had ever heard in my life, before setting off again.

Clearly our time for admiring the scenery was over.

I almost cried with joy that evening, when Swift finally announced that we were stopping to rest the horses. Selfishly, I was just glad to be out of the saddle. We'd been following a path between the undulating hills of frost, grass and rock all day.

Swift seemed to be growing nervous as we travelled and I wondered if that was in case we met any of the local fairies.

Glen and I knew nothing of the relations between the two kingdoms, but from our guide's apprehension, we were beginning to assume they weren't friendly.

I quickly excused myself and scrambled up over some jagged black boulders. I was sweating by the time I managed to heave myself over them but it was worth it for the view, and the privacy.

Although Glen and Swift had made sure to avert their eyes whenever I had to relieve myself in the valley, it was still difficult not to feel embarrassed when there is nowhere to go alone.

Our guide made no moves to hide the fact that he thought himself superior to us, which made it even worse.

Once I had finished, and my bladder was no longer close to exploding, I started making my way back down over the rocks. I considered calling Glen over so that I could just jump down and make him catch me, but the lower I got the more I could hear of their conversation.

"Swift should not be killed just so two humans can travel north," Swift was saying to a confused looking Glen.

"Hasn't King Ferchar commanded that you to take us to the castle?" Glen questioned, to which our guide laughed.

"Unfortunately, we were attacked before we could make it. The ginger human killed before my eyes whilst I battled multiple fairies. The changeling girl stolen whilst I was single handily taking out a whole team of guards."

Before either of us could grasp that that had been a threat, Swift lunged forward, kicking Glen's feet out from underneath him.

Glen fell backwards with a grunt of surprise and Swift took advantage of his shock. He pinned Glen to the ground and began attempting to strangle the life out of him.

Instead of trying to save his breath Glen shouted and cursed at Swift, swinging his arms around and getting in a few good punches. He wasn't going to die easily.

Whilst they wrestled together in the frost, I scrambled down the rocks, slipping on a patch of ice and falling to a heap below the hill.

The only thing I could think to do was jump onto Swift's back, like I did to Munro and Malcolm when we pretended to fight back home.

My sudden weight on his back surprised him enough that he released Glen's throat, giving him a chance to regain his breath and roll away.

Faster than I could believe, Swift reached behind his back, grabbed me and threw me forward onto the grass. The next thing I knew, I was winded and flailing around on the grass like a trout out of the loch.

He resumed his attempts at strangling Glen which gave me a chance to crawl back to the hillside, wheezing loudly as I went.

My panicked mind decided to grab a large rock. It made my wrists hurt to carry it, and I found myself staggering back towards the spot where our, now murderous, guide was attempting to strangle my best friend to death.

I swung the rock towards Swift, who hadn't even noticed me stumbling back over to them, with every bit of strength I possessed.

The rock met his head with a dull thud, the contact between the two jarring my arm. For a painfully long moment, nothing happened and I wondered if I'd done nothing but injure myself with this plan.

Then, thank the Others, he keeled over sideways and didn't move again.

CHAPTER

27

Freya

The King did not raise another hand to strike me after the night I met the girl, who looked exactly like Nieve. Perhaps because I spent most of my time recovering in my chambers, doing everything I could to avoid him.

As soon as I was recovered enough to resume my lessons, I jumped at the chance to ask Adair how it could be possible. The most realistic explanation I could think of was that the humans gave the King a child when they had twins, perhaps because he threatened them.

My shadow agreed with my theory but encouraged me to ask anyway. As his job was to stay with me and ensure my safety, we spent the week after I cracked my head open sharing meals and discussing the possibilities. He had asked some of the guards he was friendly with, but they all seemed as baffled by it as him.

Humans just appeared here in Culhuinn as babies. No one had any idea how, or why.

My teacher Adair had the answers, and they were so awful I wished I had never asked. His brother Laird Brochan, whom I spoke with weeks before, was highly respected. I always found him to be crude, so of course the King liked him.

His nephew Tomas lived at their family home and, much to my relief, only visited the castle for festivals. He followed me around every time he met me, asking me to visit him and doing his best to appear helpful and loving. Nieve and I had seen right through him the first time we'd met, he was ambitious and greedy.

Adair's family lived near the border with the wulver kingdom, Wulvendach, and so were often at court. On one of their visits Adair had been introduced to the King and ended up becoming my teacher. He was kinder than his brother and, as a teenager, had left his family home to explore the land. Despite what his family thought, he ventured south into the human kingdoms and so could tell me all about them.

"I could have sworn it was Nieve sitting across from me," I exclaimed, finishing my tale of that awful night.

"You are sure the head injury didn't confuse your mind?" he asked, gesturing to my forehead.

My skin was still painful and healing after its collision with the corner of the wooden table.

"This was before all of that. I know what Nieve looks like, and that girl was the same."

"She must be the changeling child," Adair said, as if that was the matter explained.

"The changeling?"

"Ah, of course the King would hide such things from you. Leaving me to tell you about the darker parts of our land once again," Adair sighed.

When he first began teaching me he was quieter, afraid to tell me the truth about our kingdom and share what he'd learned in the human kingdoms. Soon we grew to trust each other and, though he remained apprehensive, he knew he could speak against the King without consequences from me.

He looked so unhappy about having to explain what a changeling was that I considered telling him to forget the matter.

Perhaps my shadow could find out more, now that we at least knew what the girl was.

"To create workers for this kingdom, the King sends fairies south into the human lands to steal babies from their homes. That much I am sure you worked out for yourself."

I nodded silently. The thought that somewhere in the south Nieve had a family made my eyes brim with tears. How could the King be so cruel? So selfish?

"Not wanting to risk starting a war between the humans and the fairies, the King looked for a solution. A way to steal babies without the humans realising. He found it in the form of a fairy, gifted with very rare and powerful magic. As you know some people are gifted, some with the ability to see the future, to heal or to create life. Most of those who are gifted with the ability to give life can use it only to revive small plants. At most they can use it to ensure crop growth in certain soils."

I nodded again, remembering all I had learnt about the farmers and their designated fields.

"One fairy was born with the ability to create life in a human form. Those that know about this fairy speculate that he may be half fairy and half Other. Some say he was born within the standing stones between our kingdom and Wulvendach. No one knows the truth, only that the Others must be involved somehow as only they can give life and take it away."

"This fairy, he creates the changelings?" I was horrified at the thought of such a gift.

"Yes. One fairy steals the human baby away whilst he creates a replica child from his magic to be left in its place," Adair looked grim.

"So, the humans don't know what is happening? They don't realise that their babies have been stolen?"

"Oh they do, you can tell a changeling from a human. The fairy's gift may be powerful but it is not without fault. The changelings die young, as the magic is not strong enough to last a whole human lifetime. While they live, they are often missing fingers or limbs and spend much of their lives unwell."

I felt a surge of sadness for Nieve's family and her changeling twin. That girl had likely spent her whole life sick and dying, whilst Nieve had been here with me. Her biggest problem being her restricted clothing options.

"Yes, I am sure the Others are unhappy with the King, the gifted fairy and my brother who introduced them. Although they haven't seen fit to take their lives from them yet," Adair leaned forward and gripped my hand. "When you are Queen, you can stop this."

I tried to smile and assure him that I would. Of course, I would do whatever I could to stop this horror from continuing. However, it was hard to smile when the thought of being crowned, and the responsibility for a whole kingdom resting on my shoulders, made me want to leave the castle and never return.

"Why would the changeling be travelling north?" I changed the subject before I could panic further about my future.

"That I do not know," Adair's brow furrowed in confusion, "Let's just hope she avoids the Queens, it is said that one of them hates humans."

I knew that the changeling girl was not Nieve, she was not the girl I had grown up with and loved more than anything else in my life.

Still, the thought of her being executed by the Queens in Norbroch made my blood run cold. I knew her severed head would join Alasdair's to haunt my dreams.

As I watched the servants bring out multiple courses of food, I had to fight the urge to scream out everything I knew about the changelings. To tell them all to leave the castle and flee south to the human kingdoms, where they had families waiting for them.

It made me sick to think that every human here had a weak, dying, changeling twin somewhere else. So many stolen babies. So many heartbroken families.

To my disappointment, Nieve had not served us since the night when the King first struck me. Perhaps mother had persuaded him not to allow her back, or perhaps he had harmed her.

My shadow and I had had no further chances to spy on Berwin and were never fortunate enough to stumble across Nieve in the halls. Nieve could be dead for all I knew and the thought made my head spin.

Instead I focused on my mother who sat across from me at the table. She was looking older in recent months. Perhaps the pressure of being married to such a disgustingly cruel fairy was finally catching up with her. As a mother herself, it sickened me that she did nothing to try and stop him from ruining the lives of other mothers across the land.

Instantly I felt guilty for that thought. I had failed to protect the one person I loved, how could I expect her to protect all those humans.

The meal was thankfully almost at an end, after one last course of wine and pointless conversation I would be free to return to my chambers with the last two people I cared about, Mae and my shadow.

A servant brought out a flagon of hawthorn berry wine for us and three cups. With his usual dramatic flair, the King poured each of us a drink.

I never cared much for wine and so I took a small sip, whilst father downed his glass in one go. Mother took a few large gulps but not the whole glass. I had noticed her drinking more as time went on. Perhaps to help her cope.

Mere moments after I swallowed, I felt a burning, gnawing pain in my mouth and my stomach. Father dropped like a stone to the ground and the burning intensified, so much so that I found myself sliding from my chair to the floor before I could look at mother.

"William," I attempted to scream for help.

My voice was hoarse and weak, as if I had just sipped fire itself.

Shakily supporting myself on my hands and knees I retched, my body fighting to expel whatever was poisoning me. I could hear the footsteps of the guards swarming into the room, alerted by my scream, but my body was too weak to move.

"Princess!"

"Poison," I wheezed.

By now I felt as if the wine had melted my insides, from my mouth right down into my stomach.

William's strong hands were on my jaw and around my neck forcing me to open my mouth. Then, to my horror, I felt his rough fingers on my tongue and in my throat. I tried to stop him but my sweating, shaking limbs wouldn't move as I wanted them too.

After an especially loud heave, he removed his fingers. When nothing happened, they returned.

Finally, after what felt like a lifetime it worked. It was strange that, even whilst poisoned and vomiting, I was embarrassed by my behaviour.

William supported my limp frame as I vomited up everything from our large dinner, all over us and the floor.

My vision blurred as he lifted me, then we were moving much too fast and I could no long keep track of what was happening.

I regained my senses much quicker than I would have liked, and almost fell out of the bed as I turned to avoid vomiting all over myself, again. A healer was there with Mae, helping me sit up and cleaning my face.

Their faces were grim as they explained how lucky I had been to have only ingested a small amount of poison, and that William's quick thinking saved my life. With demands that I should rest and regain my strength they left me alone with him.

"Thank you," I mumbled. My throat sore from the combination of poison, William's fingers and my own vomit.

"I'm here to protect you," William looked pale and shaken. "Freya, you were all poisoned this evening. The King died straight away but the Queen is still alive, for now. They are not confident that she will survive."

I knew that, if my mother was dying somewhere in this castle, I needed to be with her. She may not have been the bravest, or always there for me when I needed her, but I loved her. She was the last family member that I felt any love for.

William silently led me through the halls and down to the healer's chambers. A few human servants watched me as I passed, but I ignored them.

We were ushered into one of the rooms reserved for royal patients and there on the bed, looking frail and startlingly old, was my mother.

Her skin was flushed and glistening with sweat. I could sense the sickness in the air. Her lips were stained a deep purple colour and the pupils of her eyes were huge, giving her a wild look.

The healers hurried to explain things I couldn't understand about plants and poisoned wine. I had never learned about poisons in my lessons, other than that they were something to avoid at all costs. A coward's way to kill.

William pushed the babbling healer away to let me move to my mother's bedside. I grasped her hand. It was so hot I wouldn't have been surprised if she had burst into flames right before my eyes.

"It's Freya, I'm here," I told her hoarsely.

Her wide eyes darted around the room for a few moments before landing on me. Her purple mouth opened in a strange smile as she stared at my face, squeezing my hand weakly.

"My baby girl," she wheezed, her voice weak from drinking the poison.

"Yes, it's me. I love you," I told her, kissing her hand.

She smiled but was unable to move any more than that. Whatever poison this was, it worked fast. The King had dropped straight away and realised that I'd seen the man I hated most die.

"Is she in pain?" I asked the healer, who was watching and twisting his hands together nervously.

"It is difficult to know Princess, she is so delirious," he looked worried about his answer.

I was sure that the King would have punished him for being unable to cure the Queen but I knew there was nothing he could do. Whoever planned to kill us had picked a poison which worked so fast nothing could be done. It was all part of a plan.

It dawned on me that I too should be dead on the floor, my lips stained that harsh purple colour.

Mother made one final rasping noise in her throat before going limp. I watched, frozen, as she stared past me with unseeing eyes. It took me a moment to realise that she was dead.

It felt almost anticlimactic and I wasn't sure what to do. The Queen was dead and so was the King which left me, the heir to the throne. An orphan.

I should have been hysterical with grief but no tears fell. King Ferchar had shown me nothing but cruelty over the last few years, and my mother had distanced herself more and more as his cruelty escalated. Any relationship I'd once had with them had flickered out long before now.

I was more worried about being the Queen of Culhuinn as the responsibility for the people of this kingdom now lay on my shoulders.

Mainly though, I was numb.

I gently placed my mother's cooling hand onto her stomach and took a few steps back, wanting to distance myself from the death.

"May she find peace in the Otherworld."

Earlier in the day I had been sitting in my chambers despising them. Now I was alone in the world with no one to despise. I should have despised whoever poisoned us and worked to find out who murdered them, but I couldn't rouse any anger.

"Go and inform the relevant people," I told the healer with a wave of my hand.

I honestly wasn't sure who should be informed about their deaths first. Everyone would need to know.

"I don't feel sad," I admitted once the healer was gone, wanting to know what William thought about that.

"You were not close with them, it is understandable," he answered sympathetically.

"It could have been me," I said with a glance at my newly dead mother.

"Thank the Others it was not," he looked angry at the thought.

I nodded, I was glad not to be dead. Even though my life had lost much of its happiness and excitement, I was still glad to have life in my body.

"I have no idea what to do now."

"You will be crowned Queen and have the support of everyone in this kingdom. I will stand by your side. I promised you, things will get better."

And for some reason I believed him.

CHAPTER

28

Euna

10 YEARS AGO

Today was the day. King Ferchar, his family and their servants would finally be leaving Norbroch and heading south. I could barely hide my happiness.

I think even the servants and guards were glad to see the back of them. The human servants were meek and polite, probably out of fear. This meant that no real bonds had formed during the duration of their stay and very few people would be missed.

That was excluding Lachlann and I, and our love for each other. I never thought I would fall in love, but Lachlann's arrival changed everything.

It was hard to tell if the King was pleased to be leaving or not, his arrogant expression gave nothing away. Princess Freya seemed unhappy, but Aelwen promised that she could visit again, now that our kingdoms were on good terms. The Princess eagerly agreed, and promised to bring her best friend back with her.

Once our final meal was over, Aelwen winked at me and headed off to find her brood of children. She knew of the plans, and it still surprised me how easily she had agreed to trick the King of a neighbouring kingdom, and steal away one of his servants.

She was not the wholly good and innocent Queen that everyone assumed she was.

I hurried through the halls, to the room where Lachlann and I had spent our first evening together all those weeks ago. Where we drank and shared our first kiss, the first of many.

Tormod hurried along beside me, he knew about our plans and I'd longed for his approval. We had been in each other's lives for years and I could not deny that I was fond of him.

To my relief, he agreed with our plan and had even assisted us in finding the most suitable location for Lachlann to leave the group heading south. His friend Alasdair would be on the lookout to ensure that he went unnoticed.

I threw open the doors and rushed into Lachlann's waiting arms. In the few hours that we had been apart I missed him desperately. He held me tight and kissed me soundly before letting go, blushing furiously when he noticed Tormod smirking from the doorway.

He was dressed in his travelling clothes, rather than the plain clothes which he wore to work. King Ferchar did not allow his servants any coin and so they had nothing but the basics, which he grudgingly provided.

Once Lachlann was here to stay, I would give him everything he had ever wanted. I anticipated him resisting my gifts and so planned to find tasks for him to do. I would create a new position for him to fill, so that he would feel like he earned the coin I would shower him with.

The style here in Norbroch, with its thick knits and furs, would suit him well. He would look, to an outsider, like a king.

I was sure that Aelwen had already bought Lachlann gifts, to welcome him to the family and the kingdom. She had asked far too many questions about his likes and dislikes to merely be curious.

"Are you ready for today?"

"As ready as I will ever be," he answered with a smile, his nerves obvious.

"Everything will go to plan," I promised, wanting him to share my excitement. "Before you know it you will be back in these halls, completely free of the King."

Lachlann nodded, pulling me back into his arms and placing a kiss on my forehead.

"I can't help but be nervous. The King won't hesitate to kill me, should he think I am deserting him."

"He will not notice. The royals always travel at the front and there will be hundreds of servants and guards in front of you and Alasdair. He may be a fairy, but his vision is not good enough to watch hundreds of humans at once," I said confidently.

I knew in my heart that the Others would not let us fail, that they would protect true love.

"You are right, Euna," Lachlann agreed with a sigh.

"My guards and I will reach you fast, you won't need to hide for long," Tormod reminded him.

The plan was for Lachlann to leave the group travelling south at one of the locations we had chosen. Each location had a place where he could quickly move off the road and hide before being spotted; be that a forest, under a bridge, behind hills or in a trusted farm.

Tormod, and a small group of guards, would be following behind slowly and would find Lachlann wherever he had stopped to hide. He would be given armour, furs and a horse so that, if they were spotted, he would simply look like another guard.

We had numerous plans so that, even if he could only manage his escape at night, Tormod would be ready for it.

I was glad that Tormod and Lachlann had become somewhat friendly towards each other as Tormod was the only fairy I trusted to bring my love back to me safely.

We embraced for a while longer before our opportunity passed and Lachlann had to join Alasdair to get ready to depart. They were unimportant servants and so would be on foot for the journey.

I could not imagine having to walk such a distance, but it made our plan simpler. A horse without a rider would surely be noticed.

Lachlann leaned in to kiss me one final goodbye, before hesitating to glare at Tormod who laughed and exited the room to give us privacy.

We were both nervous about the next few days and so took our time to enjoy each other, one last time.

"I will see you in a few days," I whispered, my hands gripping his shirt, unwilling to let him go.

"You will," he agreed, his arms tight around my waist, equally as unwilling for us to part. "I love you so much."

"And I love you."

Far too soon for my liking, we broke apart with one final kiss. I watched him hurry down the hall and out of sight, before heading out to find Aelwen. My throat felt tight and I found myself unable to speak for fear that I would cry.

Aelwen and I lit a small bonfire behind the castle to attract the attention of the Others and hopefully protect Lachlann and Tormod during their journey.

Before last night, we had only ever lit bonfires and given offerings during festivals or births. Never having felt strongly enough about anything to need extra help and reassurance from them.

Today though, I needed help from the highest power.

"It has been an interesting visit," the King said, inclining his head to Aelwen and I.

A fairy with more respect would have bowed down to the hosts who had graciously housed him for weeks, but he had no respect for anything.

I refused to allow him to anger me as my whole body was already alight with nerves. Aelwen placed her hand on my arm to calm me and replied.

"We have all enjoyed your visit, our agreements are sure to strengthen both of our kingdoms," she said with a pleasant smile.

"Yes, I am sure they will," the King said and made to turn and mount his horse before stopping, as if suddenly remembering something.

He gestured to one of his guards, who stepped amidst the column of guards and servants to retrieve something.

I wondered if he had decided to give us a gift in thanks for our hospitality, but my curiosity turned to dread the moment the guard returned.

I watched, horrified, as two guards dragged Lachlann to where the King stood before Aelwen and I, his arms bound tight behind him.

His beautiful face was bruised, so badly that one of his eyes would barely open, and those lips I had kissed not long before were now split and bloody.

He offered me a weak smile as he was forced to his knees before us. Aelwen and Tormod stiffened on either side of me but I was too distressed by the sight of his injured face to move.

"It has come to my attention that this human has been unfaithful to me, his King and so I must deal with his punishment before leaving," the King said casually, as if talking about merely wanting to buy a loaf of bread, not injure the battered human at his feet.

"I am quite sure there is no need for that," Aelwen said when it became clear that I could not find words.

"Ah, you two rule so gently. It's a wonder anyone obeys you. Humans need fear. Fear and pain are the only things that keep them in line," he said with a malevolent grin.

I found myself staring into Lachlann's eyes and could almost hear his thoughts in my mind. He looked apologetic, as if this was somehow his fault, and sorry that now it would be more difficult for him to escape.

I hoped the King's punishment did not injure him too gravely, but I trusted that Tormod could still rescue him during the night.

I tried to convey my love for him through my eyes and hoped that he could be brave and suffer through this pain. I would give him the world once he was safe in my arms, he would never feel pain again.

Aelwen's gasp shocked me out of my thoughts, just in time to see what the King had planned.

It was as if time slowed down as we watched the King thrust his drawn sword through Lachlann's defenceless human back and out through his chest.

Lachlann's eyes went wide with pain and shock, and I felt the world crumble around me.

As quickly as it happened, the King's sword was back in its sheath and he was mounting his horse, leaving Lachlann swaying on his knees before us.

I ran forward, falling to my knees and pulling him to my chest. I uselessly pressed my hand against his wound, sickened by the feeling of his warm blood, spilling over my fingers and trickling slowly down my arms.

"I am sorry," I whispered frantically as I pushed on his chest, cursing the Others for not giving me the ability to heal.

I heard the King laughing from upon his horse.

"So, it is true. You fell in love with a human. I wasn't sure if I should believe what my guards told me, I expected more from you."

"You will never return to this kingdom," I heard Aelwen shout from beside me, shocked by the anger in her voice. "Norbroch will never deal with Culhuinn again!"

The King simply laughed, "I am sure you'll soon regret that when Norbroch needs aid from Culhuinn, but it's no skin off my back."

Lachlann coughed painfully in my arms and I watched as blood began to trickle from between his lips as he tried to speak.

"I love you." he whispered in between hacking coughs and with that, my ability to hold back my sobs vanished.

"No..." I wept, wishing I could somehow stop this. "Please... no. I love you."

"Get a healer now!"

I heard Aelwen shouting to the guards behind them and Tormod calling for supplies to be brought, but I knew it was too late.

The love of my life was bleeding to death at the entrance to my castle and there was not a single thing I could do about it.

Aelwen's shaking hands joined my futile attempt at stemming the blood flow. I could feel blood, damp and warm, on my skirts and arms. By now the flow was slowing and knew our time was running out.

I placed desperate kisses on his still warm lips not caring about the taste of blood.

"I love you," I repeated over and over not breaking eye contact with him for a second. "I am sorry. I love you."

He made one final sound, which I assumed was meant to be my name, before letting out one long pained breath. Then, he moved no more.

The cry I let out hurt my throat and ears but I could not stop it.

Lachlann was dead.

He was dead and he was never coming back to me.

I could hear Aelwen sobbing beside me, apologising for not saving him and for helping us plan this, but I did not care.

How could I ever care about anything again?

The one I loved more than life itself was gone. Journeying to the Otherworld leaving me here alone, shattered without him.

PRESENT DAY

I stood, sweeping my arms across the table, sending the cutlery and glasses smashing to the floor. There were tiny cuts and scratches along my arms, where the glass had cut through my sleeves, but the pain did not bother me. If anything, it helped me feel less numb.

Tormod followed behind me as I rushed out of the room, silently judging me and remembering everything so that he could report back to Aelwen when she returned from her travels.

Not that it mattered.

I ignored everyone we passed, though no one made a move to speak to us. Probably due to my dishevelled appearance and the blood on my hands and arms.

The thought of blood made me shudder and I made a point of not looking. Reliving his death once was bad enough, I did not want to go back to that day again so soon.

I stopped at the room I had been looking for and took a moment to gather my nerves before pushing open the door.

"Stay there," I murmured to Tormod, closing the door behind me and shutting him out in the hall.

The room was one of the finest in the healer's wing of the castle. When a member of the royal family became sick, this used to be one of the rooms they stayed in until they were healed. Not anymore.

Now I forbade anyone from entering this room. Aelwen had had trouble stopping me from banishing the last person who entered.

Inside the room there was a bed, where generations of our family's sick had rested. The room had huge windows, which overlooked the grass outside the back of the castle, and the view of the mountains was spectacular.

This was the room where I had lain with Lachlann in my arms, shortly after his death. I had refused to let him go when Tormod and the healers tried to take him from me.

I screamed at them for being too late and cursed them, as if it was somehow their fault. Aelwen had eventually managed to calm me and persuaded me to carry him inside. Though she did not want us walking through the whole castle.

She knew that, if I had been allowed, I would have wrapped Lachlann up, all warm and cosy in my bed, and never let him go. Instead we went to the healer's rooms and there I lay my poor beautiful human.

Ten years later I could still remember that he looked oddly peaceful in death. I had never laid eyes on a dead human before, but it was unnervingly easy to pretend that he was simply sleeping.

I had sent everyone from the room, then got to work.

I cleaned the blood from his cooling skin with warm cloths and wrapped his wound as if that would somehow heal it.

Washing the blood away, it dawned on me that never again would it fill those cheeks and show his embarrassment, or anger.

Never again could I lay my head against his chest and hear his heart beating rhythmically. My favourite song.

Tormod brought the new clothes I had bought him and I dressed Lachlann up, as if he had returned to me like we planned and was now my king.

Once I had finished gently brushing his curls from his face I wrapped us both in blankets, foolishly wanting to keep my poor fragile human warm.

I wrapped myself up in those blankets again now, wishing desperately that they still smelled like him and not like ten years of dust.

It made my head pound just thinking about that day and the all-encompassing grief which left me a shell of my former self, unable to cope with life alone.

As time passed the grief became easier to deal with. Although there were still days like this, where I wished hopelessly that I could join him in the Otherworld and leave this lonely kingdom behind.

I ground my teeth together and pushed my face into the pillow, refusing to let my tears fall.

Once the fog of grief began to clear, I had wanted to start a war with Culhuinn. Aelwen had refused. She felt guilty for encouraging me to get so close to Lachlann without either of us thinking about the consequences, but she could not risk the lives of our people on a needless war. At that time, I had despised her for it.

I could not think of a better reason for the people of Norbroch to give their lives

Instead of waging a war I stayed here, locked up in the castle by my own choice and did nothing. I ruled, made decisions like a mindless shell and that was it.

Festivals held no joy for me. I no longer bothered pretending to speak to, or care about, eligible males in our court.

I simply wandered around the halls, revisiting my past, thinking back to the last time I was truly happy.

Remembering our love.

CHAPTER

29
Morven

"**M**orven, I'm fine." Glen complained as I fussed and forced him to sip some more water.

"You don't look fine," I argued and I was right.

The deep purple bruises, which had quickly blossomed in the shape of fingers around Glen's neck, were concerning. I had no idea what sort of damage Swift might have done but for the moment, Glen seemed to be breathing steadily.

We had stopped just inside a small forest after spending much of the night heading north. The days were longer now that it was nearing summer.

I was hopeful that Swift would not be able to find us, especially not on foot and with a head wound. I didn't know how badly I had injured him, only that the rock in my hand had been alarmingly bloody after I'd struck him.

Shaken from his near-death experience, Glen had been no help in the moments after I knocked Swift unconscious. As quickly as possible I'd gathered our supplies, helped Glen onto his horse and then we set off, taking Swift's horse with us.

I felt a twinge of guilt for abandoning him on his own without supplies, but he was a seasoned explorer. Surely, he would be able to survive on his own.

If not, he shouldn't have tried to strangle my best friend.

I spent the night worrying about Glen, who remained silent, and struggling to remain calm despite the inescapable fear that I would turn and see Swift chasing after us.

It was only once we had stopped that I had the chance to panic about other things. Firstly, I panicked that we had left a trail behind us. Having never been hunted by anyone, I wasn't even sure what kind of trail we could have left behind us.

Secondly, I worried that Swift would recover and return home. That once he got there he would turn the King against us. Would our journey home now be halted by our arrest and possible execution? I had no idea.

There was nothing to be done about either of those things. All I could do was ensure that Glen and the horses were fed and watered, before settling down to sleep. It was warmer in the forest than it had been out in the hills. It was as if the forest was so full of life that it kept everything warm. Still, I'd wrapped us up in every blanket we had, cradling Glen's head to my chest.

I hoped that the Others would be on our side, let Glen survive the night and keep us hidden from anything that might harm us whilst we slept.

The Others seemed to hear me and I was glad when we both woke a few hours later, the horses nearby and no sign of Swift anywhere.

Glen and I ate some of the food we were given and I forced him to drink more water before we checked the map. It was hard to tell how far away the castle in

Norbroch was, but we were hopeful that we could reach it before nightfall.

Before we continued heading north, I forced Glen to sit down on a fallen tree trunk so that I could have another look at his neck. I poked and prodded at his bruises making him wince. The bruises were now so dark you could make out two full handprints around his neck.

His breathing still seemed to be normal, so I hoped that meant he was okay. Ma wasn't a healer, though she could fix most ailments, so she had never passed on any advice about what to do should someone try to strangle you. I felt helpless.

"Leave it alone," Glen eventually shouted, losing his patience with my fussing and startling me out of my thoughts.

There was silence for a moment, as if the forest was observing, waiting for me to react. Well react I did. I pushed myself up off the ground and stormed away, bursting into tears as I went.

I heard Glen swear behind me and moments later he pulled me into a hug.

"I'm sorry," he whispered, swaying us from side to side while I cried.

"You almost died," I accused, saying it out loud made me realise just how close I had been to losing my best friend.

"I wouldn't let someone with a name as stupid as Swift kill me."

"He almost did," I pointed out in between sobs.

The thought of being left alone up here in the fairy kingdoms with nothing but Glen's dead body and a couple of horses just made me cry harder.

"I promise I won't die Morven." Glen said taking my face in his hands.

"I promise too." I hiccupped, letting him brush the tears from my face with his thumbs.

"It's almost over, in a few days we will be heading back down to the village with the answers to all your questions. We'll be back home in the village before you know it."

I made Glen cuddle me a while longer before we left. Following a well-worn road heading towards the snow-capped mountains, under which the castle lay.

I remembered all that the King had told us about how they stole human babies and forced them to work, but I was too exhausted to worry much about what our fate would be.

We couldn't turn back and go south, not with Swift out there somewhere, looking for revenge. Our journey had led us here to this castle and so we had to face whatever was waiting for us.

I just hoped we would make it out alive.

Two fairies on horseback rode out to meet us on the final stretch of road before the castle. The two women were wearing dark thick wool and furs, which made me realise just how foolish Glen and I must look in our double layer of clothes. It was no wonder we were both freezing.

"What is your business in Norbroch?" demanded the blonde fairy whom I noticed, with a twinge of fear, was heavily armed.

"We wish to speak with one of the Queens of Norbroch," I answered nervously, too which the blonde laughed, making me blush.

"The Queens do not simply meet with anyone who demands it," said the other guard, who's defining feature was a scar on her cheek, so deep it looked like someone had once stabbed her in the face.

My heart sank in desperation. We had travelled all the way to Norbroch, through mountains and forests, been attacked and enchanted, only to be turned away before we could reach the castle where the answers lay.

Whilst I panicked, Glen replied. "We've been sent to Norbroch by the King of Culhuinn."

The guards shared a glance, clearly surprised. They stared at each other for a few moments, deliberating what to do, before the heavily armed one tilted her head towards the castle and the scarred one nodded. The first guard then turned, galloping off towards the castle at an alarming pace.

"Follow me." the scarred guard said, allowing us to continue down the road at a much slower speed.

When we arrived at the courtyard of the castle, we were hurried off our horses and taken into a small hallway.

We were greeted by guards which made me feel sick with nerves. It was just like being arrested in Culhuinn except this time it was much more dangerous. If the King had been right about their hatred of humans we were really in danger.

"Hands." The scarred guard demanded and after a moment of confusion we held up our hands, only to have our wrists bound tightly with thick scratchy rope.

We were then searched for weapons and our only defence, Glen's small dagger was taken from us. Not that it ever did us any good. We had both forgotten about it when Swift attacked.

I kept my eyes on Glen, who was attempting to appear calm, whilst the guards spoke about us in hushed voices.

I was struggling to control my breathing and not pass out when they finally came to a decision.

"Walk." The blonde guard gestured towards another set of guards who began leading us through the halls.

I pressed close to Glen so that we were walking shoulder to shoulder, begging the Others not let them lead us down towards the castle dungeons.

"What brings you to my kingdom?" The Queen asked, moments after Glen and I were forced to our knees before her.

Despite being completely terrified, I noticed that the Queen was beautiful. Her skin was so pale I doubted she had ever seen the sun, which clashed with her thick black hair. Her poised demeanour made me feel like a child.

Her clothes were dark and, whilst they looked warm, they had none of the decoration that the fairies in Culhuinn wore. Her cheeks were hollow and her hands looked thin and pale, which made me wonder if she was sick.

"We were sent by King Ferchar," I hurried to explain, but was cut off before I could continue.

The glass she had been holding shattered in her hand, sending shards of glass and water to the floor.

I risked a glance at Glen, who looked as stricken as I felt. I could hear my heartbeat pounding in my ears as my heart raced and stomach continued to churn nervously as we waited for her response.

The longer the silence lasted, the surer I was that I was either going to vomit, or something much worse.

The stone hall was painfully silent, except for the sound of Glen and I's panicked breaths. The expression on the Queen's face was completely unnerving and I focused on the trickle of blood, slowly dripping from her hand onto the stone floor.

When the blood began to make me feel even sicker, I turned my attention to the guard beside her stone throne. The guard looked younger than the Queen and was watching her closely.

As the moments passed by, I wondered if he too was unsure what she was thinking.

He wore a jacket, which was lined with fur around his broad shoulders, and reminded me of the people who lived to the east of Loch Fai. He was so muscular even Finnian would have looked weak beside him.

He remained expressionless and stoic until the Queen spoke and confirmed my fears.

I had angered her.

"Tormod, take them to a cell." she said quietly.

"Wait... please we just want to ask you some questions," I pleaded as the guards, and the one she called Tormod, came to collect us.

The Queen ignored my explanation and sat expressionless as Glen and I were helped to our feet and marched out of the hall, through a small door I had not noticed before.

We were taken along a dim and sparsely decorated hallway until we came to a thick wooden door, which the guard Tormod had to unlock before we could continue.

From there we were taken down a winding set of stone steps, the sound of rushing water growing louder the further beneath the castle we descended.

Far too soon, we came to a corridor with four wooden doors. We could hear no movement from behind any of them and one of the guards had to light torches on the walls so we could see.

It seemed like castle's prison was empty. I wished it was staying that way.

Tormod unlocked the first wooden door and opened it to reveal a stone cell. Rather than throw us in he gestured that we should enter.

I'd once thought the mountain valleys felt suffocating, but now I wished to be back there more than ever. Despite our many troubles, this was the first time I'd ever truly regretted coming on this journey.

I cursed myself for being so eager to find answers and save my own life. I should have remained at home, content with what little life I had left.

"Please, if you would just let us explain," Glen tried, but the guard shook his head.

"Queen Euna has ordered that you be imprisoned for the time being," he said, and a flicker of hope sparked in my mind at his words.

I'm not sure I could have stopped myself from sobbing if he'd said that we were to be imprisoned forever.

Glen took a step forward and I hastily closed the distance between us, not wanting to risk separation. Another guard, who had remained silent, stepped forward and cut the rope that bound our wrists with a small dagger.

The moment we were unbound Glen and I grabbed onto each other's hands, fingers intertwining so we wouldn't be separated.

Tormod gave us a pitying look before saying "in" with such finality that we could not resist any longer.

With that final word, our freedom was gone.

CHAPTER

30

Freya

The King and the Queen were buried side by side in a small courtyard, alongside generations of those who ruled before them.

The King had been organised, as well as egotistical, whilst alive and had their gravestones carved years before his death. Each was carved with a figure vaguely resembling them, not that anyone would ever visit the courtyard to see them.

It was strange to watch as their personal guards lowered their lifeless bodies down into the graves, filled them with rocks and then lay the gravestones flat over the top.

I felt like I should be crying. Should throw myself on top of the graves, wailing at the loss of the two people who brought me into this world, but I didn't. I couldn't bring myself to shed a tear.

When I confided in William he told me that the Lairds and Ladies were gossiping about my strength and bravery, despite losing both parents so young. Brave and strong were two emotions I did not feel. I wasn't sure I had ever felt brave or strong.

Instead I simply felt sick, as my stomach continued to cramp due to the poison. The healers said it would be a few days before it was completely out of my body.

The same day as the burial, my coronation took place. The Kings and Queens of Culhuinn were crowned in a simple ceremony in the great hall. Every Laird, Lady, and the most important common fairies, were invited to watch the spectacle, before joining what was left of the royal family for a feast.

I had always assumed that I would be older when I took the throne. Older, wiser and more prepared.

It was only as I walked through the excited crowd, towards the throne, that I finally felt the urge to cry. I was in no way ready for this.

William by my side gave me strength. He had promised to help me, and that the kingdom would support me. I held onto those promises and hoped desperately that the Others would ensure his words came true. The thought of being alone on the throne was too much to bear.

In Culhuinn we had no intricate rituals. To be crowned, one simply had to don the crown in front of an approving audience. Adair once told me that in some human kingdoms they had to climb mountains before being crowned. With trembling hands, I lifted the crown. Its weight surprising me so much that I almost dropped it.

It was a thin band of metal, carved with runes to ensure that the wearer would be protected by the Others. I knew the runes were a lie. The King had been wearing the crown the night he was poisoned.

I turned towards the eager crowd, placed the far too heavy crown atop my head and sat down on my cold stone throne.

The crown felt heavy and wrong, sat in amongst the plaits Mae had spent all morning working on. I kept my chin up and smiled to the crowd, breathing slowly through my nose whilst my heart raced in my chest.

There was a moment's hesitation, before they erupted into cheers and applause. Each Laird and Lady shouted well wishes and thanked the Others. The noise in the hall built to such a level that I could barely focus, the heavy crown all that was holding me together.

I raised a hand and a blissful silence descended on the hall.

"Let us begin the feast," I called, thanking the Others when my voice didn't shake.

With that, they forgot all about their plans to win my approval and hurried out into the stone courtyard, where Alasdair had been beheaded, for the feast.

As I watched them go, I was painfully aware of the lack of human presence at my coronation, specifically the lack of Nieves presence.

Foolishly I had convinced myself that she would appear. Sneak away from her work to see me and prove that she still loved me the way I loved her.

I had tried to visit the kitchens, under the lie that I was simply greeting the humans and overseeing work, but was quickly shooed away every time. Usually with a pocket full of bannocks or a pie for my trouble.

Nieve did not want to see me, and the rest of the humans were helping her avoid me.

The feast seemed to last all night.

I lost track of how many times a Laird or Lady would wish me well as Queen, before suddenly remembering why I was crowned and hurrying to offer their condolences.

I couldn't even use food as a distraction, every time I raised a glass to my lips or took a bite of food, my stomach burned in anticipation. Just waiting to be poisoned once again.

There wasn't a drop of hawthorn wine left in the castle. William had ensured that it was all poured out the day after we were poisoned. He had also placed guards in the kitchens, to oversee the production of my meals and ensure that no one tried to take my life again.

We were still investigating who had poisoned our wine. The girl who served the wine had been distraught at the accusation and begged me to spare her life. It was clear that she knew nothing about it and so we let her go.

I could not muster the energy to care who the culprit was. Whomever it was likely had a good reason to want King Ferchar dead, and they wouldn't have been the only one considering murder.

If I hunted down and executed our attacker, the King would once again win and another family would be left devastated.

It didn't matter what I did. I couldn't win.

I found that being Queen meant the loss of my freedom. I hadn't even realised that I had any freedom left, until it was suddenly ripped away.

I could no longer escape to my meadow, spend my days in lessons with Adair or roam the halls with William. Instead I had an endless stream of meetings to attend.

Lairds and Ladies from all over Culhuinn were desperate to meet me and gain my approval. How I was supposed to know a person's character after a few moments I had no idea, but my smiles and compliments seemed to placate them all.

One unexpected pleasure of those meetings was finally getting to meet William's father and brother Urraig. They looked so similar that I would have known they were related right away, I couldn't help but stare. Although as Queen, perhaps I had the right to stare.

My first change to the court was appointing Adair as my advisor, much to the King's old advisor's disgust. He was a horrible old man who cared more about profit than anyone in Culhuinn. I easily ignored his complaints and allowed William to remove him from my sight.

It would have been foolish of me to start making drastic changes to the ruling of the kingdom before I'd had a chance to speak with the Lairds, Ladies and common fairies, but I could not resist getting rid of him.

"My son, Tomas, asks that you visit him," Laird Brochan announced after our meeting.

The meeting had consisted of him boasting about the crops and livestock from the farms near his home, and me fighting the urge to point out that it was the farmers who should be boasting, not him.

"Give him my thanks," I said with a forced smile. "As you know, I have much to do here in the castle."

He nodded and looked thoughtful for a moment.

"It was a bold choice, picking my brother, Adair, as your advisor."

"A good choice," I replied simply, desperate to avoid conversation with a man that aided in the creation of the changelings.

"Might I suggest a new choice? I know I would be a far greater help than that..."

"I have made my decision."

As I glared at him, wondering how two brothers could be so different, I was struck by an idea. An idea so great that I was oddly proud of myself.

Perhaps I was fit to be Queen.

"There is one issue with which I need your assistance," I said as sweetly as I could manage.

"Anything my Queen," he hurried to assure me. Likely already imaging the reward he would demand in exchange for his help.

I glanced cautiously at the other members of the court, who were still mingling nearby. Hoping to make it appear as if what I was about to say was meant only for Laird Brochan's ears only.

"I need to find a certain fairy. A fairy with a very specific gift."

He nodded, looking eager. To my frustration, it was clear that he had no clue who I meant. I fought back a sigh. I had hoped to be subtle about my request rather than say it outright.

"Bring me the fairy that can create the changelings," I demanded, and to my surprise his face lit up.

"Yes. Yes, my Queen. I can do that," he hurried to assure me.

His excitement was sickening.

It baffled me that he made no attempt to hide what he was part of. Stealing babies from their families and forcing them into servitude clearly wasn't something he felt any remorse about.

The Laird left the castle shortly after our meeting, returning home to collect the gifted fairy and bring him to me. Whilst he was away Adair, William and I had time to plan what we would do.

Change was coming to Culhuinn. I would make sure of it.

"The King and Queen of Culhuinn were poisoned and killed within their halls. The culprit has been apprehended and dealt with. Queen Freya sends a message of friendship and hopes to maintain the close bond between our two kingdoms." the two women before me repeated for what felt like the hundredth time.

Messengers were sent between castles and kingdoms to spread news throughout the land. These two women were travelling to Wulvendach, to inform the wulver that I was the new Queen.

The messengers I'd sent to Norbroch the day before travelled in a much larger group, armed and ready to defend themselves against an attack.

The King had ensured that relations between Culhuinn and Norbroch were completely ruined, so no messages of friendship were sent up north. The messengers were simply to deliver the news and then retreat. I hoped that the group made it back alive.

Although the King had despised the wulver and looked down on them, the relationship between our two kingdoms remained surprisingly strong.

The wulver are a peaceful race, who keep to themselves and stay amongst their mountains. They had never been involved in any of the previous wars. Not even those that tore down the old kingdoms and built up the ones that stood today.

The benefit of that was I wouldn't have to worry about hosting them here in the castle. They would simply send back my messengers with good wishes and a token gift.

Adair and I had discussed the possibility that the King's death could mean improved relations between our kingdom and Norbroch, as it would be beneficial for us both. But I wasn't counting on it.

If our messengers returned unharmed I would thank the Others and be done with it.

The changeling and the human would have arrived in Norbroch by now. I just hoped that whatever they did in the castle didn't reflect too badly on me before I could even announce my new title.

I was plagued by thoughts of my messengers running into an army of northerners marching down south, enraged by whatever the King told the changeling to do there.

All I could do was wait.

CHAPTER

31

Morven

"I never thought I would be so thankful for a hole in the ground," Glen said, making me laugh.

The hole in the ground he referred to was where we relieved ourselves. The hole had been carved down through the thick rock in the corner of our cell and, to my surprise, led to an underground river.

Being trapped in the dark cold cell was bad enough without having to deal with the smell of waste. I truly was thankful. Not that we needed to relieve ourselves often. Queen Euna seemed determined to starve us both to death.

The water rushing past beneath the ground was something else to be thankful for. Not only because it carried waste away, but also because it provided us with a distraction and something to listen to.

As we sat, leaning against each other for warmth, I let my mind wander. I imagined the water rushing through rocky tunnels for days and days. Emerging somewhere along the coast which Malcolm and Bonnie loved to tell stories about, or perhaps down at Loch Fai with Finnian.

Trapped in the silent cell, without a window or visits from guards, we had no way of knowing how much time had passed, or what day it was.

All we had was the flowing water. The only proof that life was continuing outside of our cell.

"I reckon that in a few days we will be skinny enough to jump through and be washed away from this prison," I commented which made Glen laugh.

Either of us fitting through that hole would be a cause for concern, it wasn't big enough to fit a leg through.

"Knowing our luck, it would wash us back down to the Fairy Forest. We'd be back under that fairy's enchantment before we could blink."

"At least we would be outside," I complained. "I can't believe I am missing wind and rain right now."

"Aye, suddenly a boring life trapped on da's farm doesn't seem quite so boring after all," Glen sighed, squeezing my hand.

"We will make it home..." I replied, not sure whether I was making a promise or asking a question.

"We will make it home," Glen confirmed. "Just as soon as we can fit through that hole."

As the time passed, during what we assumed was our second day in the cell, our hunger grew. I found myself imagining everything we had left in our bags.

The rolls would still be quite soft and if I focused, I could imagine sinking my teeth into one of them. The thought of the tough salted beef lying somewhere in the castle was enough to make my mouth water.

Our stomachs had been grumbling unhappily for a while and when I placed my hand on mine, I was sure it felt much flatter than before.

Soon it was hard to think rationally about the time passing, or how hungry I was, as the pain in my head had grown to a level I could no longer ignore. The water running beneath us had stopped being a source of comfort. Earlier, Glen had punched the wall a few times in desperation, and I didn't blame him.

It was torture, being so close to water but unable to drink any of it. If I'd had any water left in my body I would have cried. My mouth was dry and my lips were so sore and chapped that I didn't think they would ever heal properly.

Despite our empty stomachs and raging headaches, Glen and I told stories to pass the time. We talked about our journey so far, trying to remember every little detail, just in case we made it out of this prison and had the chance to tell our families about it.

The thought of home, my ma and da, my brothers, my Granny and the twins made my head hurt even more as I tried not to cry.

If we starved to death in this prison they would never know what happened to us. I imagined them at home, their eyes darting to the road, hoping to see us return. Eventually giving up as they realised we weren't coming home.

Noticing my darkening mood, Glen attempted to cheer me up.

"Just think about seeing Finnian again, that'll make you feel better."

"The thought of someone I knew for less than two weeks and only kissed once does not make starving to death in a cold prison any easier to cope with," I grumbled, rolling my eyes. Though I appreciated his effort.

"He was an attractive someone," Glen insisted.

Rather than respond I lay down beside him, patting his stomach sympathetically as it growled and complained.

I woke groggily sometime later. The rock-hard floor made my back ache and my cheek was sore from being pressed into it whilst I slept. To make things worse, my thighs still ached from our ride north with Swift.

My only source of comfort was Glen's warm body beside me. I rolled over to face him, the sudden movement making my vision swim and blur.

I lay there for a few moments and realised something was missing. My head no longer pounded as if someone was smashing a hammer around inside my skull. Instead it had faded to a dull ache.

I still longed for a drink of water, but food didn't hold the same appeal as it had the day before. Had the Queen opened the door and thrown in a freshly baked loaf, or even some of ma's stew, I wouldn't have made any moves towards it.

Food was such a distant memory that I reckoned I could go on without it forever.

"I'm so empty," I mumbled, my voice sounding raspy and dry as it broke the silence.

"If I had any, I would probably drink my own piss right now," Glen replied seriously.

"If we don't starve and die in this cell, I am telling your brothers that."

"Donal and Dougal would bloody love that," he agreed.

We lay there uncomfortably for an unfathomable amount of time until I felt Glen's chest hitch beneath my cheek as he began to cry.

I stared at his slightly blurred form in confusion for a few moments, trying to make sense of what I was seeing in the dark. Glen never cried. Well, he did cry sometimes, but I couldn't think of a response.

Fortunately, he didn't wait for my poor hungry mind to catch up. Instead he lifted me into his lap and wrapped his arms around me.

"We are going to die here," he whispered in between hoarse sobs.

That thought had been lingering in the back of my mind since we were first locked in this prison. All of a sudden it was terrifying and I found myself dissolving into tears as well. Apparently, my body wasn't dry as a bone after all.

"I'm sorry I brought you here," I whispered.

"I would rather starve to death with you than anyone else," Glen said, which startled a dry laugh out of me.

The rest of, what we assumed was day two, passed much the same. Glen switched between sarcasm and crying until eventually he wore himself out and managed to get some more sleep.

Whilst I did my fair share of crying, I felt otherwise emotionless about our situation. I couldn't muster up the energy to feel as much regret as I did the day before.

Soon I found myself falling back asleep. It was odd how tired doing nothing was making us.

The next time I pried my dry eyes open, I didn't bother moving. I could feel Glen's warm body beside my own and that was enough.

I lay on my back, mindlessly running my fingertips over the cold hard rock beneath me, listening to the water rushing below us. I felt almost content.

Glen too seemed a lot more enthusiastic after his emotional breakdown the day before.

"They will probably come for us today," he explained sitting upright beside me.

He glanced over at the door every few moments, saying something about weakening the defences of prisoners before they were questioned. I didn't try too hard to follow what he was saying.

He propped himself up against the rough stone wall and pulled me so that I was sitting between his legs. Resting back against his chest.

I let him move me like I was a child, before laying my head back down on his shoulder and closing my eyes.

"Tired," I mumbled hoarsely and felt my lips crack and bleed in a new place.

My throat was sore now, not just from the lack of water but from sickness. As a changeling, I had spent much of my childhood sick with various colds and once a cough so violent, da had had to abandon his farming to travel to the town to find a healer for me.

My head felt heavy and I couldn't stop my teeth from chattering.

"I'll tell you another story about the village while you rest," Glen said, wrapping his arms around me to keep me warm.

3 YEARS AGO

"I am going to punch you if you don't stop pacing," Munro complained, only half joking.

We were perched on one of the stone walls that divided our fields from the neighbours. In front of us, Malcolm had been pacing up and down and up and down for what felt like hours. Just watching him made me feel exhausted and I doubted it was doing him any good.

Malcolm stopped and stared at us, as if only just remembering that we were watching.

"Bonnie is having a baby."

Munro and I groaned dramatically.

For months, Malcolm had been overjoyed about their child. That was until Bonnie started feeling pains in her stomach and went into labour.

Ma had quickly thrown us out of the cottage with instructions to fetch Glen's ma, Martha, and his eldest brother's wife, Ceitidh.

All night and all morning Munro and I had to put up with Malcolm's ridiculous behaviour which included pacing, blurting out that Bonnie was giving birth and staring ominously into the small bonfire we had lit to attract the Others.

To my relief, Glen and his brother, Donal, came ambling through the grass towards us before Munro started punching.

"You better get back up to the cottage Malcolm," said Donal.

To which Malcolm paled worryingly and ran off in the direction of our cottage.

"I was so close to punching him right in the face," Munro said far too seriously.

"Your da would have punched you in the face if he heard that you punched Malcolm in the face on the day that he became a da," Glen laughed.

We spent the rest of the morning sprawled on the grass. Once the baby was born it would be hectic on the farm. Ma wouldn't let Bonnie lift a finger until the baby was least a month old, so I was anticipating us all having a lot more work to do.

Glen and Donal had brought out a few boiled eggs, some bread and a jug of water, which was blissfully cold, so we ate lunch whilst we waited.

I felt confident that the Others were watching our little cottage that day. The weather was unusually warm with barely a cloud in the sky. It made a pleasant change from the grey skies and rain that we were used to.

My skin grew hotter and hotter as we lay there and I hoped that the new baby would be enough to distract ma from the four of us getting sunburn. If not, we would spend our afternoon out collecting honeysuckle flowers to bathe in it.

The four of us dozed lazily until da appeared, shouting for us to come back. We scrambled to our feet and raced back to the cottage. Unsurprisingly I came last, panting and wheezing.

Another fire had been lit outside the cottage. This one, da explained, was for the afterbirth to stop any wicked fairies getting it and using it for magic. The explanation made Munro heave loudly beside me.

The moment ma stepped out of the cottage, looking haggard and tired, her eyes drifted to our sunburnt noses and foreheads with a frown. To my relief, she didn't say anything about it.

We were ushered inside and what I saw made me squeal in delight before I could stop myself. Bonnie was reclining against Malcolm and in her arms she held two perfect little babies.

"Twins!" Munro blurted out.

"Two baby girls," Malcolm explained, prouder than I had ever heard him before.

His eyes were pink as if he had been crying and I couldn't blame him. The sight of the two healthy, squirming babies made me want to cry as well.

It seemed the Others had noticed our fires and truly blessed our little family.

As was tradition, da placed a shiny coin in each of the babies' hands and a kiss on their foreheads. It was hoped that beginning life with a coin would ensure that they never went without.

"What names have you given them?" Granny Athol asked.

The most important tradition, other than bathing the new borns in milk, was to name new babies quickly. It was thought that a baby named quickly couldn't be affected by fairy magic.

For obvious reasons, I didn't believe in that tradition. Ma and da had picked my name before I was born, and still their original baby had been stolen.

"Morag and Mildred," Bonnie said, her eyes never leaving the two little babies in her arms.

The announcement was met by cries of happiness from ma and Glen's ma, which woke the twins. We were quickly herded out of the room to let them rest.

Malcolm would stay with Bonnie for the next few days, to ensure that Morag and Mildred were never left alone, and never replaced with changelings. That wasn't said out loud, but we all knew the reason.

Instead of pestering Bonnie and Malcolm, we squished around the fire our cottage. The rest of Glen's family coming to join.

That night we feasted on a thick vegetable soup and, as per tradition when a baby is born, bread and cheese flavoured with caraway seeds.

PRESENT DAY

By the end of the story I felt like the room was spinning uncontrollably around us. If I had anything in my stomach I was sure I would have vomited.

Instead, I found myself retching painfully whilst Glen rubbed my back and tried to comfort me. Once my body had stopped I found myself cradled in his arms once again.

"They will come for us soon," he promised, nodding to himself as he spoke. His eyes focused on the wooden door.

As I watched him watching the door my vision began to blur. It had been blurred the past few days, but now it was fading fast.

I tried to shake my head, to clear the specks of light that were blocking my vision, but that just made me dizzy.

Distantly I could hear Glen speaking, his voice sounded loud and panicked. I felt as if I had finally slipped through that hole and was submerged in the river.

I opened my mouth to tell Glen that I couldn't see, and about the water, but all I managed was a hoarse breath.

CHAPTER

32

Freya

Unlike the King, who would hold court in the great hall in front of hundreds of people, I preferred to meet with the Lairds, Ladies and common fairies in a small private room away from everyone else.

Without pressure from their fellows, and the fear of being overheard, I found that everyone I spoke with was more truthful. Whilst I still despised being Queen, I was finding common ground with many of the fairies who visited.

My hopes for a fairer Culhuinn seemed less like a distant dream with each passing day.

William, Adair and the castle's master of coin, Drummond, were the only people who joined me during these meetings. I was initially wary of Drummond, having never even seen the fairy before. Adair assured me that he could be trusted and shared our views when it came to the changelings and the treatment of our human servants.

As the days passed and the meetings continued, everyone eager to meet the new Queen, I began to appreciate the new company. Drummond was younger than I expected, and had the ability to find amusement in the dullest of afternoons.

When the door opened for the next meeting I was surprised to see Berwin. It had been weeks since I last visited the stables, and he looked dreadful compared to my memory of him.

His curly hair was lank and looked unwashed. His skin was clammy and he fidgeted nervously in front of us, refusing to take the seat I offered him.

I remembered his meeting with Nieve that I'd overheard and wondered if perhaps she had sent him here. She was still avoiding me, but the sight of Berwin in front of me lit the first spark of hope in weeks. A spark which flickered and died as soon as he spoke.

Berwin dropped to his knees and with a shaky voice said, "I have a confession to make."

"Tell me."

My heart pounding in my chest as panic, which I had managed to avoid since the King died, crushed my hope.

"I poisoned the King, the Queen and you," Berwin blurted out.

With a shaking hand, he brought a small vial out of his pocket and placed it on the stone floor in front of him.

I felt my jaw drop. The murder of the King and Queen was the last thing I'd expected him to confess to. I didn't feel upset by this admission, nor did I feel one ounce of anger towards him. I was simply astounded.

I glanced at William and was glad to see that he looked equally as shocked by the news as I was. Drummond was making himself appear busy, not wanting to get involved.

It was Adair who regained his senses and spoke first.

"Why did you do this?" He asked softly, not a trace of anger in his voice.

"It had to be done," Berwin sounded uncomfortably close to tears.

"I am sure you did not work alone to poison them. I doubt it is you alone who is responsible for the murder of the King and Queen."

"It was me." Berwin said through gritted teeth.

His insistence only confirmed my suspicion that he was taking the blame for the murders, to hide his accomplices.

Adair nodded thoughtfully, "why did it have to occur?"

"With the old King and Queen dead we humans will finally have a chance at freedom."

"Alright my boy," Adair said soothingly. "It was brave of you to come forward."

"Have you confessed to anyone else?" William asked, to which Berwin shook his head. "Then you will come with me down to a cell, where you shall wait until we come to a decision."

Berwin nodded, looking paler than before but somewhat resigned. He stumbled to his feet and followed William to one of the smaller doors which led down to the prison.

William now had power over the guards in the castle. He had appointed those he trusted to many of the important roles, ensuring that we knew what was happening throughout the castle, and could control it.

"I think it would be best if this confession did not leave this room just yet," Adair suggested, to which Drummond and I nodded.

There was no way I would sentence Berwin to be executed for playing a small part in a larger plan. I wouldn't allow anyone to be executed ever again.

Perhaps that would finally stop my dreams from being haunted by Alasdair and his execution.

The killing of his subjects had allowed King Ferchar to rule by fear and he had earned himself quite the reputation for it.

If I had any reputation at all, I wanted it to be for the exact opposite.

"We will need someone new down in the stables," I mumbled.

"I think we will need many new servants before long, my Queen," Adair sighed.

The weather was suitably dramatic the day the gifted fairy and Laird Brochan arrived at the castle. It had been pouring since the night before and so they arrived soaked to the bone and splattered with mud.

The servant I sent to fetch them only gave them a few moments to change before insisting that they followed him down to the meeting hall.

We wanted to give the impression that I was a ruthless Queen. One who would happily ruin the lives of humans, simply to gain servants. William stood protectively to one side of my chair and Adair to the other.

"Excited to see your brother again?" I teased to distract myself from my nerves.

"Excited to see the look on his face when he realises that you are not your father," Adair replied with a smirk.

Although we had a plan to give them both a false sense of security, hear them confess to their crimes and then arrest them. I couldn't stop myself from being nervous.

We had no idea how powerful this gifted fairy was. Maybe he would be able to summon changelings with his magic and attack us.

Maybe he could somehow kill the changelings he had created in the past, like that girl identical to Nieve. I fidgeted as we waited in silence, listening to the wind howling and the rain battering off the windows.

Without waiting to be summoned, the door opened with such force that it bounced off the stone wall and swung back. Narrowly missing hitting Laird Brochan and the gifted fairy in the face.

It took every ounce of strength I possessed not to laugh.

"My Queen, I have returned," Laird Brochan cried joyfully, as if returning to a lover after years apart.

"I see that," I answered coolly. "Is this the gifted fairy?"

"Yes, this is Darach," he gestured to the fairy beside him.

Perhaps because I knew of his gifts, and the horrible things he had done in the past, I thought that he was the ugliest fairy I had ever seen in my life.

There was nothing particularly odd about him, though he had long skinny fingers which I was fully prepared to kick away should they try to touch me.

Knowing that this fairy was the reason every human in the castle was taken from their homes, and had caused the deaths of so many changelings, was almost enough to make me reconsider my thoughts on execution.

"My Queen," he croaked in a voice that sent shivers of disgust down my spine.

"I want to see demonstration of your gift," I demanded, feeling uncomfortably rude at being so abrupt.

The two of them seemed used to this kind of rudeness and didn't look at all phased.

"I am unable create a new changeling without a human life to copy," he croaked. "If you have a young human nearby then I can give you a demonstration."

"So, you are unable to create changelings from here in Culhuinn?"

"Yes, my Queen," he admitted, much to my relief.

I felt my confidence grow at his admission. Our plan was going to work.

"If we are given some time to travel down to the human kingdoms we can retrieve many human servants for you," the Laird hurried to assure me.

"Do you work alone?" I questioned.

"My Queen, I have been generous in offering my assistance to Darach as he goes on these missions. I have also provided many fairies over the years, to help collect the humans."

"Why have you had to provide many? Is it dangerous down south?"

"No, Darach is careful to work his magic during the night so that the humans never see him. The companions I have provided have often been... weak. Many have had to be disposed of."

"You killed them?" I barely managed to hide my revulsion.

"Yes of course, they cannot be trusted to keep our secret. A gift such as Darach's must be hidden, protected."

"Of course," I agreed.

Hidden from the world and never used again.

The pounding rain outside filled the silence as I thought for a moment. Laird Brochan and Darach waiting for me to reveal my plans to acquire a whole new population of human servants.

"Do neither of you feel any sympathy towards the human families, whose lives you destroy?" I asked.

It was amusing to watch their faces change from smug and eager to bewildered. Never in my life had I felt so powerful.

"Sympathy?" Darach muttered.

It was as if he had never heard of such an emotion.

"My Queen, those humans, they aren't the same as you and me," Laird Brochan attempted to explain, as if speaking to a child.

And so, the two of them sealed their fate.

I would not execute them. I swore not to become a ruler like King Ferchar. However, they would never be free again. Both were old, older than the King had been, and so would spend the last few remaining years of their lives in prison.

Clearly neither felt any remorse for their actions and I doubted that a command from me would stop them from stealing more babies.

"Have you announced an heir yet?" I asked, knowing Laird Brochan had but one son, Tomas.

"No, my Queen I am still young," he spluttered, I had to fight the urge to smile.

It looked as if the Laird was not at all ready to grow old and meet the Others.

"Perfect." I said and, with a clap of my hands, the guards who had silently entered the room behind them moved forward to restrain them.

"The creation of changelings is hereby banned in Culhuinn and, as the two of you are the only ones able to do so, you shall be spending a long time in prison."

"I am a Laird!" he shouted, trying to wriggle away from the guards to no avail.

"Do not fret, a new Laird will ensure that your village and farms thrive under his watch," I said with a smile. "Tomas will be allowed to remain."

"You can't arrest us for creating changelings. It is a gift from the Others themselves!" Darach protested.

"No?" I paused thoughtfully, "then I arrest you for murdering the countless fairies in your employment."

With that, they were taken down to the prison. I pitied the guards who would have to deal with their demands and complaints.

"Remind me to give the guards dealing with them a raised wage. They definitely aren't receiving enough coin to make that a worthwhile job."

"I'll let Drummond know," Adair smirked.

I felt thrilled as I left the room with William at my side. We had successfully tricked Laird Brochan and prevented the creation of any new changelings.

It upset me to think of all the changelings, weak and dying, throughout the human kingdoms, but I had no way to save them. All I could do was prevent it from ever happening again.

By now a messenger would be well on her way to William's brother, who would inform him that he was needed here at the castle.

Urraig was well liked and famous across Culhuinn, after doing well in the few games the King allowed to be held. There was a chance some would hate me for replacing their Laird, but Adair assured me that very few people held any love for Laird Brochan.

"This is going well for the two of you," I joked to William and Adair. "New jobs and the chance to change your brothers' lives forever."

"Queen Freya!" A voice called and I turned to see a skinny human boy, bright red and panting like he had ran the entire length of the castle. "I have a message for you. The leader of the humans is waiting for you in the main hall."

"Leader?" I asked, since when did they have a leader? And more importantly, why did they want to speak with me?

"Yes, Queen Freya. Chosen by us humans to lead us, she wants to meet with you," the boy said before running off again.

"They are so serious about wanting freedom that they now have a leader?" I questioned as we hurried through the castle to the main hall.

"It's not very surprising. The way King Ferchar treated them was disgusting. No wonder they want to go," William commented, looking troubled.

I felt dread pool in my stomach with every step we took.

I was embarrassed to realise that I could barely think of any of the human's names. I could only picture their faces. Knowing them as the ones who washed the clothes, served the food, tended the garden.

Had I really spoken to them so little that I could name no more than a handful?

I paused outside the doors and took a deep breath to steady myself. I was the Queen now. I had to be able to deal with these things. I had no choice.

Before I could change my mind, and run back to my chambers to hide, I pushed the door open and entered.

My heart almost stopped when I saw who stood inside.

"Nieve?"

CHAPTER

33

Euna

I was sat by the fire, watching the flames flicker and dance, when there was a knock at my door. I could not stop myself from flinching at the noise. It had been two days since the humans had arrived in Norbroch and I was still afraid.

I had spent the last few days watching from the windows, wondering if at any moment I would see King Ferchar charging towards our castle with an army. Tormod had sent out extra guards to watch the border, but so far none of them had reported any activity from Culhuinn.

"Enter," I called.

I knew who it would be, and what they would ask, before the door even opened.

"Shall I send someone down to the cells with food tonight?" Tormod asked once again.

Just like every time he asked me, I did not even consider it. Why should I feed the two humans that King Ferchar sent north to torment me?

If he wanted them fed and pampered, he should have kept them down south in Culhuinn.

"Not tonight Tormod," I replied, not bothering to turn around and see the disappointment on his face.

Three days after the humans arrived, a messenger arrived with news that Aelwen and her family would be returning later that afternoon. I sent Tormod, and a few of his most trusted guards, out to meet them and was spared another full day of his complaining about the humans. Why he was so eager to help the two humans sent to torment us I had no idea.

As happy as I was to escape his disapproving gaze, I found myself missing his company. I wandered the halls for a while before returning to my cold stone throne to await Aelwen's return. My hands clenched painfully to try and stop them from shaking.

I did not care about how the meeting with the wulver went. They were peaceful people, unlikely to ever start a war. I knew she would not have had any problems. Any issues they did encounter would have been quickly resolved after pleasant conversation and a nice meal.

The day crept by torturously slow as I sat, waiting for Tormod and Aelwen to return. With nothing to distract me, I spent the day battling against my own mind. Refusing to be pulled back down into my memories of Lachlann so soon.

When the doors at the end of the hall did finally open, I sprang from my seat and hurried down the steps and towards Aelwen.

She still wore her thick woollen riding cloak which made me smile. Clearly she had come straight to me, rather than returning to her rooms first.

I noticed Tormod slip in behind her and signal for the guards who had followed me all day to leave the room, he too was still dressed for riding.

We met in the middle of the hall and, rather than embrace each other as I had expected, Aelwen struck me hard across the face.

The hall was silent as I stared at her in shock, unable to hide how betrayed, and small, I felt.

I blinked furiously, trying to dispel the tears that the stinging pain brought and turned on my heel to hurry away from her.

Her hand around my arm stopped me.

"Let go." I hissed, attempting to wrench my arm out of her grip.

As a mother of three she had experience wrangling squirming fairies and refused to let me free.

"What in the name of the Others have you done?" she demanded, grabbing onto my other arm and forcing me to face her.

"Me? You are the one storming in here after weeks apart and striking me for no good reason."

"No good reason?" she shouted, closing her eyes and taking a deep breath. "Tell me you are not attempting to starve two humans to death."

"I..." as I went to correct her I felt my stomach sink. "They are prisoners," I reasoned.

"It has been decades since Norbroch last held prisoners, and even longer still since they were sentenced to die without a trial. Have you lost your mind?" she was shouting again by the time she finished.

The burning on the left side of my face, and her accusations, made the tears I had been fighting since the two humans walked into our hall spill over.

My breath hitched in a sob and at once her expression softened.

Releasing my arms from her unbreakable grip she pulled me close, wrapping her arms around me.

"He sent them," I wept, whilst she hushed me and rubbed my back soothingly.

My cheek ached, where it was pressed against her shoulder, but I did not bother to move away. I felt something inside of me calm and heal the longer she held me close.

Before she could shout, or comfort, me further the door, which led down to the cells, burst open and a frantic guard hurried through.

"The prisoner... You better... He's shouting..." the guard gasped out in between breaths.

Whatever was happening down in the cell had scared him so badly he had run all the way up here, desperate for help.

Tormod was shoving the guard out of the way and running down the stairs before the fairy had even finished telling us what was happening. Aelwen grabbed my hand and then we too hurried down the stairs and along to the cells.

I tried to dig my heels in and stop her from dragging me along, but her grip was like iron.

"You did this, and so you must face it," she said, her face softening as more tears escaped. "I won't leave you alone with them."

As we approached the cells we could hear shouting and I felt dizzier the closer we got to the humans and the unknown threat.

What if the humans attacked us? What if they killed Tormod? Killed Aelwen?

When we arrived, it was clear that the human man was attempting to break the door from inside. He was shouting and screaming at the top of his lungs. Pounding and kicking on the door as hard as he could.

I squeezed Aelwen's hand tighter to try and find some strength.

"Open the door," she demanded, and Tormod moved forward to do so. Barking instructions for his fellow guards to be ready, should the human attempt to attack.

He pounded on the outside of the door which made it go quiet inside.

"I am opening the door," he shouted before doing so.

I braced myself for an attack which never came. I did not have a chance to feel relieved as Aelwen moved to stand beside Tormod, dragging me with her. Inside the cell, the red-haired human was cradling the unconscious girl in his bleeding hands. He was crying unashamedly and I was almost floored by my guilt.

It was like suddenly breaking free from an enchantment as I realised what I had done. The two of them were dirty and shivering from the cold. The girl was deathly pale and the man didn't look much better.

"Please," he cried. "She'll die if she doesn't eat. I beg you. Kill me. Let her go."

I had to cover my mouth with my free hand to stifle my sob.

For a decade, I had hated King Ferchar for what he did to me. What he did to the humans under his rule.

Then, when the first humans in a decade entered Norbroch, I locked away and starved them close to death.

I had never seen a more pitiful sight in my life and it was entirely my fault. I was a monster.

My head swam as I thought of what Lachlann would say if he knew what I had done. He would hate me. He should hate me.

Through my tears, I noticed Tormod attempt to take the girl from the man. This only made him cry harder so he stopped. We were all at a loss about what to do, all of us except Aelwen.

"Come," she said reaching towards him, her voice gentle as if speaking to one of her children. "Let's get you both some food."

"Food?" he mumbled, to which she nodded.

Tormod gestured for the other guards to leave, it was clear that the humans posed us no threat.

I was the threat.

After much coaxing from Aelwen, he left the cell carrying the girl. We slowly made our way up the stairs and into the healing wing of the castle, Aelwen squeezing my hand again as we passed Lachlann's room.

The human's arms were shaking from hunger, and the weight of the girl in his arms, but he would not allow Tormod to take her. Instead Tormod ended up gently pushing and guiding the human as he stumbled and staggered to the room.

I watched guiltily from the doorway as Aelwen and one of the healers helped the man lay the girl down on one of the beds. Immediately the healer began using her gift to help heal the girl of all the hurt I had caused. Aelwen helped him onto the bed beside her gently tending to his injured hands.

Neither of them looked at me, but still my guilt rose and rose until I was sure it would suffocate me.

"My Queen," Tormod said, rousing me from my thoughts and gently pushing me to the side. Allowing a servant from the kitchens to hurry in with a thin watery soup.

"I did this."

"No, the King did this," Tormod said fiercely. "He knew what he was doing when he sent those two humans into Norbroch. He knew how you would react to seeing them."

I could not think of a response, although I felt my guilt loosen just a little. I would do everything I could to atone for what I had done to them, though I knew it would never be enough.

I would make sure that I never let King Ferchar affect me this way again. I did not expect the humans to forgive me. I just desperately hoped that the Others did not punish the whole of Norbroch for my actions.

I'd face the consequences in the Otherworld, I welcomed them.

CHAPTER

34

Freya

"Queen Freya," Nieve greeted me with a respectful nod, her eyes never meeting mine.

I was struck by how much she had changed since that day at the stables. Her cheekbones and jaw were sharper than ever and her hair was tied back from her face, half of it plaited down her back.

She wore her usual plain dress, but had added a leather vest and a scarf. The most noticeable addition was the dagger on her belt. My mind whirled with more questions than I could count. I wanted to know all about our time apart.

What had she been doing? Where had she been? Where did she and her human companions find the leather and wool for new clothes? Why did she carry a weapon? Most importantly, did she miss me?

William nudged me forward slightly and I remembered that this was supposed to be a meeting. I hurried forward to take my seat.

The first time Nieve had laid eyes on me in months and I simply stood there, staring at her. No wonder she didn't want to see me.

"I am told you are the leader," I commented, to which she nodded. "The leader of what?"

"We have learned that the humans residing in Culhuinn were stolen from their homes throughout the human kingdoms. I am here to negotiate our freedom," her voice was completely devoid of warmth, as if she was talking to an enemy.

Did she really think I was her enemy?

"Freedom?" I blurted out.

Berwin had spoken of the humans, and their desire for freedom, just a few days before when he confessed to poisoning us. I had not realised quite how serious they were, despite the King and Queen being murdered.

"As payment for years of servitude we want land in the south. Above the northernmost human kingdom there is place with mountains, forests and rivers. We want this land as our own, where we will be free to build our own kingdom," Nieve said, pulling out a roughly drawn map and handing it to William, who brought it over to me.

"You don't need to leave," I insisted, after studying the rough and inaccurate map. "We will pay a fair amount of coin for your work here."

"We will not work here any longer," Nieve said with a shake of her head. "We are not members of this kingdom. I ask that you allow us to leave and spread word that we are our own free and independent kingdom," her blunt demands sent a flicker of dread through me.

I had no idea how to deal with this.

"And what if I don't?"

"Then we will simply leave. Even if we have to fight our way out," Nieve replied, completely unfazed.

"I need time to think about this. There are fairies living down south in the land you are demanding," I said after a glance at William and Adair, who both looked equally as shocked by their requests.

"You do not have time. Either you grant us this land or we fight."

A pounding headache began as I realised that she had me backed into a corner. There was no way I could persuade her to change her mind. For a fleeting moment, I almost wished that Berwin's poison had killed me that night.

If the whole royal family had died, the humans could have left and I would have known nothing about it. The court would have spent weeks arguing over who the appropriate heir was and wouldn't have been organised enough to prevent the humans from taking their freedom.

I didn't know what to do. I didn't want to deal with this. I just wanted Nieve to stay with me and for these problems to disappear.

"I need time," I exclaimed, horrified to hear that my voice sounded shaky and choked with emotion.

Nieve sighed impatiently and nodded to her two fellow humans to leave the room.

My mood lifted slightly, distracted by the hope that she wanted to speak to me alone. I quickly gestured for William and Adair to leave us alone.

"What happened to Berwin?" she asked in a quiet voice.

"What?" I spluttered.

This is what she wanted to talk about alone?!

"Berwin confessed to his crime, what has become of him?"

"He is in prison?" I explained, "but I won't execute him." I hurried to assure her when she looked pained.

"Thank you, I did not approve of his methods," she replied dully before turning to leave.

Before I could stop and think about what was appropriate behaviour for a Queen, I was hurrying towards her.

I tried to take her hand in mine, like I had the first day she served us, but she pulled away from me as my fingertips grazed her warm skin.

"Please Nieve, don't do this," I mumbled, losing the battle to stop my tears from escaping.

"We need to be free."

"You can be. They can be. Just stay with me, stay here in Culhuinn. I'll do whatever you want."

"My people are more important," she said simply. "We will meet again to discuss the plans once you have had time," and without a backwards glance, she left the hall.

My legs stopped supporting me and I crumpled to the floor as the door shut, the love of my life leaving me. I struggled to draw breath as I sobbed.

I should have felt embarrassed, crumpled on the floor, weeping like a selfish child. No doubt the guards outside the door could hear me and thought their Queen was pathetic.

"It's okay," William whispered, pulling me into his lap sometime later.

I clutched the fabric of his shirt, anchoring myself to him as I shed the last of my tears. Nieve had grown strong in our time apart whereas I floundered and failed.

If she no longer loved me, the best I could do was be strong as I helped her escape. If I could not make myself happy, at least I could ensure her happiness.

Eventually, my tears dried and I noticed that William was rocking us gently, patting my back in a soothing rhythm.

"You must think I am hopeless," I whispered.

"I think you are a lonely young woman, forced into a difficult position, one which you have never wanted. I would be more concerned if you weren't upset."

His understanding made me feel less alone.

There was nothing he could do to erase my problems, but his unflinching support made all the difference. So often during the last few months he had proven himself trustworthy and selfless.

My heart still ached at the thought of Nieve leaving, but I felt like I could survive it with William there to hold me up when I could not cope.

I had to help the humans escape.

One day my life would be at an end. I would travel through to the Otherworld, my pain and sorrow erased from this world the moment the life left my body.

A new human kingdom, free from servitude and oppressive fairy rulers would survive for centuries after my death.

Generations of humans, free to live their lives without fear, who was I to deny them that?

I frowned at the roughly drawn map in front of me. The area of land we were allowing the humans to claim was much smaller than what they had asked for. They expected to claim the land running from the border with Wulvendach, all the way to the sea in the east, but we could only offer a small area in the south.

The land included part of the forest, where they could hunt, and access to the large river, which would take them to the loch in the human kingdoms.

Wulvendach would trade with them, they hadn't fought anyone in living memory so we could rest assured that they wouldn't attack.

After discussions with the Lady of our most southern town, who was luckily still up north after the coronation, it became clear that this was the only land we could spare.

The forest down south was home to many fairies whom were not part of any kingdom. They practised their magic as they wished and were completely ignorant of our laws. Adair doubted that they even knew they were part of a kingdom, their lives focused solely to their magic.

We could not ask them to leave their homes, and even if we did, they would fight us for them. We didn't have time for that. Not with Nieve threatening to take the humans and leave as soon as possible.

Once we had the new kingdom mapped out, we had to decide what the humans would be allowed to take south with them. The castle had enough food to feed the hundreds of humans within, so we had to split the food and livestock between our two kingdoms.

The Lady from the south agreed to trade with the humans once they were settled, even offering to aid them in building their first village.

I thanked the Others that their population was relatively small. If there had been more humans it would have been a disaster to organise.

While we worked on the maps and organising the food supplies, William had the job of meeting with humans in the kitchens, the stables, the gardens, the ones who washed the clothes, cleaned the halls, looked after the children, all of them.

He learned that many of those who were old planned to stay. They had lives here in the castle and didn't want to move so late in life.

Fortunately, there were fairies working in each part of the castle, meaning that once the humans left we would be able to survive on our own.

We would all just have to get our hands dirty for a while.

"This will be where you can build your own kingdom," I pointed to the pitifully small area of land Adair had marked on the map.

"That's it?" Nieve looked both baffled and furious.

"The fairies that far south don't listen to the crown," Adair explained, pointing to the depth of the vast forest. "If you tried to take that much land you would need to fight for it. You don't have the strength for that."

Nieve sighed but she agreed with what he was saying. Adair had been teaching the both of us about the kingdoms, and ruling, for years.

For a moment, I wished that King Ferchar was still alive, so he could realise that he had accidentally raised two queens.

"We will not start our new kingdom with a war. We accept the offered land."

She didn't confer with the two guards that were with her again. It seemed that the humans were content to let her lead.

"I will inform the Lairds and Ladies of your new kingdoms shortly, but we will need more time to finish arranging your supplies," I explained, selfishly wishing she hadn't accepted so that we could continue delaying her departure forever.

"Will they accept it?" she asked, looking far too young to have so much to deal with.

"Those we have discussed it with have accepted. The others have no choice," I tried to build up her confidence again.

If anyone could build a new kingdom it was Nieve.

Once she was gone, I returned to my chambers. I was exhausted from the day, first arresting Darach and the Laird and then frantically helping the woman I loved to escape. William left me outside and I made him promise to put someone else on guard that night.

It had been a long day for both of us.

The rain was still pouring down outside and I couldn't wait to curl up in my bed. Sleep would not come easily, but it would be better than nothing.

I had only just shut the door behind me when Mae appeared and threw her arms around me, pulling me in for a hug.

"I am so proud of you," she cried and I was instantly worried. I couldn't ever remember seeing her cry. "You've freed us all."

I couldn't have stopped the sob that escaped me if I'd tried. I had been so caught up, selfishly worrying about Nieve, that I'd forgotten Mae was also a human.

Mae, the woman who had been more of a mother to me than the Queen ever was, she was also leaving.

I truly would be alone. It seemed like nothing I could do would ever stop the Others from punishing me. Mae seemed to realise that I was not crying out of happiness like she was and tried to reassure me.

Just like she always did.

"I am sure she will visit you once everything is settled."

"Will you?"

She pulled back from the hug. I tried to turn away so she wouldn't see me cry, but she didn't let me.

"Will I do what?"

"Will you come back and visit me? Please," I managed to choke out.

She stared at me for a long moment, as if she couldn't believe what I had just asked, before gently taking my face in her hands.

"I have been with you since the day you were born. Not even the Others could make me leave you now."

With that, she pulled me back into her arms and let me cry, this time out of relief rather than sadness.

CHAPTER

35

Morven

"What happened?" I croaked, my throat burning. The last thing I could remember was Glen and I slowly starving to death in a cold stone cell.

Glen was lying on his back beside me so I didn't let myself panic. I was too hungry and exhausted to worry.

Glen laughed bitterly, "you passed out and I lost it. Decided to try and break down the wooden door."

"Did you break it?" I asked, astonished.

"I broke my baby toe but not the door."

"So, how did we get here then? Where even are we?"

"The guards heard me battering the door. Next thing I knew the second Queen of Norbroch opened the door and brought us up here. I think it's a healer's room."

"Oh... that's not very exciting," I frowned, which made Glen laugh again, this time in amusement.

"Aye, it won't make the best story. I'll have to pretend I did break down the door and fight off a dozen guards to free us."

"I'll pretend that I woke up just in time to see the door wrenched off its hinges."

"Thanks Morven." He went silent for a moment, debating whether to speak his mind. "I really thought I'd lost you down there."

I turned onto my side so I could squeeze him tight.

"You can't get rid of me that easily."

Before he could say more, the door opened and the most ethereal fairy I had ever seen entered.

Her hair was white blonde which matched her pale white skin. I hadn't even realised it was possible for people to be paler than us down in Tirwood.

She carried a tray with two wooden bowls of a thin broth and two mugs of weak tea. Wary that this was just another trick, Glen and I made no moves towards the food, despite the smell making my mouth water.

"The food is for you," she said cheerfully. When we still didn't eat, she sighed. "What my sister did to you both was unfair and unjust. I promise that you are no longer prisoners here. Once you have regained enough of your strength, you may leave."

"Your sister?" I asked, confused.

"Queen Euna is my sister, I am Queen Aelwen," she explained patiently.

I glanced at Glen who looked just as confused as I was. It made no sense. Why would one Queen try to starve us to death, only for the other Queen to free us and brings us food?

Without wasting another moment, we ate our broth. Hunger winning over the fear that it was a trick. I couldn't tell what was in the broth as I ate so fast I barely tasted it.

When I was finished, I felt my face burn with embarrassment. I'd managed to spill broth down my chin and all over my shift.

The Queen hurried over with a damp cloth and gently washed my face. I stiffened nervously as she approached, but soon relaxed under her care.

"I have three children of my own. I am used to cleaning up after messy eaters," she smiled.

Once I was clean, and Glen had finished his broth at a much more reasonable pace, she brought us clean clothes from the wooden chest in the corner of the room. She instructed us to change into them and then leave our dirty clothes in a basket to be collected for washing.

"I'll send a healer in to you soon. Once you are both rested and recovered we can try and find you the answers you seek."

With that she was gone, leaving Glen and I feeling baffled but oddly reassured.

How could she be Queen Euna's sister? The two couldn't be more different.

I wondered what she knew about the changelings here in the north. A queen, who'd happily wash broth from a stranger's face, didn't seem like someone who would allow hundreds of human babies to be stolen from their homes.

"Nothing makes sense up here." Glen grumbled, and I couldn't help but agree.

Nighean was a gifted fairy who could use her magic to heal. It took a lot of gentle coaxing from her, and nagging from me before, Glen agreed to let her heal him further.

His fingers and knuckles were bruised and cut after his fight with the door. After a few moments of Nighean holding his hands the bruises receded and the cuts closed over. She then straightened his baby toe and, with a crack that made me jump, she mended the break.

"Can you heal everything?" I asked, awestruck.

"Humans are easy to heal, but there is nothing I can do for fatal wounds, poison or serious sickness. A few cuts and a broken toe is easy work," she explained with a smile, looking very pleased with herself.

"Are fairies difficult to heal?" Glen asked, once he got over the shock of his bone snapping back into place.

"Well, it's not that humans are simple, it is just that we fairies are made of much more complex magic. It takes a lot more energy for me to heal a fairy toe than it does to heal a human toe. That is the just the way the Others made us."

Much to my disappointment, another healer had healed much of my sickness while I was unconscious. I'd be feeling braw once I had more to drink and gained back a bit of weight, apparently. This meant that we didn't get to see how her magic worked on changelings.

"Do you heal many humans?" I asked.

If I couldn't see how fairy magic worked on changelings, I could at least try to get some information from her. As a healer, she would know all about the humans here in the north.

My excitement was short lived.

"Oh no, you two are the first," she said, tapping Glen reassuringly on the leg and standing up. "You are the first humans to step foot in Norbroch in a decade."

The first humans in a decade.

Nothing made sense anymore.

I didn't know why King Ferchar sent us north into Norbroch, or why Queen Euna hated us so much. Once we were alone I voiced my confusion.

"If there hasn't been a human here in over a decade, where do the human babies go?" I complained, frowning so hard my head began to ache.

"I have no idea, but I think it's time we get some answers from the Queens."

We spent the next few days recovering from our imprisonment. As the days passed our appetites increased and soon we were managing to eat proper meals without feeling sick.

The Queens agreed to meet us and so a few evenings later Nighean returned. She helped us dress in new clothes which were much finer than anything I had ever worn before.

I had a dark navy dress and a thick knitted cardigan to keep me warm. Glen looked like a prince with his dark grey clothes, complete with a knitted jumper. He was even given a leather belt for his dagger, which was returned to him when we were given our belongings.

We were meeting with the Queens for an evening meal and apparently, our travelling clothes were inappropriate. Nighean had burst out laughing at the thought of us wearing them to dinner.

"If only your ma could see you dressed all fancy," I teased gently as we walked through the halls.

"If only your Finnian could see you," Glen winked suggestively, to which I blushed and aimed a kick at his shins.

"We have more important things to think about than him," I scolded, trying to stop my traitorous mind from remembering his tattoos, and our kisses.

"We can think about him once we've survived dinner with the fairy who tried to starve us to death," Glen laughed, humourlessly.

As we followed a fairy through the halls I admired the intricately carved wooden furniture. The castle was smaller than the one in Culhuinn, but no less grand.

Remembering what Nighean said, I was on the lookout for any signs of other humans, but from what I could see everyone who lived and worked in the castle was a fairy. Each fairy we passed did a double take, as if they couldn't believe they were seeing two humans in Norbroch.

All too soon, we arrived at the hall and the door was opened by the guard who had imprisoned us not long ago.

Glen grabbed my arm to halt my progress and I stood awkwardly as he glared at the guard. My gaze wandered between the two of them, the tension growing more and more uncomfortable the longer he glared. It was strange to see Glen holding a grudge. Usually he was the first to forgive anyone for their wrongdoings.

Eventually the guard spoke and eased the tension enough for Glen to release my arm.

"You are here for dinner, not to be imprisoned." The guard said, never breaking eye contact with Glen.

"How can I trust you?" Glen demanded.

It was as if they had forgotten I was there.

"I give you my word that neither of you will be imprisoned this evening."

Glen paused for a moment, perhaps like me he realised how ominous that promise was.

We would not be thrown back into that cell tonight, but would be find ourselves back there tomorrow?

"Your word means nothing to me."

With that Glen pushed his way past the guard and headed into the hall. I could hear Queen Aelwen inside, her chair scraping against the stone as she stood to greet him.

Glen and I were both understandably upset about being starved half to death, but it looked as if he held this guard personally responsible for what happened to us.

"You had better join them."

Queen Aelwen met me at the door and quickly ushered me to a seat beside Glen. The guard, whom I remembered Queen Euna had called Tormod, entered the room as well but remained at the door. Thankfully out of Glen's line of sight.

I didn't want him starting a fight, not with the two Queens in the room. That would surely land us both back in the cell.

Queen Aelwen took a seat across from me and her sister Queen Euna was sat across from Glen.

"To prevent us from being interrupted I had the servants prepare a small meal, rather than have them bring in multiple courses. I hope you do not mind," Queen Aelwen explained.

The table before us was filled with all sorts of food. We could have fed both Glen and I's families with the food on this table. The thought made me feel oddly guilty.

The conversation flowed easily as we made a start on the food. Queen Aelwen was eager to learn all about our travels and our village back home.

Glen tried to remain aloof and angry, but the temptation to tell his stories to a new set of eager ears was too much to resist. Queen Euna remained silent throughout, sipping occasionally at the soup in front of her.

"We promised you answers, so let us not waste any more time," Queen Aelwen eventually said.

This was the moment I had been waiting for since we left the village. The chance to finally find out why the fairies steal our babies, and what they do to them.

The chance to find out if I could save my life, and the lives of the countless other changelings scattered throughout the human kingdoms.

All of our travelling and suffering had led to this moment, and I found myself completely lost for words.

"How about you start by telling us why you travelled to Norbroch?" Queen Aelwen said after a few uncomfortable moments of silence. "You may speak freely. There will be no consequences for your words," she added, noting our nervous glances towards the silent Queen beside her.

"King Ferchar told us that we would find answers here in Norbroch. That here in the north a gifted fairy creates changelings to replace the babies you steal. He told us that you keep the humans and use them, for unknown reasons," I took a shaky breath. "You're the reason that I'm going to die and you're the reason that hundreds of humans are dead."

There was silence after my outburst and I feared that I had overstepped. My plan had been to simply tell them what the King had told us, but instead I found myself blaming them for the deaths of so many children and fighting back tears.

Glens hand found mine and gave it a reassuring squeeze. I'd said what needed to be said. I would not apologise.

"King Ferchar has lied to you about many things," Queen Aelwen said sadly, her sister beside her remained silent, though she looked livid.

"So, you don't have the answers we are looking for?" Glen questioned as my heart sank.

"Here in Norbroch there are no changelings and there are no humans," she explained. "Despite this, I do not think your journey has been pointless. It seems that the

King has given you the answers you seek, shrouded in lies."

"Explain." Glen said bluntly.

"The idea that there is a fairy gifted with the power to create new life, and so able to create changelings, is reasonable. We have never seen a gift such as that here in Norbroch, but that does not mean it does not exist. The King must have found the only fairy with this gift."

"We met a man in Tirwood who could bring flowers back to life," I explained, suddenly remembering the man in the inn all those weeks ago.

"We have fairies here in Norbroch with similar gifts, who help ensure that our crops grow well, if the Others will it of course."

"So, King Ferchar steals human babies and his gifted fairy makes changelings to replace them. What does he do with the humans he steals?"

"Ten years ago, the royals from Culhuinn visited us and with them they brought over a hundred human servants, each of them only just clothed and fed well enough to ensure that they worked," Aelwen explained sadly.

It was beginning to dawn on me just how badly we had been tricked.

"Why would he send us here?" Glen asked while I slumped forward, resting my head in my hands.

"He once killed a human who was... very close to us. He saw your innocence and took advantage of how little you knew about our two kingdoms. Sending you here in the hope that it would anger us."

King Ferchar's plan to anger the Queen had worked perfectly, but I didn't dare voice that thought.

Queen Euna looked ready to murder someone and I hoped that it wouldn't be me or Glen. Looking back at our time in Culhuinn, it was so clear that the King was toying with us.

After our encounter with Swift, we should have realised then that something wasn't right. It hit me just how foolish our whole journey had been.

Glen and I knew nothing about these fairy kingdoms. We'd barely manage to survive as we travelled and didn't even know where we were going most of the time.

Our journey had been for nothing. We knew who was creating the changelings, and why, but that meant nothing.

Not when we could do nothing to stop it.

CHAPTER

36

Freya

Mae was helping me change when a serving girl, whom I often saw cleaning the hallways outside my chambers, ran in looking terrified.

"My Queen, the humans, they're leaving." She exclaimed, looking horrified.

Just as she finished speaking we became aware of raised voices outside. My chambers overlooked the front of the castle and when we looked out I understood her horror.

Hundreds of humans were heading towards the gates where a patrol of guards had gathered, their swords and weapons aimed towards the humans.

As we watched, the first few humans charged at the fairies and then, the fighting began. It became hard to distinguish between humans and fairies as blood was shed and people began to fall.

I wondered why the guards were fighting the humans until I it dawned on me that I had not yet told the kingdom of our plans. The guards assumed that the humans were still our servants and would no doubt hack through them all for trying to leave.

I'd never given them new instructions and so they were doing whatever the sadistic King Ferchar had told them to do in such a situation.

I was a fool, and now people were dying for it.

William shouting my name and shaking my shoulders made me realise that I had frozen.

Standing idly, watching as people died right outside my window. The pained look on his face made my heart race. I pulled myself out of his grip and headed for the door.

As I ran through the halls, I realised that I was still in my thin shift and hadn't even stopped to put shoes on. The stone floors hurt my feet as I ran but I hurried on.

From the window, it had been difficult to see any faces, but the thought of Nieve being one of the humans struck down made me stumble and collide painfully with the wall. William helpfully shoved me forward, not allowing me to stop.

"Tell your guards," I shouted to him as we reached the main hallway. The last thing we needed was more guards rushing in to join the fight.

The looks on the faces of the fairies I passed would have been amusing, was I not hurrying to stop the slaughter of hundreds of innocent humans. What must they think of me running through the halls with my hair loose, practically naked for the whole castle to see.

A few fairies tried to shout and tell what was happening but I ignored them. When I reached the main doors, the doormen tried to stop me.

"There is a fight occurring outside my Queen," one of them told me, doing his best to avert his eyes.

"The humans are free to go. Open the door!"

The scene in the courtyard had worsened considerably in the time it took me to run through the halls. There were screams of anger and pain echoing all around and I could see numerous bodies strewn across the stone.

I pushed past the guards blocking the other side of the door and rushed into the crowd.

My feet slipped on the stones which were now wet with blood in many places. The fight continued as if I was not there. No one noticed one more body amongst the masses.

I grabbed the arm of a fairy next to me, stopping him from stabbing the human he held by the hair.

"Stop." I screeched, to which he laughed and made to continue.

I grabbed onto the blade, trying to ignore the way it sliced my palm and fingers. I was only just strong enough to stop him from driving the blade into the human's soft belly.

"I am your Queen," I shouted and I was glad to see the realisation pass across his face.

He quickly let go of the dagger and the human before backing away, glancing with horror at my bleeding hand.

"The humans are free to leave, under my orders. Tell the other fairies now," I gestured at his fellow guards, still fighting around us.

He hurried to do as I asked, pulling his companions away from the humans.

Fighting the urge to sob at the pain in my hand, I continued on through the crowd. The dead and injured I passed made me heave.

There was so much blood.

As I approached the gates, I realised that I didn't have a plan. I just needed to stop this somehow.

I needed the fairies to see me and listen. To stop their attack.

I was knocked to the ground by one of those guards, my face colliding painfully with the stones. When she turned me onto my back I felt blood running from my nostrils.

"My Queen," she gasped in shock, aborting her attempt to strangle the life from me.

"Stop your fellow guards. The humans are free to leave," I spat blood from my mouth as I scrambled to my feet.

She looked at me in disbelief until I screamed at her to go.

The fighting was thickest near the gates so I hurried forward. I was knocked to the ground by oblivious fighters so many times that I gave up and crawled the rest of the distance.

The guards at the gate looked horrified to see their Queen appear in the middle of a fight, wearing nothing but a muddy shift, bleeding in multiple places.

"The humans are free to leave," I called as loud as I could. "Stop the fight."

Thankfully they were guards William knew and so hurried to obey my command, throwing themselves into the middle of fights. Ripping humans and fairies away from each other.

I turned to face the devastation behind me, four guards in amongst hundreds wasn't enough.

Half of the people in this courtyard would be dead before the message spread far enough. The humans were good at fighting that much was obvious, but they hadn't the stamina or strength and would soon weaken.

If I didn't stop this fight it would be a bloodbath.

My heart pounded as I struggled to take slow breaths through my mouth and fight down the panic which threatened to overwhelm me. My nose was still bleeding freely down my face.

I put a hand against the wooden gate to steady myself and was struck with an idea.

The wooden gate had horizontal beams which could easily be climbed. A surprisingly awful design for a gate, but just what I needed to make myself noticed.

I whimpered as I used my hands, one of them deeply cut, to pull myself up onto the gate. My arms trembled as I pulled myself up two, then three beams, until I could see over the heads of everyone in the courtyard.

"Stop." I screamed as loud as I could.

Those nearest me noticed and stopped to stare in confusion.

"The humans are free to leave."

My voice cracked as I tried desperately to make myself heard.

Those who heard me hurried to obey, calming down those fighting and dragging the injured out of further harm's way.

"I command you to stop," I cried desperately, as loud as I could manage, breathless from panic.

My throat burned so fiercely that I wasn't sure I could shout again. More noticed my cry and, from this height, I could see gaps appearing in the crowd where my guards had successfully managed to disperse fights.

A sudden wailing drone from a set of pipes made me flinch and almost lose my grip.

William appeared on the steps and with him, a piper. The reason became clear as many stopped their fights to look towards the noise in surprise.

"The humans are free to go, Queen Freya orders you to stop this fight," he shouted, his voice carrying across the courtyard now that the screaming and clash of swords had lessened.

He gestured towards the gate, where I held on weakly, and suddenly all eyes were on me.

"The humans are free," I said faintly, my voice a hoarse whisper.

At those words, there were cries of happiness and joy from the humans all around me. I could see them crying and hugging, ecstatic that they could now leave Culhuinn behind forever.

It was impossible to tell how many were injured or dead from here, there didn't seem to be as many bodies as my panicked mind had imagined.

I let go of the gate, too exhausted to climb back down, and collapsed in a heap at the base.

My palm and fingers burned, and my nose throbbed painfully with every beat of my heart. My feet were bleeding and dirty, as were my knees. My shift was torn and disgusting where before it had been crisp, white and fresh.

Despite doing nothing but rush through a crowd, I felt as if I had battled through a whole army on my own. I couldn't muster up the will to move.

The guards from earlier returned, glancing at each other in alarm. Unsure what to do about their bloody, dirty Queen who was slumped beneath the gate.

"Open the gate," I whispered and so they busied themselves with that and left me alone.

Arms wrapped around my chest and carried me away from the crowds, into the stables. I expected to see William but instead it was Nieve.

Her face was splattered with blood, as if she had stabbed or slashed someone. It mixed with the dark blue woad she had around her eye and smeared down her face.

She propped me up against the wall and then sighed at the state of me.

"Look at you," she said unhappily, using her sleeve to try and wipe some of the blood away from my mouth.

"Look at you," I whispered back.

"Free." She laughed, tears brimming in her eyes. "Thank you."

"Leaving me," I was unable to stop my lips quivering pathetically.

I was already covered in mud and blood. Why not add tears to the mix? My appearance would portray how battered and broken I truly felt.

"Hey," she attempting to wipe my tears away. "You are okay. We are okay."

She rested her warm comforting hand on my cheek and I reached for the dagger in her belt.

It was bloody and I felt sickened at the thought of her having to defend herself with it.

Nieve watched me curiously, absentmindedly rubbing her thumb across my cheek, as I held onto the blade and offered her the hilt.

"Do this for me." I whispered, feeling strengthened by my decision.

She wrapped her other hand around the hilt, looking completely bemused.

"Do what Freya?" She asked in a whisper, my tears continued to fall silently down my face.

To die with Nieve smiling at me for the first time in months, knowing that I had set her free. It was perfect. I gave the dagger a tug in the direction of my chest to explain what I wanted her to do.

A blade through the heart from the woman who owned my heart.

The moment she understood what I wanted her beautiful smile faded. She let go of the dagger. Letting it fall with a clatter to the stable floor.

She took my head between her hands and pressed our foreheads together. I could feel her shaky breath against my lips and longed for her to close the gap between us.

"Freya no," her voice was thick with emotion. "Please."

Before I could plead, her hands were in my hair and she finally closed the distance between us.

The kiss was slow and made my eyes sting with tears as her nose brushed painfully against my own broken one.

This kiss would be the last time the two of us would ever share our love again, and we knew it.

We took our time, conveying the love we had been unable to share for months through our bodies.

Eventually, she pulled away from me and I let my hands drop from around her neck.

"Be strong for me," she pleaded, placing one last kiss on my lips and leaving the stables.

I sat there alone for what could have been hours. My lips tingling from the kiss.

Outside I could hear the hooves of horses, and the livestock which we'd arranged for the humans to take south. Adair and William must have joined the humans, helping them organise their departure now that the fight was over.

I could hear laughter outside the stable and the sound of children, running and playing as they went.

By now, my nose had stopped bleeding and the cuts on my hand were only bleeding sluggishly from the deepest areas. My throat still ached from my earlier screaming. I resisted the temptation to cry again, giving in to my heartbreak would not help me.

The door of the stables creaked open and William appeared with a worried looking Mae.

"Nieve said you were here," he explained as they wrapped a warm cloak around my shoulders. "It seems some of the humans weren't prepared to wait for their new leader to organise their departure, decided they'd risk fighting their way out instead."

Mae fussed and tried to make me drink water. Doing her best to clean the blood from me, obviously remembering my reaction to the beheading months ago.

"Mae stop, let's get her inside first." William said, lifting me up into his arms.

I expected the courtyard to be like something from my nightmares, with rivers of blood flowing across the stones, piles of bodies and weeping children.

Instead, the courtyard that greeted me couldn't have been more different.

There were bodies, covered with blankets to hide them from view, but only a handful. The castle's healers, and those gifted with healing magic, were loading injured humans up into wagons.

It seemed that, once the fairies saw me declaring that the humans were free, they accepted it. Helping them leave as if they were visitors journeying back home.

It scared me that I had the power to change their actions so drastically.

I couldn't see Nieve anywhere in the courtyard but I assumed that she would remain until everyone had been sent on their way south.

William mentioned that he had spoken with her earlier so I guessed he knew about my request. My desire to die faded as the rush of panic from the fight settled.

I was glad that Nieve had refused.

If he did know, he did not mention it. Not even when we were back in my chambers and Mae was distracted, giving instructions to the remaining servant girls.

It was for the best that I did not see Nieve again.

Better that I did not watch her ride away from Culhuinn, and me, for I knew that sight would haunt my dreams until the day I died.

CHAPTER

37

Euna

Aelwen continued to insist that the humans joined us for meals, even introducing them to Ronan and the children. I could not understand why she did not send them back down south as soon as they had their answers. Though seeing them become steadily less gaunt and sickly was helping to ease my guilt.

The humans had made no comment about their imprisonment and starvation, but I knew that they thought of it each time they looked at me, especially Glen. I still could not believe what I had done.

Aelwen tried to reassure me, blaming my actions on grief and anger, but we both knew it did not justify the suffering I caused.

Other than Aelwen striking me, there had been no punishment for my actions. Though meals with Morven and Glen night after night felt like a punishment.

I took no part in their conversations, simply listening as Aelwen shared stories about our kingdom and the fairies. The human, Glen, in turn shared stories about the humans and the ridiculous rumours that they believed about us here in the north.

I watched as their cheeks flushed red while they laughed and drank, counted their freckles and thought of my love. How different this would be with Lachlann by my side.

It would have been easy to slip away into my memories, but I forced myself to listen.

I held onto the hope that, when I passed into the Otherworld, I would find Lachlann there waiting for me. I would share all I had learned about the humans when I got to him.

Teach him everything he should have known. Everything he would have known, had he not been murdered.

I was making my way through a bowl of broth, listening to Glen talk about their encounter with the enchantress in the forest, when the door opened and a messenger entered.

It was not the usual messenger from Wulvendach or someone from Selport bringing news of the selkies, which meant that the news was from Culhuinn.

I dropped my spoon back into the bowl, splattering broth all over the table.

"What news do you bring?" Aelwen demanded.

The messenger looked at the humans anxiously but Aelwen nodded for him to speak anyway.

This was the first direct contact Culhuinn had made with Norbroch since they stabbed Lachlann through the chest and left him bleeding to death in my arms.

To hide my shaking hands, I clenched the table so hard I felt a nail split and break.

"King Ferchar is dead, poisoned at his table. The Queen is also dead. Princess Freya survived the attempt on her life and now rules as the Queen of Culhuinn," he said hurriedly.

There was a moment of stillness. Tormod, who was usually good at concealing his emotions, looked completely astounded. The humans were glancing between us and the messenger nervously whilst Aelwen seemed completely lost for words.

Slumping back down in my seat I let out a burst of laughter so loud and hysterical that it made Morven jump.

King Ferchar was dead.

The thought made me laugh again. Oh, it felt so good to truly laugh for the first time in a decade. Tears begin to stream down my face as I laughed and I laughed.

He was dead.

"Euna!" I heard Aelwen shout and when I opened my eyes she was in front of me, shaking me gently by the shoulders.

"He is dead," I whispered, my speech interrupted by sobs.

When had I stopped laughing and started sobbing?

She guided my head forward until she was cradling it against her stomach and let me cry. I heard Tormod hurrying the humans, and the messenger, out of the hall but I did not care what they saw.

Finally, the man who killed the love of my life was dead. I hoped that the poison had brought him a slow and painful death.

I hoped that the Others would remember all that he had done when he arrived in the Otherworld. That they would make him suffer for what he did to Lachlann.

"Let's get you up to your chambers," Aelwen said eventually, brushing my hair out of my face and placed a kiss on my forehead.

Tormod must have told Ronan about the state I was in, for he came hurrying into the hall. Together they half guided and half carried me up to my chambers. From there they helped me dress for bed and tucked me under the covers as if I was one of their children.

I had expected to feel joyous at the death of the man I hated most, and for a moment I had. Rather than drinking and dancing until the sun rose, I felt drained. Like I had climbed a mountain and had nothing left to give. My hatred for King Ferchar had been the only thing holding me together all these years.

"Sleep well," Aelwen whispered. "You can find peace now that he is dead, knowing that the Others will punish him for what he did."

I nodded, curling myself up into a ball under the thick blankets, watching the shadows flicker in the candlelight.

Although we knew that the Others created life and helped protect our crops and livestock, little was known about the Otherworld. We knew that when you died you travelled to the Otherworld, leaving your bones behind. However, no one knew what you would find once you got there.

I wanted to imagine the awful things that would happen to the King now that he was dead, but I found no joy in it.

I just hoped that somehow Lachlann could find a way to get revenge. That perhaps he could rest easier, knowing that the fairy who killed him no longer drew breath.

The pain of losing Lachlann lingered, but it became easier to live without retreating into my memories. I still remembered Lachlann every day. His smile, his laugh, our love. They would stay with me always.

Aelwen and I stood watching as her children showed Glen and Morven around the sparse garden at the back of the castle, near to where festivals were held.

The Princesses, Elspie and Aoife, were having the time of their lives, pointing out flowers and making up facts as they went along. There was very little of note out here, but they were still managing to make the tour drag on. Prince Elath was shy around the humans, so was content to silently follow them with his father.

The humans were good with the children, and I remembered Morven mentioning that she had two nieces back home in their village.

We were steadily heading into summer now. The Others clearly wanted the two humans to see every inch of the garden as there was not a single cloud in the sky and no sign of rain, for once.

I felt oddly fragile since receiving the news of King Ferchar's death. The hatred I had spent ten years running on had finally burnt out.

As that hatred burned out, it cauterized the wound that Lachlann's death had left behind. Finally allowing me to begin healing.

"What shall we do now?" I asked Aelwen, who was smiling, watching her children gesture wildly at trees as if the humans had never seen one before.

"I think perhaps it is time we visit Culhuinn."

"Surely you are not taking the children?"

"Not the children, I mean you and me. Perhaps it is time you leave this castle."

"Do you think it is safe?"

My stomach twisted at the thought of leaving Norbroch after so many years. Rather than answering she turned to Tormod, who was also watching the humans.

"Did the messenger tell you anything about the new Queen?"

"The messenger believed that change is coming to Culhuinn, he told me that this new Queen is unlike her father in every way. It was well known that there was no love between the two of them, especially in recent years." Tormod explained.

Tormod may not have been gifted by the Others, but he was still very skilled. Without having to resort to torture or blackmail he could gain information from people without them realising.

People were always happy to share news with him so he made sure to have a thorough conversation with every messenger who arrived in Norbroch.

"Do you think it's safe?" I repeated, unsure which answer I was hoping for.

"There is no such thing as safety," he said dramatically, which made Aelwen laugh. "However, I do think we would survive a journey south. This Queen Freya seems less quick to anger than her father."

"I think it would be beneficial to pay the new Queen a visit. We can fix the relations between our two kingdoms once and for all. Whilst we are there we can try to prevent any more human children being stolen, for Lachlann," Aelwen said, and Tormod nodded in agreement.

We went back to silently watching the children and the humans. Glen was now demonstrating his cartwheels to the two girls and the sight was almost enough to startle a laugh from me.

My palms grew sweaty at the thought of leaving Norbroch for Culhuinn, but if I could stop humans from going through what Lachlann did then it would be worth it.

I wanted to see where he lived and worked his whole life. My desire to connect with his early life was much stronger than my fear.

I could tell that Aelwen and Tormod were waiting for my answer and soon I had to break the silence.

"I think we should go," I blurted out before I could change my mind.

Aelwen wrapped her arm around my shoulders. "We won't let anything or anyone harm you."

CHAPTER

38

Morven

To our surprise, Queen Aelwen announced that we would all be heading south to Culhuinn. Beside her at the table Queen Euna was as stony faced, although for once, instead of looking like she was silently simmering with rage, she looked worried.

As if it was eating away at her, distracting her from everything else.

Queen Aelwen explained that with the King and Queen of Culhuinn dead, and Queen Freya now ruling, it was the perfect time to find answers. Possibly even put a stop to the creation of the changelings.

The last time we saw the new Queen Freya she was sitting silently across the table from us. I could not imagine what she would be like as a Queen.

I was excited that finally Glen and I might find the answers we had been searching for, and in doing so save my life. We'd wasted so much time as King Ferchar sent us on a wild goose chase into Norbroch.

I was eager to finally leave this kingdom, and the constant gut churning fear that Queen Euna would decide to imprison us again, forever.

Every step south would take us closer to returning to our village. I longed to see my family again, but I could not dwell on it or else I would cry. I knew Glen felt the same and was desperate to return, especially after his emotional outburst when we were locked in the cell.

The days between the announcement that we would travel south, and us actually leaving to travel south, were long and torturous.

For both Queens to leave the kingdom, plans had to be put in place, which took days. Then food had to be prepared and packed, to ensure that the Queens did not go hungry, and finally they had to pack their belongings and pick which guards would be escorting them on their journey.

Glen informed me that their guard Tormod would be joining us and I could not tell if he was happy or sad about that. After our imprisonment, he seemed to blame Tormod personally, as well as Queen Euna.

He acted like he loathed him, yet he often spoke to him, and told me all about the stories they shared. I had no clue what to think about the two of them.

When we did finally leave the castle behind I was ecstatic. Unlike our journey into Norbroch, we were leaving with full bellies, warm clothes and protection all around us.

The journey seemed to go much faster with company and guides who actually spoke with us. They were eager to point out farms and distant villages which we had missed on our journey north.

As we travelled I could not help but look over my shoulder, just waiting for the moment Swift would come charging over the hill, ready to kill us.

"He will be long gone," Glen tried to reassure me.

We were sitting down for a quick meal and allowing the horses to rest. I had still not mastered riding a horse, but fortunately we travelled at a much slower pace with so many guards and servants alongside us.

Glen went to relieve himself and I almost jumped out of my skin when he returned, thinking he was Swift ready to attack.

"He could be anywhere," I said, feeling shaken. "Hiding in the hills watching us."

"I'll tell Tormod that you're worried, he has guards riding ahead to scout out the landscape and look for danger. If Swift was waiting to attack us they would see him."

"I thought you hated Tormod?" I accused gently, wanting to change the subject.

"He fascinates me. It's not every day you get to speak to a fairy and he is more honest than the Queens. Less formal," he explained and I supposed that it made sense.

Glen had been obsessed with the fairies since we were children. From the very moment he heard about the fairies in the north, with their magical powers and grand castles, he was hooked. Of course he would take the opportunity to speak to a fairy and learn all he could about them.

I felt a little better, knowing that the guards were on the lookout for Swift, but I wasn't sure I'd get a good night's sleep until we reached Culhuinn.

We paused for the night, just outside the valley, and I tried my best not to look at the dark, ominous path we would have to travel along in the morning.

Instead, I went off in search of Glen. He had ridden ahead as we travelled and then, in the chaos of setting up camp and getting fires lit, I could not find him.

I tried to tell myself that he was simply lost, but all I could imagine was Swift strangling him. I clambered over the dark jagged rocks, to the spot where Glen and I had planned to sleep for the night, and almost fell to my death in surprise.

Glen had Tormod pushed up against one of the rocks and they were kissing enthusiastically.

An embarrassingly loud gasp escaped me before I could stop it, which made Tormod flinch and begin to push Glen away. Glen simply grinned and gently placed his hands to either side of Tormod's hips.

"I'm sorry. I didn't mean to gasp so loud." I apologised, probably bright red with embarrassment.

It wasn't like I'd never seen two people kiss before.

"It's understandable. I imagine we are quite the sight," Glen said with a weird look on his face that I assumed was supposed to be flirty.

"Why didn't you tell me?" I demanded, surprised by my own anger.

"This is only our second kiss Morven."

"You still should have told me," I complained. The thought of us keeping secrets from each other made my stomach ache.

We were on this adventure together, so far away from home. We were supposed to be a team.

Glen must have heard the hurt in my voice as his expression lost its smug flirty look.

"I promise to tell you about everyone I kiss from now on," he said seriously, to which Tormod laughed. "Although it might just be Tormod for a while."

"Thanks," I mumbled, now angry at myself for not noticing this blossoming romance before. "I'll leave you to it then."

I clambered back over the rocks and headed back to the main camp. Queen Aelwen was sitting beside one of the fires and called me over with a wave the moment she spotted me, stomping through the damp grass.

I hurried over and sat myself down beside her on the blanket, the warmth of the fire making me feel cosier instantly. Another reason I could not wait to pass through the valley and reach Culhuinn was that it was much warmer.

They kept talking about it being summer, but it was nothing like the summers we had down in the village. Summer didn't usually involve so much frost. I would take a few days of rain over this icy summer any day.

"I take it you spotted Tormod and Glen?" She teased which made me sigh.

Why was I the only person who didn't know?

"So, everyone knows?" I complained, to which she gave a soft laugh.

"Tormod has only ever shown romantic interest in a handful of men since the day I met him, and he began working for us when he was young. Much too young. I noticed his feelings towards Glen the moment they blossomed."

"Glen didn't even bother to tell me," I found myself complaining.

Something about Queen Aelwen made me want to share my problems, like I had with Eithrig in Tirwood.

"New love is exciting, especially when it is a secret. I am sure he would have told you soon enough. The friendship the two of you share is a rare gift, and I think you know that."

"I can't help but feel annoyed anyway," I grumbled.

"They are a good pair, though it will be short-lived. Let them have their romance whilst they can. I know only too well how quickly it can be ripped away," her gaze drifted over to Queen Euna, watching as she approached us.

"Lovely evening, is it not?" She asked, to which Queen Euna nodded.

Her expression making it clear that she thought this evening was anything but lovely.

Although I still hated her for locking Glen and I away, I could not help but feel sorry for her. Her sobs the day we heard that King Ferchar was dead, and her obvious fear of travelling south, made me pity her. I also knew we were partially to blame.

It had only taken one meal for the King to convince us that Norbroch was responsible for the changelings.

Perhaps if Glen and I had thought more about the humans we saw in Culhuinn, or paid attention the King and his amusement, we could have saved the Queen, and ourselves, a whole world of grief.

We made it through the valley without a problem. With so much company to distract me I worried less about the stone walls toppling in and crushing us.

I did not spot Glen and Tormod kissing again, perhaps because in the valley there were no places to find privacy.

As Glen and I had huddled together by a fire, finding a rare moment alone, I admitted a thought that was plaguing me the longer we went without spotting Swift.

"I think I killed him," I whispered as quietly as I could. As if admitting it would make it more real.

"Well he bloody deserved it if you did.," Glen said, to which I frowned.

I wasn't sure anyone deserved to die, and it certainly wasn't for us to decide who lived and who didn't.

"Do you think the Others will punish me for it?"

He frowned at me for a moment, before hauling me up into his lap and hugging me close.

I buried my face in his neck and let myself relax into his hold, safe in his arms.

"If you hadn't hit him with that rock we would both be dead. Swift chose to try and kill me that day, unlike you. You chose to save me and the Others know it as well as I do," he murmured, ignoring the tears he must have felt on his neck.

After the valley, it was a short ride south to the town and the castle. It was warm enough that we could finally take off our thick cloaks and scarves.

All around us wildflowers blossomed in the warmer weather and to the south I could see the forest where we were enchanted.

As I rode beside Glen, the two of us content to stay silent and watch the sun sink lower in the sky, I let myself feel optimistic.

We were so close to finding the answers we'd been searching for. So close to saving me from an early death. Each step the horse beneath me took brought us closer and closer to home.

CHAPTER

39
Freya

Now that the majority of the humans had left Culhuinn, travelling south to build their own kingdom and live a life of freedom, things were very different in the castle.

Drummond and I had discussed at length how many human servants we had and how much work they did for us, but still, we were unprepared for the sudden workload thrust upon us all.

I was busy sending messengers back and forth to the Lairds and Ladies, informing them of the humans' freedom and their new kingdom. Some responded with anger and others with indifference. I could easily tell which households the King had been close to as they were the ones infuriated by the news.

Laird Brochan's son, Tomas, had sent many messengers, each more demanding than the last. Urging me to make him Laird now that his father was imprisoned. My reply was always the same, William's brother Urraig was the new Laird.

As Laird Brochan had never chosen an heir, Tomas had no claim to the land. He had been persistent in the past, urging me to visit him. Having something to complain about had, unfortunately, only increased that persistence.

William, Adair and Drummond had been lifesavers after the departure of the humans. I was sore for a few days after the struggle in the courtyard, as my body healed my cuts, bruises and broken nose, but soon the physical wounds were gone. All that was left were the emotional wounds.

King Ferchar's death had been liberating and, now that I was not being waited on hand and foot by humans, my days were much busier. Being busy helped me to keep my mind off my pain.

Whenever I felt dark thoughts, like the ones I had in the stable, creeping in I made excuses to spend more time with William. Me remaining alive was important, not only for Culhuinn but for Nieve's new kingdom as well.

The castle did not remain empty for long. Adair suggested that we send messengers to some of the poorest known villages in the kingdom, telling the people that we needed new workers.

This saw many poor families leaving behind their failing farms, and lives of poverty, to work in the castle where they would be fed, clothed, have a roof over their heads and receive coin.

King Ferchar was no doubt rolling in his grave as I slowly but surely tried to heal Culhuinn and right his wrongs.

The arrival of a messenger from Norbroch put a dampener on my new-found contentment. He brought news that the two Queens were heading down to Culhuinn and would be arriving at the castle the next evening.

He could not say why they suddenly wanted to travel south. Though he took great care to ensure that we understood they were not coming to attack.

They simply wanted to speak with the new Queen.

The next evening, I stood out on the stone steps and watched as they rode into the courtyard, which held no traces of the bloodshed, thanks to heavy rain.

Queen Aelwen rode in first, her striking white blonde hair making her instantly recognisable.

I'd once visited Norbroch as a child, and could vaguely remember the Queens. Queen Euna had soot black hair and unlike her sister, who looked cheerful and full of life, she looked gaunt and unhappy.

It was clear that she felt as uneasy about this meeting as I did.

The King had complained loudly and often about the fairies in the north, but without ever explaining why he hated them so much. I hoped to the Others that I wouldn't find out he was right about them.

In amongst the guards I saw two humans, the changeling who looked identical to Nieve and her ginger friend. I backed away a step, bumping into William before I could stop myself.

I distantly remembered a meal with the two humans, that night the King knocked me unconscious and I dreamt of the Queen's Dark festival. King Ferchar had sent them north with lies about the creation of the changelings.

I hoped they weren't here for revenge.

"Welcome to Culhuinn." I called, once they dismounted, and felt William stiffen beside me as I foolishly forgot to address them by their titles.

"Thank you, Queen Freya, it is our pleasure to finally return," Queen Aelwen said, her sister remained silent and stony faced beside her.

"I am afraid you will find us rather understaffed currently. Please forgive any problems you encounter during your stay, your majesties." I made sure to correct my earlier mistake.

"Understaffed?" Queen Aelwen looked apprehensive.

"The human servants of Culhuinn have been released from their roles here. They have been given land in the south, close to the border with the human kingdoms," I explained, amused to watch their expressions of shock. "So, we are currently working to bring in replacements from some of our poorer outlying villages."

"Well, that is a wonderful change," Queen Aelwen exclaimed happily.

The changeling and the human made no moves to hide their frantic whispering, but I let it go. News about their fellow humans would interest them greatly.

I wondered how the changeling girl would react, if she knew that it was the human she replaced who was now ruling the new human kingdom, but I pushed the thought away.

"Indeed, one that will take a lot of getting used to," I smiled before we made our way into the castle.

Queen Aelwen made pleasant conversation as I showed them to their chambers. Her sister followed silently, sticking close to their guard.

It seemed that I was not the only one with a shadow to rely on.

After they had time to settle into their chambers, we met in the hall for a meal. We had no time to prepare a feast, but even without human help we managed to cook up enough food.

The King had only ever trusted fairies to oversee the kitchen and so we still had enough servants left to prepare bread, chicken and chunky vegetable soup for us. There was not a drop of wine in sight, even the thought of it made my stomach cramp. I was avoiding it like the plague.

I took my seat at the head of the table, where the King dropped dead, and William sat to my left. Queen Aelwen had looked delighted about this idea and invited their personal guard, Tormod, to eat with us as well. Though rather than sit beside her, he sat further down the table with the human, Glen.

"It has been years since we last saw you Queen Freya, you have grown into a beautiful young fairy," Queen Aelwen beamed. "We were saddened to hear the news of your mother and father."

"No one in this kingdom was saddened by the death of the King," I said bluntly, to which Glen not so subtly choked on his mouthful of food.

"Well, it seems things have certainly changed for the better since his death," Queen Aelwen replied, not bothered by my bluntness.

"They have." I agreed, spooning some of the soup into my mouth and hoping that the subject would be dropped.

When it became clear that I was not planning to add anything, the Queen finally explained their reasons for visiting Culhuinn. As I predicted, they were not simply here to congratulate me on ascending to the throne.

"King Ferchar sent Morven and Glen up north into Norbroch after filling their heads with lies about us and the creation of the changelings. We are here to learn what you know of this practise."

"The King tricked many people," I said, wanting to put Morven and Glen at ease as the two of them were flushed red with embarrassment.

Seeing Morven sitting there, eating food and attempting to avoid eye contact made my heart stutter.

I could not bear to see her look so embarrassed and uncomfortable in my presence. I had to remind myself constantly that it was not my love sitting at the table.

Nieve was free.

"I assume that, as the human servants have been freed, Culhuinn will no longer be creating changelings?" Queen Euna asked hesitantly, and I realised that I had stopped before I explained.

"Never again." I replied sharply, somewhat offended that she thought I might allow such a thing to happen. "The gifted fairy, who has the power to create the changelings, currently resides in the prison beneath this castle."

A clatter at the bottom of the table made me flinch and when I looked, it was Morven.

She had dropped her spoon and was now attempting to cry quietly into her hands. I panicked, wondering what I could have had said to upset her so much. It was difficult not to see her as Nieve the more upset she became. Glen hurried to comfort her but I could not understand what she was saying.

I wanted to rush down to the bottom of the table and comfort her myself. I wondered if holding her close would feel the same as embracing Nieve.

I looked at William for assistance, but he seemed to be equally as bemused by her crying. Queen Aelwen was the only one watching her fondly.

"I would not worry. It has been a long journey for the two of them," she explained gently.

"Perhaps we should retire to our chambers for the night. We can meet again tomorrow," I suggested, eager to retire back to Mae's care and gather my wits.

Tormod and Glen must have been waiting for me to say that. Mere moments after I finished speaking, they hurried from their seats, whisking Morven off to their chambers.

"Thank you for the meal. It was wonderful," Queen Aelwen thanked us earnestly, as if she had just eaten the best meal of her life.

I wondered if she was genuinely as nice as she seemed, or if it was all an act. How two sisters could be so different, I had no idea.

We left our seats and were making our way to the door when Queen Euna spoke, making me jump in surprise once again. Having new people in the castle made me more anxious than I'd expected.

"Do you know what became of a human called Alasdair? The last I saw him he wore his hair in blonde plaits," she enquired and I felt myself sway on the spot.

For weeks, I had been so busy that I fell into my bed exhausted and slept soundly each night. It had been weeks since I last felt his warm blood pooling around my toes, saw it dripping from my fingertips.

I heard his head hit the ground with a dull thud, and watched it roll towards me in my mind.

"Alasdair was executed by King Ferchar many months ago, your majesty," William explained.

He knew I could not calmly tell the Queen that her acquaintance had been beheaded at my feet.

"I am sad to hear that," Queen Euna said, and the way her voice cracked as she spoke made me believe she truly was.

"He was very dear to us," Queen Aelwen added, reaching out to grip her sister's hand.

"I am sorry," I choked out.

I felt as if someone had thrown open the doors which had been keeping the guilt out. Now the storm was back and I once again found myself caught up in it.

"Oh, it's not your fault," Queen Aelwen hurried to reassure me, taking my hand in her free hand.

"You don't understand. He killed him because of me," I whispered.

How could I sit and share meals with them when I was the one who got their friend executed?

Beside me, William began to object to my confession until Queen Euna who cut him off.

"It is not your fault," she said with more conviction than I had ever heard from her. "One day, you will be able to accept that."

CHAPTER

40

Morven

Unlike the last time we stayed in this castle, Glen and I slept until nearly midday. Last night had been emotional for us both. Our journey north, which had led to us being enchanted, tricked by the King, almost murdered and then imprisoned, was almost over. Now we were exhausted.

Not the good kind of exhaustion, that comes from a hard day's work, but a bone deep tiredness that permeated throughout my whole body and mind.

After learning that Queen Freya had the fairy responsible for creating changelings locked away in her prison, I broke down. I cried out of happiness and sorrow and relief. I was an exhausted, emotional shell of the Morven who left her village just as spring was beginning.

As most of the humans had left Culhuinn and moved south to build their own kingdom, we didn't have to put up with servants waking us and hurrying us out of bed. The servants that remained were far too busy trying to run the castle to bother us, so we were left alone to sleep.

It felt good to relax for a while. To bask in our new-found knowledge that we were no longer racing against time. No longer hurrying north to try and stop any more changelings from being created.

It wasn't until the burden was lifted, that I realised how heavily it had weighed on both of us.

Although Glen joked that it would ruin his stories, it was nice knowing that neither of us were responsible for stopping the fairy that created the changelings. We had simply wandered into the castle and been told about it.

It should have felt like an anti-climactic and disappointing end to our journey, but we were too exhausted to really care.

We were relieved, knowing that never again would a human baby be stolen by fairies and replaced with a changeling.

Never again would a child have to grow up knowing that their life would be cut short. Knowing that, despite their parents' constant reassurances, they were created by magic, not the parents they looked so much like.

We were allowed to spend the day recovering and relaxing. The servant, Mae, who brought us steaming hot water to bathe in, explained that the Queens had been discussing relations between their two kingdoms since breakfast. With King Ferchar dead everything would be improving, not only for us humans, but for the fairies in the north as well.

"The Queen looks better than she did last time we saw her," Glen said from where he lounged on the bed.

I was bathing in the corner of the room, letting the warm water ease my aches and pains.

"She does, it's strange to see her talking. The last time we saw her I wasn't even sure if she could talk."

"It's almost impressive, how one king managed to affect all of our lives, despite us all living in different kingdoms. He damaged so many families, not even his own was spared," Glen mused.

"He was a prick."

A few hours later Tormod appeared. He guided us through the castle to a hall where the Queens, as well as the guard who had sat with Queen Freya, were speaking together.

I watched Glen and Tormod out of the corner of my eye as we walked through the long stone corridors. Neither of them made a move to kiss the other, or act like they were anything more than friends

It looked like their short-lived romance was over now that we were in the castle. It reminded me of Finnian and I, we too had shared kisses then easily parted ways.

"You two look like you slept well," Queen Aelwen said cheerfully.

She did not look as if she had been up since before breakfast, negotiating the relations between two kingdoms, but I supposed she was simply a natural. Ruling came easily to her.

"Yes, thank you," I thanked Queen Freya who simply smiled in response.

It looked as if the morning's discussions had tired her out more, perhaps because she had to deal with Queens who had been ruling for over a decade.

There were a few moments of awkward silence as Glen and I took our seats at the table. Then, not wanting to waste another moment, Queen Aelwen spoke.

"Do you have many prisoners here in Culhuinn?" She inquired.

"The prison currently only holds Laird Brochan and Darach, the gifted fairy," Queen Freya's guard answered. "King Ferchar preferred to execute rather than imprison."

"That does not surprise me," Queen Euna sighed, the first time I'd heard her speak since we arrived.

Clearly after Glen, Tormod and I left the table the previous night, a bond had formed between Queen Freya and Queen Euna.

Perhaps it was their mutual hatred of the late King that had sparked this new friendship. I remained wary of Queen Euna, but I was oddly pleased to see her looking more cheerful.

"We have not questioned either of them since they were imprisoned," Queen Freya admitted and I could understand her reluctance.

"Well, perhaps now is the perfect time to get some answers," Queen Aelwen said, smiling encouragingly at me and Glen.

Not even the thought of questioning fairies, who had ruined lives throughout the human kingdoms, was enough to dull her spirits.

We entered the castle prisons through a door to the side of the chamber. Although Queen Aelwen had suggested it, she and Queen Euna stayed behind, claiming they had no right to question the prisoner of another kingdom.

The guard, whose name was William, led us all down some stone steps, the temperature lowering as we went. I felt Glen grow tenser and tenser as we descended and I realised just how similar it was to the prisons in Norbroch. However, here they did not have an underground river and so the silence was thick and oppressive.

Not caring that we were surrounded by royalty I reached out and grabbed Glen's hand, wanting to remind him that I was there, and that we would be leaving this place.

William led us to a cell near the foot of the stairs. The guard at the door seemed awestruck at the sight of his Queen. I had to bite my lip to stop myself from laughing as he fumbled to open the door and allow us in.

William entered the cell first, with Queen Freya following close behind him. I was about to enter, when I noticed that Glen was not moving. I turned to nag at him to hurry up but the look on his face stopped me.

Even down in the dimly lit prison I could see how pale he was. His posture was tense and he was rhythmically clenching and unclenching his other hand, trying to work up the courage to enter the cell.

It broke my heart to see him so afraid. I floundered, trying to think of something reassuring to say but Tormod beat me to it.

"Glen," he said sharply, rousing Glen from whatever thoughts he was trapped in. "You hold the door."

He pointed to where the door was being held open by the still awestruck guard.

"Make sure it doesn't shut on us," I added, with a look I hoped was encouraging and didn't betray how sad I felt for him.

I knew he wouldn't want my pity.

Glen looked like he might refuse but Tormod cut him off again, knowing what he was going to say.

"I'll stay with Morven and make sure nothing happens," Tormod promised and with that, he gently placed a hand on my back and ushered me into the cell.

I glanced back to see Glen take over the guard's post holding the door.

Unlike our cell in Norbroch, this one had a small wooden bed, a pitcher of water for the prisoner and a few blankets. I couldn't imagine Queen Freya wanting to starve anyone and it made me feel safer, knowing that they treated their prisoners well.

Sat on the bench, allowing his hands to be bound with rope, was the fairy that had ruined the lives of so many humans. The fairy who stole the baby my ma gave birth to and left me in her place.

He was the reason humans all over the land were afraid to leave their new-borns alone. The cause of so much death and grief.

Since learning how changelings were created, I'd expected the fairy responsible to look like something straight out of my worst nightmares. A fairy so evil that even the sight of him would terrify me.

Instead, the fairy before us was a round little man with long spindly fingers. The first thing that popped into my mind was that he almost resembled a toad, which started a laugh from me.

He didn't look frightening at all.

My laugh drew his attention and when he saw me he stood abruptly, pointing his long thin fingers at me with a look of surprise, and hunger.

"It's you!" He cried and I couldn't tell if he was angry or delighted.

He made to hurry towards me but William anticipated it and pushed him back down onto the bench, whilst Tormod pulled me back a few paces.

All eyes in the cell were on me and I hurried to explain myself.

"I've never seen him before in my life!" I exclaimed, feeling my hands beginning to sweat.

There were far too many of us in this cell and I felt my face burning with embarrassment. The tension made me want to grab Glen. run back up the stairs and escape out into the courtyard.

"Explain yourself," William said, in a tone which allowed no arguments.

I found myself wondering what they would do if he didn't explain himself. I couldn't imagine Queen Freya allowing others to be tortured inside her castle.

"I remember all of my children, but never has one come to visit," he said with a smile. "Never before has my magic returned to me."

Tormod pulled me back even further as I felt my stomach drop.

"I am not your child." I hissed, disgusted at the thought.

My parents were down south in our village. Ma and da and Malcolm and Munro, they were my family. Not this disgusting toad-like fairy.

"I made you. That makes you mine."

"No, it doesn't!" Glen shouted from his spot at the door.

"Tell us how we can stop the changelings you created from dying so young," Queen Freya said, moving the conversation on.

"There is no way." Darach said bluntly and I felt as if someone had punched the air out of my chest.

"There must be a way!" I blurted out, unable to leave the questioning to William and the Queen.

Darach let out a bark of laughter.

"You, of all changelings, want more time?"

Again, all eyes looked at me to explain, but I simply shrugged. I felt my heart sink further when Darach laughed again.

Nothing he had said so far made any sense.

"Explain." William demanded to which Darach looked smug. Clearly, he was enjoying being the one with all the answers.

"Each time I create a changeling, I give forth a small piece of the gift I was born with. Each time a changeling dies that part of the gift returns to me. My gift is not infinite. Much to King Ferchar's dismay, I could not create as many changelings as he wanted over the last decade," he paused with a smirk. "You, my child, took a much larger piece of the gift. Have you never wondered why you lived so long whilst around you, your fellow changelings sickened and died?"

I thought back to every changeling I had ever known or heard about. I thought of Ailsa, the boy who lived to be fifteen, Wallace's children, Eithrig's sisters, Finnian's family. Each of them had died so young, some not making it past four or five.

But here I stood, eighteen years old and aging with every passing day. Though I got sick easily and struggled with my breathing on occasion, I was still healthy enough to travel for weeks through forests and mountains.

"The Others wanted you to have a much larger piece of the gift. Wanted you to live a longer life than the other changelings I created. I can feel it right here, the gift that flows through your body. It calls to me."

"Why would they do that?" I whispered, sickened.

"Why is the sky blue? Why is the grass green? None of us mortals know why the Others do anything. While I can control who I use my gift on, it is the Others who control life. They decide how many changelings I can create and how much of my gift it takes to bring each of them life."

Standing there in that cell, listening to Darach call me his child and claim that the Others had given me life for a reason, I longed for my parents.

Da would have marched over to him and broke his nose for daring to say that I wasn't their child.

I felt like part of a game. Just a human shaped bundle of magic for Darach and the Others to play with. It made me want to claw at my own skin and escape. If it even was my own skin, perhaps I was nothing. Every part of me was created by someone else.

I couldn't stand to be there any longer. I couldn't hear any more.

If this was the truth we'd been searching for this whole time, then I didn't want the truth.

I turned on my heel and ran out of the cell.

I wanted to go home.

CHAPTER

41

Euna

20 YEARS AGO

"Stop it Euna!" Aelwen complained after trying to take a drink of her nettle tea, only to find that I had frozen it solid once again.

"Euna, be kind." Mother chided gently, and I let the tea turn back to liquid.

Aelwen smiled, took a sip and promptly looked disgusted.

"It is cold now!"

"We can swap. I like it cold," I hurried to reassure her, swapping our cups as she smiled gratefully.

She lifted the cup to her lips, only to be met once again with frozen tea. She threw it down on the table with a screech whilst I laughed hysterically beside her.

She fell for it every time.

It had been years since I discovered that I was gifted by the Others and able to control the temperature of small things. Freezing liquid was easy, but warming it back up took a lot more energy.

"Stop using your gift on me!" Aelwen reached out to push me playfully.

The moment her hand touched my shoulder I felt it. It was as if someone had submerged me in an icy cold bath, or thrown me into a burning bonfire.

My head spun and I felt as if I was falling.

Then, from the very tips of my toes I felt my gift leaving me. Rushing through my veins and rattling through my bones to the point where Aelwen's skin touched mine.

I could not describe what my gift felt like, but now I felt it leave me. Like water sinking down through grass and soil. My gift was trickling away.

As quickly as it started, it was over. I realised that I was sprawled on the floor beside the wooden chairs, feeling too hot and too cold all at once.

Mother had wrenched Aelwen away from me. I took a deep breath to complain about the shrill noise echoing throughout the hall and as I inhaled it stopped. It had been me, screaming.

"I'm sorry, I'm sorry!" Aelwen was apologising between sobs.

She pushed mother away and crawled under the table away from the two of us.

"My princess, what happened?" Mother asked, frantically checking me over for injuries.

"Gone." I whispered, my throat sore from screaming.

"What has gone?" Mother pulled me to her chest and began rocking me gently.

I let her comfort me, although I knew it was Aelwen who needed her right now. Aelwen who was sobbing so hard I thought she might be sick. Watching her sob and apologise from under the table, I could see how disgusted she was in herself. I knew that she had not meant for this to happen.

For years, we thought that Aelwen had been born without a gift. Now I wished desperately that was true.

Although my body ached, I could not bring myself to blame her. The Others gave gifts, and we fairies just had to live with it.

I could not muster up the energy to hate her for this. I was empty, numb.

"My gift, it's gone."

At my confirmation, I heard Aelwen wail and I knew that she must have felt it happen. Felt the gift I had been born with as it was dragged reluctantly from my body.

Mother was frantically calling for healers and trying to soothe Aelwen while she cradled me close. I did not want to deal with what happened, could not bear to think about it.

I closed my eyes and sank into her embrace, shutting out everything and everyone.

PRESENT DAY

Aelwen and I listened in silence as Queen Freya explained what they had learned when they questioned the gifted fairy, Darach.

After their visit to the cells, Glen looked shaken and I felt a flicker of guilt at that. I still could not believe what I had done to the two of them.

The changeling, Morven, looked even worse than Glen. Her skin was pale and clammy, which made her freckles stand out. Her hands were faintly trembling as she sipped the tea which Adair, Queen Freya's advisor, had brewed after seeing the state she was in.

It was understandable. I felt out of depth dealing with the workings of the Others. To a human and a changeling, it must have been near impossible to comprehend what we were dealing with.

This was bigger than us all.

"So, we have no way to give the changelings a longer life," Adair sighed, running his hand over his face.

"There is no way for us to give the changelings more of his powers. We are just lucky that the Others saw fit to bless Morven with enough for a long life," Queen Freya said with a sad smile.

Morven laughed humourlessly and slammed her mug down on the table, not noticing when the tea splashed out over her hand and dress.

"Lucky?" she spat.

"I'm sorry. I did not mean to cause offence," Queen Freya hurried to assure her, fumbling for words. "I simply mean... isn't it good that you will be able to live your life without the fear of death?"

"We know you didn't mean any offence." Glen said, rubbing soothing circles on Morven's back.

Morven simply gritted her teeth and remained silent, staring down at the now half empty mug, watching the tea cooling on the table.

I felt helpless watching someone else struggle to cope and I wondered if this was what Aelwen felt all those years watching me suffer.

Morven had every right to be furious with Darach and with the Others, but Queen Freya still looked upset, as if she alone had been the one to cause her harm.

"It seems that the best thing we can do is keep Darach imprisoned and ensure that he is never able to use his gift again," William said from where he was leaning against the wall.

Watching Morven glare at the cold nettle tea and listening to Queen Freya and her advisors discuss ways to ensure that Darach never got free, I was struck with an idea.

There was nothing more to be done for Morven. She simply had to live her life with the truth she did not want to accept. But something could be done to stop Darach from ever creating another changeling.

"Aelwen..." I started, but she cut me off.

"I cannot." She said, and I noticed just how strained she looked.

"You would be protecting so many humans, stopping so many families from suffering," she let me take one of her hands and grip it tight. "You could finally use it to do good."

"Use what for good?" The ever-observant William asked and I silently cursed.

I should have waited until we were alone to voice my idea.

"My gift." Aelwen sighed, she sounded pained to admit that she was gifted and I feel even guiltier about bringing it up.

The last time she used her gift had been when we were children. She had been annoyed by my teasing and wanted my powers to stop for a moment. Back then we did not realise that she was gifted and so the moment her skin touched mine, she leeched my gift from me forever.

It was months before she touched anyone again, scared that she would take the gifts of ever fairy she met. Thankfully she had control over her gift, unless she wanted to take someone's gift it would not happen.

I thanked the Others for not burdening her with that. Mine was the only gift she had ever taken. It took months for us to convince her that she was not a monster. That she still deserved our love.

Despite sometimes yearning to feel that power flowing through my veins again, I always believed that there was a reason the Others gave her that gift.

Finally, the reason was clear.

"What can you do?" Glen asked, unable to hide how curious he was.

He looked so eager to hear about it that I knew she would not resist. In the brief time that we had known the human and the changeling she had grown fond.

"I can remove gifts. I did it once as a child by mistake and the power has been slumbering inside me ever since," Aelwen admitted as I squeezed her hand, trying to silently show my support and remind her that I did not blame her for what happened.

"So, you could remove Darach's gift and stop him from ever creating another changeling?" Adair asked, to which Aelwen nodded.

I was glad he did not ask her about what happened when we were children.

"Wouldn't that mean you could create changelings yourself?" Morven frowned, understandably suspicious.

"No, it is like releasing a bird from a cage. The magic does not linger here, it returns to the Otherworld."

"Would you do it? Take away his gift as punishment for what he has done to the humans?" Queen Freya asked gently, not wanting to anger anyone else.

Aelwen sighed, a battle raging in her mind.

She had spent so much of her life pretending that she had no gift, not even her children knew what she was capable of. I was sure that she must have told her husband, Ronan, but we never discussed it.

I think she had always hoped that if she ignored it for long enough it would disappear.

374

The silence lasted so long that I grew concerned and was ready to call for our meeting to end.

We could meet again once Aelwen had time to make her decision. It was not fair for us to expect this of her.

Before I could voice my thoughts, Morven spoke.

"Please," she begged, her voice thick with emotion. "You're a mother, think of all the human babies stolen. All the parents who have to watch their changeling children die." She took a shaky breath, "I'm not even human. I shouldn't exist. Please, don't let anyone else be born into this life."

With that, I knew the decision was made.

I was not sure if Morven brought up that Aelwen was a mother so that she would feel guilty and accept, or if she truly was appealing to her motherly side.

Either way, it had worked.

Aelwen sprang from her seat and rushed to comfort Morven, whispering promises to stop him and hurrying to reassure her of her worth.

I knew all too well what it was like to truly despise yourself. From the distraught look on her face as she watched Morven, I could tell that Queen Freya did too.

Not for the first time I hoped that the King was being punished in the Otherworld. Nothing would ever be enough to make him pay for all the suffering he caused.

Freya 42

The next afternoon we gathered again in the meeting hall. Adair suggested that it would be best to deliver Darach's punishment in a formal setting.

Berwin had been discretely released when the humans were freed, so this would be my first sentencing since being crowned. I felt sick with nerves.

I did not deserve to decide the fate of other fairies simply because my father had been the king. As bad as I felt, I knew I did not feel as sick as Queen Aelwen looked. She would be the one removing Darach's gift.

Usually it was as if light shone from within her, brightening the lives of everyone she encountered. This afternoon she looked miserable and resigned, we could all see that she was reluctant to do it.

I wasn't gifted so I couldn't imagine the toll using such power must take on a person, especially for a gift such as hers.

The hall was filled with people.

Glen and Morven were present, wanting to see justice carried out. The afternoon's sentencing was the reason they'd journeyed north, to put a stop to the creation of the changelings.

Queen Aelwen was accompanied by Queen Euna, who seemed to have put aside her own unhappiness in favour of supporting her sister. Their guard Tormod was the only one from Norbroch present. They did not want the news of her gift to spread.

Queen Aelwen's one condition was that no one was to ever learn of the gift she possessed.

William was by my side, as per usual, and so was Adair. We waited, listening to the rain battering down on the roof, for Darach to be brought in. Everyone was tense, no one daring to break the silence.

As we waited, I could not help but let my gaze drift over to Morven. She had been unhappy since we questioned Darach, but I hoped that seeing justice served would help put her at ease. If not for her sake, then for Nieve's sake. I knew she would have wanted the changeling who replaced her to be happy.

I was roused from those thoughts as the doors to the prison opened and Darach was led in. He was escorted by four of William's most trusted guards, his hands bound behind his back, before being forced to his knees before my throne.

I had watched countless fairies be sentenced by King Ferchar over the years, to all manner of horrific punishments. Never had I felt any desire to be the one doing the sentencing.

I noticed Darach looking smugly towards Morven every few moments, so I spoke to drag his attention away and protect her from his gaze.

"Darach, you are here to be sentenced for your crimes," I began, hoping that I sounded more confident than I felt.

"I fathered many children through the gift the Others gave me, how is that a crime?" Darach asked, not the slightest bit repentant.

"You stole human babies from hundreds of families. You aided Laird Brochan in killing countless fairies. You sold human children into servitude. Almost every child you have created has suffered and died needlessly. Each of those is crime enough to deserve punishment."

"All of them suffered and died, except her," Darach amended with a nod towards Morven who was staring at the wall behind me, refusing to make eye contact with him.

Her refusal to even look at him was sharply contrasted by Glen. He was glaring at Darach with such hatred, I worried we would have to stop him from trying to kill Darach once his gift had been taken.

"As punishment for your crimes your gift shall be removed," I said simply, not wanting to draw the sentencing out any longer.

His gaze snapped back to me, his smug expression replaced by one of horror.

"That's impossible," he breathed, sounding uncertain.

"You are not the only gifted fairy."

Before I could ask Queen Aelwen to step forward from where they stood at the back of the hall, the wooden doors at the entrance beside them opened.

To my disbelief, in marched Tomas with a handful of armed men. Without so much as glancing at the Queens or Morven and Glen, he strode forward to stand beside Darach. The guards rearranged themselves to let him past, watching William for orders.

"Where is my father?" He demanded and it took me a few moments to get over my shock and reply.

"How dare you burst into my hall without invitation?" I exclaimed, embarrassed that he had simply wandered in.

What would the Queens think of me when I was being shown such clear disrespect by my subjects?

"I have sent you countless messengers asking that you release my father," Tomas continued as if I had not spoken, his voice harsh and cold.

Gone was the flirtatious fairy I had encountered at festivals and dinners in the past.

"I sent replies to each of your messengers with the same answer. Your father has committed multiple crimes and will remain in my prison until he is sentenced. Now, I'll ask that you kindly remove yourself and your men from my hall."

"I am swiftly running out of patience," Tomas spat and from the anger on his face, I believed him. "Release my father from your prison and I will say no more about this matter."

"Enough." William stepped forward, putting himself between me and Tomas who was growing angrier the longer our conversation lasted. "Queen Freya has asked you to leave this hall. Refusal to do so will see you and your men thrown out of the castle."

"This should be my hall, my castle and my kingdom," Tomas hissed. "King Ferchar promised my father that you and I would be wed, that I would become his heir."

"The King is dead and your father will reside in the cells until I see fit to free him or punish him." I felt my own temper rising the longer he refused to leave.

It did not surprise me that King Ferchar had tried to marry me off without my permission. What did surprise me was that Tomas believed it and expected me to honour the late King's promise.

He sighed, shaking his head as if he was somehow disappointed in me. I opened my mouth, ready to shout at him, feeling my blood boil at his lack of respect, when he spoke again.

"You have left me no other choice."

He threw his arms wide and a moment later, the hall descended into chaos.

I watched, frozen in horror, as the ground cracked and exploded around his feet. I had never known that he was gifted.

There was nothing we could do as his magic gouged chunks out of my hall and ripped apart the very stones it was made of.

My heart raced in panic as the cracks shot up the walls and across the ceiling, there was no way it would support itself much longer.

"You did this." Tomas shouted over the sounds of splintering rocks.

The roof gave in and began to collapse just as the rocks beneath my feet crumbled and disappeared. Something heavy collided with my back, sending me sprawling to the floor.

I could do nothing but cower as my castle was destroyed around me. Chunks of stone pelting me as they fell, the sound of the destruction making it impossible to think.

If I had not already been on the floor, I would have fallen as I realised what he was doing.

He was going to bury us alive.

CHAPTER

43

Morven

Glen and I listened as the pompous fairy tried to convince Queen Freya to release his father. Hearing him complain that King Ferchar had promised to let him marry Queen Freya made me feel a little better about falling for his tricks. Even fairies had fallen for his lies.

As we stood there, I could feel Darach's eyes on me. Could sense him willing me to look at him.

I made sure that my eyes never strayed from Queen Freya and the wall behind her. He could call me his child all he liked, but I would not give him the satisfaction of looking at him.

Just as soon as William got rid of the interruption, Queen Aelwen would be free to use her gift and Darach would never be able to create another changeling again.

We may not have succeeded in extending my life, but we had saved the lives of countless humans and spared generations of families from heartbreak.

That was enough.

Across the hall, Queen Aelwen was standing so close to Queen Euna that she was practically being held up by her. Her beautiful face looked haunted and I felt awful that she had to use the gift she so clearly despised, but it couldn't be helped. She was the only way to ensure that no one suffered like this again.

Tormod was watching the fairy argue with Queen Freya and looked tense, as if he was expecting that the fairy would not leave quietly.

"You've left me no choice." Tomas announced, the malice in his voice instantly making me want to run.

He threw his arms wide, and as he did, the stone all around us shattered and exploded.

Glen threw us down to the ground as slabs of rock and stone from the perfectly made castle rained down all around us.

I felt shards cut my face and arms so I screwed my eyes shut. Desperately hoping that the Others didn't let us be crushed to death.

People were shouting all around us. Their cries mixing with the horrific roaring sound of a castle being ripped apart and the ground bursting up into the air.

Distantly, I remembered Granny Ethol telling us stories about a human who could make the ground crack and crumble. Never did I think I would feel the full force of that gift.

I felt as if we crouched together in the rubble for hours, clutching each other tight, when eventually it stopped. Leaving my ears ringing and my heart racing.

Where there had been a fully formed roof, now there were only a few stray beams of wood remaining. The rain was pouring down onto the chaos all around us and I let myself imagine that it was the Others, sending us help.

Everywhere I looked, the fairies that arrived with the gifted fairy were fighting with the castles guards, those who were still alive anyway.

I could make out a few limbs in between slabs of stone and forced myself not to think about the bodies trapped beneath the rubble.

The once flat hall was now a wild rocky terrain, with the colossal remains of walls and the roof separating the hall into sections.

We could no longer see Queen Freya or the Queens, who had been across the hall from us before chaos began.

The wall behind the throne had been completely knocked down. I desperately hoped that Queen Freya had not been thrown out of the castle with it, I doubted even a fairy could survive that.

My ears were still ringing from the sound of solid stone being torn apart, but I could hear Glen shouting beside me.

"Are you okay?"

I nodded, not trusting my voice.

Glen's vibrant red hair was coated in grey dust, as was his face and clothes. Seeing it made me cough and wheeze, realising just how much dust there was floating around. In amongst the dust, some of which was now running down his face because of the rain, I could see cuts and blood from the blizzard of rock we'd been caught up in.

Pulling me to my feet, Glen frantically looked around for anyone who wasn't fighting. In the chaos, it was impossible to tell who was winning the fight.

"The Queen." I shouted, my voice only just loud enough for Glen to hear over the clashing swords and fairies shouting.

Glen knew what I meant and so, hurrying as fast as we could over the uneven wet rubble, cutting our hands in the process, we scrambled to find Queen Freya and William.

As we worked to get to the other end of the hall I found myself coughing more and more. Whilst the freezing rain helped to dampen and dispel some of the dust, our movement was releasing clouds of dust from in between the bricks and roof.

Every so often we would step on an unsteady piece of stone, only for it to go crashing down, sending us toppling with it.

By the time we made it to the other side of the hall I was exhausted and ready to give up.

Though the wall was gone, the floor was more intact and so we were able to stand on relatively flat ground. It looked like the fairy had blasted the stone away from himself, that's why we were so badly affected at the back of the hall.

We still had some rubble to climb over, but by now I could see that Queen Freya was cradling her advisor, Adair, in her lap. They were talking frantically so I hoped that whatever injuries he had were not fatal.

William had unsheathed his sword and was fighting the gifted fairy. He seemed to be less skilled than William and so had to focus on defending himself, not ripping the rest of the castle apart.

We let ourselves pause for a few moments and I tried to catch my breath.

The fairies were still fighting all around us, but they appeared to be evenly matched. Screams of anger, rather than pain, echoing around us.

Pausing for breath was our biggest mistake.

"I am taking back what is mine," Darach suddenly shouted with a manic look in his eyes.

He lunged towards me from where he had been hiding, behind what looked like the remains of a wooden table, crushed by the collapsing roof.

I scrambled back onto the pile of rocks behind us, cutting my fingers to shreds as I frantically tried to put distance between us.

Glen pushed Darach away from me, shouting at him with language so foul I was glad his ma wasn't here to hear him.

My head swam as I looked at the chaos all around us. William fighting the gifted fairy, Queen Aelwen and Queen Euna separated from us by a wall of fighting fairies and Glen, trying to fight a fairy intent on taking away the magic which gave me life.

"Please, help us." I whispered, hoping that the Others were watching us.

How could this be the fate they had kept us alive so long to face?

The gifted fairy, growing bored of his fight with William, once again released his gift upon the ruined hall. With another deafening roar, rock was torn apart and flung towards the cowering Queen Freya, Adair and William.

The walls continued to crumble and the remaining wooden ceiling beams fell from their precarious position onto the fairies below. Too engaged in fighting to realise that they were about to be hit by wooden beams.

The rock I was perched on was unstable and as the fairy continued to unleash chaos, the stone beneath my feet gave way. Sending me tumbling down with it.

Glen had been caught up in the rock directed at Queen Freya and so there was nothing to stop Darach from scrambling towards me.

I cried out to Glen as I scrambled away, my hands slipping and sliding on what remained of the wet stone floor.

My back hit a wall of rock and wood. With a sob, I realised that I had nowhere left to go. Laughing in a way that made me feel sick to my stomach, Darach closed in on me.

Behind him, Glen and William were stumbling to their feet, but I knew it was too late.

They were too far away to stop Darach from ending my life.

Glen and I were the children of farmers, not meant to be here in the north, dealing with evil kings and magical abilities greater than anything we could have imagined.

The moment we'd stepped foot in the fairy lands we had made a mistake. There was no way I was getting out of this alive. I was too weak.

Glen screamed my name me as Darach sank to his knees beside me. Slowly raising his hand, chuckling gleefully.

He placed his hand forcefully on my chest, pushing me back into the rock behind me, not caring how much it hurt.

My back arched beyond my control as my heart lurched forward towards his ha...

CHAPTER

44

Euna

I thanked the Others as the last wooden support beam from the ceiling fell, sending fairies sprawling. It cleared a path through the fighting so we could get through to where Queen Freya and the humans were.

We scrambled ungracefully over the sharp slippery remains of the castle in time to see the horror unfold.

Aelwen gasped beside me as we watched Darach slam his hand onto Morven's chest. She arched unnaturally up into his touch and slumped back down onto the rock.

She did not move again.

Glen let out a roar of anger and despair, so loud I was sure the Otherworld must have heard it. Aelwen began crying angrily beside me.

Even without Aelwen's gift, I could tell that the magic, which had flowed through Morven's veins and gave her life for all these years, was gone.

The way she lay unnaturally against the rocks reminded me of the last dead human I had seen.

Lachlann.

Tormod leapt down from the pile of stone and wood we stood on and rushed to join William, who was fighting with the gifted fairy that had blown the hall apart.

Queen Freya was crying as she cradled her advisor in her lap. She was soaked through with rain, dust from the crumbling bricks of her castle and dark red blood.

I had no time to contemplate our appearance further as Aelwen grasped my hand, pulling me down from where we had frozen to take in the horror.

By now, the enraged Glen had reached Darach and was attempting to beat the life out of him. Despite fairies being stronger than humans, he was doing considerable damage.

Darach had been stunned. Not expecting the surge of magic which returned once he took Morven's life from her, and so was caught unaware by the furious redhead. Giving Glen a chance to attack before Darach could defend himself.

We ran, tripping over bricks and wood, slipping on the stones which the rain had made dangerous. Aelwen reached Glen first and tried to pry him from Darach, who was now bleeding profusely from his newly broken nose and split lip. One of his eyes was swollen and half closed.

Despite all of that, he still wore the same smug smile. Like he was drunk on the magic he had stolen from the girl he had not long ago called his child.

"Glen, stop," Aelwen begged, attempting to grab his hands and stop him from delivering any further blows.

"He. Killed. Her." He shouted, through clenched teeth, delivering a punch with each word.

His hands were bloody with both Darach's and his own blood. His human hands fracturing and breaking as he attempted to punch through tough flesh and bone.

"He can bring her back," Aelwen screamed so loud that the three of us flinched, despite the noise around us.

Thankfully her scream made Glen pause, bloody hands in the air ready to strike again.

"Back?"

It was then that I noticed the tears running down his face, leaving trails in the dust and blood.

Seeing the grief and hope on his face made me realise with a jolt just how young the two them were. They had to be less than twenty years of age, not old enough to be dragged into this fight.

As we travelled south from Norbroch, Aelwen and I had listened to countless stories about their village in the south and their family there.

The thought of Glen returning home to that village they so clearly loved, Morven's dead body his only company, made my eyes sting with tears.

"He gave her life once. He can give it to her again," Aelwen hurried to explain.

"Bring her back." He mumbled, nodding.

His anger giving way to grief and shock at the loss of his best friend.

"The fairy is dead." Tormod said quietly beside me making me flinch in fright.

It was then that I noticed how quiet the ruined hall had grown. The fairy had not planned his attack on the castle well at all. His companions had been defeated and were being bound with rope by the castle guards.

He must have assumed that Queen Freya would honour the promise King Ferchar made, to marry him and release his father from prison. Surely not even he could have been foolish enough to try and take over a whole castle with less than fifteen fairies.

Behind us, he lay in a rapidly growing pool of his own blood, whilst William was helping a shaken Queen Freya to her feet. Healers rushing to aid her advisor.

Queen Freya spotted me looking and began to stumble over to us. A head wound dripping blood down the side of her face faster than the rain could wash it away. I held out my hand and shook my head to stop her coming over.

She needed to heal and see what damage had been done to the castle. As William lifted her up into his arms and carried her over to an anxious looking maid, I turned back to Darach who was now laughing manically.

"I won't do it. I won't do it. I won't do it." He was singing, in between laughs.

"Give her back her life and we may spare yours," Aelwen attempted to threaten but the threat came out shaky, pleading.

"If you don't give it back I'll... I'll make you!" Glen's attempt was even less threatening than Aelwen's, especially as he clenched his hands back into fists to hide the shaking.

"No," Tormod said, gently pushing the shaking Glen away. "You do not need to do this."

"I do." Glen insisted, wiping tears and rain from his eyes with the back of his hand.

"Look after Morven," Tormod said, his expression hardening as he turned to Darach who was watching him nervously. "I will do this for you."

Darach tried to flinch away when Tormod reached for him, but he was not fast enough.

Tormod gripped his wrist, stopping his retreat. I felt a flicker of nausea as I realised what he planned to do, but from the bemused look on Darach's face I could tell he had not yet worked it out.

"Give her back her life." Tormod said, his voice betraying none of his emotions.

Beside him, Glen now had Morven cradled in his lap and was crying quietly. Touching her cold lifeless body had drained the last of his anger, leaving him with nothing but sorrow.

My heart ached for him as he knelt in the rain clutching Morven's body. My mind flickering back to when I had knelt just outside our castle cradling Lachlann.

Without life in her muscles and bones, Morven's neck dropped awkwardly over the back of Glen's arms. It was like Aelwen's children when they were just new-borns, not yet strong enough to hold up their own weight.

Sinking down beside Glen, I lifted my hands and helped him gently support Morven's neck.

He looked like he wanted nothing more than to push me away, but he did not. His sadness outweighing the anger he still felt for me.

"I won't do it." Darach sounded more uncertain now.

He was no longer laughing. Not now that he was faced with Tormod and had no one to rescue him from whatever was coming.

Tormod let out a small sigh, then he reached out with his other hand and snapped the smallest of Darach's long slender fingers where it joined with his hand.

There was a moment of silence, as if no one could quite believe what had just happened. Before Darach let out a cry which made us all jump and my stomach churn.

"Use your gift, and give Morven back her life." Tormod said, deceptively calm.

"I wo..."

Darach did not make it through the sentence before the next finger was snapped and he cried out once more.

I forced myself to stare at Morven's unnaturally still face, rather than watch as Darach's next finger was broken. I could hear Glen breathing heavily beside me, sounding as horrified as I felt.

"Just look at Morven," I whispered, desperately hoping that he would obey.

I knew that if I stopped staring at that freckled face below me I would lose my composure.

The cries that echoed around the half-ruined hall would haunt me for months to come, would haunt all of us. I consoled myself with the knowledge that a healer would be able to fix his fingers within minutes.

Though it did not stop the guilt from welling up inside me, until I was sure it would choke me.

I thanked the Others for not making Darach stubborn or courageous as he gave in and agreed to bring Morven back to life before Tormod could snap another finger.

If it had been the King that Tormod was torturing, we would have run out of bones to break long before he gave in.

"I'll do it. I'll do it." Darach sobbed so pitifully that I could not help but feel sorry for the fairy, despite all the heartbreak he had caused.

From the pained look on Aelwen's face I could tell that she felt the same.

Mindful of his injuries, Tormod placed Darach's injured hand in his lap and carefully helped him to shuffle over to Glen, Morven and I.

Not giving him any opportunity to change his mind, Tormod placed Darach's uninjured hand on Moven's chest.

"Give it all back." Aelwen warned, wanting to make sure that he did not simply trick us so that he could escape.

Crying still, Darach nodded. We all watched, hardly daring to breathe, as he closed his eyes and concentrated.

Morven flinched violently in Glen's arm and began taking slow rattling breaths, each deeper than the previous.

Glen once again dissolved into tears, sounding almost too exhausted to cry now. William, who had arrived without any of us noticing, helped Glen to his feet and helped him carry Morven to where healers were waiting.

"We need to see it," Glen said suddenly, stopping to look back at us. "We need to see it end."

Aelwen stared at Darach, who was weeping where he sat, not even trying to escape. It was a pitiful sight, one that made my heart ache to think about how much suffering King Ferchar had caused us all. How many people he had manipulated.

"Do it Aelwen, use the gift they gave you for good," I said softly, which seemed to be the encouragement she needed.

Slowly, she lifted her shaking hand and placed it on Darach's forearm. Unlike when she removed my gift, Darach remained silent other than a choked sob.

When she released him, he slumped to the floor, sinking into unconsciousness.

I now understood why mother had been so confused all those years before. It was as if nothing had happened.

We sat in silence, the rain falling around us, soaking us to the bone. Eventually Aelwen spoke up.

"It's done." She whispered shakily and I heard Glen give a slightly hysterical laugh behind us.

"We can go home now." I crawled forward through the growing puddles and rubble, to wrap my arm around her.

Aelwen had spent the last decade looking after me, trying desperately to save me from my own grief. Now it was my turn to look after her.

King Ferchar was dead, no longer would human children be stolen and no more changelings could be created. At last the kingdoms of Norbroch and Culhuinn were at peace.

It was time for us to go home.

CHAPTER

45

Freya

I rode towards the settlement, which would soon become the first town in the new human kingdom. My thighs were burning from such a long ride and I was glad that my journey was almost at an end.

Queen Euna and Queen Aelwen had not wanted to linger in Culhuinn, especially not after the main hall had been mostly destroyed. Queen Aelwen was shaken after using her gift on Darach, and so they quickly left to return to Norbroch and her family.

William and Tormod had managed to kill Tomas before he could do any damage to the rest of the castle. Pushing me out of the way, Adair had broken one of his legs so badly that the healers were still uncertain if he would ever walk again.

We were all lucky to have survived his attack, lucky that he had been unprepared for our resistance.

After a few days spent recovering from the fight, and putting plans in place, I travelled south with William and a group of guards.

After a surprisingly emotional farewell, Morven and Glen had continued down through a valley in the Fairy Hills, heading south to their village in Tirwood.

As we travelled I'd admitted where I was going and explained that Nieve, the human baby which Morven replaced, was now the ruler of a free human kingdom.

I had expected Morven to be angry that I'd kept the secret for so long but she simply laughed. Too relieved to be heading home to care much about anything else.

My goodbye with William or as he was known now, King William of Culhuinn, was much harder.

I couldn't stop myself from crying as we'd hugged, about half a day's ride from the human settlement. Without him the last few months would have destroyed me, and we both knew it.

I wanted to travel south and be with Nieve more than anything else, but I also wished desperately that he could come with me, like Mae, who would be traveling south once I'd sent word that it was safe.

"We will meet again. Culhuinn will always trade with the new kingdom. Either I'll travel down south or you will travel back up to the castle with Nieve." He reassured us both, his own voice thick with emotion.

"Thank you for everything," I whispered, my breath hitching as I tried not to cry anymore.

"Thank you, Freya. You've given me your whole kingdom. There is no way I can ever repay you for what you've done for my family," he replied, swiping at the tears which trickled down his face.

"You don't need to repay me. You've set me free," I answered, and it was true.

After the disaster that was Darach's sentencing, I decided that I was done with being the Queen and done with Culhuinn.

Until the day I die, I will love Culhuinn as a kingdom and love the fairies who live there, but I never wanted to rule them. The best way to put an end to King Ferchar's reign once and for all was to remove his heir from the throne, me.

I'd snuck into Adair's chambers, where he was healing, to ask his advice before going to William with my plan.

As predicted, William tried desperately to stop me and change my mind when I told him I was going to abdicate from the throne. He promised to be by my side and help me until my dying day.

I will never forget the look of surprise on his face when I offered him my crown. It took a lot of persuasion, from both me and Adair, before he finally agreed.

He loved Culhuinn as much as me, but unlike me, he did not have tainted memories of this castle and the legacy of a sadistic father behind him.

William was exactly what Culhuinn needed.

I approached the settlement at the edge of the forest, which was comprised of a mix of wooden shelters and mismatched fabric tents. I was so ready for my journey to be over. I couldn't remember the last time I'd gone on such a long ride and, with the summer sun beating down on me, I was exhausted.

As I got closer to the settlement, two humans came riding to meet me. They must have worked somewhere in the castle but I had never seen them before. To my embarrassment, I did not know either of their names.

I opened my mouth to ask where I could find Nieve but they spoke before me.

"You aren't welcome here," one of the men said, his animosity making me flinch.

"I do not mean any harm," I tried to explain.

I wanted to surprise Nieve and so did not send a messenger south to announce my arrival, much to the new King William's frustration.

The man's companion laughed and cut me off, making me wish I had followed William's suggestion and not risked coming here alone.

"If you think you can come down here and force us to work for you again, you've got another thing coming."

"I promise that is not my intention..."

"If you don't turn that horse around and ride back up north, you won't like what happens to you," the first human said and, for the first time since I left the castle, I realised just how stupid this was.

William had been right. Travelling to the settlement with no guards to protect me, and no clue what I would find, was idiotic

I frantically tried to think of some way to soothe their anger and explain that I was simply looking for Nieve, but they grew bored of my silence.

In the blink of an eye the second man pulled the short axe from his belt, flipped it in his hand and then swung for me.

The next thing I knew I was at my horse's feet, clutching my head and blinking away tears.

Later I would be grateful that he had struck me with the handle and not the sharpened side of the axe, but not whilst I was lying there seeing stars.

"I am just looking for Nieve."

"She doesn't want to see you," one of them laughed.

"She's a free woman now," the other added, as if I could have forgotten.

From my position on the ground I could feel the rumble of more horses approaching and then raised voices. I hoped it was not more humans, eager to join in the beating.

If only William could see me now. His worst fears regarding me travelling alone were coming true already. The thought made me want to laugh bitterly, but my head ached too much for that.

I rolled onto my back with a groan and took stock of my injuries. My head throbbed, but thankfully was not bleeding, and my back ached from the fall. Movement at my side made me flinch painfully and I rolled my head to see what was happening. What I saw made me lose the fight against my tears.

My beautiful Nieve was there beside me, and she looked radiant.

"I was looking for you."

"Look at you," she whispered softly, her face lined with concern.

"I'm sorry. I should have sent a messenger down. I am not the Queen anymore. I gave it up to William. Please, can I stay? I understand you might have moved on, but I...."

Her lips against mine, for the first time in what felt like a lifetime, stopped my rambling. I couldn't help but smile against them, and felt her smile in response.

Then she stood, shouting for guards to bind the two humans who had attacked me, pulling me up into her arms with ease.

"You can stay with me forever, if you want."

I was too choked with emotion to reply, instead I threw my arms around her neck. Revelling in the freedom we had to embrace, finally.

The two men who attacked me were now being escorted back to the settlement and I understood that hatred was to be expected. Many of them likely blamed me, as well as King Ferchar, for how miserable their lives were in Culhuinn.

Eventually, Nieve loosened her hold on my waist, laughing that we would be more comfortable back in her home and not standing out in the sun.

"Are you okay to ride?" She asked, helping me up into her saddle before agilely swinging up to sit behind me.

"I'm okay. I'm more than okay," I smiled, leaning back into her warmth.

I was too happy to bother complaining about my aching thighs as we rode deeper into the settlement, humans stopping what they were doing to stare at me in surprise.

As they stared, I wished that I had brought a hooded cloak to hide my face. Instead I hunched back into Nieve, letting my hair fall forward in an attempt to hide my face from their attention.

I didn't risk making eye contact with anyone, not wanting to see if they were looking at me with happiness, or with hatred.

"You don't need to be afraid. You'll never need to be afraid again." Nieve said, wrapping an arm possessively around my waist and placing a kiss on my cheek.

We rode through the settlement which had been built in a small cleared area at the edge of the forest. We came to a stop at one of the small stone cottages, wedged between the river and the edge of the clearing.

Nieve dismissed her guards, who had ridden with us, before helping me down from the horse. My legs felt shaky and unstable and so I shrieked, but did not protest, when she lifted me into her arms and carried me inside. Locking the wooden door behind her.

"It's nothing like the castle up in Culhuinn, but its home," Nieve looked almost ashamed of her modest cottage, with its crooked walls and low ceiling.

"I love it," I grinned, and then to my embarrassment blurted out. "You look beautiful."

She did look beautiful. Her hair was a wild mix of loose curls and plaits, which kept her hair away from her face. Her skin was tanned and much more freckled now that she had the freedom to go outside and enjoy the summer whenever she pleased.

Clearly she was eating well as her figure was fuller now and, even through her clothes, I could see that her arms were much more muscular.

"You look beautiful as well. Beautiful but exhausted," she smiled, helping me pull off my boots and get rid of the cloak I had worn to travel. "Let's go for a lie down, and then you can see my tattoo."

I let her pull me down into the pile of knitted blankets on the straw mattress where she slept. I had brought our patchwork blanket with me, but that could wait for now. Now we had months of catching up to do.

It was only once we were comfortable in each other's arms that I realised what she had said.

"Tattoo?!"

She laughed and gripped me tighter when I half-heartedly attempted to move, holding me close and gently kissing my neck.

Despite my curiosity about her new tattoo, I was content in my love's arms, for the first time since King Ferchar cruelly separated us and the fate of kingdoms fell on our shoulders.

I covered her hands with my own, threading our fingers together and letting myself sink into her embrace. Safe in the knowledge that we were both finally free.

CHAPTER

46

Morven

"Goodbye Glen," I gave him one last squeeze before letting him go.

"You do remember that my cottage is just down the road from yours?" He teased.

"Shut up, I'll miss being with you all the time," I admitted, giving him a shove.

"I'll miss you too, but right now my bed and a home cooked meal are much more important," Glen admitted and with that, he ran off down the path towards his family's stone cottage.

I took a deep breath to calm my nerves and began wandering home. When we arrived back in Tirwood, Finnian had been there to take us across Loch Fai. This time he made us sit down and didn't let us anywhere near the edge of the boat.

We hadn't stayed long in the villages around the loch as Finnian mentioned that the Summer's End festival was approaching and we didn't want to miss another festival. We stopped just long enough to stay overnight with Eithrig and Hamish, and for Finnian to promise to visit our village.

The closer I got to the cottage, the more nervous I felt. The whole time we were away I'd wished to be back home, and desperately missed my family. Now I was oddly anxious about what I might find when I returned.

Anything could have happened.

"Morven!" I heard a shout and turned to see Malcolm and Munro running through the field towards me and at once, my nerves disappeared.

Munro reached me first pulling me into a hug and spinning me around in circles. Then Malcolm arrived, pulling us both into a bone crushing hug.

Instantly I forgot all about my aches and pains from travelling. Gone was my exhaustion and weariness. Nothing mattered now that I was reunited with my brothers.

When we finally separated, and made it to the cottage, I was once again pulled into a hug, this time by ma who wasn't even attempting to stifle her sobs.

"My baby's home," she cried, whilst Munro loudly complained that as the youngest, he was in fact the baby.

"Welcome home lass," da whispered, placing a kiss on my forehead once ma had finally freed me.

To everyone's relief, Glen and I had made it home in time for Summer's End. Two days later, I found myself helping ma to chop vegetables, much like I had done for Winter's End, which felt like a lifetime ago.

The night I returned ma forced me into a steaming hot bath, to wash away the dirt from the road, then she'd fed me up with stew before tucking me into bed.

I fell asleep almost as soon as she finished tucking the blankets around me, exhausted from our hurried journey home.

Since being brought back to life, I felt much the same as I had before. I still got out of breath when I walked quickly or ran. Glen said that I looked a little younger and so we thought that, instead of giving me back the exact same life, Darach must had given me a new one. If that was true then I could have another eighteen years to live, and love, and enjoy myself.

I found myself unable to worry too much about when I would die. We had tried our hardest to save my life, and we now knew that changelings would never again be created.

I was content with that.

"So, tell me more about this young fisherman," ma said with a grin, making me groan and blush.

When I woke the next day, the family had pounced on me, wanting to know everything that had happened on the journey.

Glen and I had debated all the way home about how much we should tell them, eventually settling for telling them the truth. Our story was filled with sadness and fear, but also excitement and adventure.

As predicted, it made ma cry to hear about the enchantment we fell under and our imprisonment in Norbroch, but da gently reminded her that I had made it home which cheered her up.

What no one would forget though, was Finnian. I had blushed the whole time I spoke about him and given away my true feelings.

Now the whole family teased me about him constantly. I was embarrassed but also secretly pleased. I looked forward to Finnian visiting our village and was glad my family was just as excited about meeting him.

"You'll meet him soon," I said, flustered, and she let it drop with a grin.

That afternoon the whole village climbed to the top of the highest hill, where we had races and danced to the musicians who brought out their drums.

I had countless people ask me about our journey and soon Glen had taken over and was wowing the crowd with tales of our adventures in Culhuinn and Norbroch.

Instead of being inside the castle, like at Winter's End, we brought the chairs outside to make the most of the long summer night. The sky looked like it was burning a vibrant mix of pink and orange as the sun finally began to set.

There was a light rain falling, which meant that the Others had seen our festivities and bonfires, and would protect our ripening crops.

I'd wrapped myself up in a tartan blanket and sat with da, watching as Munro and Rhona, who were now a couple, danced wildly to the music.

"Do you wish you could meet her?" I asked suddenly, needing to know.

"Meet who?" Da asked with a smile, not looking up from where he was distributing blaeberries to the twins.

They would go away to dance and then come running back for more, their little hands stained red from the juice.

"Your daughter."

"My daughter is sitting right beside me, fretting needlessly," he grinned, and I rolled my eyes.

"She's the ruler of a new independent human kingdom," I reminded him.

"That's all she is to me, a name, a stranger, not the wee girl I watched grow up. I don't know what that fairy said to make you doubt it, but I'll remind you every day that we, your family, love you."

With that, the lingering worry I had carried all the way south began to ebb.

It would take me a while to forget what Darach had said, but I knew that I would get past it with my family and Glen's help.

This was my family and my village. As I sat there, my heart beating in time to the drums and the light rain cooling my face, I vowed never to let anyone make me doubt it again.

ACKNOWLEDGEMENTS

Firstly, I must thank my family. Mum, Dad, Karen, Gran and Grandpa. You all supported me from the moment I told you I had started writing a book about a changeling. Thank you for always encouraging me and supporting everything I do. It means the world to me.

Next, I must thank Mia Kuzniar, I couldn't have done this without you. You were the first person join Morven and Glen on their adventure. You put so much time and effort into editing this book, and I will never be able to thank you enough. My book couldn't ask for a better Auntie!

Lauren Cassidy, the day we met back in 2015 you came with me to buy a notebook, in which I began planning this book. Thank you for your work on the title design. As I am writing this it's been 145 weeks since we first spoke on Instagram, who would have thought we would end up here?

Nazima and Vicky, two of my favourite people in the world. Thank you for being some of the first people to read my book and supporting me throughout. You never fail to make me smile and keep me positive!

Thank you to the gals: Alexis, Alison, Andi, Carol, Laura and Samantha. I am so glad that the book community brought us together! Thank you for always being there for me and putting up with me when I was stressed.

Thank you to the wonderful people who beta-read this book, your feedback and kind words made all the difference. Melissa, Morgan, Amy-Rose, Shazina, Liv, Anna, Rebecca, Ann and Amy, thank you for joining Morven on her adventure.

A very special thank you to Brittney (reverieandink) for creating the artwork I used to reveal the title of my book, it was so wonderful to work with you.

The wonderful Liza Vasse brought my world to life when she created the map. I can't thank you enough. I will never stop being amazed by how perfectly you captured the world.

Thank you to amazingly talented Leesha Hannigan for the beautiful cover artwork. I will never get tired of staring at it. It was wonderful to work with you. Thank you for bringing Morven to life!

Josephine Boyce, author of Rebellion, Resistance and Queen, deserves a huge thank you! Thank you for putting up with me asking a million questions about self-publishing over the last year or so. I doubt I could have made it through the self-publishing process without you!

A huge thank you to Ben Alderson and C. M. Lucas, author of Mist and Whispers. You both went above and beyond to help me release this book and I will be forever grateful. I will never stop being amazed by the wonderful job Claire did on my cover design (with her book design company Eight Little Pages).

I would be here for weeks typing out the names of everyone who wished me good luck with my book, or was rooting for me in the book community online.

If you've ever tweeted me or commented on my Instagram about my book, then this is for you. If we've ever chatted about writing then this is for you. I am not sure if I would have had the courage to self-publish if it wasn't for the wonderful book community.

You can't exactly thank a country, but if I didn't live in such a beautiful place, filled with folklore and magic, then I would never have been inspired to write this book. I tried my hardest to capture Scotland in every aspect of this book. I hope that I managed to share my love of my beautiful country with you.

Finally, thank you! It means the world to me that you gave my book a chance and joined Morven on her journey. The Changeling's Journey is my introduction to this world and I hope to see you again for the next adventure.

ABOUT THE AUTHOR

Christine Spoors is a Scottish writer who recently graduated from the University of Glasgow with a B.Sc. in Geography. She wrote the first draft of The Changeling's Journey in her third year of university and edited it during her fourth. Her fantasy world was the perfect escape from journal articles and essays.

Christine has been part of the online book community since 2014 and you can find her social media links below.

Instagram - @WeeReader
Twitter - @WeeReader
Goodreads - Christine Spoors
Pinterest - weeereader
Blog - weereaderblog.wordpress.com